Sean Joseph White

I, Radio

Limited Special Edition. No. 17 of 25 Paperbacks

To Colin

Hope you enjoy.

To Colin
Hope you enjoy.

Sean Joseph White is a contractor who usually provides support to the Financial Services industry in Edinburgh. He is 48 years old and spends most of his spare time at home, painting and writing. This is his first published novel.

For Jamie

Sean Joseph White

I, Radio

Austin Macauley Publishers™
London · Cambridge · New York · Sharjah

A CIP catalogue record for this title is available from the British Library.

ISBN 9781528903141 (Paperback)
ISBN 9781528903158 (Hardback)
ISBN 9781528903165 (Kindle e-book)
ISBN 9781528957403 (ePub e-book)

www.austinmacauley.com

First Published (2019)
Austin Macauley Publishers Ltd
25 Canada Square
Canary Wharf
London
E14 5LQ

I thank Elaine Pagels for her excellent book *The Origin of Satan*.

Table of Contents

I, Radio – Book One **11**

One – The Apprentice *13*

Two – The Super Volcano *18*

Three – The Darkest Hour *23*

Four – Planta Genista *29*

Five – The Unknown Pleasures *33*

Six – The Paradox and the Plan. *37*

Seven – The Honey Pot *43*

Eight – Into the Abyss *48*

Nine – The Pillar in the Temple *52*

Ten – The Children of the Paradox *56*

Eleven – The Nexus *61*

Twelve – The Calm Before the Storm *65*

Thirteen – The Tractor Beam *68*

Fourteen – The Corner of Houston and Elm *72*

Fifteen – The Warning Shot Across the Bows *75*

Sixteen – The Robe and the Lampstand *80*

Seventeen – The Fat Man *89*

Eighteen – Operation Birth Right *93*

Nineteen – The Offer and the Citadel *98*

Twenty – Hrolfr, Duke of Normandy *103*

Twenty-One – The Dragon's Run *108*

Twenty-Two – The Saxon Invasion *111*

Twenty-Three – The Dragon's Lair *116*

Twenty-Four – The Black Viking *120*

Twenty-Five – The Fountains of Lilith *124*

Twenty-Six – The Treasures of the Earth 127

Twenty-Seven – Pontius Pilate 130

Twenty-Eight – X Marks the Spot and Other Revelations 134

Twenty-Nine – The Wisest Fool in Christendom 138

Thirty – The Philosopher's Stone 143

Thirty-One – The Spirit Quest 147

Thirty-Two – The Beast of the Sea 152

Thirty-Three – The Education of Master Jacques 156

Thirty-Four – The Wedding 160

Thirty-Five – The Mission 164

Thirty-Six – The Gene Machine 168

Thirty-Seven – The Radio Apocalypse 172

Thirty-Eight – The Golden Door 176

Thirty-Nine – The Others 180

Forty – Darkness Was upon the Face of the Deep 183

Forty-One – The Arc of Time 187

Forty-Two – The Temporal Adjustment Team 192

Forty-Three – The Gods of Old 197

Forty-Four – The Ten Plagues 201

Forty-Five – Out of Egypt 205

Forty-Six – Let There Be Light 209

Forty-Seven – The Radio WHO 211

Forty-Eight – I, Radio 214

I, Radio – Book One

One – The Apprentice

He sat down on the ox-blood, leather Cambridge sofa and picked up the tiny cup of coffee from the glass-topped coffee table in front of him. He sipped the creamy, brown mixture and put the cup back down on the saucer. A bit too sweet.

He looked at the television screen and took in the hysteria and the commotion. Universal panic. This was it, at last, his day had come. 15 years of constant streaming had brought him to this point. He was either as mad as his friends thought he was or he would very shortly be vindicated in his own mind.

The picture of a passenger aeroplane in flight flashed up on screen. The strap line on the television said, "London Terror Alert" and the plane seemed to take a plunge as if heading towards something closer to the ground.

Oh God, he thought. *They are going to do a 9/11.*

He could hear the voices of the television presenters and they sounded panicked but he couldn't make out any of the words.

He started to sweat in the heat. He could feel the droplets run down his back and he begged his brain to calm everything down. He needed to think and he needed to remember what to say. If he was right, a door would open very shortly.

Future, past and present. He found it difficult to keep track of everything now. Images in his mind were conjured easily but the time frames seemed to somehow coalesce and not be important. He closed his eyes and forced himself to breathe, to click his mind in to gear. There was a sound of swishing in front of him. A door had slid open in the middle of his living room.

"Operator, suspend plane in mid-air. Jam all weapons and diffuse all bombs." He stepped through the door and into his matrix for the first time. He left the television behind him. Where he was going, televisions were surplus to requirements.

He now stood in the middle of the matrix that he himself had designed. He had called it TIME. In front of him were the incursion windows. He was one step away from everywhere in time and space and perhaps even further if his suspicions were correct.

He put his right index finger to his temple. "Operator, upload interface." A timer appeared on the window in front of him counting down the upload. He put his left index finger to the opposite temple. "Upload Core Application Suite." Another timer appeared and started counting down. Suddenly, the interface appeared in his field of vision. Energy Display. Information box from The Operator's Head. Core Application Suite. The applications started appearing as soon as they had downloaded.

"Operator, activate ADS and lock." The Automatic Defence Software buzzed into life and he could feel a force field around his body.

"Activate DEITY. Activate TREADMILL. Activate TIMESPLICER."

He waited until The Operator displayed three green ticks on screen and then he breathed slowly out. He was online and ready. He stopped for a moment and closed his eyes again. Calm down. Please, calm down. Breathe. He opened his eyes and somehow, he was ready to go.

"Operator – spatial incursion to plane interior."

The window in front of him morphed into a haze for a second. When the haze cleared, he was looking at rows of airline passengers. He walked through in to the cabin.

The Operator had warned him that things would happen very fast and that he wouldn't have time to think. It was for this reason that he had been preparing for years. Although he felt a little bit like a ball in a pinball machine, he knew exactly where he was going and what he had to do.

"All terrorists. Please put your weapons down and come to me."

There was an initial silence and then several moments of clunking as the weapons hit the floor. They all simply walked over to him. Their faces were blank and they moved in a very matter of fact fashion. The only thing that betrayed their sentience was the curiosity in their eyes. This was the DEITY application in action. He had no desire to hurt anyone so he had designed this application to avoid any unpleasantness. DEITY stood for 'Do Everything I Tell You'.

He looked at each of them in turn, cleared his throat and said, "To save your life, you first have to lose it. That does not mean, however, that you should fly a plane in to a building and take thousands of people with you. That is, always has been and always will be considered one thing and one thing only; murder."

He had rehearsed this little speech a hundred times before in his daydreams and he was grateful that he didn't have to remember it. The words came unbidden.

"You can lose your life to other things. You can lose your life to kindness. You can lose your life to generosity. You can lose your life to charity. Most importantly of all, you can lose your life to love."

He remembered where he was supposed to send them. In his mind, he could see a village with a well. An old woman was standing next to it, waiting. He opened the TIMESPLICER and created an incursion through to the village. A door appeared in the cabin and you could see the old woman through it, as clear as day. It was a face he knew well.

He turned to the man nearest him. A medium built man of about 45, handsome and well dressed.

"You would have broken her heart. Now go."

The medium built man looked concerned and somewhat apologetic but he was under the spell of the application and he walked through the door. They all did and the door vanished. It was so simple.

All eyes in the cabin were on him now. They all had that look of awe. None of them looked scared and many of them had that same blank expression on their faces as the terrorists. He was calm.

"I need you all to calm down and not panic. There is nothing to be afraid of. I'm merely going to fly this plane into the nearest airport, which I think is Gatwick. Hold on, don't panic and listen to this music."

He opened iTunes on his interface and played 'Solid Gold' by 'The Golden Filter'. He smiled because he knew it would have them guessing when in fact, he just liked the tune. It was a favourite of an old friend.

He walked down the cabin and entered the cockpit. The Pilot and the Co-Pilot were staring at him, open mouthed but still with a smile in their eyes. Their plane was suspended in mid-air and he was responsible for it.

"Hello Thomas, hello Bernard," he said. "I need you to give me a heading to the nearest airport."

Bernard looked at him and hesitated. A voice in his head said, "You don't need a heading. Just say where you want to go and I'll take care of the rest."

"It's okay Bernard. Operator, take us to Gatwick."

The plane suddenly started rising to a few startled cries in the cabin then it banked heavily, straightened out and headed for Gatwick airport.

"You better get on the radio, Bernard and let them know that we're coming."

Bernard and Thomas looked at each other in silence for a second and when they looked back, both had raised eyebrows.

"Just one question, if you don't mind," said Bernard. "Who are you?"

He smiled and looked at them both. He had been expecting this question and he had come to an arrangement with The Operator in advance. As arranged, he would act as if his memory had been wiped regarding the details of his identity. From now on, he was to be referred to by the name agreed between him and The Operator.

"I am Radio," he said. "I'm Mother's Apprentice."

The two pilots looked at each other again.

"Who is Mother?" asked Bernard.

Radio looked at him and pointed upward. He played one very loud blast of the Wotan Leitmotif from Wagner's Ring.

"Does that answer your question?" enquired Radio.

"Yes – that answers my question."

Radio smiled at him encouragingly but did wonder how he had known that Bernard was a fan of Richard Wagner.

Bernard got on the radio, "Air Traffic Control, this is Sierra Juliet Whiskey One Niner Seven Zero, over."

"This is Air Traffic Control, reading you loud and clear please go ahead."

"Do you have your TV on?" asked Bernard.

"Yes, we're clearing the runway for you now. Stand by."

There were several moments of silence before the radio crackled in to life again.

"Runway cleared for landing, you may proceed."

Bernard turned and looked at Radio. "Why are you here, where did you come from?"

"I'm here because it is time. There is a season for everything and everything in its season.

"This year is the year that the human race on this planet is introduced to the truth. I'm here to prepare the way. I can't tell you any more than that just now but it will become clear in time.

"I'm from Edinburgh but I don't really know any more than that as my memory has been adjusted. I think there are lots of things in my head that have been adjusted but there you go. Needs must as they say."

Bernard and Thomas looked at each other incredulously.

"Good luck," said Bernard. "I think you're going to need it."

"Thanks. Now I'm going to speak to the passengers as they will be alarmed." He looked back at Bernard and Thomas and said, "Don't worry, The Operator will fly you in. You have nothing to fear."

Radio returned to the cabin to find the cabin crew trying to calm down the agitated passengers. Radio clapped his hands loudly and everyone fell silent.

"Listen to me," he began, "You have nothing to fear. We are flying the plane into Gatwick and we expect to touch down in a few minutes. The runway has been cleared for landing and you will all be safe."

"Who are you," yelled out an old American woman?

"My name is Radio, I'm Mother's apprentice. Consider yourselves very lucky today, The Creator's, Mother and Father have taken pity on you and sent me to see you safely home. There is nothing to fear. Calm down and enjoy the landing."

Radio still had the DEITY application active and the whole cabin calmed down immediately. Suddenly, the loudspeaker made a clicking noise and the sound of Bernard's voice came over the air.

"This is your Captain speaking, could all passengers fasten their seatbelts. Cabin crew prepare for landing."

Radio walked up and down the aisle calming everyone as the plane came down on the runway. He could feel the fear. The old woman had wet herself and he realised her bravado had been down to the fact that she was just scared. This heightened awareness of everyone's thoughts just confirmed in his mind what he had always known. As human beings, we are too quick to judge others.

The plane made that telltale screeching sound as the wheels hit the runway and it wasn't long before the aircraft came to a complete halt. He sensed that something was different. Outside he could hear sirens and he quietly cursed to himself. He walked back to the cockpit.

"Bernard, talk to me. What is happening?"

"Sorry, it's standard procedure. We have made an emergency landing and I'm afraid that's what an emergency landing looks like."

Radio looked out of the cockpit window and could see fire engines everywhere. It wasn't the fire engines that worried him. It was the unmarked police cars. He cursed under his breath again.

He walked back into the cabin where the crew had already opened the doors and released the emergency chutes. The passengers were now emptying the cabin at an efficient rate. *They'll be glad to see the back of this plane*, he thought.

At last it was just Thomas and Bernard.

"After you gents," said Radio.

They jumped on to the chute and Radio followed them down. First preliminary down and no casualties. He quietly congratulated himself out of relief and thanked The Operator.

"No problem," she whispered.

A man in a black suit and tie approached. *Here we go*, thought Radio.

"Hello Sir, my name is Commander Bridgewater, MI5. I wonder if you would kindly come with us?"

What a cheek, thought Radio. *Why does this man think this is any of his business?* Radio decided that he would like to play a game.

"I would not like to go with you, Commander. I'm far too busy."

"I'm afraid I insist, Sir," said Bridgewater.

"I just don't care that you insist, Commander. I insist that I'm too busy to go with you."

The Commanders smile faded and he looked at Radio seriously.

"I'm afraid we need to question you. This whole incident has played out on television and we know that you let six terrorists go. We need to know what happened."

"No, actually, you don't. I have no desire to waste any time with you and I warn you, very bad things happen to those who get in my way."

Radio had no intention of doing anything himself but he had locked the ADS software as Mother demanded he do. ADS was Mother's Automatic Defence Software and he did not really know how far it went. He suspected it was quite far.

The Commander was really unsure of himself now and started to look afraid. The game, Radio decided had taken an unfortunate turn. He had no desire to scare anyone, even this chump from MI5. He looked at the Commander and raised his hand in farewell.

"Up," he said. The TREADMILL app kicked in and he flew immediately to 1000 feet above sea level. He raised his hand again and slashed open TIMESPLICER.

He stepped through the doorway that had just appeared in front of him and found himself back in the central control room of the matrix. He smiled; it was exactly as he had dreamed it. Just like the hall in a mediaeval castle. This was The Elevator.

Up against the back wall was a vast king size double bed. In front of this were two enormous chairs. Inlaid into the backrest of each chair was a symbol. On the left-hand chair was an arrowhead pointing up and on the right, an arrowhead pointing down, (Mother and Father's he surmised).

On the wall to the left was a kitchen area and a staircase that led to a balcony and the rest of the matrix. He knew that the balcony was the gateway to a vast complex but he had no inclination to explore at the moment.

On the wall to the right were bookcases and doors leading to dressing rooms and bathrooms. The dressing rooms were dedicated to different time periods and it reminded him of a children's programme he used to watch when he was young. Mr Benn would have some adventures here, he laughed.

Finally, on the front wall were a series of tall windows, each looking on to a different time in human history. This was known as TIM or the Temporal Incursion Matrix. Together with the Elevator, they made up part of the solution known as TIME. Intriguingly, one of the time windows was looking on to a scene he suspected was 1940. Interesting.

There were symbols and flags everywhere just as he had designed and imagined.

A skull and crossed thighbones, loads of St Andrew crosses in different colours, the cross of St George, the Compass and Set Square and several variations, the heart and crown, the lion, the Maltese cross, and many others. It could have been a who's who of mediaeval heraldry.

The hall was dark and just a little bit cold. *First things first*, he thought.

"Operator, let there be light." There was light.

"And put the bloody heating on, I'm freezing." The Operator laughed and a large fire kicked in to life in between the bookcases. He was warm almost immediately.

In front of the time windows there was a highly polished large and round wooden table. On the surface, a white envelope. It was addressed to 'Radio'.

Two - The Super Volcano

He picked up the envelope, opened it and started reading.
Radio,

Don't worry about a thing.

I know you are concerned about your mental health but there is nothing to fear.

Mother, Father, and The Operator have been bombarding your brain with information for longer than you can imagine and this is bound to have some consequences. Things will settle and you will feel a lot better soon.

My advice, in the short term, is to keep busy. Open some of your operations and start work.

There is no need to prepare for the testing. Your whole life has been spent in preparation and there are high hopes that you will pass. The tests will be completely obvious to you. This is why you were put on The Earth to grow up.

As far as the other candidates are concerned, the tests will be impossible!

Remember, don't worry, it will all work out.

Radio sat down and breathed out. He was calming down and was surprised at just how easily he was thinking. He had just received a letter from his older self who had sent the message back through time. It was curious that this felt normal to him. He wondered if he needed to take his medication until the voice intervened in his head.

"No need to medicate now, I'm fixing it as we speak."

"Hello, Operator," he breathed. He wasn't sure if he had said that aloud but he knew he didn't need to.

"Hello, Radio. Make yourself a pot of coffee and have a few chocolates. Then, we'll get started."

He filled the kettle and flicked the switch. The kitchen was full of his stuff and he seemed to know exactly where everything was. He found his coffee pot and added coffee, sugar, and powdered milk. Just how he liked it.

There was a click as the kettle boiled and he filled the pot with boiling water, stirring the mixture as he went.

He opened the treat cupboard and grabbed a box of chocolates.

"What will we do first?" he asked.

"Open up Super Volcano and Battle for Britain," said The Operator. "They are really good ones to start."

Radio took a sip of his coffee. Perfect.

"Operator, open Super Volcano and Battle for Britain."

One of the time windows flashed and went blank. At first, nothing seemed to happen but then a project plan started to appear on screen. He looked at the sub headings.

Super Volcano

- Part One – Recruit the boy.
- Part Two – Yellow Stone National Park.
- Part Three – The Exclusion Zone.

- Part Four – The Tractor Beam.

Battle for Britain

- Preparation – Recruit the right people and set the scene.
- Part One – Bring the tribes to Great Britain.
- Part Two – Create the United Kingdom.
- Part Three – The Darkest Hour.

He laughed. It was funny that you could summarise so much work in to 4 short bullet points. He shrugged. He had done the very same thing so often in the past when he had worked in IT.

Recruitment. Fair enough. He surmised that he was about to do quite a lot of that.

"Are you there?" he said it aloud without thinking.

"Of course, I'll be with you all the time from now on. Our awareness' are merging in to one. You have made a very good start today but don't get too satisfied. Satisfaction leads to pride and laziness."

"I know. I'm trying. This is all happening so fast I don't know what to think."

He could feel the Operator pause for a moment while she considered her response.

"It isn't really happening fast, you know. I've been preparing you for 15 years now. Don't be surprised that you are suddenly aware of what is going on. I've been putting the information in your head. Radio, you need to get used to this and fast. Mother and Father have already started testing you in preparation of the main event. You need to just respond. It will feel like instinct but in fact, everything has been thought out well in advance. I'll be here to guide you, just listen to my warnings."

"I will." He stopped for a second. "I do love you, you know." He felt he had to say it. He wanted to say it. He sensed there had been sacrifices and he wanted her to feel that they had been worth it.

"I know Radio. I think what you think and I can feel it. Thank you. Now finish your coffee and let's get started."

He knew where he wanted to go and the image filled his mind. He didn't need to say anything.

The time window morphed in front of him and he could see a terraced house on a housing estate in North East England. Just what he was expecting. He walked through and left the matrix.

Suddenly there was a scream and a loud voice, "I'm going to kill you."

The back door of the house burst open and a boy of about 15 careered into the back garden. He was followed by his mother who was holding a frying pan.

"I'll knock some bloody sense into you," she shouted. She was obviously at the end of her tether.

Radio stepped forward and loudly cleared his throat. They both stopped and stared at him. It was clear that they knew who he was. He grabbed the frying pan out of the mother's hand.

"The only thing you're going to knock into him with this, is Teflon," he held up the frying pan.

"Where have you been?" she said.

This was not the response he was expecting.

"You flew up into the air at the airport and nobody has seen you since!"

"Calm down," he responded." I've only been gone half an hour."

"That was three days ago."

Radio was stunned. It confirmed his theories about time travel and he knew he would have to have a serious think about it later.

"Oh. Doesn't time just fly?" He recovered quickly. "Right, I'm here to pick up the boy and take him off your hands for a few days. Clearly, you could do with a break and I know he can be a bit of a handful." He turned to the child and winked at him. The boy cheekily winked back.

"My name is Jamie, by the way. I haven't been called boy for some time." He winked again.

Radio chuckled.

"Why do you want Jamie?" she asked.

"He's supposed to come with me for some training. I don't know any more than that other than the fact that I'm his great grandfather, and yours for that matter." He looked at her persuasively.

"Really?"

"Yes. I'm everybody's grandfather, actually."

"I believe you," she said. "Alright, take him for a few days. I could do with the break. He's driving me half daft."

"I know. Here," he went into his pocket and pulled out a wad of notes.

"Take this and treat yourself to some shopping and a night out with the girls." He handed her what appeared to be about a thousand pounds.

"Bloody hell," she said, looking like the cat that got the cream. She turned to Jamie and looked at him sternly.

"Be good for once in your life. Please don't let me down. I'll be watching you."

With that she pocketed the notes and walked off into the house, slamming the back door behind her.

Jamie looked at him. "She played hard to get," he said disappointedly.

"She can't help it. I've got an application that forces others to agree to my suggestions."

Radio turned to Jamie and looked him up and down. It was all there, even at this young age. The boy was very wiry and his face had that look of superintelligence. At about five feet six inches tall, he wasn't the mediaeval knight that Radio would come to rely on so heavily but he was definitely getting there. Standing before him was a time agent.

He beckoned him to follow. When they were out of sight of the house, Radio turned to the boy and said, "What do you know about Fire Mountains?"

"Well, they're called volcanoes, for a start."

Radio burst out laughing. This was going to be easy.

"Indeed, they are! What do you call the chamber below the vent?"

"The magma chamber," responded the boy.

"And when the side of a volcano collapses and sends gas and ejecta down the mountainside?"

"Pyroclastic flow," he responded.

"Excellent. You pass the test. Recognise this place?"

Whilst they had been talking, Radio had opened the TIMESPLICER and moved them half way across the Earth. The boy looked around in utter disbelief.

"This is Yellowstone National Park," he said.

"Yes, that is correct. What are we standing on?"

"A Super Volcano," he exclaimed nervously.

"Exactly so. Guess what?"

"It's about to flip its lid."

"Ten out of ten," congratulated Radio.

"Are you right or left handed?" he asked the young man.

"Left."

Radio, who was right and left dyslexic had to think about it for several seconds. The Operator was laughing in his head. He expediently turned the boy away from him and lifted his right index finger to the boy's right temple. It was extremely important that the interface was on the correct side for usability purposes.

"Operator, upload interface. Upload Core Application Suite. Show me."

A screen appeared in mid-air in front of him and showed the interface being downloaded. It also showed the applications that The Operator was giving to Jamie. Radio knew that The Operator could only give applications which were exactly commensurate with how much he could be trusted.

Jamie was given ADS and Radio locked it. He warned the boy not to defend himself and that the application would take care of everything.

"Okay, let's see what you have been given. You are very young so don't be disappointed with your lot."

Radio scanned through the applications and started explaining them to the boy. He had designed this so that he could train someone in about 15 minutes. He turned to Jamie.

"You have the following:

TWIX – Turn Water into X. This application is designed to turn water into another liquid. Don't try to do anything other than drinking liquids. This application perfectly illustrates how a knowledge of science can be helpful. If, for example, you tried to turn water in to gold, the application would attempt to do it. Gold has a liquid state, molten, so the application would turn the drinking water into molten metal which is dangerous. Do you understand?"

Jamie nodded and he looked as if he was taking this seriously. Radio relaxed.

"WOW – Walk on water. The application turns the water beneath your feet into a non-Newtonian fluid. It helps if you hit the water hard and move quickly.

TREADMILL – The flying application. The command is 'up' and as you are rising state the height you want to be at. The default setting is 1000 feet above sea level. When you are finished say 'down' and the app will take you to six feet. To come down to the floor you move your legs as if you were on a treadmill. You follow?"

He gave the thumbs up.

"And finally, you have MEDIC – This app cures all ailments and diseases. There is a power bar which shows how much power you need to cure each condition. The more complex the problem, the more power you need. Don't over exert yourself or you will go hypoglycaemic. Do you understand?"

"Not enough sugar in the blood," he said.

"Gosh, you are clever. When you launch each app, the application itself will guide you with instructions that appear on your interface. To launch an app simply wave your hand over the icon on the interface itself."

Jamie looked at him and smiled.

Suddenly they could hear the sound of approaching vehicles. It was the Park Rangers in their SUVs.

"Where did they come from?" Jamie asked.

"Good question. They don't even know themselves. The Operator, which is the universe's Oversoul is forcing them to come down here. They will have jumped into their cars and driven here without really thinking about it."

Three cars pulled up and six rangers got out of the vehicles. One of them looked to be in charge.

“Hello Sir, I’m Ranger Graham. What are you guys doin’ out here?” He held out his hand which Radio shook.

“We are here,” said Radio,” because the super volcano beneath your feet has a full magma chamber and is about to erupt with catastrophic consequences.”

“Shoot.” They all looked appalled.

“Luckily for you, I have a plan. I have brought my assistant Jamie with me who is going to organise an exclusion zone around the park of 100 kilometres. He will also help you arrange a withdrawal. By my reckoning you have about 72 hours to relocate every living thing within the exclusion zone. The eruption is long overdue and it is going to be massive.”

“Holy moly,” exclaimed the ranger. “We need to inform the government.”

“I’ll leave that to you. However, I will say this. It is my intention to use a tractor beam to redirect the ejecta in to the atmosphere. This will do two things. On the one hand, it will limit the damage on Earth, which I expect to be minimal. On the other hand, it will help plug the hole in the atmosphere as the ejecta from a super volcano is rich in ozone.”

Radio signalled the lead ranger to move away from the group so that he could converse privately with him.

“Listen to me. I need you to look after the boy. He is a genius but doesn’t know it yet. In the future, he will come and work for me and will be a very important agent for us. This is just a part of his training. Mentor him please and make sure he treats others well.”

Ranger Graham looked at him seriously.

“Don’t you worry about a thing. I’ve been waiting for you for a long time.”

He held up his right hand. On the finger, next to the pinkie was a ring with a symbol on it that he knew very well. It was Mother and Father’s symbol. It was his symbol.

“Good grief,” said Radio chuckling. “I’m afraid there have been so many plans made of which I know nothing.”

“I know,” responded the ranger. “Leave this to me, the boy is in good hands. You should be aware that there is a huge network of people on the Earth who have been preparing for this moment for a very long time. They are everywhere and they will do everything they can to make sure that your passage is smooth. Don’t worry!”

“Thanks for letting me know.” Radio turned to Jamie. “Right, I’m leaving you in the hands of Ranger Graham, who will look after you. Knock ‘em dead, Jamie. It’s all in your head.”

“I will grandfather. I won’t let you down.”

Radio turned, opened a spatial incursion, and headed back into the matrix.

One down, one to go.

He looked at the plan for Battle for Britain and sighed. He expected this to be a bit more difficult. *No time like the present*, he thought.

“Operator, the study at Chartwell, 25 May 1940.”

The time window morphed for just a split second and he could see the scene he had observed earlier. Winston Churchill sitting at his desk, deep in thought.

Radio moved very close to the window.

“Winston!”

The man at the desk started looking around with a very hopeful look on his face.

“Winston, I have a desire to help you defeat these Nazis but to do so I need to bring you into my matrix. Grab my hand and I’ll pull you through.”

Radio put his arm through the window. A very excited Mr Churchill grabbed his arm and walked out of 1940 and straight in to the future.

Three – The Darkest Hour

"Master, I knew you would come, we're in a terrible mess."

Winston enfolded him in a bear hug and was obviously very relieved. This was a bit awkward. Churchill had obviously met him before but this was the first time that Radio had ever met Britain's wartime Prime Minister. Luckily, The Operator had shown him the past and the future so he knew what he was supposed to do.

"Winston, don't be afraid. I'm here to help. First things first." Radio held up his hand and a thick book flew into it.

"I've brought you into The Matrix for three reasons:

1. You are in a fight. It is a tough one but you are going to win. It will take you five years but you will defeat them in the end. I will prepare you for what you need to do. I'm going to train you Winston. You won't be able to take all the magic back to Earth with you but you will be able to take some and it will prove very useful.
2. You need a holiday. A change is as good as a rest and I need to make sure that your mind is ready for the fight ahead.
3. You will read this."

Radio held up the book he'd just conjured out of nowhere and allowed Winston to read the spine.

"The Second World War by Winston S Churchill," he read. Then he burst out laughing. "I take it I'm in the future, Master?" he asked.

"Yes, Winston, you are about 80 years into the future. You vanquished your foes long ago and the world is free of the Nazi menace. However, we can't rest on our laurels. The Operator has recorded all the help that was given to you and I need to make sure that your future is secured by going back in to my past and delivering the help you need. I know this sounds dreadfully complicated but the universe was created on the same principle. For creation to be a success, the past had to borrow from the future. My job in life is to resolve the resultant paradoxes."

Winston's eyes opened wide and he breathed, "Christ."

"Today is my first day, Winston. I've brought you back to my beginning so that you can see things from the start. Call it my gift for services rendered."

"Thanks. If this is your first day then you haven't met me before. How do you know what to do?"

"You were always quick on the uptake, Winston. The operator has been recording events as they happen. When time travel takes place, the event actually happens at the appointed time in recorded history. All the operator must do is record all the interventions in Chronological order and make sure that I resolve all the paradoxes. There are many time agents helping me, including yourself. As for what to do next, well, read the book obviously. You may take notes but write each event on a separate card. That way as each event takes place, you can burn the card that relates to it. To be on the safe side, you best write the notes in code. Make this your night-time reading.

"In the meantime, you can follow me around. There are a number of things we need to do pertaining to the war so, for you, a lot of this will be very relevant."

"Right. You've explained this to me more than once," said Winston." Five years ago, for me anyway, you told me that we would one day, deal with Hitler. I hope we are planning this soon."

"Funny you should mention that, Winston, I'm right in the middle of arranging that very thing."

Right on cue, the left most time window morphed again and 2 girls appeared carrying bundles between them. They looked to be about 12 years old but Radio knew that they were much older and extremely powerful. One had blonde hair and the other golden.

"Winston, meet the twins. Blondie and Goldilocks. They do all my dirty work and a lot more besides."

"Er...we've met before," admitted Winston, looking slightly embarrassed.

"Ah!" said Radio, understanding. "They've done some dirty work for you too!"

"For Great Britain, to be precise," said Blondie. "Our duty is to the paradox, not to any individual."

"Quite right," said Radio, nodding. "What have you got there?" he pointed at the bundles they were carrying.

"We are getting ready for you know who," said Goldilocks. "This is a uniform which will form part of the disguise." She laid the bundle she was carrying on the table.

"And these are identity papers, cash, newspapers, helpful documents et cetera," said Blondie as she divested herself of her burden. "He'll need all of this if he is to be successful."

"Who are we talking about here?" asked Winston.

"A time agent that I haven't recruited yet but will soon. We are just making sure we have everything ready to go. We are going to place him in the Reichskanzlerei so that he can launch a whispering campaign against Hitler. History records that Adolf went a bit mad as the war progressed. I'm betting my bottom dollar that we are responsible for that. I can't say any more than that, just now. We just have to wait. In the meantime, however, we can have lunch and talk about 'Battle for Britain'."

Radio went over to the kitchen area and opened the fridge door. It was packed. He decided to make Bruschetta and took a whole carton of vine tomatoes from the salad drawer and a bag of grated mozzarella.

"I'm making two types of Italian toast. Tomato and basil and Cheese and garlic butter. Somebody put on the kettle and we'll make a pot of coffee."

Blondie filled the kettle with cold water from the tap and placed it back on the docking station and flicked the switch. She went to the cupboard and produced small coffee cups and saucers with little jugs for the coffee.

Goldilocks set the table with plates and cutlery and Winston filled water jugs and put glasses at each setting.

The toast only took 5 minutes to make and this was placed on the table with a bowl full of the tomato and basil mixture. They all sat round.

"Right," said Radio, helping himself to some cheese toast. "Tonight, we have a very important task to attend to. I'm taking you back to September 1940 and the height of the blitzkrieg on London."

"That's the future for me," said Winston.

"Don't worry, you'll get used to it. In September 1940, London is on its knees and there is a very real danger that the British people are going to break. The Luftwaffe hit them 76 nights on the trot and destroyed most of the homes in the East End killing six thousand Londoners.

“In truth, it is my desire to help them but I can’t change what is already a part of history. The blitzkrieg happened and it could be argued that the attack on civilians stiffened Britain’s resolve.

“However, we can give them hope and a little bit of encouragement.

“Tonight, during a thousand-bomber raid, we are all going to fly above London batting bombs away from all the public buildings and dumping them in the Thames. Winston, you will protect the Palace of Westminster. I will protect Buckingham Palace. Blondie, you take St Paul’s Cathedral and Goldilocks, you take the Tower of London.

“When the Londoners wake up tomorrow they will see that none of their major buildings have been hit and they will know that somebody up there likes them. We will have given them the one thing more than anything else that will help them go on to win the war. Do you know what it is Winston?”

“Yes, Master. We will have given them hope.”

“Spot on. Now, all I need to do is train you, if I haven’t done so already.”

They all spent the next half an hour eating lunch and chatting. Radio discovered that this was the first time that Blondie and Goldilocks had been in the matrix which, rather interestingly, they referred to as ‘his matrix’. He put that bit of information away. He was dying to ask if there were other matrices but didn’t want to show his ignorance. There was plenty of time to investigate. He would get The Operator to make enquiries.

At the end of lunch, Radio collected the dishes and loaded the dishwasher. He then asked everyone to gather round.

“Alright, as you know, this is my first day but as The Operator has been showing me the future, I have a good idea about things but I don’t know all the detail so apologies if some of these questions seem a bit odd.”

He looked at each of them in turn and said, “Have I trained you before?”

The three of them burst out laughing and answered in the affirmative.

“All you need to do is to activate all our applications and we’ll be ready,” said Blondie.

“Operator, activate all applications. Lock ADS. Lock DIME. DIME is the Do Ignore ME application. You can move around freely and nobody will notice you.”

“Spatial incursion to 10 September 1940, 20:00 hours, Big Ben.”

The time window morphed and when the haze cleared, they were staring on to a deserted Palace of Westminster in a glorious September twilight.

They grouped together and walked through.

Radio looked at them again and said, “Call me, if you need me and good luck. Remember to send the bombs into the Thames. When we are done, you will hear the all clear. As soon as you hear the siren, come back here and I will take us back to the matrix.”

Radio activated Treadmill, the flying app and said “up.”

He shot up from the pavement until he got to about 1000 feet and said, “Stop.”

He looked around. He could see Blondie and Goldilocks disappearing to their destinations and Winston was stationing himself over the commons. He picked out Buckingham Palace in the middle distance and headed for it.

When he got above the palace he stopped. He had come deliberately early to give him time to think. Things were moving very fast and he was surprised by how smoothly things were going. He had never met Winston before but already he felt like an old friend. Something was making him feel slightly uncomfortable.

“Don’t fret; it was ‘The Operator’. You are the best-prepared person in history and I should know. Don’t forget that we have been at this for 15 years now and in that time,

I have streamed information in to your brain every day. Scenes from history, the future, information from Mother and Father and knowledge of what to do. I'm surprised your head hasn't exploded."

"I know, and I'm very grateful, it's just so odd."

"You will get used to it and very soon it will seem like second nature. You are going to blow everyone away, Radio."

"Thanks. I've been thinking about Radio. The right thing to do is to hand over that responsibility to someone better suited. I think I'm merely leading the way."

"Excellent, hold that thought. You were born to resolve my paradoxes and there are many. You will fix the big ones first, like this and then you will spend the rest of your life making everything right.

"Do the right thing at the right time. I will guide you when the time comes. In the meantime, the right thing to do is to defend this palace. Here they come!"

Suddenly, the air raid sirens wailed out across London and searchlights ripped up through the descending darkness. In the distance, Radio could hear the drone of German bombers coming his way. He smiled, he'd always wanted to do this since he was a child. He was just missing his Spitfire.

The air was so cool and clean. He had wondered if the air might be cleaner in the past and he was forced to conclude that at street level it had been a bit of a stink but up here above the palace it was quite lovely.

At 1000 feet, he had plenty of time to bounce any ordnance into the Thames, even from this distance. He launched the BATAWAY application and waited for the first bomb to appear through the clouds. He didn't have to wait long. Suddenly 4 unmistakeable shapes appeared in a row. He'd forgotten that they dropped the damned things in batches. He used the application to select all 4 lozenges and flicked them off into the water. So far so good.

The next hour and a half passed without incident. From his position high in the sky, he could see the East End take a hammering. He would have loved to have gone down there but he knew better than to break the rules concerning time travel. He had written most of them himself. What happened, happened and that was that. Still painful to watch. When the all clear sounded, he headed back towards Westminster.

Just as he reached Big Ben, he saw a German Bomber head towards the water. In the cockpit, he could see the pilot trying to release the windshield so that he could bail out but it was too late, the plane was too close to the ground.

"Save him." The Operator screamed in his head.

Radio knew what to do without even thinking. He slowed time with a thought and blew the windshield off the craft. He rushed to the cockpit and pulled the pilot out by the jacket. When he looked at his face, he experienced that telltale shock of recognition. He said "sleep" in his ear. The pilot slumped.

When Radio reached the ground, he found the others already waiting.

"Who's that?" asked Winston.

"His name is Klaus. He is a time agent who is going to work for us in the future."

Radio opened the time window and they all walked through, back into the matrix.

When they got back, Radio laid Klaus in a chair knowing that he would wake up naturally in a little while. He had something to show Winston and he knew it was important. He knew it would make a difference.

"Winston," he called. "Come here."

Winston came over and stood beside him.

"I want to show you something. What we have just done will make a huge difference. When London wakes up in the morning, they will feel defended. Look."

One of the time windows morphed and looked on to a scene which was obviously the following morning in the bright sunlight. In the background, The Operator was playing Elgar's Enigma Variation number 15, 'Nimrod'. Just as the music reached its crescendo, The Operator closed in on The Palace of Westminster just as the remaining smoke parted. It didn't have a scratch. Radio looked at Winston and he was smiling from ear to ear.

"Hope, Winston. Never forget the power of hope. Now, let's see to our German friend."

They stood over the sleeping airman. He was almost a caricature of the perfect German. Blond hair, blue eyes and fit as a fiddle. Radio wondered what to do with him next when, suddenly, he opened his eyes. He looked amused.

"Do you speak English?" enquired Radio.

"Yes," replied Klaus. "Where Am I?" he asked.

"You are in heaven," responded Radio. "I have brought you into the future to get you away from the Nazi's and the war. You are supposed to work for me. I've seen the future."

"Thank God," said Klaus unsurprised. "It will come as no shock to you when I tell you that I've actually had a dream about this on several occasions." He looked around at the matrix and nodded his head enthusiastically. Eventually his eyes alighted on Winston.

"So, Winston Churchill works for you," he said "I knew I was on the wrong side."

Everyone laughed and Radio asserted, "Well, you're on the right side now. Welcome to my matrix. From this room, we can go anywhere in time and space. You work for me now. Get settled in and we'll find something for you to do. Your rooms are at the top of the stairs." Radio pointed towards the balcony.

Winston piped up, "I could do with freshening up too, come on." They both headed for the stairs.

Radio headed for the kettle, filled it with water and flicked the switch. A nice cup of coffee would help him think.

The whole of time and space. Saying it again had given him a thrill because he knew the possibilities and he knew the thing he wanted the most in the world was there in front of him. Waiting beyond the time windows. His family.

He sat down at the table and started sipping his coffee. He could see no reason at all why he couldn't go to them. He was dying to see them. The more he thought about it, the more he wanted to do it.

"It is all right," said The Operator. "They are dying to see you too. They have waited a very long time and I'm so happy that you want to go to them on your first day. They'll be happy too. You must go to her first. It is in your head. You need to go to Planta Genista. There is a famine there and I need you to resolve it."

"I'll do it." He spent the next ten minutes relishing his coffee. He finished just as Winston and Klaus returned to the matrix.

"Right everyone. We are all going to take an important side trip. There is a planet in the Planta Genista system that needs our help. The Operator has already advised me what I need to do and all arrangements have been made in advance. You will come as observers and medical help only. Klaus, you stay close to me. Try not to show your surprise as I don't want to confuse anyone. Are we clear?"

They all signalled their understanding.

Radio collected his thoughts and stepped up to the time windows. He closed his eyes and breathed. He had to remember what to say.

"Operator. The Church on Plantagenet, please."

The time window morphed and they could see what appeared to be a mediaeval priest. He looked like he was calling for aid. He had the pallid look of someone suffering from malnutrition.

"Just as you helped us with the plague, save us from this blight which has destroyed our crops."

Radio walked through the time window and the others followed.

Four - Planta Genista

"How may I help you?" enquired Radio.

The priest fell to his knees and the congregation gasped out loud. There were cries and feeble cheers. It was clear that everyone was very weak.

"Lord," began the priest, "We are dying from starvation. Our crops have failed and we have not eaten in weeks."

"First of all, you can stand up. I require no obeisance and your actions are unseemly."

The priest stood rather weakly and Radio helped him to his feet. He was a relatively young man but the famine had made him look older. Radio would fix this.

"Sorry Lord."

"Secondly, I am not a Lord. I am Radio. I work for GOD."

This admission was met with further expressions of shock. Radio signalled for them all to calm down.

He turned to the priest.

"What year is it?" he asked.

The priest looked a bit confused but answered.

"It is 1360 anno Domini."

Radio heard a sharp intake of breath behind him and shot them all a warning glance.

"That means you have been here for 11 years, am I correct?"

"Yes, it has been 11 summers since we were delivered from the Black Death."

"Can you remember what happened?" asked Radio.

"The plague was sweeping the land. We all went to the village church to pray for our deliverance. When we awoke the next morning, we found ourselves here. We appear to be the only community in the area."

"That is because you are the only community in the area," said Radio. "Eleven years ago, the black death was destroying everything in its path. GOD was fearful that the children of the earth would be wiped out. I was sent to save as many as I could. I brought you here, to the planet of the yellow flower to save your lives." Radio went to the altar and picked up a yellow flower. He raised it above his head so that everyone could see it.

"Your King was called Edward Plantagenet, after his symbol, the yellow flower. In the ancient tongue, yellow flower is Planta Genista. This planet is called Plantagenet after the King and the flower. It is the only way I can keep track of everyone."

There was a universal sound of understanding which sounded like a prolonged 'OOOHHH'.

"First things first. Let's get you something to eat. Make sure you feed the children first and be sure not to gulp down the food or you will be sick. When you have managed to eat something, if you are ill, can you form a line in front of us and we will cure your ailments. Don't be shy. Ready."

"Operator, open spatial incursion to the refectory."

A time window appeared to howls of fright from the congregation. Radio silenced them all with a look. He lifted his hand and pulled through the wheeled trellis tables that he knew were waiting on the other side. They were laden with all sorts of food.

The congregation formed a stately queue and the children were pushed to the front. Radio was impressed. They were starving and he had expected a scrum. *If this had been 2018,* he thought, *there would have been a riot.*

The priest hadn't moved and Radio suspected there would be questions. There were.

"Tell me," said the priest, "Have you met the Lord?"

Radio had seen the sign of the cross behind the altar so he surmised he meant The Christ.

"Yes, I know Yeshua," he said casually, "He works for GOD too."

"I know that," said the priest. "What's he like?"

Radio chuckled. "He's a good laugh, actually. He likes a glass of wine. He's very generous. Doesn't judge others. Just make sure you're not the arrogant type. He'll lull you into a false sense of security and whip the rug out from under you."

The old man laughed. "That's just how I imagined him to be."

Radio thought, *Me too*. It was beginning to dawn on him why the Operator had spent 15 years preparing him. He hadn't met Yeshua in real life, yet but he had seen him in his dreams a thousand times. He had just described him to a tee.

"If you're good," said Radio, "I'll bring you to him and you can meet him. However, before I can do that, I need you to be a leader, will you do that for me, John?"

The priest looked at him eagerly. "What do you need me to do?"

"I suspect that your crops have failed because you are not rotating them. When you grow a crop in a field, you remove goodness from the earth. If you keep growing the same crop in the same field, you will deplete the goodness that the crop needs to grow.

"By changing the crops each year, the new crop will replace some of the goodness that another crop has taken out. Every few years you should let a field lie fallow for a while so that the goodness can be replaced completely. This should not only protect your crops from blight, it should improve their quality. Can you arrange that for me?"

"It makes sense. I'll see that it is done. I take it, then, that God just doesn't wave his hand?"

"All things are possible for GOD," said Radio seriously, "However, GOD relies on science." Radio winked at him. "Now go and get something to eat."

Radio turned to the others.

"I need all of you to launch your MEDIC applications. I think we are going to be busy."

Winston, Blondie and Goldilocks all nodded their heads and prepared for the queues to form.

"Klaus, time to start your training. Operator, upload interface and core application suite." Radio held his index finger to Klaus' temple until the apps downloaded. "Watch what I do for a while then start doing it yourself."

He held up his hand in front of Klaus and said, "See what I see."

"Es ist doch nicht möglich," said Klaus.

Radio laughed. "It is definitely possible, Klaus."

The first in the queue was a woman with a little boy.

Radio could see what was wrong but remembered The Operator's advice.

"Always ask the patient what is wrong. You may cure all their ailments but they have to believe that you've cured what they think is wrong."

"What's wrong little man?" asked Radio.

The little boy looked at his Mother and she nodded her head.

"I've got a sore toof."

Radio looked at the on-screen diagnosis and could see that the boy had a nasty abscess.

“I’m afraid it’s a bit worse than a sore tooth.” He looked at the Mother who had paled a little.

“Don’t worry, Matthew has an abscess in his gum which is full of poison. It will be causing him a lot of pain. I’ll fix it now.”

Radio laid his hands on the boy’s temples and kissed his forehead. The application instructed the patients’ brain to affect the cure. The closer he could get to the brain, the quicker he could instruct. Kissing on the forehead was an ideal way of doing it.

The little boy heaved a sigh of relief.

“Pain gone?” asked Radio.

“Gone.”

Radio felt an all too familiar feeling at the nape of his neck. It was like the hairs were standing on end and he had an inexplicable desire to shiver. It was the Operator’s warning. Get ready, this is important.

The next in line was a young woman. This was the reason he was here. She was young and wasn’t the woman he would come to know, yet there was still an obvious appeal.

He quickly quashed any desires he harboured for this girl, remembering what The Operator had warned him of. Always maintain a professional remoteness when dealing with the temporal paradox. *Good advice*, he thought.

“What’s wrong, Miriam?” he asked.

He hated treating young women as the problem was all too often personal and it was just so awkward.

The young woman hesitated.

“Don’t worry,” said Radio, “Come here.”

He kissed her on the forehead until he could hear the telltale bell sound in his mind which told him that he had just cured a hideous case of thrush.

She looked relieved and then he did the thing he was there to do. He put his index finger to her temple and uploaded the interface and the core application suite as arranged. It would lie there dormant for now but The Operator would wake it up when the time was right.

“Do I know you?” she asked. Her eyes were drilling in to his and there was a flash of recognition.

Radio was concerned. She had probably already started dreaming but it was too early for her.

He looked her in the eye and smiled. “Forget,” he said. She stopped and shook her head then put her hand against her temple. Eventually she looked up, said “thanks” and walked off in a daze.

Radio watched her leave. It would be twenty years until this woman saw him again, yet he was absolutely certain that he would see her before the week was out. Perhaps even sooner.

Over the next half hour, they dealt with all the conditions that you would expect to be associated with malnutrition. Low potassium was common, as was diarrhoea.

Radio kept an eye on Klaus’ power bar. The danger with this application was that you could deplete yourself very easily. Hypoglycaemia was a regular occurrence.

They cleared the queues and Radio realised that they all needed something to eat. He motioned for them to help themselves from the tables which were still groaning with food. He grabbed a plate and stacked it high, then sauntered over to John who was looking curiously at the food.

“What are these things called?” he held up a small filo parcel.

“They are called spring rolls. They’re from Cathay.”

"Good God, I thought Cathay was a myth. They are delicious."

"Hunger is, without doubt, the best sauce. Now listen. Most of this food has been selected because it will last a while, so don't let it go to waste. I'm going to check on you in a few days and I'll be measuring your performance. If I suspect you have not been doing your job, I'll be most annoyed."

"I won't let you down," said John. "I have wanted to meet Yeshua all my life and I'm not going to pass up that opportunity."

Radio finished his food and addressed the congregation.

"Tonight, may not be a good night for you, you may feel a little bit queasy. Do not worry, this is quite normal. You have not eaten for a few days, so your bodies are getting reused to food.

"I have given Father John some advice on how to manage your crops and how to keep the food and not let it go to waste.

"Help has been arranged and we will monitor and maintain the food levels.

"I am leaving you all in John's capable hands. I will come back in three days to make sure you are all right. You have enough food to keep you going in the meantime."

He turned to John. "Remember, I'll be watching."

As he was about to leave, a little girl came running towards him. When she reached him, she held out her hand. It was a little yellow flower. He smiled at her and took the bloom. He knew that he would keep the flower for a long time. It was incidents like these that made everything worthwhile.

The Operator opened the time window and they all walked back into the matrix.

Radio turned to his crew. They all looked a bit tired so he let them have a twenty-minute coffee break and then he assembled them again.

"I know this is difficult but when we are travelling through time and space it is important that you give the impression that you know exactly what you are doing. When you all gasped at the date back there, you betrayed yourselves a little.

"Our next little trip is into deep space. Does anyone have any questions?"

"Where are we going?" asked Klaus.

"You'll like this one," he said smiling.

Five - The Unknown Pleasures

"Operator, locate The Unknown Pleasures."

The time window flashed in to life. 'The Unknown Pleasures is mining the planet Mephistopheles in the Draco system.' The words flashed on screen, arriving like the football scores on a video printer. He quite liked the look of it. "You designed it," The Operator chuckled in his head.

"Hail the Unknown Pleasures. On screen."

The time window flashed into life and suddenly, he was looking at the bridge of an intergalactic spacecraft. The image of the radio waves from Pulsar CP1919 were displayed on the wall behind The Captain's chair. Just as he had imagined it. Just as he had designed it.

The Ensign to The Captain's left announced, "We are being hailed by The Operator."

"On screen," replied The Captain. It was just like Star Trek.

"Hello, Eve," said Radio, looking at The Captain directly in the eye.

The woman looked every inch the Captain of an intergalactic mother ship. Smart in her uniform, disciplined in her demeanour and sharp in her eye.

The Captain lifted her left hand to her open mouth. She was silent for several moments, in complete shock. Then she remembered who she was. "Hello, Father," she said.

"I wonder if you could send a message to the intergalactic fleet on my behalf," said Radio.

The Captain looked slightly confused for a heartbeat then collected herself. "Yes, of course. What message do you want me to send?" Her hand hovered over the communications panel on the arm of her chair.

"This is London Calling," announced Radio.

There was a stunned silence for all of three seconds and then all hell broke loose. All officers on the bridge started jumping up and down. There was cheering, hugging, clapping and lots of back slapping. Radio had never seen a crowd so happy. The Captain relayed the message to the galaxy.

"I take it the embargo on The Earth has been lifted?" enquired Eve.

"Yes," responded Radio, "Today is the day when the children of the paradox start to come home. The embargo on the home system was lifted by Mother and Father this morning. However, you can't just rush in, we'll have to manage your arrival."

Eve looked up at him. "The fleet are starting to respond, I'll patch them through."

Radio looked at the screen and another bridge appeared in front of him.

"This is The Golden Fox. Message received and understood."

The screen blurred and another captain appeared.

"This is The Twenty-Four Hours. Message received and understood."

In total, there were just over 40 ships who responded to the message until finally the screen blurred one last time. This was the one he had been waiting for.

"This is The Atrocity Exhibition. Message received and understood."

"Hello Adam," said Radio.

"Hello Master," responded The Captain.

"Where are you?"

"We are about one hour from the Sumer home world, we are heading there now."

"Can you make your way to Mephistopheles? I need to speak to you on The Unknown Pleasures."

Adam looked doubtful.

"It would take six months to get to the Draco system alone."

"I can bring you here instantly," said Radio. "Get ready, in a few hours I will open a spatial incursion which will bring you directly to the planet itself."

The Captain's eyes opened wide.

"Master, if it was anybody else but you, I'd say that was impossible. Happily, I know better!"

Radio chuckled. "Two hours."

Radio turned back to the Unknown Pleasures.

"Permission to come aboard."

The Captain, again, looked surprised but replied, "By all means."

The Operator formalised the spatial incursion and Radio turned to the others.

"Who wants a shot on an intergalactic mother ship?"

They all shouted "Me", so Radio took the lead and they all walked on to the bridge of The Unknown Pleasures.

The Captain looked unsure of herself. She looked like someone caught between two stools and it was at this point that the penny dropped with Radio. His daughter had known him when he was older and, although she knew about the paradox, she was obviously unsure how much he knew. Radio looked at her, smiled and opened wide his arms. She flew into his embrace. Problem solved.

He held her tight and positioned her head just under his chin so that he could tilt her ear towards his mouth.

"The Operator has asked me to go by the call sign Radio for the time being, can you let the others know?"

Captain Tsedeq smiled and nodded her head almost imperceptibly.

"I know the plan," she whispered, "Don't worry, we won't blow your cover."

"This is all happening so fast," admitted Radio. "I feel like a hurricane and I can't slow down."

"You'd better get used to it," Eve warned. "This is your life from now on."

"You need to send a message to the fleet and ask them all to assemble here."

"I'll arrange it."

She untangled herself from him and stood up straight in a very business-like sort of fashion.

"Right," she announced. "Introductions."

Radio turned to Winston. "This is Winston Churchill, Prime Minister of Great Britain."

There were gasps from every corner of the bridge as all eyes turned to Winston. To say the crew looked at him with respect was an understatement. Winston gathered himself and bowed flamboyantly.

The captain murmured, "Prime Minister."

Radio turned to the girls and announced, "This is Blondie and Goldilocks."

The gasps turned into outbursts of complete and utter disbelief.

The captain turned to her bridge crew and said sternly, "That will do. Remember who you are."

She then turned to Blondie and Goldilocks and bowed deeply. “Archangels, welcome aboard the Unknown Pleasures.”

It was radio’s turn to be surprised. Archangels. He made a mental note to enquire later. For the past fifteen years he had solved all his troubles in his sleep. At first, he had been unable to understand how he woke up with all his questions answered until he realised that The Operator simply fed him the data overnight.

The Archangels nodded their heads in acknowledgement.

Finally, Radio turned to his new friend. “This is Klaus. He is a time agent in our employ.”

Klaus performed the curt German bow.

“Right, let’s have tea and coffee on the observation deck.” The captain led them to a set of double doors to the side of the bridge which swished open as she approached. Radio grinned. Just like Star Trek.

They all sat round a large rectangular table of deeply polished oak. Almost immediately stewards arrived carrying tea and coffee together with various plates filled with nibbles. These were laid silently on the table. The stewards bowed and left through the same double doors.

The captain made him a cup of coffee, just how he liked it and turned to the others. “It is our custom to ask guests to help themselves.”

Everybody helped themselves to what they wanted and settled down.

The captain turned to Radio. “I have so many questions and I think after all these years I deserve some answers.”

“Ask,” said Radio.

“Tell me your story up to now,” she said simply.

Radio closed his eyes and breathed. He had been expecting this and knew there was a fine line to walk. He wanted to tell her everything but knew that this wasn’t the time. He and The Operator had worked on a truthful story which left some of the detail out. The detail that he himself wasn’t supposed to know. This was the story he would tell. This was the story he was supposed to tell.

All eyes turned to him expectantly.

He cleared his throat.

“Fifteen years ago, I started dreaming. They were different dreams. The sort of dreams you jump out of bed in the morning and enquire, to no one in particular, what on earth was that about? They were in glorious Technicolour, 3D, surround sound, HD, smell-o-vision, you get the picture. It took me days to work out that they were not dreams. The Operator was feeding me the recordings of events which had occurred in earth’s history. I was seeing time through the eyes of the people who had witnessed the events. It is not difficult to see that this is possible, especially when, in 2018, we can Bluetooth a video clip into a smart phone. The brain is a much more powerful computer than a smart phone, as I have discovered.”

Radio paused and took a sip of his coffee.

“I asked myself the obvious questions. What was I seeing and why? As soon as I asked the question, I was hurtled back in time, 14 billion years to before the start of the universe and that is where I found them.”

Radio paused again and took another sip.

“Who did you find?” asked Klaus.

“The Creators of this universe.”

They all looked at each other and whistled.

“The Operator showed me the laboratory in which the containment fields for the universe were constructed. It was vast and very dark, like a massive cave. The Creators were there and something was wrong. Don't ask me how I know this, I just do. It's not that they were stuck, it's that they were disheartened.

"As I understand it, they had to create a universe to evolve. A chaos system finds a balance which requires little maintenance. A suspended universe requires constant intervention. The thing that had disheartened them was evolution itself. They were creating the universe to contain life but they knew that they would have to wait for evolution to take its course. The wait would be a long one."

Suddenly tears welled up in his eyes and they started to wind their way down his cheeks.

"As I stood there watching them, I realised that I was supposed to intervene, I knew I could help them. The answers were all in my head. Then something wonderful happened."

"The Creators turned to me, in the dream and they said, 'Hello, Radio', I said, 'Hello', and they smiled at me and I felt loved like I've never been loved before."

He stopped and breathed and took another sip of his coffee. The captain handed him a handkerchief and he wiped his eyes.

"The Creators looked at me and said, 'What do we need to do'.

"I looked at the leader and I told her that she needed to write a computer programme called 'Mother's apprentice' and give it to the sentient Alpha-Omega they had created to maintain creation. I told them that the programme would find all the answers and that it would culminate in a single life form who would be able to provide the solution to their evolutionary problem.

"That's me. I've spent the last fifteen years of my life being prepared by the Operator. I'm the computer programme 'Mother's apprentice'. I don't know everything. The Operator has been feeding me information and visions in my dreams over and over again but she seems to do it on a need to know basis.

"I now I have access to the databases within the solution and I know that knowledge can be dropped in to my head at a moment's notice.

"My primary job, at the moment, is to recruit all of the time agents who will help me resolve the temporal paradox. The paradox has two main strands, ensure the integrity of the timeline and resolve the human evolutionary problem.

"It is vast and it is complex and I know it is going to take years to resolve. However, there are parts to the paradox which the Operator wants resolved as soon as possible. There are priorities.

"It is my belief that we are being tested and the Creators are on their way to me.

"I think I'm supposed to show Mother and Father the Radio WHO."

Radio stopped to allow all of that to sink in. The complexity of the situation made him feel that he was blurting everything out. He had to start somewhere.

Six - The Paradox and the Plan

There was silence in the room.

"Well say something."

"What is The Radio WHO?" asked The Captain.

"The Radio Who is the information technology solution which resolves the Creator's evolutionary problem. The secret to the solution is to circumvent the need to wait for life to evolve. The only way to do that is to enable time travel. Although, time travel is possible in a normal universe, there remains one thorny problem. If a misadventure occurs, there is no way to resolve it. In other words, should an irresoluble temporal paradox occur, there must be a way to set it aside. For that, you need a back up system. The IT solution provides just that. This is The Radio WHO."

"Why is it called The Radio WHO?" asked The Captain.

Radio smiled and shook his head.

"I have created a guessing game for Mother and Father to keep them interested and to relieve their boredom. I'm afraid you'll have to wait for that explanation."

"Can you at least explain the time travel solution?"

"Yes, up to a point. Time travel enables Mother and Father to come forward in to the solution and it enables me to go back and intervene in the evolution of the human race. At certain points in time, the human race has made inexplicable leaps forward in their development. Those leaps are when I have intervened with an injection of DNA. The past has essentially borrowed from the future. It has also allowed me to spread the species across nine planets in this galaxy alone, including your own. All human beings in this sector of the galaxy are descended from me and from The Earth."

It was Winston's turn to gasp. "Are you saying that there are nine planets populated with humans from The Earth?"

"Yes, in this sector of The Galaxy. This Galaxy is called Domus after the Latin for home. Although, the distances are vast from a human perspective, the planets in question are relatively close by from a universal perspective. Bear in mind that this Galaxy is one in a trillion.

"Domus is being used as a production environment. All life is developed outside of the solution and then evolved to a recipe in any one of the galaxies in the universe. If a life form is deemed viable for interaction with human species on an M class planet, it is tested first on the Honey Pot before it is released in to our reality.

"I'm certain that the species has now spread beyond Domus but I don't know the detail yet. I know there are humans in the neighbouring Galaxy which is called Accola."

The Captain interjected, "There are five planets in our Empire which are populated with humans from the Sumer home world. They are Sumer, Persia, Assyria, Babylon and Egypt."

Radio smiled and looked at Winston. His eyes were just about popping out of their sockets as the penny dropped with him.

"It's incredible," he said. "This is the paradox. Humans from these planets are going to go back in time and found our ancient societies on Earth. Am I right?"

The Captain looked at Radio and laughed. “Not going to Prime Minister, they have been back in time and founded the ancient cultures of Earth. I am Eve, the leader of the expedition, my husband is called Adam.”

“Jesus,” croaked Winston.

Everybody laughed and Radio continued.

“As mentioned, life has been allowed to evolve to a recipe in all of the galaxies. When a life form becomes viable, it is tested on a planet called The Honey Pot before it is released on to the M class planets which have been set aside for human life. As I understand it, none of the evolved human templates were truly satisfactory viable life forms until they were interbred and tested on The Honey Pot.

“Even then, they still required a boost of DNA from the future to get them to the standard that the Creators demanded. That is effectively what the temporal paradox is trying to achieve. Give the Creators the children they desired.”

There were mixed reactions in the room. Shock, understanding and disbelief. It was the latter that worried Radio the most.

“What is your plan now?” The Captain enquired.

“We are entering an extremely delicate time where everything converges. It is at this point where we are most vulnerable to making a mistake. If I am not careful, I run the risk of people like yourself running in to their younger selves. By my reckoning, you are due to be born within the next five years so we must be careful. In the meantime, however, we must prepare the Earth and defend creation. Our first job is to persuade the leaders of Earth’s governments to join The Sumerian Empire as the first planet of the Empire. Sumer is about to be demoted.”

“We have no problem with that, Earth is the home world after all.” The Captain looked reflective.

“Good,” said Radio. “Let’s wait for Adam and then we can get started. In my travels through time, I have seen him deal with the threat from Pelos. I have also seen him defend the Honey Pot.”

“What is Pelos?” asked the Captain.

“As I mentioned, there are nine planets in this sector alone that contain human life. Pelos is another human race, a secondary inter galactic empire that has been allowed to flourish without Mother and Father, as an experiment, to see how they turn out. In truth, they haven’t turned out too badly. However, they are slightly aggressive. They are about to attack the Honey Pot.”

“Where is the Honey Pot?” asked Winston.

“The Honey Pot is an ‘M’ class planet in the Mishpat-Tsedeq system.”

“Good grief,” exclaimed the Captain. “That system is half way across the Galaxy. How are we going to get there?”

“I will take us there.” said Radio. “Now, perhaps you could answer some of my questions?”

“Of course,” said the Captain.

“Can you give me a status report?”

“We have completed our mining expedition on the planet below and our hold is full. We have everything you need to execute your plan.”

“What is your plan?” asked Klaus.

“My plan is to free the people of the Earth from the lives they have enslaved themselves in. Mother and Father need recruits to help maintain the universe. Those recruits need power. To acquire power, they must pass my interview. To pass my interview, they need to behave well. To behave well, they can’t be at work all day chasing the money they need to pay their mortgages. I'm going to use the vast wealth that exists on Mephistopheles to buy them out of slavery. It is the path of least resistance."

"I assume it is no accident that the planet is called Mephistopheles," suggested Winston.

Radio looked at Winston directly in the eye.

"You have really impressed me today Winston with your insight. The planet is called Mephistopheles for a reason and it is no accident. Nor is it an accident that it is in the Draco system."

Winston laughed, "I think I'm getting the hang of this."

Radio chuckled and turned to his daughter.

"Now, it is time to instruct the intergalactic fleet to head for the Earth.

The Golden Fleet will sail up the Thames estuary to the Houses of Parliament where they will be met by the UK Government.

"The Closer Fleet will sail up the Clyde to The Scottish Exhibition Centre where The Scottish Government will meet them.

"The Opera Fleet will split in two with Italian sailing up the Bristol Channel where members of the Welsh Assembly will meet them and German will fly in to Belfast over Lough Neagh where they will be met by representatives from Stormont.

"The Unknown Pleasures fleet has the honour of sailing up the Forth to the Rail Bridge. From there I will show you my home town of Edinburgh and take you for a feed at my favourite restaurant."

One of the young Ensigns who had followed them into the room looked excitedly at the Captain. Suddenly, he knew, for a fact, that this was the Captain's daughter and his own grandchild. He also knew her nickname was Haggis on account of a fascination with Scotland.

"What is going on?" he asked the Operator silently.

"Our awareness's are merging. You have full access to all the databases and I'm releasing information to you when you need it. You need to adjust to this very quickly. We'll talk in more detail when you go to bed."

Radio looked at his grandchild.

"Is everything all right, Haggis?" he asked.

His granddaughter looked utterly astonished.

"Yes, I'm just excited, that's all. I've always wanted to see Edinburgh and I wasn't sure if I ever would. Does it really have a castle?"

"Yes, a rather large one on top of an extinct volcano."

"What's it like?" she asked excitedly.

Radio scratched his head.

"I can't remember," he said. "I haven't been there since I was five."

Everybody burst out laughing.

"I live there." He exclaimed. "You don't visit the tourist attractions when you live in a town."

"But it's a castle," the Ensign spluttered.

"Next you'll be wanting me to introduce you to The Loch Ness Monster." It was artfully done. He knew she had a fascination for this as well. Little did she know that he could make it happen. Sort of.

"There's no such thing," she scoffed.

Radio put on his straightest face and turned to her, looking her seriously in the eye.

"Er…that isn't true. I've met her on several occasions. The first time, she stole my salmon sandwiches."

Everybody in the room stopped. He had been convincing and when he spoke like that, people listened. He could feel the Operator giggling in his head. "I love you," she whispered.

Haggis didn't know what to think. Her face went from incredulous to hopeful in the blink of an eye.

"You're not serious," she said.

"I'm perfectly serious. Twenty-five years ago, when I was in my early twenties, I was fishing on the shore by Urquhart Castle. At lunchtime, I put down my rod and went in to my rucksack for my lunch.

"I got out my sandwiches and laid them on a rock and went back in to the sack for my flask. When I went to get my sarnies, they were gone.

I turned around and there she was. Munching away."

"No way," she exclaimed.

"Way," he retorted. "When we get the chance, I'll take you to see her. I'll see if she'll give us a ride on her back."

Haggis was stunned. She looked at her Mother who could only shrug her shoulders indicating that she wasn't sure. She turned back to Radio.

"I'd be honoured to meet the monster," she said finally.

"The beast is no monster but one of the most ancient and powerful entities in this universe."

The room was completely silent now.

"What?" he demanded.

They all laughed again.

"Father, you are full of surprises," said the Captain.

"Just keeping you on your toes. Now, who wants to see the Matrix?" he asked.

There was a universal showing of hands. Radio turned to the nearest blank wall and opened the TIMESPLICER application.

"Operator, spatial incursion to the Matrix, please."

The wall in front of him warped and a door swished open in front of him. He held out his hand for his daughter to take and then walked through beckoning the others to follow.

When they were all safely back in the Matrix his daughter started to pace around, taking it all in.

"This is where I grew up," she said finally.

Radio hadn't thought of that but of course, she must have grown up here, in the Matrix.

"That hasn't happened yet," murmured Radio.

"I know that," she said, "It's completely crazy yet it all makes sense now."

She turned to her father. "Do you have any idea how clever you really are?"

Radio stopped for a moment and scratched his head. He hated having to speculate on this topic but, as usual, he had prepared a statement.

"I don't think I am clever in the traditional sense. I think I was designed to be different. My forte is being able to take a myriad of disconnected ideas, put forward by others, and merge them all together in to a single coherent solution. I am the person who stands on the shoulders of giants."

"Yes," she said. "That makes complete sense."

"Right," said Radio, in a very business-like fashion. "Time to get down to some work."

"Archangels," he called for Blondie and Goldilocks.

They appeared out of nowhere and stood in front of him.

“Will you kindly advise the various governments of the United Kingdom that a very large inter galactic fleet is about to arrive on their doorsteps. I will be very grateful if they could all send representatives to greet them. Ask them to treat it like a state visit.”

“On our way,” they responded in unison and disappeared through the matrix.

Radio turned to his daughter. “Now we need to wait for Adam. I have a plan for defending The Honey Pot and he is the key.”

“Why Adam?” enquired The Captain.

Again, Radio scratched his head. “I have seen him in time defending the planet.”

“Do you mean that you can see the future?”

“Yes, sort of. I have no idea how it works but when I get very drunk on alcohol, I appear to be able to send my awareness through time and space. I got the idea from the native Americans.”

“Are you serious?” she asked incredulously.

“Yes, quite serious. There are traditions from the Native Americans where members of their tribes, known as Shamen, would take some form of narcotic, and go on what was known as a spirit quest. I think they were seeing the possible futures laid out before them which helped them make the right choices for the tribes they served.

“My experiences have been very similar. I get drunk on whisky and I can see events as they may happen. I can discard the choices that lead to an unfavourable outcome and select the way I want things to turn out.”

“That is incredible.”

“In every scenario, I have seen Adam defeat The Pelosians. I have drawn up my plans based on what I have seen.”

“What else have you seen?” she asked curiously.

“What I’m about to tell you is really important, so listen carefully. In the not too distant future, you will believe that my life will be threatened. I don’t want you to worry. I want you to remember that I have been everywhere in time and space and I have seen a myriad of futures. I have even seen the testing. Unlike the native Americans who had animals to lead them on their quests, I have The Operator, the greatest, kindest, cleverest sentient Alpha-Omega in existence.”

“Good grief, it’s all so hard to take in,” she said breathlessly.

“I know it is difficult but you have to get up to speed quickly. There are so many people looking to you for leadership. There are so many who rely on you for their existence.”

Klaus, who was standing nearby, interrupted.

“I hope you don’t mind me asking but what is an Alpha-Omega?”

“Klaus, I don’t mind you asking, in fact, I demand that you ask questions if you are unsure of something. An Alpha-Omega or AO is an operating system invented by Mother and Father. It stands for Automatic Operator. It is the system which maintains the universe. It does a huge amount of maintenance automatically, without even thinking and then it intervenes sentinel when required.

“Now Klaus, here is the thing that will really blow you away. You have one, as does every human being.”

Everybody in the room was listening now and they all gasped.

“You see, when a baby is born, The Operator writes a very small version of itself and places it in the baby’s brain. Think about it. Your brain is maintaining your body without the need for you to think about it. The small version that The Operator writes is called a Software Upload.

“You call it a soul from **SO**ftware **U**p**L**oad.”

“Father, how do you know all this?”

"I designed it all for Mother and Father. It is all part of my Radio Who? The Operator is the universe's Oversoul."

It was Winston's turn for a question. "Master, you talked about the testing, what do you mean by the testing?"

"It is my understanding that Mother and Father want to retire and turn responsibility for the universe over to someone else. As I understand it, there are five candidates and I'm one of them.

"Normally, I would have no interest in assuming control but I think Mother and Father know that. To motivate me, they have selected a couple of complete bastards as candidates who seemingly have a good chance. Rather than let the universe be controlled by these chumps, I'm really going to go for it. The Operator has been preparing me for years. I don't mind telling you Winston, I'm absolutely shitting myself."

Radio eased the tension with this admission and everyone in the room laughed.

"I don't think you have anything to worry about," his daughter interjected. As she said it, she smiled and winked at him. Of course, she knew him after the tests. This was a very good sign.

"Before the testing can begin, I need to deal with Pelos and recruit The Earth."

Radio knew that both these tasks were preliminary rounds. He was being tested already to see how he would deal with difficult situations. He knew that he must ensure that nobody died and that everyone had free choice. It was Mother and Father's way.

He turned to his daughter. "I think we should contact Adam. I don't think I can wait. We'll get him to join us and we'll decide what to do."

Seven - The Honey Pot

"Operator, Hail Adam. On screen."

The time window morphed and the bridge of The Atrocity Exhibition appeared out of the haze.

"Hello Adam. I'm afraid I'm under a little bit of time pressure. Can you join us please?"

Without saying a word, Adam walked through the TIME door and into the matrix. Haggis walked over and kissed his cheek and The Captain embraced him.

"What can I do for you, Master?"

"It is my belief that I am about to be tested by Mother and Father along with several other candidates. To that end, I believe that Mother and Father have arranged for their experimental garden to be attacked by an aggressive inter galactic empire called Pelos.

"The planet in question orbits around the star El-Elion in the Mishpat-Tsedeq system. It is an M class planet called the Honey Pot and it is administered by angels working for Mother and Father. The entity in charge is a scientist known as The Beekeeper.

"Our job is to defend the Honey Pot and ensure that the planet remains inviolate thus protecting thousands of years of experiments.

"It is my belief that this is one of three preliminaries to the testing proper, a qualification round, if you will, to show worthiness."

Everyone was silent for a moment and then Adam cleared his throat.

"How do you know this?"

"Apparently," Eve interjected, "My father can send his awareness through time and space by getting drunk on Scotch whisky."

Adam looked at Radio and burst out laughing. "That's handy, very handy. Killing two birds with one stone."

Eve looked at her father. "My husband is well acquainted with the properties of Scotch Whisky."

Ouch, thought Radio. *Clearly a bone of contention.* "When we have time, Adam, I can show you how to do it too. One has to get very, very drunk." He smiled.

Eve looked annoyed and gave a rather sickly smile.

"I'll look forward to that. What is your plan?"

"My plan is to take the Lookfar and the Atrocity Exhibition to the Mishpat-Tsedeq system and defend the Honey Pot. Things are a bit more complicated then they first appear. The Pelosian plan is to denude the planet of its minerals. My plan is to offer them an alternative. If they agree, I will open a spatial incursion to Draco and allow them to mine Mephistopheles."

"And if they disagree?"

"Here is the slight complication. If they disagree, we have a problem. Their ships are not particularly well defended. The Atrocity Exhibition will easily destroy their entire fleet. My fall back plan is to arm 2 of your shuttlecraft with phased canon and use them to disable their fleet. We will then teleport the survivors to your hold and drop them off at the nearest uninhabited M class planet which is Tsedeq itself, in the same star system. I expect there to be no casualties whatsoever. This is important and is the key to negotiating this round."

"Understood. When do you want to start?"

"Straight away. Eve, Haggis, Winston and Klaus, you will join me on the Lookfar. Adam, return to your ship and we will join you in about 5 minutes."

Radio beckoned for the group to follow. They mounted the stairwell from the Elevator floor and turned away from the opening which led to the rest of the matrix. Before them was a silver staircase which Radio climbed. When they reached the top, there was a doorway in to a small cabin with a cockpit in the front. There were three seats in the cockpit and seven seats arranged behind.

"Eve, Winston, join me at the front. Haggis, you and Klaus can sit there." He indicated the two seats directly behind the Pilot.

"Secure your seatbelts. This is going to be hairy."

"Don't you have inertial dampeners," asked The Captain.

"Of course. However, we will still be travelling at great speed. Everyone ready?"

Before them, through the windshield was black space. No stars. Nothing.

"Operator, take us out."

The door behind them sealed shut with a clunk and the ship gingerly unattached itself from its mooring. It moved forward slowly until it was clear of the matrix.

"Operator, spatial incursion to Sumer."

In front of them a giant black hole appeared like a spiral of emptiness. There was a juddering motion and then they flew forward at great speed. Radio was thrown deep into the bowels of his chair.

"Oh my God," Winston shouted.

Radio laughed. Winston hadn't even been on a modern rollercoaster let alone a spaceship travelling through time and space. The experience, he had to admit, was somewhat disorienting.

There was a flash of bright light and then they slowed very quickly and came to a gentle stop. In front of them was the Atrocity Exhibition in orbit around Sumer.

"Operator, hail and on screen."

The viewer in front of them morphed in that recognisable way and they were looking at the bridge.

"Are you ready, Adam?" he asked.

"As ready as we'll ever be, Master."

"Hang on to your hat!"

Radio manoeuvred the craft so that they were pointing into deep space away from the planet.

"Operator, spatial incursion to the Honey Pot."

The same black hole appeared in front of them and they were off. Just as before, they slowed down gently and came to a stop. In front of them was the most beautiful thing Radio had ever seen. The Honey Pot.

The planet was blue and gold and there was a rainbow corona surrounding it.

Suddenly, The Operator's voice appeared over the loudspeaker.

"We are being hailed by The Beekeeper."

"On screen."

A beautiful woman appeared in his field of vision. It was the face he had dreamed about for a long time.

"My knight in shining armour. Come halfway across the galaxy to rescue me from despicable thugs."

He didn't know what to say. He couldn't speak.

"Cat got your tongue?" she enquired.

"Hello, Miriam," he said. "Fancy meeting you here?"

"Do you mean, fancy meeting the woman you fancy here?"

Everyone on board laughed out loud and so did others on the planet who were slightly out of view.

Radio chuckled. *Who would blame me*, he thought.

"Well I don't blame you," she said. "I rather like it."

Shit, she can read my thoughts, he thought.

Miriam looked at him and it was her turn to burst out laughing.

"Coming through," she said.

There was that familiar swishing sound behind him and there she was. She was in the cabin with him.

Radio unfastened himself from his seatbelt and walked over to her. He put his arms around her and held her tightly. After about a minute she spoke again.

"You can let go now."

"I want to," responded Radio, "But my arms won't let me."

She cupped his face in her hands and looked him directly in the eye.

"I know darling, but you are going to have to let me go for a while. I'm not going anywhere."

"How can you be in two places at once?" he enquired.

"I'm not. I had a dream the other night and I've been dying to speak to you. I have some information which you may find interesting. When you ask The Operator something, she responds in my voice, am I correct?"

"Yes. I hear your voice as clear as day."

"When I ask The Operator something, I hear your voice in response." She looked at him with her eyebrows raised, challenging him to find an answer.

Radio looked at her in shock and then, suddenly, a massive penny dropped and it felt like the final piece in an extremely difficult jigsaw fell in to place.

"Christ," he said aloud, "We are both linked to The Operator."

The look she gave him was one of understanding finally. He imagined his face must have looked exactly the same.

"Yes, we are both linked to The Operator. Your thoughts are my thoughts now and vice versa but there is something more. I can't quite explain it but I think we are on the edge of it. The something else is eluding us at the moment."

"Yes, there is something bigger and you are right on the edge of it, as you say." It was The Operator speaking in their heads.

They looked at each other and said, "Was that you?" They both spoke at the same time and both found it very funny. Both found it terrifying.

Radio looked at Miriam. "I want to conduct a small experiment. Please say out loud what I'm thinking. If I can be absolutely sure you know my thoughts straight away, we can use this to our advantage."

She nodded in acquiescence.

Radio closed his eyes and said, "Go."

"You are thinking about a Mint Aero."

He smiled and changed tack.

"St Agur cheese."

He nodded.

"Joy Division."

He gave her the thumbs up.

"Shah Jahan Rezala Chicken, Pilau Rice, Garlic Naan."

He chortled.

"Do you think of nothing other than food?"

"You obviously know the answer to that."

She laughed.

"This is fantastic," he said seriously. "I think our minds have been married."

She looked at him and he felt a wave of pure love emanating from her. He had obviously said the right thing. He put that information away for a later date although what difference it would make he didn't know. She already knew what he was thinking.

There was a very loud clearing of a throat behind them. It was Eve.

"Mother, Father, if you don't mind, I think we should get going."

"Right," said Radio. He created a loop with his arm for Miriam and she put her arm through it. He couldn't bear being separated from her, especially when she was in the immediate vicinity.

"Spatial incursion to Atrocity Exhibition."

The door swished open and they all walked through on to the bridge.

"Welcome," said Adam. "What now?"

"We wait. I expect the Pelosian fleet anytime in the next few hours. Do you have long range sensors?"

"We do," responded Adam, "But they are not very accurate."

"Captain, we are picking up the fleet on sensors. ETA two hours." It was one of the Ensigns sitting at what looked like a science station.

"Two hours. That gives us plenty of time. Have you armed your shuttle craft?"

"We are in the process of doing it now."

"Right." He turned to Miriam. "Do you think the planet is in any danger?"

"I doubt it. Although I know this to be a test, I don't think Mother and Father would allow their experiments to be affected in any way. The research is too valuable."

"Yes, that is my belief also. I need a straight answer." He looked at Miriam. "Am I being tested or are we being tested?"

She took a deep breath.

"I'm not sure. If you and I are linked now, as we suspect, then I think we are being tested."

"That answers my question. I think we are linked and I think I can prove it"

"How can you prove it?" she asked.

"When I saw the Creators in my dreams, I saw the design of the solution, from what I could piece together, the AO should write small discrete versions of itself to be uploaded into the human population.

"Before upload, the SOUL was to be placed in the GUF or The General Upload Facility where it would be split into its male and female components. When the bodies died the two parts would meet up in the afterlife and become an ANGEL. A Non-Genetically Engineered Life form.

"I think we are the same soul. When our bodies eventually die, we will be together in the afterlife. That's why I think The Operator is pushing us together. I think we have a better chance of passing the tests if we are together."

From nowhere came the sound of music. It was The Operator giving him a clue that he was on the right track. Radio had worked a part of it out. However, he just knew there was more.

"Can you hear that?" he asked his daughter.

"Ye" she said, "I believe it is Beethoven's 9th Symphony. Well done, Father. I think you are getting there."

She was smiling from ear to ear and so was Adam. Everyone was smiling and the penny dropped.

"Are you in on this?" he asked Eve.

"Yes, Father. We are all in on it. We all work for Mother and Father, the creators. You are doing very well, by the way. I would proceed as you are. You are going to blow them all away, Father."

"Are you in on it?" he turned to Miriam.

"I thought I was, at first, but now I'm not sure. I think I have a choice to make. Do what Mother and Father tell me to do or just forget that and go with you."

"Well?" He already knew the answer. She had been waiting for him as long as he had waited for her.

"I'm going with you and hang the consequences."

He looked at her and put as much love in his glance as he could muster. "There won't be any consequences. You are supposed to do this. I'm certain of it."

The look she gave him showed that she believed him.

There was a sudden crackling noise as the ships communication system came alive.

"Engineering to the bridge. Captain, the shuttlecraft are ready for inspection."

"On my way." Adam turned to the others. "Let's go take a look."

They all made their way to the shuttle bay via an elevator.

The shuttlecraft were a bit bigger than Radio had expected and were easily the same size as The Lookfar. With the enhanced weaponry, they looked mean.

"I'm having second thoughts about this. Are you sure you can disable their fleet without casualties?"

One of the engineers stepped forward.

"Don't worry, Master. We have very exact targeting computers on board. Our plan is to hit their engines with the phased canon. It will disable their propulsion systems but will cause minimal damage?"

"Right. I really can't afford to have casualties. I think Mother and Father will be very upset if anyone is hurt."

Adam turned to Radio.

"Listen, it may not come to that. I think your plan is a good one and if I was a betting man, I'd be fairly certain that they will take you up on your offer of mining Mephistopheles. It is, by far, the largest mineral giant in this galaxy."

"I hope you're right. Time will tell, I guess."

Eight - Into the Abyss

They all returned to the bridge where they didn't have long to wait.

The Pelosian fleet sailed in to view at great speed and when they slowed, it was obvious which the Mother Ship was.

"Operator, hail the Mother Ship. On screen."

The viewer morphed as The Operator took control and they found themselves looking on to a bridge of a very similar size to The Atrocity Exhibition. Standing before them was a man who was obviously in charge. The Operator informed Radio that his name was Admiral Apollyon. Radio smirked inwardly. He knew who Apollyon worked for and he now knew that this was definitely a test.

"Welcome Admiral Apollyon, I trust you are well?" Radio smiled.

Apollyon looked shocked for a split second then he relaxed.

"Hello Radio," said Apollyon.

Radio continued, "The Planet yonder, you plan to denude of mineral, is The Honey Pot and is your Masters' experimental garden. It must remain inviolate or thousands of years of experiments will be lost. I believe this will make your masters very cross indeed.

"I have been gifted a planet in the Draco system called Mephistopheles which I am very sure you are acquainted with. You are welcome to mine there and you may satisfy all your needs. I will even open a spatial incursion and let your fleet pass through without harm."

The Admiral looked at him and burst out laughing. He held his hands up.

"In my defence, Radio, I warned Mother and Father that this exercise was a complete waste of time and that you'd pass with flying colours. I am delighted to say that I was right, for once. You have passed the test with flying colours."

He looked at Adam. "Permission to come aboard?"

"Granted," said Adam.

There was a flash of light and the sound of a teleport beam. Apollyon was with them on the bridge.

Radio walked over and held out his hand. "Apollyon, really?"

"It is an old one and we weren't sure if you had heard of it. We were pretty sure you would have heard of the others. Where did you hear about it?"

"Nostradamus predicted it 400 years ago."

Apollyon looked at Radio approvingly.

"Your TIME solution is outstanding. You are going to blow them all away."

Radio chuckled. "So, everyone keeps saying. You can stop. If you think for one second that I'm going to be fooled by your attempt to give me a hubris and make me overconfident then you are sadly mistaken. I will not be hoodwinked so easily."

Apollyon looked up at the ceiling. "What's the point?" he asked of no one in particular.

"Now let's get down to business and the real reason I'm here," said Radio.

Suddenly everyone stopped and he could tell that he had caught them all off guard. A little smile was playing about Miriam's lips and he winked at her.

Radio looked at Apollyon.

"I'd like to offer you a job."

There was utter silence. There was fear. Adam and Eve looked terrified. Miriam looked unconcerned.

"You play a dangerous game, Radio," said Apollyon. "I like dangerous games. What's in it for me?"

"In the old days, you were accorded the number 2 because you are of the sea and of the land. I see the sea but I do not see the land. I will bring you the land and you will be one."

Apollyon's face went stark white and he looked like a man about to faint.

"If anyone else had said that to me I would have considered it impossible. As you have said it to me, I choose to believe you. I must give you this warning. If you are lying to me, I will not rest until I see you defeated and dead. Do I make myself clear to you?"

"You do and I would expect nothing less from you. However, I already know where the land can be found and I know how to win the kingdom."

"You may consider myself recruited."

"Thank you, Archangel," said Radio.

"Operator, open spatial incursion to Draco and let the Pelosian fleet pass through."

He turned to Apollyon. "Give the fleet their final instructions."

When Apollyon was done, Radio opened an incursion to the matrix.

"Winston, Klaus, Eve, Adam, Haggis and Apollyon. Return to the matrix and wait for me there. Miriam and I will return with the Lookfar. We have loads to do."

When they were all safely back in the matrix, Radio decided that he would put on a slow casserole for dinner. He was still digesting the food he had eaten on Plantagenet but in a few hours, he knew that they would all be hungry. Dinner would also be a good opportunity to check up on Jamie and Ranger Graham. He would invite them to supper.

"Need any help?" It was Eve offering her services. Normally, he hated having someone in the kitchen as he felt that too many cooks definitely spoiled the broth, however, he suspected that, for Eve, it was quite normal for her to help out.

"You can peel the spuds and put them on to boil," he said.

She collected the potatoes and started peeling them. Soon, between the two of them, they had everything in the slow cooker. Radio secured the lid.

"Smells good. I've never asked this before but where did you learn to cook?"

Radio laughed. All his adult life, he had received compliments on his cooking skills and people assumed that he must have been trained in France or something but the truth was a lot more prosaic.

"When I left home, I was only eighteen and once I'd paid all my bills, I had very little money left over to feed and clothe myself. I taught myself to cook out of necessity. If I didn't become very good, very quickly, I'd go hungry. It was a great learning curve. There were times when I had so little money, I literally had to make a silk purse out of a sow's ear."

"It's amazing," she said, "But I'm not surprised. You are very creative. I hate to think of you grubbing about like that though."

"Don't pity me. I think the best way of learning is to do it under difficult circumstances. Mother and Father have always known this and I never complained because I instinctively knew what they were doing."

They made their way back to the group who had all found seats at the round table.

"Dinner will be in two hours. I think we should use that time to reflect on what has happened so far and decide what to do next." Radio announced.

"Let's start with Winston. As things stand, Winston is in a bit of a pickle. He has nearly 400,000 troops languishing on the beach at Dunkirk surrounded by the Wehrmacht. France has effectively fallen and the Germans are a whisker away from winning the war, although they themselves have no idea just how close they actually are. A flotilla of small boats is on its way to Dunkirk to rescue the BEF and the Luftwaffe are about to start a blitzkrieg on London.

"I can tell you that the evacuation of Dunkirk will be a great success and you do not require any help from us. The British need to do it all themselves as it will give them hope. Your job is to hammer that message of hope home. I want you to use the radio as much as possible.

"You will go on to the end, Winston. You shall fight in France, you shall fight on the seas and oceans, you shall fight with growing confidence and growing strength in the air, you shall defend my Island, whatever the cost may be, you shall fight on the beaches, you shall fight on the landing grounds, you shall fight in the fields and in the streets, you shall fight in the hills; you shall never surrender.

You can quote me on that, Winston."

There was a moment of silence and then everybody fell about.

"I think I'll write that down," laughed Winston.

"As far as the blitz is concerned, we have done as much as I dare. That only leaves the promise I made to you five years ago."

"Which was?" enquired Apollyon.

"I'm so glad you asked. Gabriel, Uriel, get the stuff."

Blondie and Goldilocks had returned from their errand and ran off to get their packages. When they returned, they started laying everything out on the table.

"Here is your first task, Lucifer," Radio announced, waving his hands over the contents of the table. "A time hatchet job."

Radio's mentioning of Apollyon's name caused a few raised eyebrows but not any real shock. *Good,* he thought, *they already suspected.*

Lucifer was curious and interested. Another good sign.

"Tell me," said Radio, "Do you know what whispers in the dark are?"

Lucifer smiled and it was a brilliant wicked smile. "I think you'll find that I invented them."

"Do you know this man?"

Radio turned and pointed towards the TIME windows. The Operator had put up a portrait of the most notorious criminal of the 20th century.

"Him, I know," said Lucifer.

Radio went to the table and picked up some of the papers left there by Uriel.

"You are Julius Schaub, Hitler's Nazi Party adjutant, shit." Radio stopped. He had heard of Schaub and wondered if he was too high profile. He turned to Gabriel and Uriel. He had a very bad feeling.

"Where is the real Julius Schaub?"

"He is in our rooms. Don't worry, we got him completely nuggets on schnapps. He hasn't a clue. When Lucifer is finished, we'll get him pissed again and dump him at the bunker in Berlin at the end of the war."

Radio thought for a moment and decided it was a great plan. He smiled at the archangels. They purred.

"When did you get him pissed?"

"July 21, 1943. One year before the assassination attempt."

"Do you have his DNA?"

They held out a lock of hair. Radio gathered up the strands and held it up.

"Operator, scan DNA and upload into the transform application."

The hair disappeared and Radio turned back to Lucifer.

"You will go back to July 21, 1943 and take up your position as Hitler's adjutant. How good is your German?"

"Ausgezeichnet," he responded.

"Fantastic, you will whisper in Hitler's ear and you will take him to the edge of reason. When he is completely mad you will take him to the precipice and you will show him the abyss."

"Then what?" asked Lucifer.

"You will throw him in." Radio said it with a note of finality.

"And why would I do this?"

"He murdered 6.2 million of your children."

Lucifer looked at the uniform and started dressing at once. When he was done, he looked the part.

"Klaus, I need you to go with Lucifer and give him inside information on the Third Reich. The culture, the currency, manners, you know the type of thing. You can stay in Schaub's apartment. Will you do that for me?"

"Yes, master. I'd be delighted."

Radio raised his index finger to Lucifer's temple and said "Operator, upload the transform application and activate."

A timer appeared in the time window followed by a green tick.

Lucifer concentrated for a moment and he transformed in to Julius Schaub.

"Ready?" asked Radio. "Operator, temporal incursion to Reichskanzlerei, July 21, 1943."

The time window morphed and looked on to wartime Berlin.

Lucifer gathered all the papers and without a backward glance, he and Klaus walked in to 1943.

Nine – The Pillar in the Temple

It was dinner time and Radio walked over to the time windows to collect Jamie and Ranger Graham.

"Operator, spatial incursion to Yellow Stone National Park."

The time window morphed and Radio looked on to a scene of utter bedlam. The world's media were camped outside the Ranger's offices in the park. He cursed under his breath. He hated the press, for no other reason than he thought them extremely badly behaved. He walked through.

As he appeared the crowd screamed and he realised he was going to have to talk to them. He stood on the stairs in front of the crowd and said, "Silence."

The crowd shut up immediately. Radio addressed them.

"I have fifteen minutes to spare so please choose your questions carefully."

He looked around and recognised one of the logos on a reporter's microphone.

"NBC," he said.

"Sir," said a young woman of about 30. "Can you give us some idea of the size of the immanent volcanic eruption?"

"Certainly. Our expectation is that the eruption will eject 250 cubic miles of debris and will be at least 2500 times the size of the 1980 eruption at Mt St Helen's. Left unchecked it is potentially an extinction level event. However, we are going to use alien technology to stream some of the ejecta into the atmosphere. The rest of the ejecta will be teleported in to space where it will be collected and removed. There is nothing to fear. You still have 2.5 days to evacuate the exclusion zone. If you remain outside of the exclusion zone for the duration of the event, I can personally guarantee your safety. If you venture inside, then you risk injury and death. Nobody will try to save you if you get in to trouble."

"KTWO." Radio knew this was a local station on the ABC network.

"Do you think it dangerous to make a pact with Satan?" It was a middle-aged man with a look of fear on his face.

Radio considered the question. He realised that The Operator had warned him she would televise the day's events but he had forgotten in all the commotion. Probably just as well as he realised it would have been a distraction.

"I see you've been paying attention, for once." A small titter ran through the crowd. "If I thought it was dangerous then I wouldn't have made it in the first place. I realise that you have a very warped idea of the truth and that is not your fault. I cannot answer all of your questions on this topic just now as I fear it would take too long. However, please approach a reputable Rabbi who I'm sure will be able to explain it to you. If you have no access to a Rabbi then please refer to Job chapter one."

"Fox."

"Is it significant that the ships in the inter galactic fleet are named after Joy Division albums and songs." It was a man about the same age as himself and he was wearing an earring. *I bet he was a fan,* thought Radio.

"I named the fleet after my favourite music. That is the only significance. Thanks for the question."

He laughed and so did everyone else.

"BBC." *What are you doing here*, he thought?

"How extensive have your travels in time been?" It was the million-dollar question.

"Now I'm really going to give you all a headache." They laughed again. "My travels have been extensive but I haven't made all the trips yet. This is the year when the paradoxes are resolved so all the major time interventions should be completed over the next few months. For obvious reasons, The Operator isn't keen on time travel so the quicker we complete our adventures the better."

Radio held up both his hands. The all stop sign.

"Listen. I know you are curious but the next few weeks have been meticulously planned so that the truth is revealed to you slowly. By asking your questions now you are merely spoiling what should be very interesting television. Don't ruin it for yourselves and everybody else. Keep an eye on the TV and enjoy yourselves. There is nothing to fear. I really must go now as I have too much to do."

Radio turned around and was ushered inside.

"Whoosh," he said to Jamie. "How are you getting on?"

"Good," he smiled, "We've cleared the park already and we have a plan to evacuate all the urban settlements. In fact, there was already a plan in place, we are merely acting on it. I have been on TV and given everyone the warnings they need to get out of Dodge. Luckily, the figures I gave them were exactly the same as the one's you have just given so at least we sound joined up."

Radio turned to Ranger Graham, "Hasn't he done well?"

"This boy is a certified Genius, Master. A certified Genius."

Radio heaved a sigh of relief. He was very pleased.

"Right, let's get you both fed. It's dinner time."

"Good," said Jamie, "I'm bleedin' starving."

"Operator, the matrix, if you please."

When they got back, Lucifer and Klaus were waiting for them, still in uniform.

"That was quick," said Radio. "I take it, our Nazi friend took the easy way out?"

"Strangely enough, he did. I don't think he could take the voices in his head anymore. I came back as quickly as I could. I'm not missing one of your dinners. It's the main reason I decided to work for you."

"This is the most delicious casserole I have ever eaten," said Winston when they had sat round to dinner. "It is utterly sublime." Winston had been in a good mood since he had received news from Lucifer.

Radio smiled. He loved hearing people enjoy his food. It was one of life's real pleasures.

"I didn't think I liked casserole," said Jamie, "But I'm liking this. It's tremendous."

They sat round the table for ages and finished off with a bowl of vanilla ice cream from the fridge. It was Winston's favourite and he rather liked it too.

At the end of the meal, they all helped to clear away the dishes and when he was about to suggest a game of cards he noticed that everyone had gone quiet.

Standing at the time window was Gabriel and Uriel.

"Are you ready?" Gabriel asked.

"Yes, I'm ready."

"Then come with us."

Radio walked behind them, through the time window, into the hall. He was calm. The Operator had taken him into this hall one hundred times in his dreams. It was packed.

Standing room only and every entity of power in the universe was in attendance. Sitting at the end of the hall on a massive throne was Father.

In his dreams, he had met him at least a hundred times but that did not prepare Radio for the reality of meeting him in person. He was 9 feet tall and extremely robust. His face betrayed the wisdom of ages and He looked every inch the Father.

Radio walked right up to him and looked him directly in the eyes. His face was stern but His eyes were smiling.

"Hello Father," said Radio.

There were murmurings throughout the hall. "Outrageous," "Who does the boy think he is," "No manners," "Jumped up, little twit."

"Hello Radio," said Father.

Radio took a deep breath and asked the question he knew would change the universe forever.

"Where's Mother?"

There were shouts of derision and there were outbursts of shock and disbelief. Most of the audience simply burst out laughing. In the rush to pour scorn on him, they didn't notice the flaring of an incandescent light behind him. Then all sound stopped.

"I'm right here," said a voice. An unmistakably familiar female voice.

Radio looked up, she smiled at him and he ran in to her arms. She picked him up and looked at him.

"Do you love me, little boy?"

"Let me show you how much."

He grabbed her face between his hands and gave her the all over face kiss. She laughed.

"I want one of them," said Father. She handed him over and he repeated the process with Father.

"Glad you could join us dear," said Father.

"Good to be here, at last," said Mother. "I was beginning to wonder if I actually existed. If it wasn't for my young apprentice, I think I'd still be living in the shadows."

Radio launched the chuck a chair application and created a throne out of mid-air for Mother to sit on. Every bit as large as the one occupied by his Father.

"Thank you darling." Mother sat down.

If Father had been impressive then Radio found it difficult to find the word that described Mother. For Radio, it was like when television went from black and white to colour or when jumbo jets became Concorde. She was, without doubt, supersonic.

Radio turned to look at the crowd. They were stunned. He was chuffed. Pay-back time.

Mother began. "Radio, you have told the Earth that you are my apprentice and therefore my candidate for the testing. Your Father and I would like to know why?"

Everyone in the room was looking at him now and they looked worried. They looked like recalcitrant children who had been caught in the act of wrongdoing and were now being forced to suffer. They looked frightened.

Radio cleared his throat.

"When You and Father first introduced yourselves to me 15 years ago, I wondered why nobody on Earth had heard of you. After a period of consideration, I realised that this was not true.

"There are two pillars in the temple. It wasn't that they had not heard of you, it was that they had forgotten about you. I did not realise that this forgetfulness extended to the whole universe.

"I decided there and then that I would make it my personal responsibility to reintroduce you to those who had forgotten. I understood that this would not bother my Father as you are a loving couple and He would want you both to be together.

"I also realised that, as a student, I should apprentice myself to the master that I needed the most."

They both nodded. "Why do you need Mother the most?" asked Father curiously.

"Because Mother's a girl and I'm a boy," replied Radio.

He had said it as if it was the most obvious thing in the world and it made Mother and Father chuckle.

"Why did you think it your responsibility to reintroduce me to the universe?" asked Mother.

Radio thought for a second and gave the most honest answer that he could come up with.

"When I saw you both in my dreams, I realised that I loved you very much. It felt the right thing to do."

Father stood up followed by Mother. They looked sternly round the hall.

"This is our son, Radio, Mother's apprentice. You will give him a standing ovation."

Mother and Father started clapping and so did his group. Winston was cheering and Eve was crying. The others in the hall were less than enthusiastic but eventually they joined in but with not much enthusiasm.

Then he saw them. Four individuals who were looking at him with complete and utter hatred. These were the candidates. Radio relaxed. It was clear to him and he didn't know how he knew but he was sure, in that moment, that Mother and Father had selected them to teach them a lesson. At least, that was his hope.

Mother came forward to address the gathered throng. She spoke to him.

"Radio, you have qualified for the testing with flying colours. These tests have been conducted for Millennia and nobody has ever passed. There is help and advice available from those who have been tested before. Will you avail yourself of this help?"

Six robed individuals stepped forward. Three men and three women. They looked sure of themselves. Confident and arrogant. Radio smiled to himself. He already had help. He cleared his throat.

"I require no help," he announced.

There were shouts and groans from the crowd. The six robed individuals looked astonished and then offended and then they looked at him in that way he had seen so many times before. "This guy is a smart ass."

Mother looked at Gabriel and nodded. "You may return to your matrix and await instructions."

Ten – The Children of the Paradox

When they were safely back in the matrix, Eve turned to him and she looked exasperated.

"Father, are you mad," she spluttered. "You could have had help there from people who have sat the tests before."

"Calm down," said Radio. "You clearly weren't listening. Mother said that no one has ever passed the tests. The help is a diversion. It is the blind leading the blind. You can only pass the tests by listening to your heart. Not by listening to complete failures."

Eve calmed down. "Oh," she said.

"Besides. I've had lots of help from The Operator. Time for coffee."

Radio went over to the kitchen and made a pot of coffee which he placed on the round table. They all sat.

"Right, let's get back to our review of where we are now. Winston, all that remains for you is to read your book and take notes. There is no further help available at the moment."

"Master, I am content with the help given. Yesterday, I had no hope but today…"

"Good. Now Jamie. Arrangements are in place to clear the exclusion zone and instructions have been given to the general public through the media. All that remains is to tractor beam the eruption in to the atmosphere. What are you going to do?"

Jamie turned to Eve.

"Captain, can you provide a tractor beam to stream the ejecta from the eruption in to the hole in the ozone layer above the Earth?"

Radio was pleased. The boy was extremely quick on the uptake.

"We can do better than that. Our fleet has travelled from Mephistopheles to the Earth and there are currently 40 ships monitoring the activity beneath the park. We will use The Gotterdammerung to tractor beam the eruption and The Wilderness to remove any excess rubble. The Closer, which is a hospital ship will attend to any casualties. How's that?"

"Fantastic," replied Jamie.

"What time is it?" asked Radio.

"It is 22.00 GMT," replied Adam.

"Okay. I think it is too late to do anything now and I am exhausted. It has been a very long day. I suggest we all call it a day and start again in the morning."

"Yes, I'm very tired too." It was Miriam. "Besides, I think we need to talk."

Radio understood. There was so much going on and he needed to check in with Miriam. He had to make sense of all the images in his head that were not necessarily his own.

"Gabriel, will you make sure that Jamie and Ranger Graham are seen to their guest bedrooms, we will all meet up tomorrow at 07.00 for breakfast."

"Leave everything to us," said Gabriel.

Radio and Miriam went over to the massive double bed at the far end of the room. Above the bed there was a portrait of The Green Man in all his fecund glory. Radio recognised the artist and smiled. Either side of the bed there was doorway which led to a bathroom and changing room.

Radio pointed to the left-hand door as they approached.

“Those are your rooms, I’ll see you in a minute.”

The bathroom was just as he had imagined. A huge bath, shower cubicle, wash basins and wardrobes with changing rooms just leading off to the side. He stripped off and had a quick shower.

When he was dry, he found his pyjamas, laundered, and neatly laid out. He climbed into them and returned to the bed. Miriam was already waiting and he jumped in.

They snuggled close and closed their eyes.

“Are you there?” said Radio.

“Yes, we are here.”

“Was I right, are we now linked as one SOUL?”

“Yes, of course you are right. In the future, your SOULS will merge completely and you will be one, just as you were when you were written. Don’t worry, it is a wonderful thing.

“At the moment, you are in a state of flux. On the one hand, there is a desire to maintain your individuality and on the other, a yearning to be together. It takes a while to marry but you have made a very good start. You are both already experiencing each other’s direct thoughts. This should not frighten you as this has been going on for some time now. In fact, ever since you uploaded Miriam’s interface on Plantagenet.”

Radio could sense that Miriam had already worked that out.

“What happened after that?” asked Radio.

“I started experiencing visions in the same way that you have been. After a few months, Mother and Father came and got me. I was trained as a biologist on The Honey Pot and put in charge of The Operation. That was 20 years ago. Since then, I have been acquiring various skills presumably as you have acquired them and I’ve learnt to use the applications with the help of The Operator.”

“That makes complete sense,” said Radio. “There have been occasions when I’ve suddenly known how to do something that I couldn’t possibly have known before. I guessed the skill must have come from somewhere. Now I know from where.”

“This is going to be great,” she said. “Do you want to kiss me?”

“Gee, let me think,” said Radio.

They both laughed and fell into each other’s arms. Radio had never felt closer to another human being and he thought it was better than…

“A chunky Kit-Kat?” she asked. She really could read his mind!

They all arrived at the round table for seven the next morning where Radio and Miriam had laid out Cereal, milk, and fruit. There was also toast, tea and coffee.

“Isn’t there any bacon and egg?” asked Winston.

“Don’t eat too much Winston, I’m taking you all out for lunch in Edinburgh. I’ve booked out my favourite restaurant.”

“I think you’d better have a look at breakfast television,” said Eve. “We had a look in our room. I think someone is going to have a heart attack.”

Sweet Jesus, thought Radio. *What now.*

“Operator, turn on BBC Breakfast.”

The middle time window morphed and it was a reporter doing a piece to camera at the Houses of Parliament in London. Behind her were a row of massive space ships,

“There appear to be eight ships hovering over The Thames, here, just outside The Palace of Westminster. They are, The Golden Fox, The Golden Door, The Golden Key,

The Golden Hall, The Golden Filter, The Golden Light, The Golden Chance, and The Solid Gold. This, I guess, is the Golden Fleet that Radio was referring to yesterday."

"How big are the ships?" asked the presenter from the studio.

"They are absolutely massive. I don't know how they can just hang there in mid-air."

Radio could see that the ships were indeed massive. It was only when you compared them with buildings on the ground that you got some idea of the scale. He had an idea.

"Everyone tuck into breakfast. I've got an idea." He turned to Miriam, "Coming dear?"

"I'll come too," said Eve.

The three of them walked through the window in to the BBC studio and sat down on the couch. The presenter was still talking to the reporter and his back was turned.

"Do we have any idea what they are doing here?" asked the presenter.

The reporter whose eyes were bulging was looking behind him. "Why don't you ask them yourself. They're sitting behind you."

The presenter turned slowly around and stared at them for a few seconds in disbelief.

"Hello Charlie," said Radio.

"Hello Radio. Is it okay if we call you Radio, there has been a lot of debate here about what to call you? Winston Churchill, for instance, calls you Master."

"It is okay to call me Radio. I am, after all, the responsible person at the moment. Winston calls me Master because he is one of my apprentices. I've known him since he was a little boy."

"What do you mean by the person responsible?" asked Charlie.

"At any given time, in this galaxy, there is always someone responsible for a planet or a group of planets. They are there to protect the life on the planet and make sure that the environment is safe for life to flourish. The person responsible is called, Radio, which is short for Radio Operator. I imagined that the person responsible would be in the control room receiving emergency calls from around the universe. I can't be on duty 24/7, I will have to hand over responsibility to someone else at some point."

"Oh, I see. So, Radio is more of a title than a name?"

"I think I'd rather describe it as a job description."

"Why are the space ships here?"

Radio kept silent because he knew that Eve wanted to assert herself.

"We are here because we were invited to come home. My name is Captain Eve Tsedeq and I am the head of the intergalactic fleet which is based on the Sumer home world. Every human being in the Sumerian Empire is descended from an ancestor who came from Earth. In fact, the majority came from a multi culturally diverse United Kingdom. My crew are desperate to discover their origins. It is like you having the chance to go back in time and live in England during the Middle Ages."

"Gosh, I take it this is the result of the temporal paradox you keep mentioning?"

"Yes," said Radio, "To circumvent the evolutionary time frame, the past had to borrow from the future. To do that, we had to send time agents back into Earth's past to inject DNA into the indigenous population. They also introduced basic science, farming and the like. It was never our intention to leave the expedition stranded. The space ships you see across the United Kingdom this morning are the children of the paradox coming home. I would esteem it a great favour if the people of the United Kingdom would welcome them with open arms."

"I'm sure everybody will do that. I don't think I've seen the country so excited. Will they have the chance to see inside the ships?"

"Yes, of course," said Eve. "Our crews will be happy to show you round. My advice would be to create a system which manages the numbers. Each fleet can easily cope with about 5000 visitors per day and we'll be here for at least 2 months. I don't care how you do it but the system must not be based on wealth. Admission will be free and everybody must be allowed a chance. I warn you now, if I detect any bad behaviour from you, I will withdraw the offer. Mother and Father do not allow their servants to facilitate any kind of unfairness in any way."

"Understood," said Charlie. "The names of the Golden Fleet have gotten everyone talking. What is the significance?"

"I'm afraid you'll have to ask my father that question. He appears to love guessing games and we have been guessing since the ships were launched."

Radio smiled. "I can't answer all your questions as it would spoil it for those who want to work it out for themselves."

"What are your plans for today?" he asked Radio.

"I'm taking the Unknown Pleasures fleet into Edinburgh where I am taking the Captains to lunch at my favourite restaurant. After that, we will be heading back to Yellowstone to monitor the super volcano. If they have managed to clear the exclusion zone, I may decide to kick off the eruption early. It is like the sword of Damocles hanging over my head at the moment. I want to get it over and done with."

"I can understand that completely," said Charlie. "Are you here to take control?"

"Mother and Father do not believe in imposing their will. They believe in choices. You are either with us or you are against us, it is as simple as that. Being with us means that you have a desire to protect the universe. The universe was created so that life could develop here. Mother and Father require us to protect life, to move it forward. Ever onwards and ever upwards."

"You talked yesterday about passing an interview. How is that achieved?"

"You pass the interview by making a choice to follow Mother and Father. Not in the dysfunctional way you do it here on Earth. They are not in to worship and they require no obeisance. They view it as unseemly behaviour. The only way to worship Mother and Father is by doing the right thing.

"Making mistakes is allowed. Nobody was born perfect. It is Mother and Father's preferred method of teaching to throw people in at the deep end so that they can learn faster. My advice is to join in with life and learn from any mistakes you make.

"Make sure your heart is in the right place and when you conclude that protecting creation is the right thing to do and you are prepared to put your money where your mouth is then you will be ready to pass the interview."

"You make it sound very easy," said Charlie.

"It is and it isn't. I have found in my life that doing the right thing is almost always the hard choice. When you make easy choices, they are usually selfish ones. Selfish does not fit in with protecting creation and moving life onwards. Passing the interview is always others, it is never me, me, me. The Earth, especially in the western sphere of influence is far to me oriented for my liking."

"There are very few people who would disagree with that."

"Mother and Father's response to that would be 'Do something about it then'."

"The way you talk about Mother and Father makes it sound that they are quite tough."

"They believe in tough love. They are disciplined but discipline does not mean punishment. I love them very much and I am always respectful but I am also always on my toes. I know that if they felt I was behaving badly, they would not hesitate to discipline me. For them that means lulling me in to a false sense of security and whipping the rug out from under me. It would embarrass me and I hate being embarrassed. However, I would not make the same mistake twice. If you are ever lucky enough to meet them you must show them the respect that they are due. They broke their backs to create life in this universe and they deserve our love for all they have done."

"I will bear that in mind as I'm sure everyone will."

"Now if you will excuse us, we have lots to do."

It was time to go. He had said all that he needed to say to prepare the way.

"Thanks for dropping by," said Charlie. "You are welcome at any time."

"Thank you, Charlie."

Radio, Miriam, and Eve got up and returned to the matrix.

Jamie was waiting for them.

"You are really good on TV," he said. "Would it be okay if I came to Edinburgh with you? I've never been and I'd like to see the castle."

"Yes, of course you can. I think a certain Haggis might like to go too."

Haggis looked up from her cereal and nodded. "We can go together if you like. My name is Ruth by the way. I don't mind Haggis but it can get a bit weary."

Radio filed that bit of information. He had noted this phenomenon before. Nick names always have a time and a place.

He looked at his watch. Three hours to lunch. He wondered. He turned to Miriam whose eyes were glowing. She nodded in the affirmative.

"Let's make a packed lunch for him," said Radio. The two of them got an old cloth bag from one of the dressing rooms and filled it with delicious bites. Radio made his favourite sandwich from a baguette and poured a tin of coke in to an old bottle. Chocolate, an apple, a banana, and sweets all went in to the bag.

They then ran in to the dressing rooms and stripped off all their modern clothing. When they returned to the elevator they looked like Arabs.

"What on Earth are you two up to?" asked Eve.

"You'll see. Your Mother and I are making a small side trip before lunch."

They walked up to the TIME windows. Radio instructed the Operator in his head. The window morphed. They activated TREADMILL and flew into the past.

Eleven – The Nexus

Radio whizzed along a dusty road at about ten feet above the ground. Miriam had her legs around his waist in the 'piggy back' position. He loved having her there. He could feel her cheek against the nape of his neck and he could smell her perfume. She leaned forward and kissed his mouth to show that she could feel what he felt.

About 100 yards in front of them, a young man was walking along the road with a bag over his shoulder. He held a staff in his left hand.

Radio launched the ANCHOR application in readiness and deftly hid behind a rock to the side of the road. The man stopped at the brow of a small incline and turned around.

"I know you're there," he shouted. He had a well-spoken Scottish accent. That was a turn up for the books.

"No, you don't," Radio shouted back.

The man chortled. "Yes, I do."

"No, you don't. How do you know we're here?"

"I can smell your perfume. You're wearing an after shave."

Well I never, thought Radio.

"Where are we then?"

"You're behind that rock."

Radio made a rock explode about a hundred yards to his left and launched the VENTRILOQUIST application.

"Are you sure?" he threw his voice.

"No, now that you mention it."

Radio and Miriam shot 80 feet up and behind him in the space of a second and anchored themselves to his back. Every time he turned to look, the ANCHOR application would move them when he moved. They were always just out of his field of vision. They laughed aloud which made him laugh.

Radio sneaked in incrementally until they were right behind him. He tapped his shoulder.

The man turned around and looked at them with eyes which were blue within blue.

"How do you do that?" he demanded.

"Hello Yeshua," said Radio.

"Hello Radio, hello Miriam."

"We thought you might like a spot of lunch. Let's find a pool of clear water. There's a cave over there with one."

They walked up a small slope and into a cave out of the sun. The space was bright with the sunlight reflected from the quartz on the walls and ceiling.

"Sit here, beside me," said Miriam, patting a flat stone beside her.

Yeshua took off his bag and sat down beside her. Radio went in to his pack and removed the baguette.

"I've made you my favourite sandwich," announced Radio, Scottish Mature Cheddar with Chorizo and Mayonnaise. He handed it over.

"What about my favourite sandwich?" enquired Yeshua.

"Oh, that's you all over, isn't it, you think of nobody but yourself."

They all howled with laughter.

Yeshua was clearly hungry and he immediately ploughed in to the baguette.

"Where do you get this bread?" he said after several mouthfuls, "It's delicious."

"In Gallia. In the future, it is THE place to go for all sorts of foods. Their wine is considered to be the best in the world."

"You're kidding me?" Yeshua sounded surprised. "Better than Falernian?"

"Way better," said Radio. He'd never heard of Falernian but assumed it was a popular wine from Rome. He'd check it when he got back.

"Now speaking of wine, I assume you will be partaking of it in large quantities when you get to this wedding you are going to?" Radio asserted.

"Er...well, yes, it is the done thing. Do you see a problem?" responded Yeshua, somewhat evasively.

"Yes. I do have a problem. They are going to run out and you are going to resolve it."

"How am I going to do that?"

"The TWIX application," announced Radio.

"Operator, show me Yeshua's interface and his Core Application Suite."

A screen appeared in front of them with a list of the applications Yeshua had uploaded.

He had MEDIC, WOW, TONGUETWISTER and DEITY.

Radio looked at him and said, "So, you can cure the sick, walk on water, speak all languages and get people to do your bidding. Are you comfortable with all of these applications?"

"Yes," he replied. "The MEDIC app is a work of real genius. You can even cure people without them knowing."

Radio smiled. "Operator, upload TWIX and activate."

The timer appeared followed by the usual green tick.

"Right, let me show you how to use the app."

Radio created three empty buckets out of thin air using the CREATEME application and filled each of them from the pool.

"When you get to the wedding, you will be asked to change three barrels of water into wine. This story is told to all children in the future so it is important that you follow my instructions to the letter.

"When you are ready, launch the application. Hold your hand over the first barrel and say 'Marques de Riscal'." Radio held his hand over the first bucket and turned the water into wine. He took a cup from his pack, dipped it in the bucket and handed it to Yeshua.

Yeshua tasted it gingerly at first, then downed the whole cup.

"Steady on," said Radio. "It hasn't been watered down."

Yeshua chuckled. "That is an outstanding wine, is it from Gallia?"

"No, that one is from Rioja in northern Hispania."

Radio went to the next bucket and said, "Châteauneuf-du-Pape." He passed a cup to Yeshua.

This time he sipped it carefully.

"Good God, that is very good. Complex and delicious."

Finally, Radio approached the third bucket, "Chateau Petrus." He handed Yeshua the cup.

"Always make sure you leave the best to last. You have in your hand the greatest wine ever produced on the face of Earth."

Yeshua lifted the cup and sniffed the contents. He then sipped the wine slowly.

"This is heady and amazing," he said finally. "I take it that is from Gallia?"

"Yes, it is. Different years produce slightly different crops. Don't worry about that, the application always chooses the best vintage. Now repeat back to me the names of the wines in order."

"Marques de Riscal, Châteauneuf-du-Pape and Chateau Petrus."

"Excellent. Everybody is going to be completely pissed."

Yeshua finished the baguette and Radio went in to the bag and produced the chocolate and the bottle of coke. He put the other food in Yeshua's bag and handed him the chocolate and the drink.

"You'll need to finish these now as I can't leave them with you. They are from the future, you see."

Yeshua sniffed the chocolate. "What is it?" he asked.

"Try it."

He broke off a couple of squares and put them in his mouth. Immediately his face was transformed.

"Oh, that is exquisite."

"It is chocolate. It comes from a land beyond the pillars of Hercules which lies beneath a star call La Merica. It is made from a special bean called Cocoa. The drink is made from the same bean."

He finished the chocolate and drank the coke. He giggled at the tingling sensation the coke made on his tongue.

"There are air bubbles in the drink. We call it fizz."

He giggled again.

"What now?" asked Yeshua.

"Well, good question. When the wedding is over, you are going to go on a recruitment drive. There are 6 men whom you are going to make disciples. I will provide you with a further 6. They will become known as the 12 Apostles. Unfortunately, there is a slight problem."

"What's that?" Yeshua asked curiously.

"I'm rather afraid your 6 are complete idiots," Radio admitted. "In fact, I'll go further, they are mad, bad and dangerous to know."

"That's nothing new round here. Everybody is mad. Part of the problem is that they have so little. You might think that this is the land of milk and honey but in actual fact it is a desert. Add the Roman occupation in on top of that together with a priesthood which is, quite frankly, militant then you have a society on the verge of constant rebellion. They are so dissatisfied."

"Yeshua, you have just described every society from now until doomsday. What do you think is the root cause of the problem?"

"There is not enough love."

Radio smiled. "No, there is not enough love. If that is true, and it is, then there is too much of the opposite, wouldn't you say? What is the opposite of love?"

Yeshua looked at him directly in the eye. "It is greed," he said.

Radio relaxed. He was so proud of this man.

"You will change the world, Yeshua, and when you are done here, I will bring you home and make you King of the Earth."

"I don't think they'll make me King in Rome."

Radio laughed aloud. "I can tell you with absolute certainty that the Citizens of Rome are waiting for you with baited breath!"

The look Yeshua gave him told him that he didn't believe him.

“Anyway, there are two brothers called Simon and Andrew, who fish by the Sea of Galilee. They are your first recruits. Simon is extremely cynical, arrogant and he stinks of fish. Good luck with that.”

“Radio, you’ve just described every man in Judah!”

Radio looked at Yeshua very seriously and continued.

“You are entering a time now where people will listen to every word that you say and believe you. However, try to remember that you are not just speaking to those who are there, you are speaking to those that come after.

“Every word you say will be remembered and taught to the children of the future. It is best that you speak in metaphors and use allegory to your advantage. A good story is a good story regardless of when it is told.”

“I will remember. Stories are coming to me in my sleep and a few days later I get the opportunity to tell them. I already have a good store, all waiting to be told.”

“Right,” said Radio. “Time for us to go. We’ll stay in touch. Over the next few weeks, I’ll be speaking in your head. Try not to have a heart attack.”

Yeshua looked surprised. “Why would I have a heart attack, you’ve been speaking in my head for years.”

“Right,” said Radio. Of course, he had.

Miriam folded Yeshua in an embrace and kissed him and so did Radio.

“Enjoy the wedding and don’t get too pissed.”

Miriam jumped on to radio’s back and they whizzed out of the cave and back into the matrix. When they returned there was silence in the elevator. His friends were motionless with shock. It was Winston who stepped forward.

“Who is he, exactly, Master?”

“Winston, he is the nexus of the paradox. He is the person around whom all others fly.

“I need someone on Earth to help everyone pass the interview. Yeshua will come home and show you all the way. He is irreproachable, you see, and loved by all who know him. Even his enemies.

“There are entities in this universe who are waiting to flatten anyone who stands in his way. Make sure you are not one of them.”

“I wouldn’t dream of it,” said Winston. “Is it lunchtime?”

Twelve - The Calm Before the Storm

20 minutes later they all gathered at the time windows in their best clothes. Radio inspected everyone and nodded in satisfaction.

"Operator, The Unknown Pleasures."

The window morphed and they all walked through on to the bridge.

The crew were gathered around the main viewer and there was music playing in the background. Radio chuckled. They were all looking at The Forth Bridge.

"Isn't it magnificent," said the chief engineer.

Radio had to admit that it was pretty magnificent for a structure that had been built in 1890.

"Right," said Radio. "Gather together all the Captains and we'll take a shuttle in to town."

"Where are we going?" asked Eve.

"We are going for a Chinese Banquet at the Rendezvous on Queensferry St. It's the oldest Chinese restaurant in the town!"

When they had all gathered, Radio sat next to Eve as she piloted the shuttle out of the shuttle bay. South Queensferry was mobbed. There were crowds all the way to the road bridges and he could see shuttles on the shore.

"I take it, you have started showing people round the fleet?"

"Yes," she replied, "We started unofficially after the broadcast this morning. The crowds have been remarkably well behaved."

They flew over Edinburgh until they got to Queensferry Street where he noticed a large Police presence on the ground outside the restaurant. A police officer was waving them down on the road which had been cleared of traffic.

When they got out, Radio sauntered over.

"What's going on?" he asked.

"The restaurant got in touch to say you were coming. You realise you are going to cause a riot everywhere you go. It would be good to have some advance warning?"

Radio thanked the policeman and took a note to start organising some advance warning in future. He realised that his life had changed forever now. He would never have another private moment again.

He ushered everyone inside.

"Table for 20. Booking for Radio."

The young Chinese woman grabbed a pile of menus and ushered them to three large round tables which had been placed close together. He sat with Miriam, Eve, Adam, Winston, Klaus, Jamie, and Ruth. Gabriel sat with 5 of the fleet captains and Uriel with the other 5.

Radio watched as they all lifted their menus.

"May I recommend the spicy chicken goujons as a starter? They are out of this world."

Radio was full. There was one tiger prawn left on the *assiette* and it was wrapped in the salted batter that he so loved. Should he, or shouldn't he? Miriam picked it up and put it on his plate. He smiled his thanks.

"Right," said Radio, "I hope that you have not been idle this morning. I require a status report on the super volcano. Jamie, if you please."

"The Captain has been monitoring the activity in the magma chamber and the general consensus is that no one has any idea when the volcano is likely to erupt. The only word anyone agrees on is immanent.

"The exclusion zone has now been cleared after a massive operation carried out by the US government through homeland security. Ranger Graham and your good self, appear to have friends in very high places.

"The media reaction to all of this activity has been very positive and your reference to The Sword of Damocles has been received well. The general consensus is let's not wait. Sooner rather than later.

"Your comments about plugging the hole in the ozone layer has caused a mixed reaction among the science community. There are some, and it is a significant some, believe that your assertions are nonsense. However, these are the same scientists who denied we had a global warming problem."

Radio was impressed. The boy was monitoring press reaction so that he could manage opinion and that boded well for the future.

"What do you want to do?"

"Ruth and I would like to visit the castle for an hour. When we return, I would like to return to Yellowstone and resolve the situation once and for all. The Captain says that she can start the eruption by sending a controlled explosive through the tractor beam.

"There are two ships in the Unknown Pleasures fleet which have been built to easily withstand the forces of a volcano and a tractor beam. They are the Wilderness and the Disorder, I suggest we use these ships to cruise over the exclusion zone during the event and deal with any emergency as it comes up. The Closer will be on permanent standby for the duration of the event and will deal with any casualties."

"Okay, let's do it your way. You and Ruth have one hour."

"I'll take them," said Gabriel. "I want to see the castle too."

Radio and the others had coffee and dessert whilst they waited for Jamie and Ruth to return. When they got back they were both full of excitement.

"It's like a fairy tale," said Ruth.

Jamie was a bit more down to Earth. "The man who showed us round was very knowledgeable. The history was very interesting. I didn't realise it was still an army base."

Radio was embarrassed, he hadn't visited the castle since he was five and that was 42 years ago. He made a note to drop by soon.

The Captains of the fleet wanted to stay on in Edinburgh and have a look around and they agreed to pilot the shuttle back to the Unknown Pleasures. Radio returned the Captains of the Disorder and the Wilderness to their own ships. He then opened a spatial incursion to the Gotterdammerung, which was in orbit around the Earth, and they all walked on to the bridge.

Mother and Father were waiting for him.

"Do we have Radio silence?"

The man who had been at Father's side in the hall nodded in the affirmative.

Mother and Father both turned to him.

“We need to talk for a little while with nobody observing or listening in.” Mother said. “This is the Adjudicator,” she indicated the man at Father’s side. “He monitors the tests and scores the points for each candidate. He has a few questions for you.”

“Hello Radio. The testing is extremely dangerous and it is not unknown for the candidates to die whilst attempting to pass the tests. We have to be sure that a candidate has a good chance of passing or at least not injuring themselves before we allow them to even make the attempt. The question I have for you is this, can you pass the Dragon’s Lair?”

“Yes,” responded Radio.

Mother, Father and The Adjudicator exchanged glances.

“How?” he asked.

“The Dragon happens to be one of my best friends.”

Radio realised that there was no way he could explain things to them. He had to show them. He held out his hand and produced a bottle of orange juice out of thin air. He turned to the viewer.

“Operator, The Dragon’s Lair.”

The viewer morphed and he could see The Dragon sprawled on a pile of treasure. He laughed.

“Lilith, orange juice, your favourite,” he shouted.

Her head shot up and she came trotting through on to the bridge. She was huge and could only get her top half through.

He walked over and kissed her snout, opened the bottle and poured it down her throat.

“Oh, that’s glorious,” she purred. “How long have I got now?” she asked.

“No more than two weeks. I’ll try to arrange things so that I’m first. That way you won’t be bothered by the others.” Radio stopped and looked at The Adjudicator.

“You’ll have to forgive him, Lilith, he has no idea just how much pain he has caused you over the years. I’ll make it up to you, I promise.”

“I believe you my darling,” she replied.

“Go back to your nest and have a sleep. I won’t be long now.”

She bowed her head and kissed him and trotted back to her treasure.

The window morphed and she was gone.

He looked at The Adjudicator who had gone pale. “Are we alright?” he asked.

The Adjudicator was speechless. He turned and nodded at Mother and Father.

“How are you doing this?” asked Father.

“I worked out why you and Mother created the universe and once I knew that, I was able to work out everything else.”

Mother and Father beamed at him.

“Don’t tell anyone else,” said Mother. “We require them to work it out for themselves.”

“Your secret is safe with me.”

There was a flash of light and they were gone.

Lucifer stepped forward and bowed deeply to Radio.

“How could I ever have doubted you?” he said.

Thirteen – The Tractor Beam

"Operator, hail the Disorder."

The viewer immediately looked on to the bridge of the Disorder.

"Captain Glass, please trawl the park and ensure that the exclusion zone is clear. How long will it take you to report back?"

"Give us 15 minutes in case there are any stragglers."

Radio turned to Eve. "Jamie mentioned an explosive device to precipitate the eruption. How big are we talking?"

"There is a rock shelf below the caldera. We intend to send a 1-megaton torpedo through the tractor beam to break through the rock. When you consider that the resultant eruption will be at least 200 times that, it is nothing."

Radio suddenly had a very bad feeling. Had he thought of everything or was this going to be an ecological disaster? He remembered the Icelandic eruption of 2010 which was 1 on the Volcanic Explosivity Index. Krakatoa was 6. This was bigger.

In 2010, all flights in Europe were cancelled for 6 days. Was this going to be worse? Had he underestimated everything?

"What is it?" asked Eve. She looked concerned.

Radio looked at Jamie.

"I think I've underestimated the effect of this event. I haven't spoken to Air Traffic Control and my expectation is that air travel will be impossible for some time."

Ranger Graham stepped forward. "Don't worry. Homeland Security have cancelled all flights in and out of the United States for the next two weeks.

"You are forgetting that we already had a plan and that plan was based upon receiving no help. You are streaming the ejecta away from any built-up area. Trust me we are in good shape."

Radio relaxed a bit. "I think I'm experiencing a fit of nerves."

They all chuckled.

After 10 minutes, Captain Glass reported back.

"The exclusion zone is clear. We picked up one traveller with his two dogs. It seems that the events of the last few days have passed him by. He thinks he's been abducted by aliens."

Radio laughed. He couldn't wait to see that interview on YouTube.

"Right, are we agreed that we are ready?"

They all nodded their assent.

"Over to you," he said to Eve.

"Engage Tractor Beam."

"Engaged."

"Fire torpedo."

"Away."

They all waited. The viewer showed a satellite map of the North Western United States centred on the State of Wyoming.

Suddenly there was a very small distortion on the map. Radio wasn't fooled. In the context of the size of the US, the explosion must have been massive.

"Is that it?" asked Jamie.

Radio smiled and he walked over to the map beckoning Jamie to follow. He circled a relatively small area of land and turned to Jamie.

"The land within the circle is the same size as the United Kingdom," he said.

"Oh my God," exclaimed Jamie, "It is huge."

"Yes. They will be able to hear that explosion in India."

Radio turned to the bridge crew. "Let us monitor the media reporting, that way, we will be able to respond to any unforeseen emergencies."

Over the next few hours, Radio and the others watched nervously as the event unfolded. They were three hours in when the first concerns started to become apparent.

"We are receiving news from New York State. There are reports of debris falling between Buffalo and Albany."

Eve immediately took control.

"Hail the Valkyrie and the Siegfried."

The viewer split into two and Radio could see the bridges of the two ships. He was encouraged by the fact that everybody was on full alert.

"Make your way to New York State, we are receiving reports of debris falling between Buffalo and Albany."

"On our way. ETA two minutes."

Radio was impressed. 2 minutes from Belfast to New York. He'd make that commute any day of the week.

"Captain, I have reports of damage to buildings in Buffalo from falling trees."

Radio stepped forward. "What's happening?" he asked Eve.

"Listen," she explained, "We expected this. The Tractor Beam is streaming all the debris in to the atmosphere. The volcanic dust and smaller rocks will stay there but the larger items will start to fall.

"It is our expectation that most of that will be over the Atlantic but some of the heavier items are starting to fall now."

"Fine." Radio turned to Miriam, Jamie, Winston and Klaus. "I think we should go down and help. Activate your MEDIC applications. TREADMILL will also be useful."

"Operator, take us to where we are needed the most."

The air in front of him morphed and they walked through into the city of Buffalo.

The scene of destruction in front of him made Radio blanche. He had not expected this disaster.

"Stop." It was the Operator. "You are getting upset and that is not going to help the people that need you now. The measure of a person is how they deal with things when they go badly. This is your no-win scenario.

"My advice is to deal with each situation in turn. I am opening up all of the applications to you and Miriam. We will execute your commands without the usual protocols, just think what needs to be done and we will make it happen. Trust us, it is straight forward."

Miriam was at his side and the look she gave him showed that she had heard the exchange. She ushered him forward towards a large building which had been devastated by a falling rock. A large tree had also crushed what looked like a conservatory. Radio cursed. It was a doctor's surgery.

With a thought, he lifted all of the debris from the structure and looked for the nearest uninhabited space. He found a desolate wood about 400 meters away and hurled all of the debris in to the trees.

Miriam raised her right arm and the building suddenly rose up out of the ground. The glass from the shattered windows streaked back to where they belonged and the roof righted itself. It was like watching an explosion in reverse. When they were done the building was as good as new.

Jamie, Winston and Klaus looked on in astonishment.

Radio went over to them. “Find any casualties and fix them. Use the MEDIC application.”

He went in to his pocket and produced a Mars bar. He gave it to Jamie. “Make sure you eat this. Remember what I said about hypoglycaemia.”

Jamie nodded and all three started looking for casualties.

Radio caught up with Miriam and they went inside the building.

Most of the damage had been to a waiting room and there were several bodies lying on the floor. The nurses and doctors were frantically trying to revive as many as they could. Radio and Miriam went through the crowd curing everyone as fast as was possible. After ten minutes, everyone was back to full health. Apart from the dead. There were four corpses lying on the floor.

“What do we do?” asked Miriam in his head.

Radio spoke aloud so that the conversation could be heard by everyone.

“The old man has passed the interview. To resurrect him now would be to do him a great disservice. He has gone to join his partner who has also passed the interview. Mother and Father have a new recruit.”

Radio looked at the other three. ”As for these three reprobates, they will have their work cut out.”

Radio raised his hand and brought each of them back from the dead.

One of the Doctors walked up to him. “Sorry to interrupt but we’re hearing that the shopping mall has been hit. There are a number of casualties. I’d like to help.”

Radio knew this would happen. He knew that he would be approached by people saying they wanted to help when in reality they were merely hungry for power. He looked at the man and instantly knew everything about him.

This young Doctor was a career person who had entered the medical profession for kudos and to earn money. He was also someone who took great satisfaction from bullying those who worked for him.

“I am disappointed, Doctor, that you think me dumb. You have failed the interview and the universe can invest no trust in you. You are odious.”

The young man staggered back as if he’d been punched.

Radio knew that he had been harsh but he also knew that this exchange will have been seen by billions around the Earth. It would be a warning to everyone. It was not easy to pass this interview.

Radio and Miriam went to look for the others. They found them all outside the surgery.

“Have we seen to all the casualties?” he asked.

“We think so,” said Jamie.

Radio checked with the Operator who confirmed that the situation had been dealt with. On to the shopping mall.

If the surgery was bad, the scene at the mall was devastating. Radio and Miriam moved through the building repairing shops, seeing to casualties and raising people from the dead. On the one hand, he was grateful for the fact that he didn’t have to make any decisions about resurrecting anyone as nobody else had passed the interview. On the other, it was slightly concerning that there was so much failure. He vowed to fix it and soon.

The five of them were at it for eight hours when eventually the Operator was satisfied that everything had been done. Radio was exhausted.

"Operator, the matrix, please."

When they got back they found Mother and Father waiting for them.

Mother stepped forward and lifted him up in to her arms. "Well done, my darling. You must be exhausted. Let's get you something to eat." She kissed him and put him down at the round table.

It had been transformed. There were groaning platters of food from all over the Earth. Every single one of his favourite things (and there were many) were there. He sat down and attacked a plate of spicy chicken wings. He was starving.

When he had satiated his immediate hunger, he looked around at his companions. He could sense that something was wrong.

Jamie was very subdued.

"What's wrong?" he asked.

"It's over isn't it," he replied. "The super volcano is dealt with and I'll have to go home."

Radio had been thinking about this and wondered how much to tell the boy. He decided that the best thing to do was to make him feel better.

"It's not over, Jamie, it has only just begun. I have seen the future and you will come and work for me for the rest of your life."

Jamie suddenly looked very hopeful. "Is this true?" he asked.

"Yes, it is true. However, in the short term, I need you to go back to school and complete your education. I've had a thought and with your Mother's permission I would like to offer you a paid weekend job.

"During the week, you will stay at home and at the weekend you can come and train with me. I warn you now, it will not be easy and you will be asked to do tasks which you may find tedious from time to time.

"I'm afraid I cannot make it easy for you. The things we acquire easily in life are never valued. There is a lot of power and responsibility on offer and Mother and Father require you to always value the gifts you are given. What do you say?"

There were tears in his eyes. "I'd love to. I won't let you down."

Radio chuckled. "Lesson number one. Don't make promises you can't keep."

"Come here, Jamie." It was Mother. She was sitting on the large chair that Radio had seen when he first entered the matrix.

Jamie dutifully trotted over.

"You did well, today and I'm very grateful for all the help you gave my children."

She took hold of his collar and with her free hand, burned a mark in to the fabric. When he turned around, Radio could see a golden arrow pointing towards the Earth. Mother's symbol.

Fourteen - The Corner of Houston and Elm

Radio could tell that Jamie was pleased. He continually pulled the collar of his shirt so that he could get a look at the symbol Mother had burned in to the garment.

"You're definitely one of us now," said Radio. "You will now spend the rest of your life trying to live up to the expectations that one symbol has set.

"Congratulations. To mark the occasion and as my reward for services rendered, you may now select any event in time and space and I will show you what happened in glorious Technicolour through the time window.

"Think carefully. There is so much to see. We could go back to 1783 and watch the Montgolfier brothers go up in the first hot air balloon. Perhaps, the summer of 1966, when England won the world cup or maybe you would like to go back to the beginning and observe the big bang. The choice, today, is yours."

Jamie sat down at the round table and his face transformed in to the look of a person giving a problem some serious thought. Radio smiled. It would be very interesting to see where the boy would go.

There were depths to Jamie that very few people could ever fathom. Nobody would ever have thought that this boy from a housing estate in South Shields would become the greatest knight of the middle age. The most effective and diligent time agent in history. A man that people would follow knowingly to their deaths. Radio suspected that he would choose a belter. He did.

"The sixth floor of the Texas School Book Depository on the corner of Houston and Elm, Dallas, Texas, 22 November 1963, 12.28 central standard time."

The room fell silent and every eye turned to Radio. The others in the room must have thought that the boy's choice was controversial. Radio couldn't care less. He was exultant. He'd been dying to have a look since he had arrived in the matrix but somehow, he had always been diverted. There was no stopping it now.

"Take it away Jamie. Instruct the Operator. You know what to do." Radio sat down and let the boy take over.

Jamie stepped carefully up to the time window. He was going slowly on purpose because he wanted to get everything right. This opportunity to find out the truth might not come again. The time window morphed and they were suddenly looking on to a room full of packing cases. At the window was a man of about twenty-five. He had a rifle in his hands and he was leaning against a stack of cases that he had wedged up against an open window. It was Lee Harvey Oswald.

Jamie cleared his throat. "Operator, play the scene at one quarter speed and please show the trajectory of each bullet fired from the rifle. Remove the wall so that we can see the whole of Dealy Plaza."

Radio could see the motorcade turn right from main street on to Houston. The assassin stole a glance down the street. If he fired now, he would have an easy killing shot. John F Kennedy could be seen clearly in the limousine waving at the crowds either side of the street.

Oswald didn't take the shot and Radio knew why. It would be obvious where the shot came from and he would expose the sniper's nest. Clearly, the culprit wanted to get away.

Radio looked closely at the assassin. The young man was as cool as a cucumber. There was no sweat and no panic. His face was completely implacable. His movements were utterly methodical and his handling of the weapon completely competent. Lee Harvey Oswald was a trained assassin.

The limousine made its stately progress to the corner of the plaza and slowly turned left on to Elm Street. It was a terrible turn. The elongated limousine could barely make the transition at such a sharp angle. When the car was almost directly below the window, Oswald took aim and fired his first shot.

A red trace like a laser beam captured the progress of the bullet. It hit a traffic light suspended from a post above the car and ricocheted down Elm Street towards the triple underpass. It hit a kerb and fragmented with a piece of shrapnel striking a passer-by. James Tague. First bullet a miss with collateral damage.

The assassin took aim again. The limo continued down Elm Street and reached the Stemmons Freeway sign when Oswald fired his second shot. The red trace passed through the back of the President and straight in to Governor Connally who was turned at an awkward angle to his right. The President could be seen raising both his arms to his throat.

So much for the magic bullet theory. This was no magic bullet. It was an actual bullet and it hit both men. Second shot a hit.

The limo slowed down to a stop. At one quarter the speed, it was very clear that the driver had put on the brake. Oswald took aim and fired again. The shot sailed over the President's head and disappeared under the triple underpass. Third shot a miss.

Suddenly, there was another gunshot sound coming from the picket fence beyond the grassy knoll.

"Operator, rewind five seconds and show me the shooter on the grassy knoll." Jamie was beside himself with excitement.

The time window morphed and they were suddenly in the car park. A man dressed in a Dallas police officer's uniform was standing beside a railroad worker wearing a hard hat. The police officer was aiming a rifle, through the trees, at the motorcade. He fired a shot and the trace went straight through the head of the President who jerked back and slumped to his right.

Mrs Kennedy could be seen climbing on to the trunk where a secret service agent quickly hustled her back in to the car. The limousine suddenly accelerated and headed off through the underpass.

The police officer handed the gun to the man with the hard hat who immediately locked it in what looked like an electrical hub or power generator. The man with the hat walked away to a truck, got in the driver's seat and rode away. The police officer turned around and casually started walking towards the crowds that had started to stream up from the plaza. Radio recognised the police officer. It was David Farrie.

The police officer casually started directing the crowd, occasionally showing them his identification. The man was calm and collected and appeared completely unruffled. It was a superb piece of acting.

"Oh my god," said Jamie. "Who is the police officer?"

Radio stepped forward and put his hand on Jamie's shoulder. "The police officer was a CIA agent called David Farrie. He was subpoenaed to give evidence in New Orleans at the Shaw trial conducted by Jim Garrison but he died in mysterious circumstance on the day he was due to appear. What are your conclusions?"

Jamie stopped dead and Radio could see that he was gathering his thoughts.

"If a CIA agent fired the shot that killed the President, then I think we can conclude that this was a CIA conspiracy. Unfortunately, that is all we can conclude. It may well have gone further or higher up the chain but we can't prove that from what we've seen today. The only thing we have proven is that Lee Harvey Oswald was NOT the lone gunman."

"Excellent. You have not fallen in to the trap of making assumptions. In cases like this, believe only what your eye can see and what you can prove definitively. It is my opinion that the truth will come out after this and there are a few people who will have some explaining to do."

"Is there any chance we could follow up on some of the possibilities?" asked Jamie.

"Another time, perhaps. My advice is to do your research first and then come to me with the things that you really need to find out and then we'll talk about it. Alright?"

"Yes," said Jamie excitedly. "I'll do exactly that."

"Now off to bed with you!"

Radio turned to Winston, who had watched the whole thing with a cool interest.

"What you have seen today cannot be stopped. At some point in the future, you will meet Jack Kennedy and you cannot change a thing. He died in Dallas and that is an immutable fact.

"The consequences of this assassination were far reaching and we don't know for certain if his death changed the world for the better or for the worse. It is too complex from a temporal perspective.

"What we do know is that his death is a part of Earth's history now and we must live with that. Do you understand?"

Winston looked at Radio with great sadness. "I understand completely. I've already met the young man who will become President. My impression of the boy was that he had huge potential. It is a great shame. A great shame."

"Yes," replied Radio. "There are few people who would disagree with you."

Fifteen – The Warning Shot Across the Bows

When everyone else had gone to their rooms, Radio and Miriam got ready for bed. They returned to the elevator and walked over to where Mother and Father were still sitting. Radio climbed in to Mother's lap and Miriam in to Father's.

"Now that we are properly alone, your Father and I are intrigued to find out how you worked out the reason we created the universe. We'd be very grateful if you could take us through it step by step."

Radio gathered his thoughts. He had expected this question and felt he had as good an answer as anyone.

"The simple truth is that I borrowed Occam's Razor to answer the question.

William of Occam was an English philosopher who lived in the 14th century. He postulated the idea that complex problems are usually solved by finding the simplest explanation. This is exactly what I did.

"I held out my hand and imagined that it was full of all the possible reasons why you created the universe. I then borrowed Occam's Razor and shaved away all the reasons that could be classed as impossible.

"For example, I asked the question, did Mother and Father create the universe to increase their wealth? The answer is no because you had the sum total of the universe before you precipitated the big bang. I can therefore render the wealth argument impossible and I shaved it away.

"At the end of this process, I was left with very little and I asked myself the question. Why would I go to such lengths and endure such agony to create this universe? There was only one reason why I would do it so I was able to shave away what was left in my hand.

"This is the reason you created the universe."

Radio held out a hand which was clearly empty.

"There is nothing there," said Mother.

"Exactly," replied Radio. "To truly understand the meaning of the word nothing in this context, you have to play a game of tennis on the Earth."

Mother and Father looked at each other and smiled triumphantly.

"I guessed that you wanted a specific type. I hope we haven't let you down?"

"Actually, darling, most of you have. However, we have you, to make up for all the rest."

"Does it bother you that I've been written to your requirements?"

Mother held him tightly. "No, it does not. You still had free choice and you chose correctly. I don't mind telling you it's been a bit of a roller coaster but you got there in the end."

Radio heaved a sigh of relief. Mother continued.

"Nobody was born knowing the truth. This universe is a cesspool and at its heart, a darkness. To understand the truth, you have to allow yourself to be swallowed by the dark for that is the only way you come to understand the truth, especially about yourself. It was ever thus and ever thus will be.

“You are not a saint, Radio and you were never meant to be one. I thank my lucky stars that you are who you are.”

Radio chuckled. He remembered the Paris incident and it still caused him some discomfort.

Miriam guffawed. “Put it behind you for Gawd’s sake!”

Mother smiled.

“Sadly, he can’t. It is the memory of incidents like this that make him who he is.”

“But it was nothing,” argued Miriam.

“No,” replied Mother. “It was definitely something.”

They all laughed.

“Now that you have dealt with the preliminaries, what are your plans for tomorrow?” asked Mother.

“I’m going to give a man a warning. I want to see how he reacts.”

“Yes, it is a justified and deserved warning. However, don’t be too hard on him. His heart is in the right place and that’s nine tenths of the way there.”

“Yes, I agree.” Radio mused for a moment before asking his next question.

“How many preliminaries were there, exactly?”

Mother laughed. “There are only two but you’ve made extra work for yourself! We wanted to see how you would deal with a crisis at home and how you would deal with a crisis abroad. The Super Volcano and The Honey Pot.

“You have a temporal paradox, however, at the heart of your solution, so you have made life very interesting indeed.”

“Right. Did the others pass?” He wasn’t sure if Mother would answer this question.

“There is no pass or fail, there is merely a measure of effectiveness. My advice is not to worry about what the others do, worry about what you do.”

“I wish it was as easy as that,” said Radio wistfully.

Mother and Father were immediately alert.

“What do you mean by that?”

“I was thinking about Lilith,” admitted Radio. “As an entity, she is unassailable. However, in the past, when candidates have attacked the Dragon’s Lair, she has been forced to defend herself. This has caused her great pain because people have been hurt and killed. She is sick of it. If you let me go first, I can free her from all of that.”

Mother and Father looked at each other again and Radio could tell that they were greatly concerned. Eventually Mother looked back at him.

“Your Father and I have missed something. We will ensure that you are first to tackle the Dragon’s Lair. Now go to bed. I have a bit of thinking to do.”

Radio slid to the ground and held out his hand for Miriam. When they got to the bed, he pulled back the covers for her and they climbed in. *Cuddles*, he thought. She laughed.

When they woke up Mother and Father had made breakfast and the round table looked as jolly as it had the night before. Radio had Granola with a banana, a black cherry yoghurt, several slices of toast and a pot of coffee.

He looked over at Winston and smiled. He was ploughing his way through his second full English and Radio wondered if he was making up for yesterday’s lack of bacon and egg.

After breakfast, Gabriel came through with a full suitcase. Radio had arranged for Jamie to have a full new wardrobe when he returned him to his Mother.

“It’s time,” said Radio,” But remember, this is not adieu. It is au revoir. I’ll pick you up again on Saturday morning.”

Jamie waved at everyone who all shouted, “See you soon.”

Jamie's Mother was waiting at the front door. She ran forward and hugged him tight. "I'm so proud of you," she said.

Radio went in to his pocket and pulled out an envelope. He handed it to the boy. "Your first week's pay," he said.

Jamie looked at him sincerely. "Are you sure?" he asked.

"Listen, through some twist of fate, you find yourself in an impecunious position. Take this money. I would like you to have it. Mother and Father gifted me the richest planet in the galaxy. I'm happy to share it around."

Jamie smiled and took the envelope. "Saturday," he said.

"Saturday," said Radio and returned to the matrix.

When Radio got back, he told everyone that they could have the day off as he and Miriam had something to attend to.

Winston looked relieved and Radio promised to remind himself that he was 66 years old now and no spring chicken.

He turned to Miriam. "Ready?"

"Operator, Rome."

The time window morphed and hand in hand, Radio and Miriam walked in on an old man having morning coffee. He looked up and smiled.

"Welcome Radio, welcome Miriam. Coffee?"

He assented and they both sat down. Radio always loved having coffee in France and Italy because they always gave you a small cup with a saucer. He thought it to be very civilised.

"Now," said The Pontiff, "What can I do for you?"

Radio decided to get to the point.

"In six to eight weeks, it is my intention to bring Yeshua back to Rome. I'm here to give you a warning.

"It is my belief that there are certain things that are going to cause him a great deal of irritation. For lots of reasons, he is not the type of person you want to irritate.

"First things first, you must stop charging people to gain access to the Vatican complex. This will be viewed as exploitation.

"Secondly, there is far too much wealth on show here, if you don't sell the things that are not nailed down. He will. Moreover, he will embarrass you in the process.

"Thirdly, you have too much wealth in your bank accounts. My advice is to give it to the poor whilst you still can.

"This is by no means the exhaustive list of grievances but I feel if you do these three things, you won't meet with disapproval and disappointment."

The old man looked at him for a moment and then handed him a parchment which looked ancient.

"This letter was handed to Leo X, exactly 500 years ago, today. It has been in our archives all this time. Read."

Radio recognised the handwriting immediately. It was his own.

It was a letter to the man sitting opposite giving him the warnings he had just delivered in person.

"What are you going to do?" he asked curiously.

"I am going to do exactly as you ask, of course."

Radio was confused. He asked the obvious question.

"Why haven't you done these things before?"

The old man smiled sadly, "Because I didn't have a mandate until I received that letter and I only received that letter yesterday morning.

"You are living under the misapprehension that I have temporal power. The truth is I don't.

"I am only The Pontiff because I am the candidate who is the acceptable balance. On the one hand, I must be seen to move the church forward in a modern age. However, if I go too far, I won't be Pope for very long."

Radio suddenly had a very bad feeling.

"Are you telling me that you are being threatened?"

The Pope laughed.

"Every single Pontiff since the renaissance has lived under the same condition. I don't want to sound like a crackpot conspiracy theorist but there are dark forces abroad on this Earth and I receive threats every day.

"In truth, I have no idea if there is a secret organisation pulling strings, quite frankly, there does not need to be. I am aware that I can only push the boundary so far.

"With this letter, however, I have received instructions from the person responsible. Now, I can act and I will."

He stopped and took a sip of his coffee. Radio could sense that the old man was annoyed and he could see why. However, Radio just couldn't let him off the hook. He leaned forward and grabbed the old man's hand.

"Let me explain things to you so that you are clear and understand. Had you acted and done the right thing regardless, you would have passed the interview with flying colours."

The old man gently removed Radio's hand from his own.

"I know that, Radio. However, I am custodian of this Church and I refuse to take it back in to the dark ages. Who would be my successor? I can assure you it would be a man with less of a mandate than me and I ask myself the question. Would he be crippled by fear?"

Finally, Radio understood. He wasn't looking at a bad man or a man that had failed to do his job. He was looking at a man that could never win. Radio could relate to that.

The old man continued.

"Don't judge me on what has happened up to now, judge me on what happens from now."

Radio smiled. "I'm not judging you. I am trying to help you. Luckily for you, in very short order, you will have Yeshua to show you the way. Passing the interview will become his responsibility."

"You are wrong, Radio. Whether you like it or not, you are already showing people the way. They are already looking to you for leadership. You are the person responsible. I wish you all the luck in the world. I think you are going to need it."

Radio realised that he was right. He took another sip of his coffee.

"You asked for something else in your letter," said the old man.

He handed Radio a printed handful of sheets. It was a timetable of events in roughly chronological order, culled from the 4 gospels, showing who met Yeshua and when. Radio was pleased as this would save him a bit of time. Although the Operator held the record of what actually happened, this was going to be handy in the event of any disputes. It was going to save him some work.

"Thank you," said Radio. "I'm very grateful."

The old man looked at him and his face was very serious.

"Setting aside what you said about him being a nexus, who is he, exactly?"

Radio breathed out. He should have expected this question.

"I'm not sure, exactly, and the Operator will not tell me. In truth, I am extremely curious myself. I have sent my awareness through time and space trying to find out and I'm afraid it's like catching water. The answer always seems to be over the next hill."

The old man laughed aloud. "Somehow, I'm not surprised."

Radio continued. "I have felt for some time now that the Operator has a desire to make a drama out of this. I think she is using these events to give everyone something to get excited about. To give them hope."

The old man smirked. "That makes complete and utter sense to me."

Radio stood up. He handed the old man a phone.

"I would like you to stay in touch. Phone me every couple of days and let me know how things are going. You will have to make plans for Yeshua's return. Aim to have those plans completed within four weeks. That way you will definitely be ready."

"I will. I am not your enemy, Radio. I wish you all the best."

"I know that Filis. Be well."

Radio took Miriam's hand and they returned to the matrix.

Sixteen – The Robe and the Lampstand

When they returned, Gabriel was waiting for them.

"Are you ready?" she asked.

"I am."

"Then come with me."

She led him back in to the hall. This time, somehow, things were a bit different.

The audience was less antagonistic towards him and he noted that there were more of Mother's supporters in the crowd. He could see her symbol everywhere.

He walked up to Mother and Father who were sitting on their thrones. They were smiling at him.

The adjudicator stepped forward.

"May I introduce the fifth candidate. Radio of Edinburgh."

There was a round of applause. Radio noted that it was more enthusiastic than his first reception.

Radio looked to Father's right. There was a small Dais with 5 seats, 4 of which were already occupied. It was the other candidates and they were all wearing the most garish robes he had ever seen. They looked like they had just walked out of a masonic ceremony. Radio smiled inwardly.

Mother stood up from her throne and clapped her hands.

Two angels appeared carrying a tailor's dummy. It was draped with a robe that Radio had to admit, looked damned impressive. It was covered, from collar to hem, in symbols that he recognised all too well but the symbols were accentuated by the largest gemstones he had ever seen. It was, at the same time, rather tasteful.

The crowd were astonished and there were lots of 'ooohs' and 'aaahs'.

Mother looked at the people in the hall and they all went silent.

"Hello darling," said Mother, "Welcome to your robing ceremony."

"Thank you," said Radio, "But if you think I am going to wear that thing. You have another thing coming. It is hideous."

The silence in the hall was frightening. Radio, who had somehow acquired the skill of picking up what other people were thinking could feel one emotion and it was universal. It was terror.

One individual broke the silence. He started laughing. It wasn't just a normal laugh it was a fit of uncontrollable belly laughing. It was Father.

Mother who had stopped dead when he spoke couldn't control herself either. She started and she couldn't stop.

Radio felt a wave of relief wash over everyone and they too started laughing. Soon the whole hall was in fits. The only people who weren't laughing were the other 4 candidates who suddenly looked less sure of themselves.

Finally, Mother spoke. "Please explain yourself," she chortled.

"I cannot wear that thing," he said. "To wear something like that is to set oneself apart from others.

You are making a statement. You are saying 'look at me, aren't I the dog's bollocks'."

If I put that on and walked into any pub in Edinburgh, they would chase me all over the town. I would have to take refuge in the Cathedral where they would probably nick it off me.

This sort of dress is reserved for people who have a desire to exert their authority over others. Let me assure you, it is not dress that exerts authority, it is how you conduct yourself. It is not clothes that make the man. Manners make the man.

"Thank you for the offer but I'm afraid I must decline."

Mother and Father stood up and started applauding. The crowd followed. Soon the whole hall was cheering.

Father looked at the Adjudicator. "Points, please."

The Adjudicator stepped forward.

"Dyer of Pelos – 0 Points.

"Grace of Assyria – 0 Points.

"Mohr of Agora – 0 Points.

"Adela of Lore – 0 Points.

"Radio of Edinburgh – 3,000 Points.

"Radio of Edinburgh takes the lead. We will meet here in 3 days to agree terms. That will be all."

The cheers resounded around the hall. For the first time in his life, Radio felt that he had everyone behind him. He wondered what had changed.

"You are a winner," said the Operator in his head. "Try to remain calm. Keep your wits about you, but very well done."

The candidate nearest Father had stood up and was calling for quiet. Radio stopped to listen.

"Lord," he addressed Father. "Permission to disrobe," he asked ruefully pointing at his ridiculous outfit.

Father looked at him. "Certainly not," he replied scornfully. "You've made your bed, now lie in it."

With that, Mother and Father left the hall.

The man, whom he assumed to be Dyer of Pelos, looked at the six experts whose advice radio had been offered by Mother. The look he gave them was one of murder.

Radio scrutinised them too. They were less sure of themselves now. He wondered if they would brazen it out. He hoped they would, he needed them to keep misinforming the other candidates.

He was sure that the next tests were so subtle and complex that he had nothing to fear. He hoped.

Radio returned with Gabriel to the matrix.

Three days, he thought. *What will I do first?*

"It is time to start giving the people of the Earth a choice." It was the Operator. "Prepare for operation birth right. Today is Wednesday. You have a test on Saturday so inform the PM that you will address parliament on Friday at noon."

Radio turned to the time windows.

"Operator, hail the PM."

The window morphed and he found himself looking down on a cabinet meeting.

"Prime Minister," he began. He hadn't meant to be loud but the Prime Minister jumped out of her skin. The cabinet ministers all laughed.

"Sorry," he continued. "I have a desire to address parliament on Friday at noon. Can you arrange for everyone to be there? Three-line whip, if you please."

She collected herself. “Of course. You are more than welcome. Do you have any special requirements?”

“No. Thank you for asking. I will take care of everything.”

Radio walked over to the kitchen and put on the kettle. He had one more thing to do before he could relax. He made a pot of coffee and brought it over to the round table where he poured Winston and Miriam a cup as well as one for himself.

He decided to act. He called for Lucifer.

“What’s up,” asked Lucifer when he arrived. He sat down and Radio poured him a coffee.

“Do you know who Lilith is?” asked Radio.

“Of course,” he replied.

“We have a problem and I need your help.”

“Go on.”

“It is my belief that Lilith has been underestimated by everyone. They have assumed that because she is unassailable she can feel no pain. What they have failed to realise is that she can feel emotional pain all too well.

“Mother and Father have promised me that I can go first on the test called Dragon’s Lair. It is my intention to free Lilith so that she does not have to participate in the testing any more.

“However, I need to make the other candidates believe that they have no chance. It is my desire to persuade them to drop out.

“Before I make my mind up, I’d like to know more about each candidate. Can you find out for me?”

Lucifer chuckled. “Yes, I can find out for you. It is just like the old days.”

He downed his coffee and disappeared.

“Operator, locate Mother and Father.”

“We’re behind you,” said Mother.

Radio turned around to find them sitting in their chairs. Their ability to come and go was starting to intrigue Radio. He’d find out how they did it when he had the time.

“I have some questions for you, if you don’t mind, and I was hoping for some advice?”

“Of course,” said Mother, “Proceed.”

“It has been said, and I don’t know if it is true, that the purpose of the testing is to find someone to hand over responsibility so that you may retire. Is this correct?”

“What do you think?” asked Mother.

Radio laughed. “I don’t think it is quite true. My understanding is that the universe is far too large to have one person constantly responsible. My belief is that you are looking for a number of individuals whom the Operator can trust.

“It is your hope that, in the not too distant future, you will have a trusted group that can be called on to take their turn at being the person responsible. You are looking for a ‘rota’.”

Mother and Father exchanged glances and Radio could tell that he was close to the truth. Mother leaned forward.

“Over the years, your Father and I have become increasingly busy. As the sentient societies of the universe have advanced, we have been called on more and more to avert disaster.

“It has gotten to the stage where we do not get any time to enjoy the purpose we created the universe for. A purpose which you have so admirably worked out.

"Our desire is to hand over responsibility to free up some of our time. If you think a rota is a good idea then I believe it can be entertained. However, my advice would be to make sure the Operator is completely satisfied with the candidates."

Radio nodded his head. It made sense. He continued.

"Let us for one moment entertain the idea that you do get the opportunity to step back. Where would you go?"

Mother looked at him curiously. "What's on your mind?"

"Well," said Radio. "You could come and live with me. This matrix is enormous and you could go anywhere you pleased but you would be near the things that you want the most."

Mother and Father looked at each other. "Agreed. We'll move in with you."

Radio chuckled. He had known for some time, that this had been the plan all along but it was good to get the issue out of the way.

"Now, what was the advice you wanted?"

"I have designed several applications which, if launched, would change the face of the Earth. If you had asked me ten years ago if I thought it was the right thing to do, I would not have hesitated. I would have launched the applications immediately. Now, I'm not so sure."

"What is concerning you?"

"I have concluded that the things we acquire easily, as human beings, are not valued. It is my concern that the acquisition of certain things will make it more difficult for the human population to pass the interview and I have to think of the long term.

"This universe, alone, will be around for several more billion years and I know that life itself will never need to end. The interview, in the context of evolutionary time, lasts for no more than a Nano second. If I give them a paradise now, with nothing to strive for, I feel I might be doing them a great injustice."

"I cannot help you, I'm afraid. You have to take each application on its own merits. My advice is to do as much research as you can so that, if things don't work out, you can at least say that you tried your best. Leadership is lonely, Radio. You have to find a way and it has to be your way."

"One final thing." Radio turned to Father. "Who is the fat man?"

It would be an understatement to say that his parents were shocked. They literally jumped.

"What do you know about the fat man?" Father demanded.

"In my travels through time and space, I have come across him several times. Here is what I have discerned so far.

"He appears to be the leader of a powerful inter galactic race from another galaxy. Over the years he has come to be an irritation. He has managed to acquire great wealth, most of which has been swindled from you. The loss of these possessions does not concern you but the bad behaviour has come to exasperate you.

"What has made things worse is that he is now boasting that you are an easy target."

Father looked furious. "Is he now?"

"Yes. What's more, he intends to use the testing to acquire more wealth for himself by way of a wager. In the past, the candidates you have supported have all started well but ultimately failed because they lacked the courage or the will for what they perceived to be a fight.

"He expects you to place a wager on me and he expects to win.

"I can assure you that I have a plan to completely bankrupt him and win everything back. All that he has defrauded from you will be yours again."

"What do you need from me?" asked Father eagerly.

“A crumpled shirt, an iron and an ironing board,” replied Radio.

Mother and Father looked at him and laughed.

“I’ve seen myself do it,” said Radio. “It is a racing certainty. Just follow my instructions and it will all be yours again.”

“Oh, we will,” said Father. “We will.”

“You have the rest of the day off,” said Mother. “What are your plans?”

Radio rubbed his hands. “Miriam, Winston, Klaus and I are off to find the buried treasure.”

Mother looked intrigued. “What are you going to do with it?”

“I’m going to give it back to the rightful owner. You see, I put it into safekeeping 1950 years ago. Time to return it I think.”

Radio and Miriam changed into Jeans and trainers and waited at the round table for Winston and Klaus to return. When they appeared, Radio had to admit, they looked a bit odd. Both were slightly uncomfortable in the modern clothes they had been given.

“Are we ready?” asked Radio.

“Master, where are we going?” asked Winston curiously.

“You’ll see. Operator, the old woman and the well.”

The time window morphed and Radio led them through.

Waiting for them were the six terrorists that Radio had let go on his first day.

He approached the old woman.

“I think, for you, it’s been a long time,” said Radio.

“Too long,” said the old woman. “By my reckoning, I think it has been 70 years for me.”

“You are right,” said Radio. “Seventy years is too long. Your work here is done. I have secured a position for you in rehab with Nicolas. You will work there from now on.”

A door opened in front of the old woman. An old man appeared and held out his arms.

The old woman looked at Radio and said, “Thank you.” She hurried over and fell into the old man’s arms. He waved at Radio. The door closed and they were gone.

Radio looked at the six men. They had the look of little boys who wanted to make up for past misdeeds. Radio smiled. It was going to be a good day.

“Today,” he began, “Is an opportunity for you to make up for the catastrophe in London. Where we are going has its dangers and I need you to do exactly as I ask you. Are you ready?”

They all nodded eagerly.

“Operator, the chamber under the mountain.”

The air distorted and a chill could be felt in the warm climate. They all walked in to the darkness.

“Operator, let there be light.”

They were in a massive space. There were classical columns supporting a flat roof and there were carvings everywhere. Scattered about the room was the wealth of nations.

Radio turned to all of them. “You will not report what you see in this room, do you understand?”

They all nodded.

Radio approached a niche in the wall where a massive golden lampstand stood. It had seven branches and as Radio got closer, the lamps started to glow. He held out his hand and touched one of the branches. The lamps flared.

Radio could hear the gasps behind him.

“Behold, the holy menorah,” said Radio. “Moses lampstand.”

The six men had fallen to their knees and were looking at the menorah in awe.

"Right, stand up and form two lines of three facing away." They immediately fell in to line.

Radio manoeuvred the lampstand on to their shoulders and opened a spatial incursion directly in front of them.

"Follow me," he said.

Radio led them through the vortex and they appeared in a large assembly hall full of people.

It was the Knesset.

He led them down and on to the dais to thunderous applause from the assembly and created a niche on the wall behind the speaker. He then lifted the lampstand from their shoulders using his mind and placed it in the space he had created for it. It fit perfectly.

The cheers rang out and Radio thought they were going to raise the roof.

When they eventually calmed down, Radio addressed the throng.

"That which was stolen by Titus has been returned by your enemies." He indicated the six men.

"I think they deserve a standing ovation."

They got one.

When the assembly had settled down there were a number of questions.

A well-dressed old man stood up. He looked like he had just walked out of 1920.

"Master, where had it been all this time?" he asked.

Radio chuckled. This was going to be good.

"Okay, I need you all to just imagine that anything is possible."

There was lots of laughter and shouts from the audience about believing anything he said. Radio realised that something had changed. The crowd was in a good mood. It felt like a cloak of despair had been lifted and people were happy again.

"During the siege of Jerusalem in AD 70, the Roman General, Titus, sacked the temple and removed the menorah from the well of souls, where it had been hidden.

"It was taken back to Rome under armed guard along with many prisoners. On the night that the rebels were crucified. The Romans held a large celebration.

"I went in under cover of darkness with some friends of mine from mediaeval times and we stole it back from The Romans. We took it to a secret hiding place in Scotland and it has been there ever since."

Radio had just told the most unbelievable story in history and nobody batted an eyelid.

"What else have you got in that secret hiding place of yours?" asked a young woman with glasses. She looked like a curator in a museum and radio knew that he had to be careful.

"Lots of things actually," he said, "But they are not all for you. This gift is for Israel, from Mother, on account of the fact that you named your country after her."

"Do you know where the Ark of the Covenant is?" asked a young man with a beard.

Radio looked at him like he was a bit daft.

"Obviously. I don't think you've been listening. I've got a time machine and a passion for antiques. Of course, I know where the Ark of the Covenant is. Especially when you consider that I stole that too!"

The young man burst out laughing as did the rest of the crowd.

"I have a question." An old lady stood with the help of her walking stick. Radio was immediately on his guard.

"I have a question for the Nazi." She looked directly at Klaus.

"Tell me, did you know that Jews were being systematically butchered in Eastern Europe?"

The crowd went silent. It wasn't the fairest question in the world as Klaus had been captured in 1940. However, Radio realised that this was an opportunity for Klaus to talk about what he did know. The question could work to his advantage. He decided to let Klaus answer.

"The short answer to that question is yes. At the start of the war, the general consensus was that the Jews were finished in Germany. Nobody knew about the plan but everyone knew that the outcome would not be good.

"When I went back to Germany with Lucifer to deal with Hitler, I discovered what was happening to them and the plan was well known. The Jews would take a train and the train would not come back. Everyone was talking about concentration camps, forced labour and shootings.

"It was only when I returned that Captain Tsedeq showed me the gas chambers.

"The master had told Lucifer that 6.2 million had been killed. That was a shock.

"I am so, so, sorry."

There was deafening silence. Then something wonderful happened. The old lady started clapping and then the whole audience applauded.

"Thank you," she said, and sat down.

Radio stepped up to the front of the dais and called for silence.

"The return of this artefact is a double-edged sword. From now on you cannot tell a lie in this room. Everything you say must be the truth, the whole truth and nothing but the truth, so bear this in mind and act accordingly.

"The presence of the menorah changes people. It changes your behaviour. You are being watched.

"My advice to you is to take a few days off and reflect on what bad behaviour really means.

"One of my great concerns is that bad behaviour has become so prevalent that it is now normal. You have forgotten what it means to be truly good.

"You need to change and change fast."

Radio looked at the audience as they took in his warning. There were encouraging signs. Nobody was surprised at being called badly behaved. Radio had hope, real hope for the first time in ages.

A man approached and introduced himself as the Prime Minister. He wondered if his group would like to have lunch.

Radio enjoyed having meals from different cultures. He sat with Benjamin as the plates were delivered to the table. There was salad, tahini, hummus, rice, mashed potatoes and all sorts of other dishes that Radio could not identify.

He scrutinised one rather large platter. "Is that schnitzel?" he asked.

The Prime Minister laughed. "Yes, do you know it?"

"Sort of. I thought it was an Austrian dish of veal, from Vienna."

"It is," replied Benjamin. "However, we make it with chicken on account of our dietary laws."

Radio helped himself to Schnitzel and rice. He had to admit, it was damn delicious.

Benjamin leaned over, "I know you must be tired of fielding questions so stop me if I bore you but there are a few things I'm dying to know."

Radio smiled at him. "I'm not tired. Since this whole thing started, I feel like I have been on a roller coaster and I haven't had time to think. In truth, I had expected more questions but I seem to have to move on just as it gets interesting. What do you want to know?"

“You said that we had named our country after Mother.”

“Yes,” replied Radio, “Israel means ruling with El. Mother’s name is El. Father is called Elion.”

“How do they speak English?”

“The question is, how do we speak English?” Radio asserted. “The Operator has been changing the language in Britain for the last 1500 years. Just a word here and there. This was always the plan so that when Mother and Father arrived, we would speak their language.”

“Wow. You said that everyone is descended from you. How is this possible?”

“You are very clearly my great grandson with lots of greats in between. You are descended from my daughter Eve as all Israelites are. The statistical likelihood of there being one person on this planet that is not descended from me is so slim that I have just decided to call you all my grandchildren.”

Benjamin thought for a second. “It is all so ridiculous yet here I am speaking to you and believing every word you say.”

“It is a question of proof,” said Radio. “I believe in cynicism when there is cause. It is preferable that cynicism is polite as odious cynicism leads to offence and argument. When there is no cause, there is no point. You know that I can prove my assertions, therefore you believe me. It is as simple as that.”

Benjamin laughed. “Yes, you are right. Do you think Yeshua is the Messiah?”

Radio raised his eyebrows. “Try to remember that the bible was written by men and it has been heavily redacted over the years. The word Messiah is just a word and I really don’t know what you mean by it. He was sent in to time to do a job. He did the job and now I’m bringing him back to finish what he started. If that is Messiah then fine.

“I don’t know all the answers yet as the solution is complex. I have spent 15 years looking through time and space and I still can’t answer all my questions. I’m sure that time will tell.”

“Like everyone else on this planet, I have a desire to pass the interview. How do I do it?”

Radio looked at the Prime Minister and realised that he was sincere.

“You do it by imagining. You imagine that your Mother and Father created this universe for all of their children. Not just you, but all of them. You imagine that they love them all equally and want all of them to succeed. That means that every sentient being in creation is your brother or sister.

“Now imagine that you can only pass the interview if you do everything that you can to make sure all of your brothers and sisters pass.

“You cannot afford to be cruel to be kind. That’s my job. You have to be kind and well behaved.

“If you can do all of these things then you will pass.”

“Can a rich man like me pass this interview?”

“Of course,” said Radio. “I have a concern that excess wealth leads to bad behaviour. Nobody minds a man having a fortune but it is a fortune in the Jane Austen sense of the word. An amount of money that makes a person a good marriage prospect.

“There are fortunes in this world which are, quite frankly, dysfunctional. When a person can pay for everything so that they have no responsibility and don’t have to lift a finger then a warning bell should sound.

“My advice to people who find themselves in that position is to invest the time and make sure you give the excess money away and ensure that it is well spent.”

“Are you GOD, Radio,” asked Benjamin.

"You are in GOD," he replied. "GOD is the General Operating Dimension. It is reality.

"My question to you is, why do you need there to be a GOD in the traditional sense?

"All you have done is use GOD to abdicate your responsibility.

"You blame him for world poverty when you are to blame for poverty. There is plenty to go around. You just don't share it in the way you should.

"You blame him for disasters when you are the architects of your own misfortune.

"Passing the interview is about being the masters of your own fortune. Work together in harmony so that you don't need a GOD."

"Some might argue that you are abdicating your responsibility."

"No, I won't accept that. Mother and Father believe in tough love and tough love will get you through the interview. If you don't want to take part then I can arrange for you to be damned. Deactivated and made null."

"If it really is as you say, then, we are either with you or against you. There is no other choice."

"Ultimately, it comes down to that."

"I choose to be with you then. Is there anything I can do?"

"Yes," said Radio. "As a matter of fact, there is. I need you to look after these six men for me and hopefully see them safely home. They are no longer a threat and I want to see how you deal with them. The world will be watching you and judging you. You decide what happens to them."

"They are heroes, now. They returned the holy menorah to Jerusalem."

"Yes," smiled Radio. "They did."

After lunch, Radio, Miriam, Winston and Klaus made their goodbyes and headed back to the matrix.

When they returned, he took Klaus aside.

"That was very well done back there," said Radio.

"Thanks," muttered Klaus. "The situation is not good, whatever way you look at it. I knew the Jews were for it and I did nothing about it. I did not even think about them. I just didn't care.

"Now I seem to care about everyone."

Radio put his arm around him. "Listen, you are going to have plenty of opportunities to make up for it. I need you to do something for me.

"In the future, Jamie will work for me and will be very important, as far as the paradox is concerned. It is my intention that you will go with him when he goes back in time.

"I would like you to mentor him in the short term and teach him German and French.

"I would also like you to learn Old German and find out as much as you can about the tribes that came to Britain during the Saxon invasion. Get the boy involved and come up with a summary of events for me. Will you do that for me?"

Klaus transformed immediately and his face lit up. "I will be delighted. Leave it to me."

Radio knew what was next on his agenda and he rubbed his hands gleefully.

The Fat Man.

Seventeen – The Fat Man

He'd been putting it off for a while but now was as good a time as any to get it done. Ironing was, without doubt his least favourite task in the universe. He didn't mind the shirts, they were easy, it was the trousers he hated.

He set up the ironing board in front of Mother and Father's chairs and got the basket. Two pairs of trousers and six shirts. Not bad.

Miriam, who was sitting in Father's lap was curious and as they were in company, she spoke aloud.

"What do you hate about trousers so much?"

Radio thought for a moment and attempted to articulate his issue.

"There is no obvious process for doing them, therefore it is very difficult to find a way to cut the time down. You just have to iron every nook and cranny, otherwise they look ridiculous."

He had managed to pique Mother and Father's curiosity.

"Do you try and find a way to always cut a process down?" Mother asked.

"Yes," Radio replied. "The ideal scenario is when you don't have to do the thing at all. Fifteen years ago, I discovered that some bright spark had invented the non-iron shirt. I was overjoyed. I went to the shops and bought ten of them. Unfortunately, there was a slight problem."

"What was that?" asked Mother.

"It was bollocks." He replied. "They needed ironed just like anything else. I foolishly went to work in one and the comments were awful. I live in Scotland, you see and they just don't let you away with anything.

"Some smart ass came up and asked if I'd slept in it."

They all laughed.

"What was it like growing up in Scotland?" Mother enquired.

"In the main, it was pretty good. They don't get too over excited about stuff. They have a great sense of humour but they can take things too far. Taking things too far, on occasion, is a national trait."

"Give me an example," said Mother.

"They don't have a stop button. I remember standing at the bar in a pub when this guy came in looking for a pint. Unfortunately, he had the most hideous boil erupting in the dead centre of his forehead.

"Before he could place his order, the barman asked him if he was here for the unicorn's reunion.

"Everyone fell about, including me. Unfortunately, it didn't stop there. There were unicorn and boil gags for the next two hours. Eventually the guy got pissed and punched someone. Massive fight ensued. That's Scotland for you."

"Do you think the Earth has a chance?" Mother asked.

Radio put the iron down and looked at her.

"The people of the Earth have forgotten what it means to behave well. They are so terrible and they have no idea just how bad they are but they have one saving grace.

"They mean well and so many of them have a heart in the right place. I think they will surprise us all with a bit of guidance."

Radio got the ten-minute warning on his interface. He turned to Father.

"The Fat Man will be here in 10 minutes. Please follow my instructions to the letter.

"When he arrives, there will be the usual pleasantries and then he will enquire if you are wagering on the testing.

"You will ask what odds will he give if your candidate breaks the record.

"He will ask me if I have any special powers and I will ask him what he means by that.

"He will then assume that I'm gormless and will give you 1000/1. You will bet your shirt on me to break the record.

"One final thing. When it comes to paying his debt. I will be the one to collect. Agreed?"

"Agreed." Father smiled at him. "Why do you want to collect?"

"I am programmed to throw bad behaviour back in people's faces. You'll see," said Radio.

Radio finished the trousers and moved on to the shirts. This was it. He was ironing the shirt that he'd seen in his dreams.

The Adjudicator appeared followed by an enormous man. He recognised him immediately.

"Lord, Caro Gantz, nice to see you."

"Welcome Caro, good to see you." Father was diplomatic and betrayed no annoyance.

"Good to see you too, Lord." The man was smooth, Radio gave him that.

"What brings you here, Caro?" asked Father.

"The testing. What else? The big ones are coming up and the real points will be won. One wonders if you would like to make a wager. I hear one of the candidates has gotten off to a very good start."

He nodded at Radio.

Radio had deliberately worn an old cardigan. He felt it made him look more of a sap.

"I'm not sure, Caro," said Father. "I don't think I have that type of candidate. The odds would have to be very good."

"Ha," laughed Caro. "We'll see. What special powers do you have, boy?" he asked Radio.

Radio looked at him. This man had called him boy. Radio wasn't a particularly proud or defensive person but there were limits. Caro Gantz was full of himself, arrogant and cruel. He deserved what was coming. Radio put on the most gormless look he could conjure.

"What do you mean by special powers?"

Caro Gantz put his head in his hands and moaned. He turned to Father.

"I'll give you 1000/1."

"A thousand to one. Don't be ridiculous Caro. You cannot afford odds like that. Think of your family. Think of your people. You'll wipe them out."

"Lord, consider it a gift for all that you have given me. You may have 1000/1."

"Done," said Father. "I'll have a trillion talents on Radio of Edinburgh to break the record."

"Done," replied Caro.

Father turned to the Adjudicator. "Draw up an agreement and give him his money."

Radio stepped forward. "There is no need to draw up an agreement and there is no need to give this buffoon a brass farthing."

Radio had put on his serious face and his terrible voice and he could feel it.

The room was filled with fear. Caro Gantz was paralysed with terror. The Adjudicator was scared. Even his parents were frightened. The only one who was not afraid was Miriam and she was crowing in his head.

"You see, Caro Gantz, I have already broken the record. No candidate has ever nailed a test until now. I passed The Robe with 3000 points. The most any previous candidate has scored is 850 and that was after the testing had been completed. You owe my father 1000 trillion talents."

"That is correct," whispered the Adjudicator. "I had forgotten." He was trembling.

Caro Gantz looked at Radio and he could see the dawning of realisation on his face. He had been swindled just as he himself had swindled his father in the past.

Radio turned to the Adjudicator. "Bring me this man's tax returns," he ordered.

The Adjudicator sent the order down the line and a functionary appeared within two minutes. The Adjudicator handed him a sheet of paper.

Radio looked at the bottom line. It was as he suspected.

"You cannot afford your debt, Caro Gantz. It says here that the sum total of your personal wealth is less than half of what you owe."

"I can assure you, it is worth more than that."

Radio looked the man in the eye and poured every ounce of evil into his stare.

"If you are telling me that you have fiddled your tax returns, I will burn you in eternal hell."

No man looking at Radio could possibly have disbelieved him. He looked like he meant every word he said and he was terrifying.

Caro Gantz did the only thing he could do. He started weeping.

"Listen to me. You will pay my father everything you own. You will return every star system you have been given. You will return every piece of wealth that you and your family possess. Every single item. Do you understand?"

"Yes," the man wailed.

Radio turned to the Adjudicator. "Will that pay off his debt?"

"No, Lord. Not by half." The Adjudicator had recovered. Curiously, he had also started calling Radio, Lord.

"Remove your clothing," said Radio.

Caro Gantz stood up. "What?" he spluttered.

"Remove your clothing and your jewellery. You may keep your underpants."

The wretch removed his clothes and put his jewellery in a bowl. He stood there chittering.

"If you ever try to swindle my father again, I will find you and I will finish you. Do you understand?"

He nodded.

Radio turned to the Adjudicator. "Give this moron a servant's tunic. You will ensure that every penny is recovered and you will dump him at his lodgings."

"Lord, it will be done." The adjudicator bowed and hustled Caro Gantz away.

When they had gone Radio relaxed. Miriam jumped out of Father's lap and threw herself on him. She kissed him on the mouth and her voice sang in his head. My Radio.

Mother and Father looked at each other and then they did something that surprised him. They high-fived each other.

"Darling," said Mother, "We didn't know you had it in you?"

Then the penny dropped with Radio. Mother and Father weren't sure what he was capable of.

"You are aware that I can do pretty much anything?" he asked.

Mother looked at him. "You need to tell me. I wrote the general program but I'm not sure how far you have gone."

"I have an application for everything, I think. I can move a planet to another solar system. I can spin a city out of nothing. I can cure all disease in the universe. I know what everyone is thinking. I can speak every language and I can make everyone do my bidding.

"I have had fifteen years to fill my app store and if I think of something else that I need to be able to do, I just create another application."

Radio looked at them. They were staring at him open mouthed.

"What?" he asked.

They just laughed.

"Right, who wants coffee and a cake?"

Eighteen – Operation Birth Right

Radio, Miriam and Winston stood in front of the time windows as they watched the house of commons assemble.

He held Miriam's hand as he loved having her close. He loved touching her skin. The truth was that they were now so close in the mind that Radio did not know where his thoughts ended and hers began. He did not care.

The house settled and they walked through.

"Prime Minister," said Radio holding out his hand.

"Radio," she said and returned the handshake.

"Prime Minister, I'd like you to meet the Prime Minister." He introduced Winston.

There was a huge cheer in the chamber as Winston shook hands with the current holder of the office. Winston and Miriam sat on the government benches as the cheers subsided. Radio began.

"Mr Speaker, Prime Ministers, honourable members. This Earth stands on the cusp and the human race on this planet at a crossroads."

Radio walked up and down the centre of the house, looking in to as many sets of eyes as he possibly could.

"If you decide to go one way. The current way. Your way. The easy way. The wrong way. Mother and Father will withdraw and you will be allowed to destroy yourselves. You are well on the way to achieving your goal."

"It is also the democratic way!" It was Dennis Skinner.

"Thanks Dennis, you big mouthed tit." Radio had expected the interruption and felt that this was the best response. It got a laugh and quite a loud one.

"If, however you decide to go the other way. The new way. Mother and Father's way. The hard way. The right way. You will be welcomed in to an intergalactic community of shared technology, trade, shared research and shared burdens.

"This Earth has caused great concern amongst the intergalactic community. Can anyone guess what has caused the concern?"

There were no takers. Even Dennis was silent. For once.

"Trinity, Hiroshima, Nagasaki, Bikini Atoll, Three Mile Island, Chernobyl and the piece de resistance, Fukushima.

"What sort of moron builds a nuclear reactor on a known geological fault line. We do, apparently.

"This Earth is one of the most beautiful and diverse planets in this galaxy and is the home planet of Empires. It was gifted to me before the beginning of time and it will not be allowed to be destroyed by you or by anyone else.

"It is time for you to make a choice.

"If you decide to go with Mother and Father, you will hand power over to me temporarily. You will complete 5 programmes of work under operation birth right and when you have completed these works to Mother and Father's satisfaction, I will hand your power back to you and you will continue as normal.

"If you decide to continue on your way. Mother and Father will withdraw from the Earth. Nobody from the Earth will be allowed to pass the interview. You will destroy yourselves. The super volcano beneath Yellowstone National Park is not the only disaster that needs to be averted. There are others and they are overdue."

"What are the five programmes of work, may I ask?" It was Dennis again. Radio had to admit he had courage despite the fact that he was a complete pain in the arse.

"They are:

"Shelter – I propose to free everyone from their domestic mortgage so that they can concentrate on passing the interview. If money is required, I have it in abundance. The Unknown Pleasures has mined Mephistopheles on my behalf. Operator, hail the Captain."

A viewer appeared on the wall above the speaker and the bridge of the Unknown Pleasures came in to view.

"Beam down three cases," ordered Radio.

There was a flash of light and three cases appeared. They were full of the largest diamonds radio had ever scene.

"As you can see. I have the wealth."

Radio continued.

"Wise Owl – I propose an adjustment to your education system so that every child is trained to pass the interview.

"Food Chain – You have a surplus of food and an excess of waste, yet there are citizens of the United Kingdom who go hungry. I propose an adjustment to your food production and distribution process to resolve these issues.

"Jigsaw – Mother and Father support unions of states. The experiment which is the United Kingdom has largely been a success. However, each state within a union must be of equal size and influence to strengthen the bond.

"The best marriages are ones where the partners are equal. I propose a redrawing of the map of the United Kingdom to bring it in line with Mother and Father's vision of equal partnership.

"I also propose that we plan for the future. It is my intention to allow other states to apply to join Mother and Father's union. New states will also have to be of equal size.

"And finally Leapfrog – There are individuals within your society who have an excess of wealth which is interfering with their ability to pass the interview.

"I propose a series of measures which, without forcing anyone, will make it easier for individuals to limit themselves and to redistribute wealth, land and property. This will enable those at the level below to leapfrog up the chain.

"Mr Speaker, before I can proceed, I need you to call a vote. You have until 4.00 to make up your mind.

"We will return to hear the result."

Radio motioned for Miriam and Winston to follow and they returned to the matrix.

Radio was nervous. He had told them as much as he could because he wanted them to have faith in him. The warnings had been pretty clear but he knew what humans could be like. It would only take one very good speech on democracy and they could vote against him. If they did, it was curtains for everyone.

He looked at his watch. 12.30. He had 3 and a half hours to wait.

His mobile phone rang. It was the Pope.

"Good speech," he said. "You have 3 hours to wait. Why don't you all come and join me for coffee and we'll wait for the result together, it will take your mind off it."

Radio couldn't think of anything else to do so he agreed.

"I'll be with you shortly."

The three of them walked through the time windows and found themselves once again with the pontiff.

"Welcome Winston," said the old man. "You look well. I think time travel agrees with you."

Winston chuckled. "A change of scene is good for any man, your holiness."

They all sat down and Radio accepted a cup of coffee. It was good to have a rest from time to time. He always seemed to be on the go.

"I realise you are very busy," the old man began, "But you should be aware that you have started a wind of change in the world. Our organisation is struggling to cope."

Radio chuckled. "May I ask what is causing you specific problems?"

"Specifically, your assertion that Mother and Father are not in to worship and require no obeisance. Congregations are turning up on Sundays in their droves and are becoming quite militant. The priests don't know what to do."

Radio was delighted. The Earth was starting to wake up from the trance they had been placed in.

"It is really quite simple," Radio asserted, "Your priests need to start doing their jobs at last. I said before, that the only way to worship is to do the right thing. People now want to do the right thing.

"In every parish, there are people that need you. Your priests need to step up to the plate and be the pastoral ministers they should always have been. They need to become the facilitators and allow the help to be distributed.

"Old people need company. Send parishioners round to their houses and make them dinner once in a while and talk to them. Sick people need to be visited. Do their washing and cleaning and tend to them.

"All sorts of people need help. Help them."

"Are you giving me a mandate to lead…?"

Radio held up his hand and stopped him.

"I am confirming the mandate that was given to you 2000 years ago. A mandate to facilitate the love in a community.

"You must change, my friend, and change quickly. Your priests are all men. There is nothing to stop women from being the facilitators. Some would argue that they might be more practical at doing a better job.

"Mother and Father share responsibility for the universe equally. So, should you."

"You make it sound so easy."

"It is, you just have to imagine."

The Pontiff looked at him and Radio could tell he was considering his next question carefully.

"Just ask the question," said Radio. "I promise not to be offended."

"Why have you recruited Lucifer?"

Radio understood why he had asked the question. His association with him was probably creating doubt and controversy.

"I recruited him to show Mother and Father that I understand and to enable me to pass the tests.

"It is probably a bit early but you will soon work out why Mother and Father created the universe. When you work that out, you will work out who Lucifer is and why he is here. Always remember that the things we acquire easily, we never value.

"He is not who you think he is. There is no devil in hell."

"You threatened Caro Gantz with eternal hell."

"Yes. Mother and Father's method of rehabilitation is to throw bad behaviour back in people's faces. Whatever you have done in life will come back to haunt you in the afterlife. Until you learn your lesson.

"Caro Gantz mistake was to show the most enormous disrespect to our parents. You cannot expect to get away with that. It will be the end of you."

"Can you give me a clue, at least, as to what Lucifer's purpose is?"

Radio thought for a minute.

"This is as much as I can tell you. Lucifer's primary job is to hide something. He is occult. You have to work out what he is hiding and why. If you can work out that then you have answered your question.

"It would also do you no harm to consider how you managed to get yourself in to this position. This dire position. You have been asleep and now you find yourself in a situation where the sleepers are awakening. What makes it worse is that you have forgotten how to deal with the wide awake."

Radio, Miriam, Winston and the Pope spent the afternoon together drinking coffee and chatting. After a while, Radio forgot where he was. So much so, the Operator had to send him a reminder.

"The vote is in. Return to the commons."

Radio stood up and informed them that the vote was in. He shook hands with the old man and they all returned to the commons.

He was met by The Speaker who was standing between the despatch boxes. "Radio, you have temporary power over the United Kingdom. 454 for, 0 against. There were a number of no shows and abstentions. Over to you."

Radio was delighted. He knew that momentum was extremely important so getting to work straight away was key. What was also the key was handing back power. Sooner rather than later.

"Thank you, Mr Speaker. Firstly, thank you all for having faith in me.

"My plan is merely to give you the money to enable you to complete a programme of work on behalf of Mother and Father which is designed to make it easier for you to pass the interview.

"To that end, I will arrange for the contents of the Unknown Pleasure's cargo hold to be transferred to HM Treasury today.

"Prime Minister, as you are the elected leader you will become the Operations Manager and will report directly in to Mother and Father once a week."

This caused an 'Oh' in the audience which got steadily louder. Despite the obvious immaturity of it, Radio could not help laughing. Of course, they would be shitting themselves to report in to Mother and Father.

"Luckily for you. Mother and Father will only entertain a maximum of 6 slides and they much prefer illustrations and bullet points. You may put supporting data in an appendix which nobody will read."

Everybody laughed but they all knew it was true.

A screen appeared above the speaker's chair and Radio delivered a pre-prepared presentation.

"Your slides will be headed up:

"Issue – Who are your stakeholders? What are the terms of reference? What issue are you trying to address?

"Measure – What is the extent of the issue?

"Problems – What problems are associated with the issues?

"Analyse – What are the root causes of the issues and problems?

"Control – How do you propose to improve and control the issues and problems?

“Take Forward – On the grounds that no one ever completely solves a problem. How do you propose we take things to the next level?

“Those of you who are on the ball will have noticed that the slides spell out IMPACT.”

There were wolf whistles and fake outbursts of astonishment. Radio thanked them and bowed to laughter and a huge round of applause.

“Your first appearance in front of Mother and Father will be next Friday at 12.00 and you will deliver a presentation at operation level.

“You will appoint programme managers and you may also appoint project leaders if you think it makes sense to split the programmes up. Do not create an unnecessary army of functionaries. It is waste.

“There should be six slides produced at each iteration of work giving more detail.

“I will let you chew on things over the weekend and I will send someone to help you get started.

“I will answer any questions you have on Monday morning. Are you clear?”

The Prime Minister nodded. “As you say, we have the weekend to think about it. I’m sure there will be lots of questions on Monday.”

“I’m sure there will be,” said Radio ruefully.

They all headed back to the Matrix where there was a welcoming committee.

Mother, Father and all the Sprogs were there and they gave him a round of applause.

A young planet builder raised a glass and announced, “It’s just like old times.”

Nineteen - The Offer and the Citadel

It was Saturday. Radio could hear Mother and Father making breakfast and he could smell bacon and eggs. Normally, he didn't have a cooked breakfast because he liked a clean start to the day but today was different. Today was the day when the tests started in earnest.

He could feel Miriam close and he snuggled in further. Their minds were merged now. When he spoke, she spoke and vice versa. They decided that they would have a cooked breakfast this morning in preparation for later.

Radio and Miriam got up and went through into his bathroom. They'd taken to showering together so that Radio could wash Miriam's hair. They dried each other and got dressed.

If an observer had seen them, they would have reported that they did not speak yet they never stopped talking to each other. Sometimes Radio had difficulty working out who had spoken.

When they came through to the round table, Miriam sat down and Radio got her breakfast. Bacon, egg, toast and coffee.

"What are you going to do this morning?" asked Mother.

"I thought I would make you all lunch," replied Radio. "I'm going to do a pot of leek and potato soup. A green bean casserole and a chocolate cake to finish."

"That sounds nice," she said. "I think I'll stay for lunch, then I must leave to prepare for the tests. When you are called today, it will be around 4.00 and it will be Father conducting the tests. Don't be alarmed."

Radio looked at her and smiled. "I am not alarmed. Everything will be fine."

After breakfast, Radio collected his shopping bags and he and Miriam headed through the matrix to pick up Jamie. He was as smart as a new pin and very excited.

Apparently, he had become something of a local celebrity judging by the small crowd that had appeared to wave him on his way.

Radio opened an incursion and headed for his local Sainsbury's. It was early Saturday and it was still quiet.

As they meandered through the aisles, he and Miriam started picking up the thoughts of the other shoppers.

"Oh my God, it's him. Calm down, he's only doing his shopping."

Radio smiled inwardly. I didn't really matter what the person looked like, their thoughts were all equally silly.

One woman looked at them and thought, *I wonder if they're having sex?*

What possible reason could she have for wondering that. Radio would have reacted differently before but he realised that Miriam had brought a new maturity to his thoughts.

A balance was now being found, where extremes were previously the norm.

He noted that he was no longer as interested in football and was more interested in his appearance. He took more care about things that he never used to care about.

Radio picked up onions and leeks and sent Jamie to find a garlic bulb.

As he was looking through an end display, he suddenly had that feeling at the nape of his neck. In front of him there was a multi pack of spicy crisps that he knew he just had to buy. He had no idea why or who they were for but he picked them up and put them in his trolley. Then he heard a voice in his mind. It was alien.

"Help me, Radio."

He turned around and saw a figure he recognised. It was a woman he used to work with. A woman who he didn't like. He had always thought of her as very badly behaved.

She was unusually wearing jeans but what really struck Radio was that her long hair had been shaved. He had a bad feeling.

What's up? he thought.

"I'm dying," she said aloud. "Cancer."

Radio launched the Medic application and had a look.

"Actually, you're not, Monique, you're in remission. However, you are very unwell. You are low in potassium and you are very weak from malnutrition. Probably the cancer treatment."

Radio placed his hands on her cheeks and kissed her forehead. He waited until he heard the bell sound and took another look at her. She had transformed before his eyes.

"Do you want me to grow your hair back in?" he asked.

"Yes, please, if you can."

He put his hand on her head and her hair flew out in glowing locks. He even styled it for her.

"Thank you. I don't know what to say."

Radio looked at her and said the most honest thing he had ever said.

"Don't thank me, thank Miriam. She is the one with all the compassion."

Monique laughed. "I believe you, you were always scary. Always a bit aloof."

Monique turned to Miriam. "Thank you, Miriam. You are really good together."

Without waiting for a response, she hurried away.

They looked at each other. "Good together." A tear streaked down his cheek and Miriam kissed it away.

There was a cough. It was Jamie and Radio could tell that public displays of affection were not on his list of cool.

There were ten for lunch. Mother, Father, Winston, Jamie, Klaus, Miriam, Radio and three planet builders who had arrived with a status report. This was going to be interesting. This was the first real interaction where events were seriously out of chronological order. No wonder the Operator had taken 15 years to prepare him.

Radio put the soupier down on the table and invited everyone to help themselves.

"This is delicious," Mother exclaimed. Radio chuckled, he was never tired of hearing that.

"It really is good," said the older planet builder as she collected her thoughts.

"Right," she began, "We have suspended a universe in the fantasy EL-PAR and we have transferred the planet templates into the solution. At the moment, the planets are unpopulated but they are ready for temporal insertion.

"As soon as you know who you want to transfer in to the solution, you can begin."

"Thank you," said Radio. "I'll send out the invitations as soon as I have a free moment."

"Who are you sending the invitations to?" asked the young one.

"Good question," replied Radio. "I want to send invitations to the dead souls who are currently in rehab. It will be an opportunity for them to make up for lost time.

"I also want to send out invites to those who are in PARADISE awaiting their partners. There are lots of powerful entities in the fantasies and they could assist with the training.

"Beyond that, anyone who would like to go."

"I'd like to go," said the young one.

There was silence. Radio had expected the request and he was not sure how to proceed. He needed to ask a few questions.

"Are you in or out of the solution at the moment?" he asked.

"Out," she replied. "My body is in the laboratory on life support at the moment. My SOUL has been uploaded in to the solution and I'm currently using the body you assigned to me from the ANGEL store."

"Are you asking to come in permanently?"

"Yes. That was always the plan. Those of us who are still in the lab are there, just to make sure the solution is completely stable before we go for permanent upload."

"How many are left?"

"304."

Radio thought about it for a moment.

"Is there any reason you shouldn't come in?"

"The only thing stopping me is you. If you have any more planetary requirements, then I will have to stay outside of the solution as all the other planet builders have now uploaded.

"We are the last three but the truth is that my colleagues don't have my skills. One is a supervisor and the other a tester."

Radio realised that he could not be selfish in light of the fact that all of his other requirements had been met.

"Fine. You may upload permanently in to the solution."

"Hurrah."

Radio laughed and then he stopped. His requirements. He looked at Miriam and she stood up from the table and looked at him. She looked frightened.

Radio turned to Mother. "We are waking up, Mother. We are starting to remember."

Mother lifted him into her lap.

"Don't be afraid darling, I've been expecting it for a while now. Let it happen. I expect it will take a while but it will be all right."

Miriam climbed in to Mother's lap also and held Radio tight. She started weeping and Radio knew why.

It was time.

Gabriel was waiting in front of the time windows. "Are you ready?" she asked.

"I am."

"Then follow me."

They walked together into the hall. A table had been placed in the centre and Father was standing next to it.

The Adjudicator stepped forward. "The fifth contestant again, Radio of Edinburgh."

There was a roar of applause and Radio glanced around the room. The other 4 contestants were seated on the dais and there was something different about them.

They were all significantly older than they had been three days ago. They were older, wiser, less arrogant and they were exhausted. *Oh dear,* thought Radio. *Some things never change*.

"Welcome Radio," said Father. "You have qualified for the testing and in line with tradition this entitles you to a significant portion of this universe. If you attempt this examination, we will give you twenty star systems in this galaxy."

"Don't worry, Father. I'll do it all for nothing."

Radio's announcements were no longer met with gasps, they were met with sounds of understanding. Dawning realisation filled the hall.

Radio looked at the piles of coin stacked on the table and the troop of men standing behind his father. He smiled.

"Moreover, I require no budget and no servants."

Father's grin was broad and there was a tear in his eye. He held up his hand and a time window opened behind him. Radio could see a citadel whose battlements were defended by an army.

"Then, my son, bring me back my treasure."

"Certainly."

Radio walked through the time window and toward the battlements. The sergeants on the wall ordered the men to stand easy. Radio knew that they would only defend the citadel if it was attacked. A single man walking towards them could hardly be described as an attack.

He reached the gate, knocked five times and waited. He didn't have to wait long.

A woman appeared followed by an armed guard.

"I wish to see the lady," said Radio.

The woman looked at him and Radio could tell that she could not believe that an unarmed man would walk up to a well-defended fortress and knock on the door.

"May I tell her who calls?" the woman asked.

"My name is Radio. I am Mother's apprentice."

The woman's face transformed into the most beautiful smile Radio had ever seen. "Then follow me, my Lord."

Radio followed her through the gate, across the courtyard and into the hall. In the middle of the hall was a 10-foot rendition of a human skull, sculpted from solid diamond. *The so-called treasure*, thought Radio.

The woman led him to a throne. Sitting there, in all her glory, was Mother.

"Father has sent me to bring you home," said Radio.

"What did he say to you?" asked Mother.

"He said, bring me back my treasure."

Mother looked at him and he realised she wasn't speaking to him but to the people in the hall and perhaps even to posterity.

"Don't you think he meant that?" She pointed at the diamond skull.

"No, Mother, he didn't mean that. Despite the fact that I marvel at the majesty of the universe, one immutable fact is true."

"What's that?" asked Mother.

"It is the dross left over from a science experiment. Father's dross," Radio pointed at the skull. "Father's treasure," He pointed at Mother. "You are Father's treasure, Mother, and mine! Who could pass this test but Mother's apprentice?"

She leaned forward "Who indeed." She picked him up and threw him in the air. "He's done it," she shouted and there was a deafening roar of exultation.

Father was there immediately and he grabbed him out of Mother's arms, kissed him and threw him up in the air.

He turned to the Adjudicator. "Points please and distribute accordingly."

"I will summarise the performance and deliver the points for all candidates tomorrow," replied the Adjudicator. "I will make sure that Radio is scored appropriately."

Radio didn't really care. He just wanted to make sure that he was so far ahead that he could persuade the others to drop out. The question of Lilith was still bothering him. *Not long now*, he thought.

Twenty - Hrolfr, Duke of Normandy

Radio had enjoyed a pleasant evening.

Mother and Father had opened champagne and most people had gotten slightly drunk.

At the breakfast table, Winston was knocking back orange juice by the litre and Radio smiled. The Prime Minister had been well oiled last night and had regaled everyone with some hilarious tales. He was regretting it now.

"When you finish that," said Mother, pointing at his cereal, "You need to make your way to the BBC. You are being interviewed on The Andrew Marr show."

Radio nodded soberly and ate his granola. He didn't mind being interviewed at all but he had noticed that there was a certain set of BBC interviewers who confused assertiveness with rudeness. He was in favour of pressing politicians to get to the truth, especially when they were being evasive.

He wasn't a politician and he had only been evasive to protect people. He hoped the man would be polite.

At 8.58 he walked through the time windows and in to the studio.

Andrew was already seated and motioned for him to join him.

"Morning. Normally we mic people up but I assume in your case, it will be unnecessary."

"Completely."

The programme started and Andrew made his introduction to camera. He then turned to Radio.

"Westminster is buzzing this weekend with birth right and IMPACT. What results are you expecting to see from this programme of work?"

"I'm expecting people to have more time to pass the interview. At the moment, the majority of people in the UK are one pay cheque away from being skint.

"They also have mortgages or rent to pay every month. My desire is to free them from that responsibility so that they can work a bit less and spend more time helping others in their community."

"There are many people who would say that what you're asking people to do is work that should be done by the government."

"Government is an abdication of responsibility. At the moment, people are slaves to their debts so they have a very good argument to say that they don't have enough time to do the things they need to do to convince Mother and Father that they are trustworthy enough to work for them."

"Saying that Government is an abdication of responsibility is a very large assertion, isn't it?"

"Sumer is the largest Empire in the galaxy and their government meets once every five years. There are only 5 members of the government and they only meet to have a review of the legislature.

"They realised, hundreds of years ago that government was pure waste. Once you have put the law in place and encourage people to adopt the law in spirit then any change is unnecessary tinkering.

"There is an administration that deals with the management of a civil society but they only do what is absolutely necessary.

"The people take care of everything else.

"There is very little crime and as a result, only a skeleton police force.

"There are no old folk's homes as they would never allow their old folk to be looked after by strangers. The old person turns up for a visit and never goes home. They are loved.

"The fact is that you have created a whole load of dysfunctional work for yourselves because you are afraid of responsibility. You are lazy and you are selfish.

"My advice to all of you is that you cannot pass this interview by being lazy and selfish."

"It really does come down to that, doesn't it? You are gearing the society to pass the interview."

"Yes, I feel that I must give everyone, one last chance to get it right. If you had actually done what Yeshua had asked you to do 2000 years ago, you wouldn't be in this mess. However, I cannot blame the people when the church has abdicated its responsibility.

"Church ministers were meant to be pastoral. Prayer is all very well but a hungry man can't eat a prayer.

"I am now spoon feeding you so that you may pass. You should be embarrassed."

Andrew didn't look embarrassed. "You talked about Wise Owl. What are your plans for the education system?"

"Every single child should leave school at the age of 18 with a basic degree. They should be able to read to a certain standard. Write to a standard and do complex arithmetic. They should also have key life skills which will enable them to do two things. Pass the interview and get a job as an apprentice anywhere.

"The education doesn't stop there. They should be able to complete modular education and be mentored in their chosen profession until they obtain their master's degree.

"My expectation is that everyone will be a master at the age of thirty. The progression is student until 18. Apprentice until 30 and then master. As master, I will expect them to become mentors for the next generation."

"That will surely put some people's noses out of joint. You can obtain a master's degree at the age of 24."

"They aren't masters," Radio looked at his interviewer. "I have come across many people who have been highly trained to master's degree level at university but every single one of them has lacked something. It is invariably something that will pass them the interview.

"Don't lose sight of the grand plan. When a candidate acquires the rank of master, we are essentially saying that they are ready to pass the interview. It is more than knowing facts."

"What do you mean by modular education?" asked Andrew.

"If a candidate gets a basic degree and wants to become a lawyer, my expectation is that he will join a law firm who will then put him through the appropriate education pertaining to the day to day tasks that he does. The candidate may start off as a solicitor conveyancing and obtain the appropriate modules which will qualify them to do that role.

"However, they may wish to go on to court law at a later date.

"My expectation is that the education will be paid for by a mixture of tax, the candidate and the law firm.

"It will cut out waste in the education system."

"Is education ever a waste?"

"It is, when you consider that there are many people who have obtained a degree in science and have ended up working in an office. There are lots of examples like that.

"I am not imposing a set of rules on you, I'm giving you some general principles which have been proven elsewhere. Societies that follow these principles, pass the interview."

"The one programme that has caused the least amount of controversy is food chain. I don't think anyone would disagree that we have a problem there. How do you see that panning out?"

"Food chain, if implemented properly, will actually cause a bit more work for people. They will spend a little bit more time cutting waste and preparing healthy food properly. However, I'm hoping that we will create time by doing other things properly.

"This is the one that interests me more than the others. I'm looking to see how you intend to solve some of the problems that face you. This could be an opportunity to show the universe the way as food chain has caused other cultures problems. It is not going to be easy. Time will tell."

"And now the one that has caused the most controversy, Jigsaw. Are we going to see the end of countries within the United Kingdom? Is this the end of England, Scotland, Wales and Northern Ireland?"

"Not necessarily. On other planets, the land is divided equally in to manageable states with wilderness given national park status.

"Our experiences have shown that a state of about 10 million people is ideal. In the UK there are 60 million, so a quick calculation tells me that another 2 states may emerge. There is nothing to stop you from resurrecting the states of the past. You could still have England, Scotland, Wales and Ireland but perhaps also Mercia and Northumberland. I'm not imposing my will, I'm merely giving you an example of how you could do it. Suit yourselves.

"Moreover, if France chose to make an application to join, they would also have to split themselves up. They could have Burgundy, Aquitaine, Ile de France, Normandy or Savoy. The opportunities and possibilities are endless.

"Equally, you could decide to change it completely and have states named after anything you like. Capital cities, dialects, heroes from the past. Do what suits you. Make it work."

"Then we come to the million dollar question. What does it mean to pass the interview? What is in it for the people of the United Kingdom?"

"If a candidate passes the interview, I will give them a Core Application Suite or CAS. The human brain is only using about 10% of its capacity. The other 90% was set aside for the application suite.

"A typical application suite contains about 15 applications depending on how big they are. The Operator gives you a suite to suit the individual. Some people may get MEDIC. If they get MEDIC then they may not get a full suite because MEDIC is huge and takes up a lot of space.

"To give you an example. This is a typical CAS."

Radio waved his hand and an interface appeared on the studio viewer.

MEDIC SAC ICEBREAKER

TREADMILL TWIX CREATEME

TIMESPLICER TONGUETWISTER DEITY

SLEEPER XEROX MUSICMAN
FEEDME

"This is a typical CAS for a candidate in the diplomatic employ of Mother and Father. There are one trillion stars in this galaxy and one trillion galaxies in the universe. You have only seen the tip of the tip of the iceberg.

"A person with this suite will be able to cure any illness, spin a city out of nothing or a dwelling or a village or a town. They will have a number of applications which will enable them to break the ice with new species in the universe.

"They will be able to fly through the air, turn water into any other drink, create objects out of thin air, travel through space and time.

"They will be able to speak any language and make anybody follow their orders.

"They will be able to put a large crowd to sleep, copy any object they see and sing any song that has ever been written, play any instrument ever invented and conjure music from the ether.

"They will also be able to feed any entity they meet. It is a huge amount of power."

"My God," said his interviewer. "It is incredible."

"And yet I have demonstrated how they are all possible and you believe me."

"I have always had a desire to travel in time. Is it possible for you to demonstrate this application?"

Radio had expected this request and was ready.

"Today is your lucky day!"

As he spoke, Gabriel and Uriel appeared carrying a set of clothes with them and a pot of hot soup. It was a monk's habit with a rope belt.

Radio handed the habit to Andrew.

"Put that on. You are Friar Andrew from Dal Riada. You will say nothing unless I give you a direct order. Do you understand?"

"Where are we going?" Andrew looked excited but also a bit nervous.

Radio chuckled. "You'll see. Operator, The Lower Seine, 918, Temporal Incursion."

The vortex that appeared before them felt different. It felt powerful and dangerous.

"Let's go. Operator launch the TONGUETWISTER app and extend."

They appeared in a valley covered in mist. Radio could see an avenue of trees extending away from him. Just as he had seen it in his dream.

He created a circle of stones and lit a fire and put the soup on a flat rock to heat.

He darkened the left lens of his spectacles and transformed himself. He could feel himself growing outwards and upwards. It was strange.

He turned to the others. "Be ready and have your wits about you. They are formidable."

He selected a tune from his interface, increased the volume to maximum and turned to the tree line.

"Hrolfr," he shouted. "Hrolfr." Nothing happened for several minutes. "Hrolfr."

And then they started to come out of the mist. They were, indeed, formidable.

They rode forward like death. If murder were a regiment of mounted men then he was looking at it.

The lead rider rode up to them and dismounted. He caught Radio in a bear hug and shouted, "Walvater."

"Put me down, Hrolfr," chuckled Radio.

Hrolfr laughed and dropped him to the ground. He looked at Gabriel and Uriel and nodded. "Well met, Archangels."

His eyes alighted on Andrew and he turned to Radio.

"Is that not the fellow from the BBC?"

Andrew jumped and Radio smiled.

"This is Friar Andrew of Dal Riada. Friar Andrew, meet Hrolfr, Duke of Normandy."

"How do you do?" said Andrew.

"I'm well Mr Marr," said Hrolfr. "Don't worry, I was trained in the matrix. We've met before but I expect that has not happened for you yet. You'll get used to it."

"First things first," said Radio. "Let's get you fed. You all look like you could do with some soup."

"That's your ham and lentil," said Hrolfr. "I could smell it coming down the hill."

The men produced their bowls and Radio ladled generous amounts of the soup to each man.

"Right, status report?" asked Radio.

"It is as you predicted," said Hrolfr around mouthfuls of soup. "The King has offered me the land from here, north to the sea in exchange for defending France against the Norsemen and the Danes. I have accepted."

"Excellent. You will name your lands Normandy after your brethren. This is the beginning. From this spot, the greatest Empire the world will ever know will grow. Your great, great, great grandson will invade Britain and will become King of England. You have done well, Hrolfr."

"Thanks. How's Master Jacques?"

"He has just started his training. Don't worry, by the time you are ready to come home to me, Master Jacques will be ready?"

"Any wine?" asked the Duke, hopefully.

Radio held out his hand and produced a pitcher of Petrus from out of nothing. He handed it to Hrolfr.

"Oh, ho, ho, ho, it's the good stuff," exclaimed Hrolfr jubilantly.

He produced a cup from his saddlebag and poured himself a large one. It disappeared.

"Oh my God, that is magnificent."

Radio and Hrolfr talked for about 15 minutes, He gave Hrolfr a number of instructions and then stood up.

"Right, we'll need to be getting back."

He hugged Hrolfr and opened the vortex.

Not one of Hrolfr's men turned a hair. They had seen it all before.

Radio ushered the others back to the BBC studio.

Andrew sat down. "That was extraordinary," he said.

Radio leaned forward. "You had better get used to it. Things are about to get very hairy indeed. The testing is about to get very serious indeed and you are about to see the completely unbelievable."

Radio turned and looked directly at the camera.

"Remember, if you all want to be a part of this. You need to pass my interview. There is so much work to be done. This universe is vast and Mother and Father need you. Don't let them down."

Radio looked at his watch. An hour had elapsed, it was time to go.

He stood up and returned to the matrix followed by Gabriel and Uriel.

Lucifer was waiting for him.

"You have nothing to fear," he said. "They are way out of their depth and dying to throw in the towel. All they need is a good excuse."

"Thank you. I have the perfect one."

Twenty-One – The Dragon's Run

Radio found himself in the hall again, awaiting the results from yesterday's tests. For the first time, he sat on the dais with the other candidates. They no longer looked at him with hatred. In fact, Radio felt that they were very subdued, very pensive.

When everybody settled, the Adjudicator stepped forward.

"Two tests were conducted yesterday, The Offer and The Citadel.

"The Offer is a test of hubris, greed and behaviour. The candidate is offered a portion of the universe by The Creator, a budget to complete the tests and servants to do their bidding.

"The Citadel is a test of understanding. The candidate is asked to find The Creator's treasure and return it to him.

"Let's take each candidate in turn.

"Dyer of Pelos.

"Dyer accepted the portion of the universe that he was offered and did not question whether he was equal to the task. He scores 100 points.

"He negotiated for a greater budget than offered arguing that he could do more good with more money. He scores 0 points.

"He accepted the offer of servants. 0 points.

"He attacked The Citadel with an army and laid siege to the castle for 5 years. There were 18,477 casualties at a cost of 400 million talents. He scores 0 points.

In total 100 points."

There was silence in the hall. No applause. No recognition at all.

Radio now knew why the candidates looked older. Mother and Father had sent them back in time to lay siege to the castle. He could see what they were doing. The candidates must have asked themselves the question, give up or carry on. Was the slaughter worth it?

No wonder the candidates looked pensive.

Grace of Assyria also scored 100 points. Mohr of Agora scored 100 bonus points for rejecting personal servants giving him a total of 200. Adela of Lore scored 500 points for asking if Father was sure she should have such a large portion of the universe. Unfortunately, she still accepted the offer.

"Radio of Edinburgh," announced the Adjudicator. All eyes were on Radio.

Radio rejected the offer receiving maximum points of 3000. He also scores 2000 bonus points for knowing the answers to two of the questions before being asked.

He successfully completed The Citadel by bringing back The Creator's treasure. 3000 points. 3000 bonus points for no casualties, no cost and no time.

11,000 points in total. No casualties. No cost. 10 minutes to pass the tests.

Radio of Edinburgh leads the way with 14,000 points.

Everybody in the hall, including the other candidates stood up and gave him a standing ovation.

When the noise had died down, Radio stood and looked at Mother and Father.

"Permission to address the other candidates?"

There was that familiar rumble in the hall. Radio smiled inwardly, he seemed to create uneasiness wherever he went.

Mother and Father nodded.

He looked at each of the candidates in turn.

“Firstly, I bear you no ill will. I say this to save you and others from further travails.

“I would like to make you an offer.

“If you withdraw from the testing, Mother and Father will allow you to remove the robes that are causing you such embarrassment and they will take you on as apprentices.

“I can see the future. The next test is The Dragon’s Lair. If you proceed to this test, you will all surely die. It is not a possibility. It is a certainty.”

There was silence, again, in the hall. After a painful pause, Dyer of Pelos stood up. He addressed Mother and Father.

“Father, Mother, I speak for only myself. I would like to withdraw from the testing. I realise that I have only been here so that I may learn a hard lesson.

“Let me assure you, the lesson has been learned. I would also point out that I am a willing student and if you have any further lessons for me, a simple note will suffice.”

In that one statement, Dyer of Pelos won everyone over, including Mother and Father. Everyone was laughing and patting him on the back. The other candidates removed their robes to show that they were taking his lead. That left Radio.

Mother stood “And then there was one. I presume you have a desire to complete the testing?”

“Yes, if that’s all right,” Radio replied.

“Blow us away, Radio. Show your Father and I that you are the person we think you are. You have no reason to be coy now. Explain everything.”

“I’m rather glad you said that,” said Radio.

At that instant, Lucifer stepped forward. He was wearing what looked like a wet suit cut short at the knees.

Radio joined him and removed his clothes to reveal a similar suit. Both suits had the same symbol over the heart. Mother and Father’s symbol.

“Are you ready,” asked Radio.

“No, I’m not bloody ready,” replied Lucifer. “I’m absolutely shitting myself and for the record I think you are officially mental.”

The buzz in the hall was one of anticipation.

“Now, remember, keep them off my back.”

“Get on with it.”

Radio moved Mother and Father’s thrones to the side of the hall and cleared the area in front of the time window.

“Operator, the Dragon’s Run.”

The sea appeared on the viewer. Radio looked at Lucifer and said, “Good luck.”

They both started running at great speed and launched themselves out over the sea. The attack came almost immediately.

Six dragons descended on them from nowhere.

Radio and Lucifer split up and Radio headed for the Island that was now dead ahead. He was followed by three of the dragons.

He increased his speed until there was distance between him and his pursuers. Thinking quickly, he sent a wind wave behind him, hurricane strength. The dragons spiralled out of control and hit the surface of the sea.

He touched down on the Island, launched DIME and slowed time down to a quarter. Four seconds for him was a single second for every other entity in the universe.

He sped along the promontory and came to the standing stones. The nest.

In the middle of the stones was the largest egg he had ever seen. He cursed inwardly, he had underestimated the size. He launched ANCHOR.

He sped toward the egg. Even with time slowed, the speed of the mother was phenomenal. She came out of nowhere and swiped her claw at Radio. He slowed time to an eighth and ducked watching it sail slowly over his head. He grabbed the egg and anchored it to his back.

She was moving again and was still fast. Radio had no option. He launched JACKINTHEBOX and hit 1000 feet in a split second.

For the first time in an age, Radio had to admit that he was scared. He looked down. Even at an eighth, the dragons were heading for him like cruise missiles. Shit.

"To me," he shouted at Lucifer in his mind.

Radio sped over the ocean at top speed and waited while Lucifer caught up with him. He was being pursued by at least 50 dragons.

Radio opened the time window and they both shot through. As he passed he shouted to the Operator, "Keep them out."

Radio and Lucifer hit the floor of the hall and rolled about 50 paces.

Behind them he could hear the dragons battering the fabric of time and space. They were a very pissed off group.

Radio got up and placed the egg on the floor.

He put his hands on the shell. "Come on little one. Please, you can do it."

The shell cracked and a small wing emerged. Radio cleared the shell. He removed the top half of his suit to reveal his naked torso. Reaching in to the egg he pulled the dragon clear.

He held the baby dragon to his chest and waited.

Nobody said a word. Everyone in the hall was white faced.

And then she did what Radio knew she would do. She spread her wings wide and cuddled him. Radio was utterly relieved. They were bonded.

"You can let them in now," said Radio. He created a seat and sat down in front of the window.

Six of them appeared and they had all transformed in to humanoid form. They looked like very tall elves.

"Welcome, Great One," he addressed the mother. "I'm afraid you are too late."

"What are you up to, Architect?"

"In the future, your daughter will become one of my best friends. There are many things that we will do together. I am sorry if I have caused you any distress but I know I have to do this. I have to bond with her. In my travels through time and space, I have seen us achieve great things."

The mother thought for a moment and looked at the man standing next to her. He smiled and nodded.

"If you have travelled through time and space and we believe that you have, then you will know her name. You may give her, her name."

"She is called Lilith."

Twenty-Two – The Saxon Invasion

It was Sunday evening and the Dragons had returned home.

Mother and Father had questioned him at length in the Great Hall. They wanted to know why he had stolen the egg.

Radio had explained that it was the only way to pass the test but not to ask too many questions as the test would reveal all the answers. They had relented but he could tell that they were intrigued.

He was now listening to a presentation delivered by Klaus and Jamie.

It had been extremely interesting and Radio was very pleased at the level of detail they had been able to provide. However, he had questions.

"Can you tell me the exact date that Cerdic landed in Britain?"

"As far as we can tell, the most likely date is 495?"

Klaus had given Jamie responsibility for the delivery of the presentation and Radio was delighted. The boy had taken to it like a duck to water.

"How many ships did he bring with him?" asked Radio.

"No more than five, however, there is something that is nagging me."

Again, Radio was pleased, Jamie was highlighting the things that didn't make sense.

"What's bothering you?"

"The records are scant but many believe that Cerdic's father was Elesa. What is puzzling me is that they have identified Elesa as the Romano-Briton Elasius who was regarded as chief of the region.

"My question is this. Why would Cerdic be living in Germany when his father was the local British chief?"

Radio thought he might know the answer.

"It is possible that Elasius may have been a mercenary. When the Romans quit Britain in 410, the British hired German mercenaries to do their fighting.

"The mercenaries revolted in about 442 and the British finally defeated them in 490 at Badon Hill. Elasius may have been a carry over and took control of the local tribes. I'll ask him."

"What?" exclaimed Jamie.

Winston, who was also listening in started chuckling.

"I'm meeting Cerdic tomorrow and I'll ask him."

Jamie looked at him and started laughing.

"Why did you ask us to do all this research if you can find out for yourself?"

"Several reasons, actually.

"One. We won't always have access to the temporal matrix. Time travel is dangerous and the Operator is keen to have it over and done with.

"Two. You will be doing research all your life so you had better get used to it.

"Three. Background information is always useful. You never know when it might come in handy."

It was time to call it a day. He was exhausted and he had a full day ahead of him.

He was heading for bed when he remembered that he had to take Jamie home. He was about to turn around when the Operator spoke in his head.

"Don't bother, let him stay here."

There was something about the tone that made him uneasy.

"What's wrong?"

"The mother is drunk and in a foul mood. If you take him back now there will be a lot of unpleasantness.

"I'm going to put her to sleep soon so that she won't remember a thing in the morning. You will be able to play the incident to your advantage."

"What will I tell the boy?" asked Radio.

"Nothing. Leave it to me. I'm going to open communications with him tonight when he goes to bed."

"Sounds familiar." Radio was taken back 15 years to the evening when the Operator first started speaking to him. The boy was in for one hell of a surprise.

The following morning, Jamie was remarkably chipper over breakfast.

"Everything all right?" asked Radio.

"Yes. The Operator shared your plan with me last night. I'm really looking forward to it. I didn't know she had a tattoo."

Radio smiled. He couldn't wait.

When they got back to Jamie's house, his mother was waiting at the door.

"What time do you call this?" she demanded. "He was supposed to be home last night."

Radio puts on the serious face.

"Get inside, Natalie." he said shortly.

Her show of bravado dropped immediately.

Radio motioned for her to sit down.

"Natalie, I did bring Jamie home last night but unfortunately, you were very drunk."

She immediately looked frightened. "I'm sorry, I can't remember."

"You don't remember the striptease?"

"Oh my God." She fell to the floor in complete embarrassment.

"Natalie, it was all over the television, last night. I checked this morning on YouTube and it's been viewed over 100 million times already."

"Oh my God." She started crying.

Jamie stood up and helped her to her feet.

"Mother, I need to ask you a question. Why have you got a tattoo on your arse?"

"Oh, my fucking God." She screamed and put her hands over her ears.

"Natalie. Listen to me." Radio paused for effect. "We are of course, only kidding."

She stopped and looked at them. Radio could tell that she was thinking about getting angry but they both maintained a look of dread seriousness.

"Natalie, you are going to have to stop drinking. I need you to pass the interview because Jamie is a certainty to pass. The last thing I want is for him never to be able to see you again.

"I'll make a deal with you. Jamie is so important to us that if you devote the rest of your life to looking after him as you should, I will let you pass the interview."

She sat down and put her head in her hands. Eventually she got up and looked at him.

"I need help. I want to stop but I think I'm an alcoholic. Help me."

"Then follow us."

Radio led them back through into the matrix.

Mother and Father were waiting.

“Natalie, let me introduce you to Mother and Father. Whilst you are here, you cannot drink alcohol or Mother and Father will know.” He turned to his parents. “Can we ban alcohol whilst Natalie is in recovery, please?”

They both smiled and said “absolutely” in unison.

Behind them he could here Winston curse. “Bugger,” he said.

Radio turned to Jamie. “Show your Mother your apartments Jamie. You can have the day off school today but you’ll be back tomorrow. Okay?”

Jamie looked at him. “Thanks, Grandfather,” he said.

After Jamie had gone, Radio considered his options.

“Operator, show me Battle for Britain please.”

The plan appeared on the viewer.

Battle for Britain

- Preparation – Recruit the right people and set the scene.
- Part One – Bring the tribes to Great Britain.
- Part Two – Create the United Kingdom.
- Part Three – The Darkest Hour.

He had already recruited Winston, Hrolfr, Jamie, Klaus and the UK parliament. That just left Cerdic.

The Normans were well on their way but he had done nothing about ensuring the Saxon invasion.

He looked at his watch. It was 8.30. He was due in parliament at noon which gave him 3 and a half hours to find Cerdic.

He would wait until Jamie returned and they would all go and find the King of Wessex.

“Winston, how are you getting on?”

“I’m more or less done,” said Winston. “I’ve written each event on a card as you suggested and I’m just reviewing my notes to make sure I understand and remember them.”

“Excellent. How would you like a trip to Saxon England? There’s a TONGUETWISTER application in it for you.”

Radio knew that he wouldn’t be able to resist. Being able to translate every language would be extremely useful where he was going.

“I think I’d like that very much.”

“We have a few choices. We could go as Romans, Saxons, Romano-Britons or Celts. Anything else would attract too much attention.”

Winston thought about it for a moment. “If we are going East, then I think Saxon. If we are going West then Celt or Romano-Briton. Roman means army at the time we are going and that could mean trouble.”

It was a good point. “Saxon, it is, then.”

When Jamie returned after showing his Mother around, they all had great fun dressing up as fifth century Germanic marauders. Winston put on a false ginger moustache and looked like Obelix from the Asterix cartoons.

Radio transformed into Wotan. The others thought he looked formidable.

When they were ready, Radio uploaded the TONGUETWISTER application into their CAS and asked the Operator to drop them on the beach as Cerdic’s ships arrived.

They walked through on to a bluff overlooking the channel.

In the middle distance, they could see Cerdic's ships making their way to the shore. They were to all intents and purposes Viking longboats. Radio smiled. He hadn't expected that.

Radio turned to the others. "Let me do the talking. I don't know if I've met Cerdic yet so this could be a bit hairy."

As the boats landed on the shore, Radio walked out. They were halfway to the water when one of the men jumped on to the sand and made their way towards them. When he was about ten feet away he pulled back his hood. Radio just about fainted.

"Well I'll be damned, if it isn't Tommy Godfrey?"

Radio had worked with the man in his days as a contract analyst.

Tommy smiled ruefully. "I guess this is what I get for looking like a Saxon, eh boss?"

"What on earth are you doing here?"

"Operators orders," said Tommy. "Five years ago, for me anyway, you offered me the job. I was single at the time and had just come out of a bad relationship.

"You got me on the rebound and told me that I could go back in time and marry my soulmate. So, I took you up on the offer. The Operator wanted to surprise you."

"Consider me surprised." Radio looked at the man. He was a good ten years older than he should have been.

"Hello Winston, you are looking very well, Sir."

"I am well, Tommy. Married life agrees with you, I think."

"Do you know, Winston, I think you might be right."

Tommy then turned to Jamie and before Radio could stop him, he ploughed ahead.

"Well, I never, look at Master Jacques. He's like an embryo."

Jamie laughed nervously but didn't say anything. Radio jumped in.

"Klaus and Jamie haven't met you yet. Have a care."

"Oops," said Tommy. "Keep forgetting. Losing track is so easy."

Tommy turned and spoke to the crowd gathering behind him. They were all looking at Radio and they were terrified. He was beginning to think the Wotan disguise was a bad idea.

Suddenly, the group knelt down, en masse. Tommy turned back to radio.

"There's no point trying to explain to them. As far as they are concerned you are Wotan and these are your retainers. It is the path of least resistance. Trust me."

When they had all gotten up. Tommy or Cerdic, to use his Saxon name, beckoned a woman forward with three children. Radio smiled. They were all gorgeous. Cerdic was a lucky man and he knew it.

"This my wife, Aefre." Radio's heart melted. Her name meant forever. She curtsied and Radio put on THE SMILE to put her at ease. She smiled back as no one in the universe could resist THE SMILE.

"This is my boy, Cynric." Radio looked at the child. He was about 10 years old and looked as strong as an ox. He would need to be as he would be King of Wessex until he was 75.

"And these are my girls, Kendra and Eldrida." Radio nodded. Their names meant Prophetess and Advisor. Radio wondered if the Operator was trying to tell him something.

He turned to Cerdic. "I'll be changing your name to spawny bastard, ya lucky sod."

They all burst out laughing.

"Listen, I've got three hours and then I have to be back in parliament. Let's build a fire and have a chat."

They got a fire going on the beach and Radio sat down with Cerdic. Cerdic's men were set to work unloading the long ships.

Nobody complained that their leader was chewing the fat with their God. How could they?

"How many men have you got coming over?"

"There are about six hundred in this wave alone," replied Cerdic. "Listen, The Operator talks to me all the time and I've been asked to tell you not to worry about a thing. We are all over it.

"You just worry about the tests and get them completed."

"Fine," replied Radio. He was grateful to put another burden to bed.

"Tell me, Tommy, are you happy?"

"I've never been happier. Things can be a bit tough but you concentrate on surviving. Every small inconvenience is made up for by the closeness you feel to everyone. We are all a family and it is so much better than living in luxury on your own.

"Once you get over the fact that you have to take a shit outside, then you are on easy street."

Radio laughed. "Why don't you invent the flush toilet?"

"I tried that but the Operator told me to pack it in. The flush toilet isn't really invented until the 19th century."

They all sat round talking for hours until it was time to go. Cerdic suggested that Radio open the time vortex on the beach as the tribe would have something to talk about for years and it would give him extra Kudos.

When they got back to the matrix, Radio turned to Jamie and Klaus.

"So much for Elasius. I met Tommy's father once and his name was 'Boaby', if I remember correctly."

Twenty-Three – The Dragon's Lair

Parliament wasn't as bad as he thought it was going to be. On arrival, he had been taken to a cabinet room where the Prime Minister had set up a large television screen to deliver her presentation.

Radio, Miriam and Winston sat down in front of the screen and Radio motioned for the PM to proceed.

"I have concentrated our efforts on the first two slides. I would be grateful if you would critique them heavily before we present them to Mother and Father."

"Don't worry," said Radio. "You are acting on our behalf. If Mother and Father have any issues, they will be raised with us, not you directly."

"That's a bit of a relief," said the PM. She seemed to relax a little.

She put up the first slide which had been headed up ISSUE.

Sponsors – Mother and Father

Executive responsible for delivery – Radio

Terms of reference – All citizens of the United Kingdom and its dependencies.

Issue – The people of the United Kingdom have not been given their birth right. As a result, they are finding it difficult to find the time to pass the interview.

Goal statement – We will give them their birth right.

Radio was pleased. The slide was exactly right and at the right level. He had hope.

"Can you change Radio to Miriam," said Radio. "Other than that, this slide can be presented to Mother and Father."

The Prime Minister looked relieved. She had understood and had delivered.

The second slide appeared under the heading MEASURE.

Total number of households in UK – 27 Million

Households owned with no property debt – 10 Million

Households with property debt – 10 Million

Total property debt – 850 Billion

Households renting – 7 Million

Cost of purchasing rented households – 600 Billion

Total cost of wiping out property debt – 1,450 Billion

Again, Radio was pleased. The figures had obviously been rounded up but that was the right thing to do. He thought the bottom line was quite cheap. He had budgeted for more.

"I'm happy," said Radio. "I think we can deliver this on Friday. If you can move on to PROBLEMS and ANALYSE and deliver two slides of this quality then we will be fine.

"My advice is to stick to the mortgage debt at the moment. When we clear this issue, we can move this data to the appendix and concentrate on some of the other issues.

"I'm really pleased. I think we have made a very good start."

Radio stood up and motioned for Winston to follow. Miriam, however, stayed seated.

“You go ahead,” she said to Winston. “I’m going to stay here to help with the resolution of this issue.”

Radio and Miriam exchanged a collaborative smile. *And so, it begins,* they thought.

Radio found himself, once again in the Great Hall. This time his arrival had been met with thunderous applause. He stood before Mother and Father and all the formality of the testing had gone. He was the only one left in the contest. Mother motioned for silence.

“As you are the only contestant left, there is no need for secrecy. Your Father and I would like you to conduct the test and when you return, we would like you to explain everything.”

She waved her hand and The Dragon’s Lair appeared in the time window. It was a tower on the edge of a cliff.

Radio said nothing and stood there waiting. After about a minute, Lucifer appeared and he was wearing what looked like a dress uniform. It was a purple tunic trimmed with gold with pressed black trousers. Over his breast was the hidden symbol.

“Are you ready?” Radio asked him.

“I am.”

“Then come with me.”

Together they walked through the time window and the door of the tower and into the lair itself.

The dragon was asleep on a pile of treasure.

Radio walked up to her and kissed her on the snout. She awoke.

“Are you kissing me awake?” she asked.

Radio smiled. “It is my preferred method of waking. I thought it might be yours.”

She laughed. “What brings you into the lair and certain death?”

“I have come to bring you home. I have made dinner for you because you have been missed.”

She stretched her neck and rose out of the pile of coins. She loomed over him.

“Give me one good reason I shouldn’t flatten you?” she asked.

Radio looked at her and smiled. It was the saddest smile she had ever seen.

“I will give you three:

One. Your tower stands on a cliff desolate and you are starved of love and surrounded by dross. Come back with me and I will surround you with real treasure.

“Two. I love you. You should never flatten the people who love you.

“Three. I have found you a mate. He would like to propose marriage to you.”

When Radio had finished she looked at him. In her eyes, there was hope.

“Who is this suitor you bring me?”

Radio held out his hand and indicated Lucifer.

“Lilith, I give you the sea, the Lord of Darkness and The Prince of Lies?”

Lucifer bowed flamboyantly. “Madame,” he said.

When Radio looked at him, his eyes started glowing a bright red colour. The colour of blood.

Lilith looked at him closely then turned to Radio. “I will come with you,” she said.

Radio lifted his right hand to her left temple. “Operator, upload interface and Core Application Suite. Activate the transform application.”

“Lilith has all the applications. She is already online and live.”

This was a bit of a surprise. “Then proceed,” said Radio.

The dragon concentrated for a moment and then transformed into one of the most beautiful women Radio had ever seen. She stepped forward into Lucifer’s embrace and they kissed.

When they separated, Lilith said, “What do you think of my horde?”

Lucifer smiled. “Father has given me an enormous dowry, it is yours now. You may never have to worry about wealth again. There are none richer than you.”

“What will I do with all of this?” She indicated the wealth scattered over the hall.

Radio stepped forward. “May I make a suggestion?”

They both nodded.

He bent down and picked up a coin. “I call this stuff, portable wealth. As you are now the richest person in the universe, you have no more need for this dross. It is beneath you. We could ask the Operator to transfer it all to the fountains of the Earth so that if a poor man needs the price of a meal, he can dip his hand in a fountain and thank the dragon for his daily bread. What say you?”

She smiled. “Do it.”

As she said the words, the music started to play. It was the pilgrims’ chorus from the third act of Tannhäuser. It was one of Radio’s favourites and he had always thought of it as romantic dancing music.

Lilith and Lucifer started to dance. As they danced a host of angels came in to the lair and formed a circle round about them. When the music reached a crescendo, the coins and trinkets all started to rise up from the ground and disappear through the ceiling.

The pilgrims sang out at the top of their voices.

“Hallelujah, hallelujah. In *ewigkeit*.”

When the song was over. Lilith and Lucifer were in each other’s arms in the Great Hall. The dragon’s lair was gone. Expunged from existence.

The cheers were deafening.

Mother and Father were smiling and there were tears in their eyes. Eventually Mother stood up.

“You are my puzzler extraordinaire, my darling. Explain it to them and leave nothing out.”

When Mother had sat down, Radio turned to the audience. He picked out a number of individuals in the crowd and looked directly in to their eyes. It was his way of saying, I’m talking to you.

“When Mother and Father created the Universe, they did it for a reason.

“I, like so many of you, wondered why. I, however, was made differently. I was made to solve problems.

“When I considered why Mother and Father had created the Universe, I turned to William of Occam and I borrowed his razor. I shaved away all the reasons that could not possibly be true until, after some considerable time, I was left with the truth.

“Mother and Father created the Universe because they wanted children. They wanted us. They wanted to love us and be loved by us, in return.”

There were the usual gasps and sounds of dawning realisation.

“When they were eventually successful, they were exhausted. Creation was not easy and they had broken their backs to do it. When you invest so much of yourselves to acquire a thing, then you will also invest to be the best.

“Mother and Father are our parents and they aspire to be the best in the Universe and because they are who they are, they are the best in the Universe.

“The best parents in the Universe know things about their children that the children themselves do not know. They know that the things a child acquires easily will not be valued.

“Mother and Father had a desire to give us their inheritance. Because they are the best parents in the universe, their inheritance would be the best.

“Father had a thing to give and Mother had a thing to give.

"Father wanted us to know the truth. Mother wanted us to know love. That is the inheritance that you will come to value more than anything else.

"However, Mother and Father knew that to just give us this inheritance would be foolish and profligate so they recruited two individuals, two angels to hide their gifts from the children.

"The two angels would hide the gifts by selling us the opposite and oh how we have lapped it up.

"The two angels are greed and lies. A Dragon and a Leviathan. A beast of the land and a beast of the sea. They are Lilith and Lucifer."

Radio looked at the audience. "A standing ovation for your Satan, if you please."

They were awarded a proper standing ovation and it was respectful.

When the crowd were done, Radio continued.

"The secret to passing the Dragon's Lair is to transform the beast. Change greed and turn it into love."

He looked at Mother and Father and bowed.

The cheers resounded around the hall.

When the audience died down, Mother and Father stood and came towards him. Mother held a tunic in her hand.

"Here, put this on. It is not a test, it is a uniform and a badge of office."

Radio removed his cardigan and put the tunic on over his shirt. It was black and completely unadorned apart from symbol over the heart. The skull and crossed thigh bones. The symbol of the call.

Father turned to the audience.

"This is my son, Radio, who has passed tests that no one has ever come near to passing. It is our desire to hand over responsibility for this universe. Mother and I appoint Radio and we are now officially retired.

"We will continue to provide guidance but you must look to him now. He is in control."

And that was that. Radio was officially in charge. *Oh shit,* he thought.

Twenty-Four – The Black Viking

Radio was busy now 24 hours per day and that wasn't the only thing that had changed. He no longer needed to eat or sleep. He was constantly full of energy and wide awake.

It made finding time for the things he wanted to do, difficult.

After three days of constantly being dragged across the universe, Mother suggested that he set aside time for other things.

"Why don't you set aside a couple of hours in the late evening when Earth is at its quietest?"

Radio decided that this was a good idea and it gave him an opportunity to see to Jamie's training.

It was after dinner and they were all gathered at the time windows. Radio addressed his motley crew.

"It's time to start training the people of the Earth. We are being televised and my intention is to show everyone how the applications are used to their best potential. That way, if someone passes the interview, the Operator can upload their application suite and they can start straight away.

"The MEDIC application is the most important weapon in our arsenal and it is for that reason that I want to start with that. Let's show everyone what can be done."

He turned to Jamie who was standing ready with a food trolley.

"Tell me what you've prepared."

"I've got loads of cheese and ham sandwiches, fruit, chocolate, fizzy drinks and sweets."

"Perfect," said Radio. "Let's go. Operator, The Royal Hospital for Sick Children in Edinburgh."

The time window morphed and they all walked on to a full ward. It was night time so the lights were off and most of the children were dozing.

"Okay, everyone eat a bit of fruit and check that the power bar on your interface is full."

Miriam, Jamie, Klaus, Winston and Natalie all picked up a Satsuma and ate a few segments. Radio had decided to give Natalie some of the applications that would help others. He needed her to work her way out of her alcohol problem.

They all checked their power and all indicated that they were at maximum.

Radio opened his interface so that everyone could see the application and how it worked.

"First things first," he said. "I'm going to make a diagnosis and then we can decide what to do."

They approached the nearest bed and Radio looked at the sleeping child. A little girl of 8 years.

The application immediately flashed a diagnosis in the information box.

Leukaemia – Malnutrition – Diarrhoea – Urinary Tract Infection. Each condition was coloured differently.

Radio turned to the others.

"This child has blood cancer. The other ailments are as a result of having the primary condition and being treated for the condition. The drugs are heavy duty.

"The application will allow you to cure all the ailments at once or one at a time."

He pointed to the power bar.

"These arrows are colour coded and point to how much your power bar will be depleted by affecting each cure. It is important that you don't over extend yourself or you will make yourself hypoglycaemic. This could result in you slipping in to a coma.

"The application will look for a power source elsewhere but if it can't find one, it will deplete yours."

In this case, all four arrows were very high up the power bar, leaving Radio at 95%.

"When you are ready to affect a cure, simply kiss the child on the forehead."

Radio bent down and kissed the little girl. He waited until he heard 4 little chimes in quick succession.

"When the application has affected each cure, it will sound a chime to say that you can stop."

They waited for a few seconds and then little girl stirred and opened her eyes.

"How are you feeling Tamara?" asked Radio.

"I feel so good."

A group of nurses had arrived to see what the commotion was. They all looked awed but ready to help.

"Would you like some ice cream?" asked Radio.

"Yes please. Chocolate."

Radio turned to the staff nurse. "Do you have any chocolate ice cream?"

"Absolutely," she said. "You cure the kids. We'll take their orders." She ran off to get some chocolate ice cream.

Radio picked up another Satsuma and ate a few segments. The power bar returned to 100% almost instantly.

"Do you all get the idea?" he asked.

They all nodded. He gave them the 'what are you waiting for' look and they got to work.

Jamie's first patient was cystic fibrosis. When he was done, he was sweating and had used 30% of his power. He ate a banana and drank a can of coke.

"That's a nasty business, CF. There's so much to fix." Radio told him.

Winston cured a teenager with lung cancer who had also broken his leg. Radio thought he would be exhausted but he jumped up like a spring lamb. He was obviously enjoying himself.

Natalie cured a black girl who had sickle cell anaemia. Her Mother had stayed with her for the night and she was obviously over the moon. Radio could easily imagine the relief a parent must feel when a child is cured.

The little girl eyed him up and down. He trotted over to see her and say hello.

"Is it true that you're my grandfather?" she asked.

"Of course, I'm everybody's grandfather, Aniyah."

"Even me?"

"Why not you?" asked Radio. He could see where this was going and was determined to give a good account of himself.

"Well, I'm black," she pointed out.

"Well, that's not strictly true," said Radio. He asked her to budge up and he jumped on to the bed beside her.

"There is nothing wrong with being black," he began, "Or yellow or red or white for that matter, but the truth is we're all a mixture. Mother and Father don't see colour, they just see the children they love. All of their children are related because they all come from the same ancestors. Observe."

Radio took hold of her arm and tapped it with his right hand. A hundred strands of DNA suddenly popped in to the air and all had different colour codes.

"I can tell who your ancestors were by looking at the acid traces in your blood. All your ancestors leave an imprint behind in you."

A little crowd had gathered at the bottom of the bed and they were all rapt.

"Let's take this group coloured red and pink. They are the royal families of West Africa."

The child's mother had jumped out of her seat and was paying very close attention.

"Is that right?" she asked.

"Yes, you are descended from Musa Keita, who was the richest King of the Mali empire."

Radio smiled. He could see a coat of arms heaving in to view.

"This group coloured purple lived in the Caribbean in the 17th and 18th centuries."

The mother nodded. This obviously came as no surprise judging by her Jamaican accent.

"This group coloured blue, and it is a significant group, lived in Scandinavia about ten centuries ago."

"What?" exclaimed the mother. "Are you telling me my daughter is a Viking?"

"Yes. Have you heard of Harald Hardrada?"

"No."

"He's your great-grandfather and the King of Norway."

"Jesus. Sweet Jesus." Radio could tell that this coat of arms was going to get bigger.

He went back to the DNA strands and plucked a silver one and highlighted it.

"Do you know who this is?" he asked.

"No idea."

"This is Charlemagne. He was King of France and Germany in 800."

The woman was struck dumb.

Radio pushed a number of the strands aside and delved deep in to the past. Eventually, after furious swiping he found it.

"And finally," he pulled out a strand coloured gold and which shone with diamonds.

"Do you know who this is?"

They shook their heads.

"This is me!"

He tapped his own shoulder and a strand of DNA appeared. It was exactly the same. Everyone round the bed was wide eyed.

"So, in summary. You are Aniyah. Mother and Father's beloved black daughter who is descended from the King of Mali, The King of Norway, The King of the Franks and the Radio. You are my granddaughter."

"Son of a gun," said the mother.

"We are all the same Aniyah. We are all brothers and sisters. Whatever happens in your life, I would like you to remember that. Will you do that?"

She looked at him with sincere, solemn eyes. "Yes, I will remember that."

Soon all the children in the ward were wide awake and had been cured.

He spoke to the nursing staff who had spent the evening delivering food and drinks to the children. "They will all be full of energy and excitement. The best thing to do is to let them tire themselves out. Now, as a reward for all your help, who would like the MEDIC application?"

They all immediately raised their hands. He uploaded the app in to every one of them and sent them off to the other wards.

He called his crew together.

"Now is everyone completely au fait with the app?"

They all nodded their assent.

"From now on, you do not need to wait for me. I would like you to go around the hospitals when you have free time and cure as many as you can. Start with the children and work your way to the elderly."

He opened a spatial incursion and they all returned to the matrix.

When they got back, Mother and Father were keen to talk to him.

"Where on Earth did you learn to do that with the DNA strands?"

Radio thought for a moment and stopped dead in his tracks.

"I have no idea." He admitted.

Something else was gnawing at him and he couldn't get it out of his mind. He decided to take a chance. He looked at Mother and Father.

"Where are the others?" he asked.

"They are waiting for you," replied Mother.

The response made sense. Images were now coming to him from further afield. Not just things from inside the solution but beyond. Radio had suspected that there were different universes for some time and he wondered if his visions were from beyond.

He knew that he could ask Mother and Father and they would answer his questions but he felt that this was the wrong thing to do. It was too easy and it was boring.

He had a problem and he wanted to solve it himself.

Was he not the puzzler extraordinaire?

Twenty-Five – The Fountains of Lilith

Radio made his way to the time windows.

"Operator, locate Lucifer and Lilith."

"Lucifer and Lilith are on Earthsea."

In all the commotion, he had forgotten that he had his fantasy EL-PAR to explore. All the books of his childhood. He was suddenly excited.

"Spatial incursion to Earthsea."

The time window morphed and he walked on to the island where he had found Lilith as an egg. Things had changed. Beside the standing stones stood what looked like a sturdy Georgian mansion. He knocked on the door and waited.

After a few moments, the door opened. It was Lilith's mother.

"Oh, it's you, Come in."

He walked through the door and into a hall. Lilith's mother closed the front door and ushered him into a large reception room. The room was full of couches and easy chairs and nearly every seat was occupied.

An easy chair was pushed forward and he was invited to sit down in between Lilith and Lucifer. He was in a circle and every eye was on him. Nobody said anything.

Lilith's mother broke the silence. "What brings you here, Architect?"

"I am on the edge of something and I'm looking for answers," said Radio.

"For someone who can send his awareness through time and space, I would have thought that answers would be easy to find." She looked at him and smiled. They were playing with him.

"Ah," said Radio.

They all laughed.

"I will play your game," he said. "Here is what I have discovered so far."

He had their attention. They were playing a game but they wanted him to win.

"All of you were born outside of the solution apart from Lilith. You were all assigned ANGELS when your SOULS were uploaded.

"When the fantasy EL-PAR came online, you chose to come here and be anything you wanted to be. As dragons, you gave birth to Lilith but she has all the powers accorded to an ANGEL. She is a special child.

"I think that when you were outside of the solution, you worked for Mother and Father in various roles. Some of you were scientists and some of you were IT.

"I think that I am describing you in human terms and from a human perspective. I think your reality was quite different from the solution. Outside you were limited in some way. Here you are completely free.

"I have a strong suspicion that you were not the only team trying to build a universe. I now suspect that there were others.

"It is my belief that the others are now calling me for some reason. I think they have been waiting for me. Unfortunately, I'm not sure why?"

There was silence in the room.

"Impressive." Again, it was Lilith's mother. "You were always so very capable."

Always. It was just a word. One insignificant word. It answered all of his questions.

He smiled. "Thanks for the information, planet builder. I have it now."

He turned to Lilith.

"Are you busy?"

"What are you up to?" She looked suspicious.

"There are a number of things I need you and Lucifer for over the next few days, I just wondered if you were up for a bit of adventure?"

"I'm on my honeymoon, you fool. However, you can pick me up from Mephistopheles. Just ask the Operator to go back about 100 years."

"Oh yes, why didn't I think of that? What about, you?" he asked Lucifer.

"You can pick me up from Mephistopheles, just ask the Operator to go back about 100 years. It must be hard to keep track, moving back and forward in time but try to remember we were recruited together. We were only allowed to marry when you uncovered the truth," They both looked at him as if they felt sorry for him.

Radio understood. There were gaps in his travels through time and space. It was as if the Operator had shown him the need to know events.

He stood up to leave and then he thought of one last thing. He turned to Lilith's mother.

"Before I go, does the word hybrid mean anything to you?"

"Oh dear."

"I'll take that as a yes. I'll let myself out."

Radio left the house and returned to the matrix. His mobile phone rang almost immediately.

It was the Pope. "Join me for coffee. I need to talk to you."

Radio walked through in to the old man's sitting room and sat down.

"What's up?" asked Radio.

"It is the fountains of Lilith." said the Pontiff. "They have caused a huge problem."

Radio laughed. He was not surprised.

"Lilith continues to do her job, I see. I take it that some of her treasure has been taken from the fountains and people are questioning whether or not the recipients are deserving of it?"

"Exactly so. It has caused a huge debate on social media and people are being outed as thieves for taking coin that others say they don't qualify for. It has gotten exceedingly nasty."

Radio thought for a moment before responding.

"My advice is to ask people to stop looking at what others are doing and concentrate on passing the interview.

"If someone takes something that they are not entitled to, then the Operator will put them in rehab. Let people make their mistakes. It is not for one to judge the other.

"I am concerned that this is being debated. In a world with 24-hour news channels, one wonders sometimes how much of this type of controversy and debate is created to fill the schedule.

"If a person has enough then it is better to just ignore what's in the fountains."

"Yes. I agree. Let's just hope that people will listen to you."

The penny dropped with Radio. This conversation was being televised across the globe and the Pope needed people to hear it from the horse's mouth. The initial hope that Radio had felt for the human race was slowly fading. They would talk themselves out of their inheritance and they would lose everything.

The old man picked up a sheaf of papers from the couch next to him.

"There are a few other issues, if you don't mind," he said apologetically.

"Don't worry. That's why I'm here."

"I have applications from several heads of state to join Mother and Father's union. They are initial statements of intent but I believe they are serious."

Radio felt a sudden elation. His mood improved exponentially.

"Who are they?"

The Pontiff smiled. "The Vatican, Italy, Portugal, Spain, France, Belgium, The Netherlands, Germany, Poland, Austria, Hungary, Romania…" He stopped. "All of Europe actually."

Radio couldn't believe it. He lifted his hand to his mouth. He couldn't speak.

"It doesn't stop there. We have all of The Americas and Australia. Most of Africa and we are starting to see applications coming in from the middle and far East. We have sent envoys to those countries that have not applied and are inviting them to join, on your behalf, of course."

Radio was beside himself. "What has happened?" he asked.

"The world is changing and people want to be part of something bigger. You were right. We do not value the things we acquire easily and because you have set the goal of passing the interview, people want to achieve the goal."

Radio knew he was right.

"I also believe that the fountains of Lilith have helped. Every single fountain on the face of the planet was filled to the brim with treasure. It is an embarrassment of riches. This was your suggestion and it showed the people of the Earth that here was somebody at last who was determined to wipe out the unfairness of life. Poverty has effectively disappeared over night.

"Let's just hope that the people of the Earth can get it right."

"Amen to that," said Radio.

Radio was relieved. The fountains were doing their job after all. He hoped he had said enough. He rather thought that he had.

"Finally," said the old man. "When are you next going to see Yeshua and have you found out any more?"

"I am going very soon but I'm waiting to collect someone first. Don't forget your Ecclesiastes. Everything in its season!

"And yes, I have found out more. The pieces of a temporal jigsaw are falling into place in my head and I now have a very good idea who he is.

"I would ask you not to press me on this. I would like to give you a big reveal at the right time.

"I do not say this to be a dramatist. I say this because you will enjoy it all the more.

When I bring him back to you, I want him to be the cold glass of water at the end of the desert. Do you understand?"

"Oh, I understand perfectly."

"Now," said Radio. "How would you like a trip through time and space? I need to collect that someone I mentioned and it might as well be now."

The old man looked at his habit and said, "I'll just change out of this. I'll be back in a minute."

When he returned he was wearing his blacks but had left the dog collar behind. Radio nodded approvingly.

"Operator. Plantagenet please."

Twenty-Six – The Treasures of the Earth

Radio and the old man walked through in to the church. Waiting for them were Blondie and Goldilocks.

"What are you doing here?" asked Radio.

"Following up," said Gabriel. "Don't worry about it but when you intervene, there is a whole team of us following after you to carry out your wishes. We've been doing it for Mother and Father and now we're doing it for you."

"That makes sense," said Radio.

John the priest came over. He looked much better and good deal younger than Radio remembered.

"It's Lazarus," exclaimed Radio. "Back from the dead."

"Yes, I do feel a lot better. I have never eaten so well in my life and some of the food we have been given is, well, out of this world."

Radio laughed. He turned to the old man. "John, I'd like you to meet the Pope."

The priest did a very small double take but took it in his stride.

"Your holiness," he said, holding out his hand.

"Nice to meet you, John." The two men shook hands.

"Now John. I need you to sit down and listen to me. I have a desire to fulfil my promise to you but it is not going to be easy."

Radio ushered him on to a pew and sat down beside him. He really didn't know where to start. He decided to just blurt it out and take it from there.

"I am able to travel through time and it has become apparent to me that you were meant to meet Yeshua all along. In fact, Yeshua would like to make you one of his disciples.

"The Pope and I come from the future, the year 2018 to be exact, 658 years from now.

"It is my intention to bring you forward in time so that the holy father may train you in preparation for your mission.

"When you are ready, I will then take you back in time to introduce you to John the Baptist who will then introduce you to Yeshua himself. You will watch over Yeshua until the crucifixion, when I will bring you both back to the future. What do you think?"

John sat stunned for several moments.

"Why me?" he asked.

"Because, you have been chosen. It is as simple as that. I don't ask questions, I follow orders when they are given me."

"What about my people here?"

"When you have completed your mission, you will have won the kingdom. The treasures of the Earth will be yours and you will be able to travel wherever you like in time and space. If you like, you will be able to come back here one minute after we leave."

"Do I need to bring anything with me?"

"No, I will give you everything you need."

“Then what are we waiting for? Let’s go.”

“Good man.” Radio opened a vortex and they disappeared through it and back to the old man’s apartments.

“Where are we?” asked John.

“This is Rome,” said the old man, “And these are my private apartments. You will stay here whilst I school you in your mission. We have an extensive library and I’m very confident that when it is time for you to go. You will be ready.”

John looked around and Radio could tell that he was impressed by the opulence of what he saw.

He waved his hand at the grandeur of his surroundings. “Is this the treasure of the Earth?”

Radio smiled and sat down.

“No, it is not. The treasures of the Earth are what Mother and Father give you by doing their bidding. Every child born in this universe will ultimately face a choice. You are either with us or you are against us.

“When you are truly with us you will help us maintain the fabric of the universe. You will protect life and you will help move it forward. Ever onwards and ever upwards.

“When you have done this, the treasures will be yours. They are a knowledge of the truth which will make you powerful and a knowledge of the value of love which will make you happy and kind.

“When you have these treasures, all of this opulence will mean one thing to you. Nothing.”

John smiled back at him. “Yes, it will mean nothing because there are things in life of far greater value than this. I am with you and I will do your bidding.”

He looked at Radio seriously. “Who is Mother?”

Radio laughed. “Mother and Father led the team of scientists that created this universe.”

John thought about this revelation for a minute and asked the question that Radio expected him to ask.

“Who is Yeshua then? I have always believed him to be the son of God but you are telling me that scientists created this universe. Is there even a God?”

Radio knew this was an awful lot to take in. John’s whole belief structure was crumbling before his very eyes.

“There is a God. It is the containment field where creation is housed. GOD stands for General Operating Dimension. It is reality.

“This reality has an operating system called Alpha-Omega, which maintains the universe.

“In the past, when people talked about a God, it was just a word they used to describe something that they didn’t quite understand.

“You know more than most people in history have ever known. You know who your parents are and what they are trying to do and you believe in them.

“That is better than blindly believing in something that you knew nothing about.”

“Yes, it is. I agree with you. That just leaves the question of Yeshua. Who is he?”

“We are not totally sure yet. I have some serious suspicions and I know I am right on the edge of it but I’m afraid we’ll just have to wait and see. I know that he is no threat. I know that he is harmless. I know that he has great understanding because I have read his work and it makes complete sense to me from an allegorical and esoteric perspective.

“I know he is meant to come back to the future and guide the people of the Earth through the interview. I know that you are meant to help him.”

“Oh, I will help him. As I have already said, I am with you now and it is my desire to save as many as I can.”

Radio stopped dead in his tracks and moved away. He closed his eyes and cleared his mind. This was happening more and more. Somebody would use a word and the significance would hit him like a runaway train. Lilith’s mother had used the word ‘always’ and now John had used the word ‘save’.

He opened his eyed. John and the old man looked concerned.

“Is everything all right?” asked the Pontiff.

“What do you think has happened to all the SOULS who have passed the interview?” asked Radio.

“I don’t know. You said they became ANGELS and went to work for Mother and Father,” responded the old man.

“Where are they, then? The only ANGELS I’ve seen so far have all been uploaded from outside of the solution. Operator, where are the SOULS that have passed the interview?”

A viewer appeared in the room. Clearly, this information was for everyone.

“They have been SAVED. I have uploaded them to PARADISE and they are now awaiting your instructions. My advice is to take your time. Make your plans and then ask them to help you execute your plans when you are ready.”

“How many are there?”

“There are 442,623 reconnected SOULS from Earth in PARADISE who have passed the interview and are fully trained.”

Radio was shocked. He went as white as a sheet.

“What’s wrong?” asked the old man.

“Think about it. Since human beings emerged on this planet there have been 100 billion people which amount to 50 billion reconnected SOULS. We are looking at a pass rate of 0.00001 %.”

The Operator flashed a response on screen.

“That is not strictly true, until 2000 years ago, all SOULS were recycled and nobody passed the interview. They were simply reincarnated. Since Yeshua opened the door about 1 in every 100 has passed the interview. There are a vast number awaiting reconnection.

“There are 1 trillion galaxies in the universe and we don’t have enough recruits from across Domus yet to manage 1 per galaxy. The number of recruits needs to significantly increase. The plan was not to release the SOULS until Mother and Father were completely satisfied with your performance. You are leading the way.”

They all sat down. The numbers were absolutely staggering.

Radio turned to the old man.

“Well, there you have it. Now you know the monumental nature of your task.”

“Don’t you mean our task?” The old man countered.

“I’m not the one who pushed myself forward as head of the church. I’m not the one who wears the big hat. I’m not the one who jumps about the place forgiving everyone their sins. You took the responsibility. Now you’ve got to deliver.

“My expectation is that the Operator will judge you in the context of your own hubris. You said you could get the job done. If you fail then on your head be it.”

He turned to the screen. ”Am I correct, Operator?”

“Yes, you are absolutely correct.”

Radio struggled to keep a straight face.

“I’ll leave you two to get started. I’ll check in on you in a couple of days.”

John and the old man looked at each other and laughed. “Right,” they said.

Twenty-Seven - Pontius Pilate

Radio returned to the matrix where he was met by Miriam. He hadn't seen her since Monday but he had been in constant communication with her. If he was being honest, it was like talking to himself.

She did not need to update him or vice versa, it was literally like being in two places at once. When they were alone, there was no need to talk but they had come to an arrangement when they were in company. They would speak aloud as they were aware that their behaviour could very easily make people paranoid.

"You go, I'll watch from here."

Radio considered the situation for a moment. He was about to get in touch with a man that he had never met before but had seen in his dreams often. He was a time agent and like Winston, he was an operative that had met him on many occasions before.

He knew what to do and what to say but he also knew that the man could be extremely funny. He was everything a time agent should be. Clever, adaptive, shameless and a first-class actor. Radio was looking forward to this. He turned around to look at Mother and Father.

"You might want to watch this." They immediately sat up and looked intrigued.

"Operator, Rome 25 A.D., the house of Pontius."

The time window morphed and Radio decided that he would stay put for now. He held Miriam's hand.

The scene in front of him was opulent. It was a lavish bedroom in a typical Roman Villa built for a patrician family. There were animal skins on the floor, golden candlesticks, and wash basin but the most impressive thing was a mosaic of Venus inlaid on a marble floor.

Pontius was in bed with two women and he looked to be enjoying himself.

Radio decided he'd have a laugh.

"Pontius," he screamed, ensuring that the volume was at maximum.

The women fell out of bed, took one look at the scary man shouting from the ceiling and dashed for the exit.

Pontius, who had rolled with the women got tangled up in the covers and fell off the side of the bed.

Mother and Father started laughing.

Pontius quickly got up, wrapped the cover around his middle and sat on the edge of the bed looking at Radio.

"Boss," he said, breathing heavily. "I think I've just shat myself."

They were all laughing freely now.

"Why, may I ask, do you remain in Rome?" said Radio.

"Because," replied Pontius, "That arsehole Tiberius refuses to make me prefect of Judea, despite the many favours I've done for him."

"Who is prefect at the moment?" enquired Radio.

"Valerius Gratus. He is popular because he keeps the Sanhedrin in check. It was Gratus who appointed Joseph son of Caiaphas to the position of high priest and Caiaphas is respected by the scribes."

"I see." Radio thought for a moment. "Get dressed Pontius. I'll arrange for you to see Tiberius at lunchtime. I think I'll come with you."

"I actually have an appointment with him at noon."

"Excellent," said Radio.

Pontius, however, didn't move. He sat at the edge of the bed and stared at the floor. Radio had to admit that this man was exceptional. He was a magnificent actor.

"What's wrong, Pontius?" asked Radio.

Pontius put on a bit of a snivelling face and looked if he was about to cry.

"Feeling a bit low," he stammered, "Missing Glasgow. Missing my life in the 21st century."

"Oh, dear," said Radio, playing along. "Is there anything I can do?"

"You could sing us a wee song whilst I get dressed," he wheedled.

"You what?" said Radio. "What song?"

Suddenly, Pontius sat up looking very chipper. "Sing the Radio Who song."

Radio laughed. "I've got Mother and Miriam here, if I'm singing, they'll want to see some dancing."

"Here, here," they both shouted.

"But, of course," he responded.

Radio opened his iTunes interface and put on Transmission by Hot Chip.

What followed was hilarious and had Mother, Father, Winston and Miriam rolling about the floor. As Radio sang, Pontius did the most ridiculous dance you have ever seen. Always keeping his private parts just out of view, he whipped off the covers and put on his Roman tunic skirt, and leather breastplate. When he was done, he looked every inch the Roman procurator.

Everyone cheered as the song finished and they both took their bows.

"Right," said Radio. "I'll meet you at the palace."

"Aren't you coming with me. I've got a chariot waiting."

"I'm afraid I won't fit," said Radio smiling.

Pontius groaned. "You're not bringing those devil dogs with you, are you?"

"Oh, yes," said Radio.

"Oh, shit," said Pontius.

The scene vanished and radio asked the Operator for Mephistopheles, 100 years ago.

He walked through into the Lair.

Lucifer and Lilith were waiting for him.

"Don't bother," they said. "We've been informed. The Operator has asked us to remind you that we don't know the future yet so you've not to say anything. We've just to do the things you need us for and then you've to bring us back here."

"All right," said Radio, "I can see why the Operator hates time travel, it's starting to give me a headache."

They walked through into the matrix with Radio.

Lucifer and Lilith, then did a curious thing. Lilith kissed Father and Lucifer kissed Mother.

Radio went white. Had he got it wrong. He couldn't think of it now, he would address the issue later.

"Lucifer, Lilith. I need Phobos and Deimos."

They both transformed into Rottweilers the size of race horses. They looked utterly frightening and as Pontius had said, like Devil dogs.

Radio opened the transform application and selected Jupiter in war attire. He grew to 9 feet and looked like a brick shithouse.

"Oh my," said Miriam who immediately transformed in to Juno. She looked like a 9-foot librarian in a toga. "I've decided to come with you after all."

"Operator, The Palatine Hill, 10 minutes to Noon."

The time window morphed again. Before them were two rows of armed guards leading to a table where an old man sat reading a scroll.

Jupiter and Juno, flanked by Phobos and Deimos walked through. The guards fled.

Tiberius looked up. "Ave Jupiter," he said laconically.

"Ave Tiberius," said Radio. "Your guards are a bit vapourish, are they not?"

"I think it might be our doggie friends that have sent them packing. Don't worry, I'll have them flogged."

Tiberius put down his scroll and rang a bell.

"Let's see if my manservant is as skittish."

The manservant appeared and Tiberius called for wine. Although the poor man looked nervous, he held it together and went off in search of a flask and goblets.

"How are you?" asked Radio. There was something about the Emperor's accent that was nagging at him.

"I'm well. How is Master Jacques?" enquired the Emperor.

Of course, he was French. There was something about the French accent that was difficult to erase completely.

"Well, I'll be damned," said Radio. "Master Jacques is well and about 15 years old. I'm meeting you for the first time. I take it you've met me before?"

"Of course. I'm Geoffrey, Preceptor of Normandy. In the future, or my past, I work for Master Jacques. I don't envy you, Lord. It must be difficult to keep track."

"I'm finding out just how difficult. This week has been a nightmare and I have a very funny feeling it's going to get worse. Tell me a little bit about yourself."

The old man laughed. "It feels like ancient history or another life."

The servant returned with goblets and a flagon of wine. They waited until he had left and The Emperor filled three goblets. He continued.

"I was born in Auvergne in 1250 and lived there until I was 12. On my twelfth birthday, I said goodbye to my parents and was taken to Paris by my uncle who was a Templar and an intermediary known as Jeanne. In Paris, I was accepted, with great ease, in to the order by Amaury de la Roche, The Preceptor of France.

"Over the years, I rose through the ranks until I became Preceptor of Normandy. By that time, Master Jacques was the Grand Master and I became his right-hand man and started working for you.

"On Friday, 13th October 1307, Master Jacques and I were arrested at the Paris temple by the forces of Philippe Le Bel. I have been in prison ever since.

"From time to time, you arrive and ask one of us or both of us to do a job for you and we go where we are asked. Sometimes the jobs take a couple of days, sometimes half a lifetime.

"When we are done, we return to prison for a well-earned rest but you are never far away. In terms of linear years, I believe I am in the region of 130 years old."

"Holy moly," exclaimed Radio. "It is astonishing."

Tiberius laughed. "I hope you don't mind me laughing but the shoe is, for once, on the other foot."

Radio understood. For once, this old man had the upper hand and was thoroughly enjoying it.

"Do you know why I'm here?"

"Yes," replied Tiberius," You want me to make Pontius Prefect in Jerusalem. He has applied on several occasions for the role. I have refused on your advice.

"Pontius is suffering from depression at the moment. It is not uncommon in a time agent. The feeling of isolation can be quite oppressive. For that reason, I have slowly been building a legion populated with recruits from 21st century Glasgow. I am going to send them to Jerusalem with Pontius. As a result, we will kill two birds with one stone.

You see, it is these men that will crucify The Nexus."

Radio was stunned. It was a great idea.

"I take it Pontius has no idea who you are."

"He hasn't a clue, although I know who he is, of course. Even Master Jacques has heard of him. I think this is partly a cause of his mental health problem.

"After Master Jacques, he is your most secret, darkest agent. He is a legend in time but when he goes home he's just Billy and nobody has any idea who he is."

Radio considered the time. He should be here by now.

The servant returned, "Pontius Pilate is here, My Lord."

"Show him in."

Pontius was ushered in an immediately took in the scene. It was clear that the dogs were making him nervous. Suddenly, Lucifer pounced on him from behind and fell to the floor with Pontius facing upwards in his paws. Lilith then jumped on top of him and started licking his face. Pontius who had started with a yelp of sheer terror, slowly started to laugh. Soon they were all roaring.

The dogs let him go and he got up. He looked apologetically at Tiberius and adjusted his uniform.

"Ave Caesar," said Pontius.

"Sit down, Billy," replied Tiberius in English.

Pontius sat down in the spare seat looking stunned.

Over the next ten minutes, Radio and Tiberius explained the situation to Pontius Pilate and when they were done he looked relieved. *In fact*, Radio thought, *he looked happy*. The news that the 10th legion was mainly from Glasgow had lifted his spirits enormously.

"It explains a lot," said Pontius. "One of the centurions in that legion keeps winking at me. I thought he was gay."

"He may well be," said Radio. "He's from Glasgow after all."

They all laughed. "Gentlemen, I believe our work here is done. I will see you in time."

With that parting shot, Jupiter, Juno, Phobos and Deimos returned to the matrix.

Twenty-Eight – X Marks the Spot and Other Revelations

When they got back to the matrix, Radio turned to Lucifer and Lilith.

"That was a wonderful thing you did back there. I think you really helped cheer him up."

"We know how he feels," said Lilith. "Unfortunately, you will find out too." She looked so sad when she said it.

Radio sighed. He knew exactly what she meant. There was so much to do and he was perfectly aware that he wouldn't always be able to rely on a squad coming in after him to tidy up. There were some things that only he could do.

One of those things was recruitment. In the not too distant future, he would have a team full of time agents adjusting the timeline to ensure this reality. All geared to bringing the human race to a level of maturity at a point in time. He had to make them ready for the others. It was the delivery of the prime requirement. It was time to go fishing.

15 minutes later, Radio stood in front of the time window dressed in his fishing gear. He had his spinning rod and a haversack with his packed lunch.

"Operator, The Unknown Pleasures, please."

The time window distorted in the usual way and he walked on to the bridge.

"Long time, no see," said Eve.

"Sorry, love. I've been all over the place this last week. I don't know if I'm coming or going."

"I know, I'm only kidding. What can I do for you."

"I'm here to deliver on my promises and the weather is perfect. Where's Haggis."

"She's in engineering. I'll call her."

5 minutes later, Ruth appeared on the bridge.

"What are you dressed like that for?" she enquired.

"We are going fishing. It is the right weather for the beastie and I thought you might like a wee history lesson in to the bargain, since you have such a fascination with my country."

"Oh my god, I'll get changed. Give me 5 minutes."

Radio and Eve laughed as she rushed off.

"What on Earth are you up to?" said Eve.

"I'm ticking off another thing on my temporal to do list. We're going to see a man about a kingdom. You'll see."

Ruth returned dressed in what Radio could only describe as futuristic outdoor gear. It was a tight fitting black suit made of a rubber like material and what looked like hiking boots. He had to admit she looked the part.

"Operator, Loch Ness, if you please."

"Have fun," shouted Eve.

They walked through on to the shore of the loch. From his vantage point he could see the ruins of Urquhart castle. He would have liked to have gone there but it was a bit mobbed with tourists.

He showed his granddaughter how to set up a spinning rod and how to bait the hook. When that was done, he added a weight to the line and a float then cast it into the loch. He wedged the end of the rod between two rocks then sat down on a flat stone.

"Now we wait," he said.

"How long?"

He could tell she was excited and it reminded him of the innocence and wonder of youth. Life was such a difficult journey when one reached adulthood that he felt it was a dreadful sin to cut short a childhood. *We make them grow up too quickly*, he thought.

"Ruth," said Radio seriously. "There is no Loch Ness Monster."

"You are kidding me. I've been looking forward to seeing the beast." She looked dejected.

Radio laughed. "It is a story, like so many of the myths on this planet there is probably a grain of truth in it but it is more likely an allegorical tale. Like Jonah and the whale. The first known and recorded sighting was by St Columba about 1500 years ago. Since then, there has been only occasional glimpses of the beast. Round here, she is known as the Kelpie, which means water horse.

"She became really famous in the 1930's when a passer-by took a mysterious photograph of a creature in the loch. It was actually the trunk of a circus elephant. Once word got out, the whole world descended on the place and that was that.

"The unfortunate thing is that every dafty on the planet has reported a sighting. I think these are the same people that get abducted by aliens."

"How ridiculous. When we abduct someone, we don't bring them back, not after we've eaten them."

This was said with such a straight face that Radio roared with laughter. There was more to this girl than he thought. He continued.

"I've brought you here for a purpose. I wanted to hammer home a point. I know you are disappointed about not seeing a monster but the memory of the disappointment will live with you and so will the lesson for today.

"Never confuse an allegorical work with the truth and learn to tell the difference between the two.

"Religion and myth have caused great strife on the Earth because the people have failed to make the distinction.

"In my youth, I was always fascinated with the search for the holy grail and for buried treasure. In almost every culture, buried treasure was a central tenet of lots of myths. I also realised that in just about every case, the treasure was marked with an X.

"In my adult life this came to fascinate me. I realised that an X was made up of two symbols. The universal symbol for the divine feminine▼, a stylised uterus and the universal symbol for the divine masculine▲, a stylised uterus. In other words, Mother and Father are the treasure because they are a symbol of universal love. It is no mistake that the flag of Scotland is an X. So buried treasure becomes something completely different than what the story suggests. You must learn to read through these stories to the layers that lie beneath the apparent tale. Do you follow?"

"Yes, I think so. Are you saying that the story of the Loch Ness Monster is a story similar to the story of Jonah?"

"I'm not sure. Why don't you have a look and let me know what your thoughts are. I'd be interested to hear your take on it."

"I will. You've got me interested now."

"I'm glad. Are you hungry?" asked Radio.

"Yes, I haven't eaten since breakfast," Ruth replied.

"Good. I hope you like salmon. Don't worry it's not the tinned stuff, it's smoked with cream cheese."

Radio went in to his bag and pulled out a packet of morning rolls. He handed her one.

"Gosh, what funny bread."

"It's a Scottish morning roll," he explained. "We put everything and anything on them. I once had a pie roll at a football match in Glasgow. Sounds disgusting but once you put brown sauce on it, was strangely delicious."

She took a large bite. "It is rather good." She mumbled round a mouthful of salmon.

Radio took one of the rolls and bit in to it. He was ravenous.

Ruth stood on the shoreline eating her roll. She was obviously glad to be out and was taking everything in.

"Is it what you expected?" asked Radio.

"I'm actually quite surprised just how close everything I've read is to the reality. When I was at Edinburgh Castle, I saw a man wearing a tartan kilt. I never thought that would be true and yet there he was walking along.

"The castles and the landscape are exactly as reported. I can't quite believe it."

She stopped and thought for a moment.

"There is one thing that is a bit of a puzzle?"

"What's that?"

"The people I've met don't seem very serious. They are all a bit devil may care and yet history tells us that they are quite clever."

Radio laughed. "They don't take themselves very seriously. It is true. Cleverness does not equal seriousness and I have found in my life, all too often, that serious isn't very kind. I think the people here, are in general, usually quite kind."

"You mentioned history, what were you going to tell me?"

"What do you want to know?" asked Radio.

"How did Scotland become part of the United Kingdom?"

"You ask questions where the answer goes on forever. Take a seat and I'll begin."

She sat down on a flat stone opposite him and took another bite of her roll.

"Once upon a time, there was a King of Scotland who got tired of fighting his English neighbours to the south. He realised that it was a drain on Scottish resources and if closer relations could be established, it could be of mutual benefit to both nations.

"His name was James IV and in 1502 he signed the treaty of perpetual peace with his English counterpart, Henry VII. As part of that settlement, he married Henry's daughter Margaret who was sister to Henry VIII. Margaret gave birth to James V and he was the father of Mary, Queen of Scots. Mary, in turn gave birth to James VI who became de facto King of Scotland in 1567, after his Mother was deposed.

"In England, the Tudor line of succession died out. Henry VIII, despite having six wives, managed only 3 legitimate children. Edward who died without issue of a lung related illness, Mary who died without issue from cancer of the uterus and Elizabeth.

"Elizabeth lived to age 70 but is known to history as the virgin queen. For various reasons, she never had any children.

"When she died in 1603, the line of succession went back to her grandfather, Henry VII. The most legitimate descendent was James VI of Scotland, his great, great, grandson. James was offered the crown of England as per Elizabeth's instruction and he accepted it. In 1603, the union of the crowns took place between England and Scotland."

"Didn't Elizabeth have Mary, Queen of Scots head chopped off?"

"Yes," replied Radio. "And it is for that very reason, that you and I are going to make a small detour this afternoon."

"Where are we going?" asked Ruth.

"In to time," he replied. They stayed for another hour and caught two brown trout.

"That will do," said Radio. "Only catch enough fish to eat and these two will feed all of us tonight."

Twenty-Nine – The Wisest Fool in Christendom

Radio and Ruth prepared the brown trout and put it in the slow cooker on a very low heat.

"When we return, we'll make the sauce. If you make the sauce now, it will curdle and dry out, even on a low heat. There is enough water in the cooker to maintain a level of moistness."

"Where are we going?" enquired Ruth.

"We are continuing your history lesson. First of all, you'll need to get changed."

Radio took her to the 16th century changing room and asked her to select a dress. Radio put on a linen shirt with ruff and a doublet. He discarded the pantaloons and went for a pair of black leather trousers which seemed to somehow transcend time. He finished the outfit with black leather boots.

When Ruth reappeared, she looked like a young Elizabethan to the core. Her dress was intricate and beautiful and she had chosen a headdress that whilst fussy, was still very tasteful.

"Excellent. You look the part."

They walked in front of the time windows.

"Operator. Holyrood House. 1587."

The time window morphed and looked on to a study filled with books. Sitting at a desk was a little man with long hair and a goatee beard. He appeared to be about twenty years old. They walked through silently.

Radio sat down in the chair opposite him. The young man looked up.

"Grandfather," he said, "I didn't hear you come in."

"Hello James. How are you?"

"I'm well. What brings you here?"

"Your mother," said Radio shortly.

The little man sighed and put down the quill he had been holding. He looked at the end of his tether.

"If you've come here to persuade me to intervene, you are too late. I received word this morning that she was beheaded at Fotheringhay yesterday morning. She apparently only had a day's notice. It's over I'm afraid."

"That's not why I'm here. Your mother was doomed from the start, I'm afraid. There was nothing anyone could have done. It is one of those moments in time which are immutable. She was executed by Elizabeth and that's that.

"I'm here because I have a desire for you to acquire the English throne and add it to your own."

Immediately, the little man sat up, He was listening all right.

"What would you have me do?"

"Elizabeth is a crowned Prince and she is not an idiot. You now have to play a political game that on the one hand, satisfies the demands of a son whose mother has been murdered but on the other hand show that the same son has the diplomatic skill to become King of England.

"In short, you have to show Elizabeth that you are a worthy successor. As far as I am concerned you are the pretender with the right pedigree. You are descended from her grandfather and you are also a King yourself. Show Elizabeth and her court that you have the maturity to rule their realm."

The little man sat back in his chair and pursed his lips in contemplation.

"Help me understand why this is so important to you," he demanded.

"Great Britain is an experiment that has already been 1000 years in the making. Ever since the Romans quit and returned home, I have been intervening on this island. It was me who brought the Saxons to these shores to boost the indigenous population. I was behind the Norman invasion which created the beginnings of a legal system and a structure to government. It is me who has a desire to create a United Kingdom for Mother and Father.

"The Creators of this universe are supportive of those who work together for the greater good. Everything they do is collaborative. They are in favour of unions and I mean both marriages of individuals and marriages of states. An individual with talent can win a game of chess but a team working together can win the kingdom.

"Join my team James and win me the kingdom. The United Kingdom."

The little man smiled. "It has been my official policy for some time to become King of England. Now that I know that you are behind me, I will double my efforts and will walk twice as carefully."

He looked at Ruth, as if seeing her for the first time.

"Are you going to introduce us?" asked the King.

"This is Ruth, my granddaughter from not only the future but also from another planet."

The king blanched visibly. "Ye gods, there are other planets in the universe?"

Radio smiled rucfully. He kept forgetting that a man from the 16th century would have a 16th-century world view.

"Yes, there are one trillion stars in this star cluster alone and one trillion star clusters in the universe. It is vast. Ruth is from a planet called Sumer."

Ruth curtsied. "Your Majesty."

"My Lady," responded James.

"I've brought Ruth with me today as she has always held a fascination for the history of Scotland."

"Have you?" smiled the King. "In that case, you might like this?"

He went to a desk and retrieved a small locket. It was circular in design, unadorned and finished in plain gold. He bowed and handed it to her.

Ruth accepted the trinket and examined it closely. "What is it?" she asked curiously.

"Open it," he commanded.

Ruth found a small catch and opened the locket. Inside was a lock of hair.

"It is a lock of my mother's hair. You can take it back to the future and say it was given you by the King of Scots."

Ruth was speechless. "Thank you, Your Majesty. I will treasure it always."

He nodded with satisfaction. "If you don't mind me asking, how do you manage to get from your Planet Sumer, to here on Earth? Do you have magic?"

Ruth thought for a minute. "There are times when a question is asked by a person, that you realise it is unanswerable. Not because I do not think you would understand, it is that the language is so alien and incomprehensible that it would sound like gibberish."

Ruth turned to her grandfather. "Can we show him?"

"I don't see why not," said Radio.

He stood up and turned to the door. "Operator. Place an interdiction on the door until we return. Open a temporal incursion to the Unknown Pleasures."

The vortex appeared in front of them and they were looking on to the bridge. Radio grabbed James' arm and walked him through on to the space ship.

Eve stood up. "Welcome to the Unknown Pleasures, Your Majesty."

The King of Scotland looked at his surroundings in total disbelief. "Where am I?" He breathed.

"You are on the Unknown Pleasures, the mother ship of the intergalactic fleet." She looked at one of the ensigns. "Take us into orbit," he nodded.

Radio felt a small amount of motion beneath his feet but the King acted like he was on a ship at sea.

"What's happening?" he asked fearfully.

"Give us one minute and we'll show you," said the captain.

After a few seconds, the ensign turned to the Captain. "We are now in orbit," he reported.

"On screen," said the captain.

The King turned around and looked at the viewer. The Planet Earth was laid out before him in all its ultramarine splendour.

"Oh my God, is that what I think it is?"

"Behold, planet Earth," said Radio. He pointed to a small island off the coast of Europe. "Look, there's Scotland."

The young man stared at the planet before him. His face was full of wonder and a small smile played around his lips. "So, it is round after all. Look at France. It is minute. That would annoy Henri if he could see this. What is that?" he pointed at Africa.

"That is Africa," said Radio.

"I suspected it was large but not that large. It is massive. And that," his eyes turned toward the Americas.

"I'm glad you mentioned that," said Radio. "That is America. When you are King of England. I would like you to encourage the British colonisation of this continent. In 400 years, it will emerge as one of the most powerful nations on Earth and will be allied to Great Britain."

"Does it float here in the night sky?"

"Basically, yes," replied Radio. "The planet spins around on its axis. When Scotland is facing the sun, it will be daytime. As it starts to turn away, it goes to twilight and then when it's facing in the opposite direction, it will be the dead of night."

"Oh, yes," he turned to Ruth. "I now see what you mean about gibberish. When you can visualise what is happening, it makes it so easy. Where is the moon?

"Take us into orbit around the moon." ordered Eve.

The ship spun away from the Earth and again, although Radio felt nothing, James acted like he was on a rocky boat.

"Can you feel that?" asked Radio.

"Yes. I think I feel a little sea sick."

The ship picked up speed gradually and then there was a gentle acceleration as it headed for the moon. It came in to view at great speed.

The king screamed. "How fast are we going?"

"About 5000 miles per second," said the captain.

"Oh my God, how far away is the damned thing?"

They all laughed. "One quarter of a million miles from the Earth."

"Me and my big mouth," he moaned.

Radio realised that the King was out of his comfort zone. He instinctively knew what was bothering him. What if they leave me out here? How will I get back? Will I have to swim through the night sky?

"There is nothing to fear. You are with your grandfather and I can assure you, everything is perfectly safe."

They went in to orbit around the moon.

"It is another planet," said the King.

"Yes, you are correct. However, when a planet goes into orbit around another planet, we call this a moon.

"Every planet in the night sky has a field of attraction which brings other things floating in space closer to it. The moon got caught in the Earth's field and has been here ever since."

Radio was careful not to mention Gravity. All he needed was that to be discovered 50 years ahead of time. He'd have another paradox on his hands.

They spent another hour, showing the king, the solar system until Radio decided it was time for brown trout. He invited the King for dinner.

When they got back to the matrix, there was another round of introductions and explanations and Radio started to believe that he was going to boggle the poor man's mind. He sat him down at the round table with Winston and he and Ruth went to make the sauce for the dinner.

Eventually, everyone was sat round the table, tucking into fillets of brown trout with potatoes and garlic lemon butter herb sauce. The general consensus in the company was that it was utterly delicious.

It was over coffee when Lilith who broke the silence. "Have you decided what you are going to do about the Loch Ness Monster."

"Not yet," Ruth replied. "I'm still thinking about it."

James was immediately interested. "What's this?" he asked.

Ruth briefly explained what had happened earlier before they had gone to meet him.

"Very interesting," he mused. "I have read several reports of a beast in the Loch. There was a Walter of Bingham, a cleric from Nottingham who reported seeing such a creature during the time of the third crusade."

"Is that right?" asked Ruth.

"Yes. He even drew a picture which seems quite laughable in light of what you have said."

"Have you heard of the Leviathan?" asked Lucifer. "The Beast of the Sea."

Immediately Ruth's head shot up. Radio smiled. She was clever and he could tell that she had made a connection. "I have definitely heard of that. Is it relevant?"

"It may well be," said Lucifer. "If I didn't know the answer I would split the problem up so that I could understand it a bit better. I would ask the following questions. Why a beast? Why the Sea? I would also take into account the fact that the story of the Loch Ness Monster is one big lie. Is that lie serving its purpose?"

Ruth looked down at her plate and her face twisted in to a look of concentration that Radio recognised all too well. She reminded him of himself. He now knew that she would not settle until she had found the answer. He smiled. He had his two recruits.

He stood up from the table and turned to James. "Time to see you home I think," he motioned for Ruth to follow.

They both got up and followed him to the time windows. He opened the vortex and walked them through to the study.

“Operator. Remove interdiction.” He looked at James. “I will be calling on you shortly as you have a massive job to do. Of all the important things you will do in your life, this will be the most important.”

The King looked at him with concern. “I will be ready. I think I know where I am going.”

“Good.”

The made their goodbyes to James and returned to the matrix.

Thirty – The Philosopher's Stone

When Ruth and Radio returned to the matrix, they were met by Gabriel and Uriel.

"What's up?" asked Radio.

"You have not completed the testing, there are still more trials to negotiate. Are you ready?"

In all the running about, Radio had forgotten that there was still more to do. He breathed deeply and calmed down.

"I'm ready."

As before, he was led in to the hall. This time there was complete silence.

In front of Mother and Father was a chest. It was the type of chest that Radio associated with pirates and buried treasure. He walked forward to take a closer look.

It was clear that he was going to be given no help and no instructions at all. He thought about it for a minute. Mother and Father were testing his assertion that he could send his awareness through time and space. If he was correct then he should know what to do next.

Radio smiled. He had been here fifty times before and the question that had always been asked was "What is in the box?"

He examined the lid of the chest. There were three scenes inlaid on the wood. A man turning water into wine. A man rising from the dead. A man attaining immortality.

What could be in the box that could achieve these three things. He thought he knew the answer. It was time to find out, once and for all, if his spirit questing was a real capability or whether it was just an excuse to get drunk.

He sat on the box and looked at Mother and Father.

"The Book of Brilliant Things."

There was silence in the hall. Many members of the audience were looking at each other in complete confusion. Mother and Father remained silent.

He looked over at the 4 candidates who were still sitting on the dais. They were smiling, triumphantly. Why? Then he saw the six advisors whose help Radio had been offered at the beginning.

They looked very frightened. Each one was biting their lips. Could it be, that after everything that had happened, they were still spouting their nonsense. Was it possible that the others had made an attempt and failed through receiving poor advice.

That was it, thought Radio. Mother and Father have reached the end of their tether and they wanted him to deal with them. Radio would oblige.

He stood up and addressed the six.

"There comes a time when Mother and Father can tolerate bad behaviour no longer.

"When Dyer of Pelos realised that Mother and Father were trying to teach him a lesson, he made a choice to listen to Mother and Father. He divested himself of his bad behaviour, he swallowed his pride, he suffocated his hubris and he admitted his mistakes. Moreover, he expressed a desire to learn and he made a promise to listen."

Radio looked over at the candidates and they all had the saintly expression of the converted. The advisors, however, were very frightened now,

"Let me explain to you what this test is about so that you understand. This test is about the understanding of allegory. When you seek the truth, it will hardly be valued if you can find it on the end of your nose. One of the devices our parents use, to make us think, to make us better, is allegory.

"In this case, a picture, that when studied closely reveals a hidden meaning.

"There are three pictures on the chest. A man turning water in to wine. A man rising from the dead. A man attaining immortality.

"There are legends in the universe that point towards an artefact that can achieve all three things. The Philosopher's Stone. But, what is The Philosopher's Stone?

"In ancient times, mankind used to write on stone but as man got more intelligent, they needed something more convenient to write on. Something lighter, something more portable. As a result of this need, they invented papyrus or as we call it today, paper.

"This papyrus was loved by Philosophers and became known as The Philosopher's Stone, where lovers of thought made their writings. It was never a magic substance that performed miracles.

"There is only one way to perform miracles and that is to read books, to educate yourselves and build your knowledge so that you can turn water into wine. So that you can raise a man from the dead. So that you can achieve eternal life.

"There is only one book in the universe where you will find documented all the things that you need to know. My Book of Brilliant Things."

He looked again at the six. They were terrified.

"You have shamed yourselves beyond endurance and Mother and Father can no longer invest any time in you. When you had the chance to redeem yourselves, rather than grab it with outstretched arms you chose to continue being what you have always been. Odious and arrogant human beings. There is no place for you in the new world. You are relieved of your duties.

"I hope you will all go home and rethink your lives and when you are ready, I hope that you will have the courage to pass the interview. You may go."

The six got up and left. Nobody made a sound.

When they were gone, Radio turned back to Mother and Father.

"Open the box, my darling," ordered Mother.

Radio bent down and opened the box. He reached in and lifted clear a huge leatherbound tome. It was The Book of Brilliant Things.

This time, it wasn't just a standing ovation. It was a riot.

Dyer of Pelos was first at his side and soon he was being carried round the hall shoulder high by the candidates. He had given them a sort of revenge. A piece of closure. They congratulated him and deposited him back on the floor, next to Miriam. *Perfect timing*, he thought.

Eventually, Mother and Father silenced the crowd.

As he stood there waiting, time windows started to appear all around the hall, just where the high walls met the ceiling. Soon the hall was completely encircled by them. In each window were a man and a woman as formidable as Mother and Father.

"Do you know who they are?" asked Father.

Radio didn't bother replying to the question, he simply looked at each in turn and addressed them directly.

"It is yours, if you want it," he began. "It is given freely and without charge. It is given with love from me to you all. Moreover, if you have a desire for me to resolve your temporal paradoxes. I have a plan for each and every one of you."

Father looked at the visitors. "Are we agreed?"

They all nodded in agreement. Then they all vanished.

Father walked towards them and handed the book to Miriam. "Yours, I believe."

"Thank you," she said.

Without saying another word, Radio and Miriam linked arms and walked back in to their matrix.

When everyone had gathered, Radio made a pot of coffee and they all sat down at the round table.

"What are you going to do with the book?" asked Mother.

Miriam thought about it for a second. "I have been preparing the Prime Minister all week to deliver a presentation to you and Father. I have been there for a reason. I wanted to see if their desire to help was genuine and whether they were prepared to deliver change speedily and without dysfunction.

"It is my belief that they will and that should come out in the presentation to you. However, it won't hurt to add another incentive. My Book of Brilliant Things is separated into 3 parts; Green, Amber and Red.

"If the people of the Earth start delivering change to my satisfaction, then I will give them the green portion so that they can educate the Earth. They will be able to publish green on the internet. It is information available to all. I will also give amber to their scientific community so that those with a master's degree in science may have access to all that it contains."

"And what do you plan to do with red?" Mother enquired.

"I will retain it until I believe that their best scientists can be trusted with the information. At the moment, far too many of their brightest are involved in programmes which do not benefit humanity."

"Such as?"

"Nuclear weaponry is a good example. They have the capability of easily destroying the earth. With the information contained in red, they could easily finish us all."

"When are they due to give their presentation?" asked Father.

"First thing tomorrow morning, I think we need to let everyone absorb and reflect on what has been said today and then they can start with enthusiasm tomorrow. Once we give them the go ahead, my expectation is that they can resolve things very quickly. There are easy ways to pay off a mortgage and there are easy ways to take people off the street. Let's hope they can find them."

Klaus, who normally remained quiet, cleared his throat. "Is it your intention to take over from Radio?"

Miriam and Radio stopped and considered for a moment. They were disappointed that someone as close to them as Klaus had been, had missed the obvious. Would the people of the Earth miss the point? They had to admit that some of them would not get it. Despite their disappointment, they kept a straight face and answered the question.

"Everyone has a job to do and each to their own," said Miriam. "Radio is about to go on a journey and he needs to concentrate on that. There is nobody else that can do it. He is the only one with the skill. He cannot be two places at once. Or can he?" she started to laugh.

The others chuckled but Radio was painfully aware, only a few of them got the joke. How many clues did he need to give them? Were they incapable of seeing what was staring them in the face? He couldn't go any further. He consoled himself with the knowledge that everyone thought the Earth was flat until somebody realised they couldn't see over the horizon. Now 500 years later, everyone knew it was a sphere orbiting the sun and the idea of flat had been consigned to history.

"Now," said Miriam, "Tomorrow is a big day. Let's us all get some sleep and we'll meet up again for breakfast."

When Miriam and Radio were finally in bed together, they held each other close. Although their minds were completely merged now, they still took some comfort from holding each other. This would be the last chance for a little while and they decided to make the most of it.

"Do you think they will work it out?" asked Miriam.

"Yes," he replied. "In the end."

Thirty-One – The Spirit Quest

When they woke up in the morning, Mother and Father had prepared a lavish breakfast.

Miriam piled high a plate for Radio. Where he was going, he was going to need it. He tucked in to his bacon and eggs and made sure he had his fair share of buttered toast.

Everyone around the table was in a pensive mood. Radio thought he knew what was wrong. They wondered where he was going and they had engaged in a fair amount of speculation. Eventually, Winston plucked up the courage to ask the question.

"Where are you going, master?"

"It is a good question, Winston," he began, "And to be perfectly truthful. I'm not entirely sure. The universe was created by virtue of a series of temporal paradoxes. Over the last few weeks, you have seen me begin to resolve these paradoxes but there is one, more than any other that has been causing me headaches.

"I have always been aware that the Operator has guided me in my travels through time and space and I have always known that information is released to me on a need to know basis. A season for everything and everything in its season.

"Despite several attempts to get to the truth, I have never been able to find out who Yeshua is. Not for certain. It is time to discover the truth and once I have done that, resolve the paradox. I need to bring him forward in time so that he can lead the people of the Earth through the interview. He is their guide, as he has been for the last 2000 years.

"First things first, I am going to go on a spirit quest to get to the truth. I am going to get extremely drunk on Scotch Whiskey and I'm going to send my awareness through time and space to see if I can discover the truth in relation to Yeshua.

"Once, I have done that and know for certain what I need to do, who knows? I suspect that I will end up in Judea to resolve the paradox. I have already made a huge amount of preparation for that but the paradox has shown us in the past that there are unexpected twists and turns.

"All I know is this. Now is the time to make a resolution. Now is the time to discover the truth."

"I want to come with you." It was Winston. Radio smiled. It was the greatest story ever told and his apprentice wanted to be a part of it. He didn't blame him.

Radio looked at everyone around the table. "I've been thinking about that and I'm pretty certain that there may be parts for us all to play. Let me have a look in time first before I commit myself to saying yes. Remember, it is still a paradox and it still needs to be resolved."

"What do you want to do first?" asked Miriam. "Spirit quest or presentation?"

"What do YOU want to do first?" countered Radio.

"I think we should get the presentation out of the way. I want to be with you when you start drinking. We don't want another Paris incident, do we?"

Mother and Father laughed but everyone else looked curiously at Radio.

"What happened in Paris?" enquired Winston.

Radio shook his head at the utter shame of it. "Four years ago, I got ill with flu but still insisted on going ahead with a spirit quest. There was so much I needed to find out that I just couldn't wait.

"I started boozing in Edinburgh and after about a bottle of whisky, I sort of blacked out. I don't remember anything after that. Four days later I woke up. I was buck naked on the floor of a nightclub in St Denis, Paris. It was horrible."

Everyone fell about. "What did you do?" asked Winston.

"I found a receipt in my back pocket for a hotel in Montmartre, which I'd stayed in before. I went there and all my stuff was in my room. Suitcase, passport, keys. It was a lucky escape. Ever since, I've been very wary of questing alone. You never know what is going to happen.

"To make it work properly, you need at least three quarters of a bottle which is a huge amount. The possibilities for disaster are endless."

"Don't worry," said Miriam, "I'll keep you out of trouble."

They finished their breakfasts and chatted over coffee until it was time for the presentation. Miriam went off to get the parliamentary delegation, while the others lined up chairs next to Mother and Father.

When the delegation came through, Radio could tell that they were extremely nervous. Miriam had uploaded the presentation to the Operator and the first slide now appeared on the main viewer. Radio had to admit that it looked really professional.

The Prime Minister delivered the first two slides which Radio had already seen and they went to PROBLEMS and ANALYSE. Radio was pleased. They had addressed some of the issues that he himself had expected in connection to housing falling very short of standard and there was a detailed analysis of what would be considered as acceptable going forward. All in all, Radio thought that they had done a good job.

The Prime Minister asked if they had any comments or questions.

Mother did. "I am pleased to see that you have done a very good job. However, I want you to consider this. Why did you not address these issues before? Why did it take Radio to bully you in to action?

"I am not expecting you to answer this question. I would like you, as a nation, to reflect on this. This is your last chance. Must you always have someone standing over you to pass the interview? Reflect."

Radio stood up. "All in all, a good job. You have a mandate to proceed. I would like you to use the money I have given you to pay off the mortgages at source. The banks will have a bottom line. Clear the bottom line.

"You will give advice today, to the people of the UK to cancel their rent and mortgage Direct Debits. From now, they are free of this debt. We will tidy up in the background."

The Prime Minister looked pleased and a bit relieved.

Radio turned to Miriam. "What next?"

"We will move this work to the appendix and start on food chain. My expectation is that I will be needed less and less but I will continue to support whilst you are on your travels."

The delegation got ready to leave and just as Miriam was about to take them through the time window, the Prime Minister turned to Radio.

"Good luck. I want you to know that the country is behind you and we are all praying for you."

"Thank you," said Radio. Maybe, just maybe, it had dawned on them.

When Miriam returned, they all gathered at the round table. Radio had prepared a bottle of Petrus and two bottles of whisky.

"What now?" asked Mother.

"I'm going to start off with the wine. Once I've drunk a bottle of that, the whisky should slide down quite easily. The secret is to get drunk as quickly as possible. If I start with the scotch, I won't be able to drink it as quickly as it is too harsh."

"I'll join you," said Winston. "There's nothing worse than having to drink alone."

Radio burst out laughing. When he had banned alcohol, he had been absolutely certain that Winston would find some glorious excuse to carry on. He produced two bottles of champagne from the ether and handed them over. Winston's look of triumph was beautiful.

"Here goes." He poured himself a glass of the Bordeaux and downed it. He shivered and poured himself another. Radio hadn't drunk for quite some time so the booze was going down like a dream. He was loving it. The second glass disappeared. He poured a third.

Winston downed a few glasses of champagne and started to tell a few tales. Soon the wine had gone and Radio started in on the whisky. The first couple were appalling but by the time he hit the third he was on easy street. He stopped hearing the gaggle of voices around him and soon he was in a world of his own. Nearly there. Another whisky and he was gone.

He was standing on a lawn in front of a wall with a golden door. Beside him was Miriam.

"How did you do that?" he asked.

"I've no idea. I closed my eyes as you closed yours and here I am."

As Radio expected, the golden fox appeared in front of him. It was the Operator. "When you were younger, I used music as a device to separate you from your body, so that you could travel through time and space. It is merely a means to an end. It will enable you to do what you need to do. Follow me."

Just as he had done, all those times before, Radio listened to the song and went through the golden door and collected the golden key. They went down the golden hall. At the end of the golden hall was a doorway. Gold dust was falling from the lintel like water in a shower. The golden filter. He walked through with Miriam and their eyes were blinded by the golden light.

When they opened them again, Radio's heart sank. They were in the temple. Not the ancient one in Judah but the replica built in Edinburgh.

"Why so disappointed?" asked the golden fox.

"I'm not. It's just that so much nonsense has been spouted about this place that when I come to explain it, people will just pour scorn on the whole thing."

The golden fox laughed. "Think on this. It was built for one person and it was built in Edinburgh for a reason."

Radio felt shocked but, in his heart of hearts, knew it to be true.

"Explain this place to me," said the fox.

"It is Mother and Father's temple. It explains how the traditional God of old is both male and female. Mother and Father. It is a temple dedicated to collaboration, to union, to working together, to marriage. It is about pooled resources and how the whole is greater than the sum of its parts. It is dedicated to the inheritance of the Earth. To truth and to love."

"Tell me about the pillars?" asked the fox.

"The pillars represent Mother and Father and the gifts they hold in trust for their children. This is why you have brought me here. I got them the wrong way around. I allowed the traditional view of the male and female roles to infect my thinking. I won't make that mistake again.

"I originally thought that the beautiful pillar was Mother but it isn't. The pillars represent their attitudes and way of thinking.

"The plain pillar, or Master pillar is actually Mother because Mother is the Master. Look at the strength at the base of the pillar and see how the pillar stands staunch and true. It is the pillar of a King. It is the pillar of daily bread. It is practicality and it is the truth.

"The beautiful pillar is the pillar of the apprentice. It is a pillar of dreams and has no practicality at all. It is always looking to the future and rarely at the here and now. It dreams of what could be and draws all who see it. It is a fatal attraction and transmits the power of love. It is Father."

"Excellent," said the golden fox. "I require you to think, you will not make this mistake again, do you understand?"

"Yes."

"Give me one clue to tell me that you have gotten to the root of this problem?" asked the fox.

"I am not Radio, WHO am I?"

"Excellent. You are my greatest ever student. Never forget that."

The golden light engulfed them and they found themselves in a desert town. It was an ancient dusty place. Radio recognised it. He'd been here before. A young woman was washing a blanket in a wooden tub.

"Who is she?" asked the golden fox.

"She is Yeshua's mother," answered Radio.

"Who is she?" the golden fox was looking at him.

Radio walked toward her and tapped her shoulder. She did not move and did not even see that he was there. Hundreds of DNA strands leapt out from her shoulder and Radio rifled through them.

He then tapped her abdomen and repeated the process.

When he returned, the golden fox was amused. "Excellent, excellent. Who is she?"

"She is my granddaughter. She is descended from the others, from Eve and from all the patriarchs. She is a gene machine."

The golden fox laughed. "And the boy?"

"He has exactly the same DNA as the mother. There is no father. He has been created in the womb by you as a result of the work completed by the others."

The golden fox bowed. "Well done, Radio. It was true after all."

The golden light engulfed them again.

This time, they were in brightly lit room looking on to a morning sunrise. It was Yeshua and his twelve disciples gathered together for breakfast. At Yeshua's side was a woman. Once you had seen one gene machine, you had seen them all. The woman looked up at him and smiled.

The golden fox looked expectantly at him. "Amaze me, Radio."

He smiled. "Leonardo Da Vinci's, The Last Supper."

The golden fox chortled. "He was a very good student, too! And the girl?"

"Descended from the renegade Pharaoh, as her name suggests."

"Stunning."

The golden light bathed them in its intense vermilion.

This time they were in ancient Rouen. Again, Radio recognised the place, he had also been there before. It was Hrolfr's banqueting hall. He was at the head of the table and next to him were Jamie, Natalie and Klaus. They were all wearing mediaeval garments.

"Do you follow?" asked the fox.

“Yes, I am supposed to take Jamie, Klaus and Natalie back in time to Hrolfr. He will ensure that they are trained in ancient languages and Jamie will be given training as a fighting man. He will be one of the most formidable knights of the middle age and it will prepare him for his training as a Templar.”

“And Hrolfr?”

Radio looked more closely. If there was a clue, it would be about his person otherwise the golden fox would not have brought him here. Hrolfr reached out and picked up a goblet. There, on his finger. A ring.

Radio smiled. “He will lead the temporal raiding force and bring ancient artefacts back to the future. He is wearing a ring that was worn by the eighteenth dynasty pharaoh, Akhenaten.”

“Excellent. Why is it important?” asked the fox.

“It is a revelation of the truth. The people of the Earth will, once and for all, be able to put their myths to bed and understand the real histories and the allegories for what they are. Stories with a hidden moral. It is part of their inheritance.”

“Well done. You have my permission to have a party and get blind drunk.”

Radio opened his eyes. He was back at the round table and all eyes were on him.

“Well?” asked Mother.

“Mission accomplished, my Master. Now if you don’t mind, I think I’ll get squiffy. Let’s put on some tunes.”

Everybody laughed. It wasn’t long before Radio realised that everybody was taking the opportunity have a party. All things considered, he thought they deserved it.

Thirty-Two – The Beast of the Sea

When Radio woke up the next morning, he had a dreadful headache and he felt sick. Miriam was no better. He snuggled in under the covers and settled in for a morning of doing nothing.

Just as he was about to doze off, he was picked up by Mother and carried in her arms. He thought she had taken pity on him and was going to nurse him in his misery. She wasn't. She threw him in to a pool of cold water.

Radio knew he had a pool but, because he had been busy, he hadn't bothered exploring the matrix. Miriam landed next to him. They were both naked and it was freezing.

They swam to the side of the pool and got out. Mother and Father were standing there with towels and a glass of ice cold lemonade. They both drained the glass. They felt much, much better.

"I take it you don't believe in hangovers?" asked Radio, chittering.

"I was tempted to let you lie in but your Father and I have made plans. You have a test today and things are heading towards their denouement. We have invited some very important people to join us. People who have waited a long time to meet you. It would look awful if we let you get behind in any way."

She was gently towelling him dry when she stopped and sighed.

"Radio, I'm nervous. You are not the most talkative person in the world which I realise is my fault but could you give me just a clue that you know what is going on."

Radio smiled and kissed her. "You have invited the others to join us. The Operator has always worked in this way. As I get closer to an event, the rope winds and the possibilities solidify in to one eventuality. It's just like Wagner said in his prelude to Gotterdammerung."

She heaved a sigh of relief. "Thank goodness for that."

Radio continued. "I don't blame you for what happened all those years ago. It was not your fault, it was mine. My hubris was the root cause. I want you to put it all behind you. It is forgotten and I am happy."

She lifted him in to her arms and kissed him again. "Let's get you dressed."

When they returned to the elevator, Radio noticed that the time window had already been prepared for the test. Mother and Father had obviously thought there was no point in going to the Great Hall if he was the only candidate.

The window looked on to a still grey blue lake surrounded by black hills. It appeared as if night had fallen but the quality of light was slightly different. The scene looked eerily familiar.

He and Miriam sat down at the round table for breakfast when they were joined by Lilith.

"You're back, I see."

She laughed. "I'm back from my honeymoon. Your trip to Rome was a hundred years ago for me and may I say, I have never forgotten it. What do you need me to do?" she asked cheerfully.

“I need you to tell that husband of yours that there will be two passengers today and I’m expecting a very smooth trip indeed.”

“Don’t worry. I’ll tell him. May I ask you a question?” she said.

“Of course, you may.”

“How did you work this test out? I would have sworn that nobody would work it out but you obviously have.”

“Jonah and the whale,” replied Radio around mouthfuls of granola. “I’ve come to the conclusion that some biblical stories have been written as a letter to the initiated. I guess you could say that I am initiated.”

“Oh, yes. That makes complete sense.”

When breakfast was over, the crowd started to gather and very soon filled the elevator. The room was smaller than the great hall so gave the impression of being more tightly packed. It felt like a football match where the crowd was right on the touchline.

Those closest to him had seats at the round table. Eve, Adam, Ruth, Winston, Jamie, Klaus, Natalie and the 4 candidates. When the time came, the room fell silent.

Mother and Father sat in their chairs and did not say a word. There were no instructions now.

Radio smiled inwardly. He knew he was about to cause another one of those rumbling noises in the crowd. Sure enough, as she started to walk across the floor toward him there was the low humming of whispered questions. And then she was there at his side, wearing the same outfit as Radio. A black tunic with the skull and crossed thighbones over the heart.

Radio and Miriam held hands and waited.

Out of the black mist, they could hear the rippling of the waves and then a head broke the surface of the blue grey water. It was enormous. The head appeared through the time window and the creature laid its chin on the floor. It opened wide its mouth and waited.

“NO.” It was Ruth. She ran forward and grabbed Radio by the wrist. “Don’t!”

Radio smiled. He knelt down to her, so that their faces were inches apart.

“The truth is esoteric. It is hidden in the darkness. To understand the truth, especially about yourself, you have to allow yourself to be swallowed by the dark.”

There were gasps in the crowd. Radio patted his granddaughter on the cheek and holding Miriam’s hand he walked forward. They both laid down on the creature’s tongue and folded their arms. The beast closed its mouth and its head disappeared under the surface of the water.

Radio and Miriam lay there for what seemed like an age. The mouth was shut tight around them and they could feel the force of intense acceleration. They shut their eyes tight as light started to flood through the creature’s skull. There was a feeling of being stretched as if put through an old mangle and then a deceleration as fierce as the speeding up had been. The creature came to a stop.

When it opened its mouth, Radio knew exactly where they were. They were in the cave where he had found Mother and Father all those years ago. He grabbed Miriam’s hand and they walked on to dry land.

Behind them, there was an audible ‘whoosh’ and Lucifer appeared at their side.

Radio turned to him. “In the beginning, were you in or out of the solution?”

“Out,” he replied. “I was uploaded at the same time as Mother and Father.”

“What was your job?”

“I was responsible for safety, ethics and compliance. I fought with Mother and Father every day. I was appointed to this role on your advice.”

“That makes total sense to me.”

“Yes, it does, doesn’t it?” he laughed.

In the distance Radio could see a vast silo like object rising out of the gloom. It was enormous.

As they got closer, Radio could see a small door surrounded by dim light at the bottom of the silo. It looked minute against the sheer scale of the edifice. When they reached the door, Radio could see the word GOD written on a sign directly at the centre.

Lucifer grabbed his arm. "Whatever you see in there, I want you to understand that there was no choice. It was the only way we knew how." He looked so sad and Radio detected an element of fear.

He nodded. "Don't worry."

Lucifer waited outside. Radio held Miriam's hand tightly, took a deep breath and went inside.

The room was very small and dimly lit. It was a control room of some sort but the technology was very alien. The wall was lined with what looked like workstations and over it all he could hear the faint thrum of an electrical generator. There was a sign on the largest machine which looked like a hub. Alpha-Omega.

At the end of the room was a bed and in the bed, was a body asleep. The body was attached to what Radio could only assume were life support systems. This is why he had come.

Miriam and Radio walked to the side of the bed and looked down.

The sleeping body was neither male nor female and the age was indeterminate. What was apparent was that this alien person had been badly burnt down one side. The left-hand side of the body was a mass of black flesh and bloody contusions.

"Hello Operator," said Radio.

"Hello Radio," said the Operator in his head. "Don't worry, it is only partly what's left of me. As you have already worked out, an Alpha-Omega can maintain itself. This is the part that maintains the universe. The aware part of me is in the solution, along with everybody else."

"Who were you?" asked Radio.

"I was Mother and Father's son. My name is Eloidh and I was Head of Operations. Quite literally, the Operator."

"What happened?"

The Operator laughed. "Something terrible, something wonderful. You know better than to ask too many questions. I would like you to work it out before the others arrive. It is important for a number of reasons. Are you not Mother's puzzler extraordinaire."

"I am indeed," said Radio. "Sleep well, Golden Fox."

"I can assure you that I am both fast asleep and wide awake at the same time. I thought that someone who sends his awareness through time and space when he's as pissed as a fart would have worked that out!"

"Aye, right enough. I know more than I let on, you know."

"I obviously know that, Radio. Now get going. You can't be here too long. You'll catch your death."

Radio and Miriam turned around and walked back out of the door and into the cave. Lucifer was waiting.

"Well?" he asked.

"No surprises," said Radio.

Lucifer smiled and looked relieved. "There is more to you than meets the eye. Let's go."

He rushed them back to the lake. Radio peered down into the water and a dreadful suspicion started to dawn on him. Was it really water?

When they walked out of the creature's mouth, Radio let go of Miriam's hand and ran at top speed to Mother. She knelt down and swept him in to her arms. He kissed her fiercely.

"You see," he said. "No big deal and a wonderful solution."

The tears were streaming down her face.

Thirty-Three – The Education of Master Jacques

For the next couple of days, Radio and Miriam were inseparable. They held hands wherever they went and they were never apart. Radio was going in to time to complete the mission that was causing the Operator the greatest concern. It was the mission that was number one on the temporal priority list. Operation Jesus of Nazareth.

Radio had decided that he would stay with Yeshua as much as possible throughout his mission to make sure that all the applications were available to him when needed. Miriam would monitor from the matrix in real time and arrange to provide extra support if it was needed. In the event of an emergency, she would walk into the past and help out.

The Operator had advised that they should start at the Wedding in Cana and that all affected time agents should assemble, in the matrix, to agree their plans.

Radio wrote down a list of key personnel and Gabriel and Uriel were sent to collect them from time.

When they left, Radio decided that it was time to make his famous Chinese banquet. He collected his bags, linked arms with Miriam and headed through the matrix to Pat's Chung Ying in Edinburgh.

"Time for a bit of shopping and a bit of recruitment," laughed Radio.

Radio loved food shopping, largely because he loved cooking. Over the years he had honed his recipes and only ever allowed the best ingredients in to his concoctions.

"What are we going to make?" asked Miriam.

"I think we'll start with chicken noodle soup followed by a selection of Chinese starters. Spiced chicken wings on a bed of wilted savoy cabbage with soy sauce, Tsingtao cocktail spring rolls, spare ribs and crispy duck with hoisin sauce."

"Oh, that sounds wonderful. Main courses?"

"I think we'll do two. Beef, green peppers and black bean sauce together with Lily Kwok's Chinese chicken curry."

"And dessert?"

"Let's go for Mango Pudding served with ice cream. You can buy a whole one right here."

They started filling their basket with all the required ingredients. Radio smiled as Miriam picked up the Kum Kee brand of black bean sauce. It was a classic and it had taken him years to perfect that recipe.

As he bent over the freezer to pick up the box of Tsingtao spring rolls, there was a tap on his shoulder. He turned around. Standing before him was a red-haired man of about 35. He was about 5'8'' and quite robust.

"Can I help you?" asked Radio.

The man tapped his temple. "Operator sent me. Tells me your looking for a treacherous and contrary individual to betray saviour of the Earth. A man who can do his job with no sense of shame and walk away at the end of it with no regrets. I think I'm your man." He smiled.

Radio looked him up and down. He was well dressed. Intelligent, matter of fact. "Credentials?" asked Radio.

"I'm a Hearts supporter living in Leith. My neighbours call me Judas to my face."

"You're hired," laughed Radio. "Welcome to the Temporal Incursion Team."

"Er…that spells out TIT."

"Oh, so it does," chortled Radio. "Welcome to the Temporal Adjustment Team."

"TIT for TAT. I can see why you're the boss." The man laughed.

Radio was delighted. He was obviously very clever and it resolved a headache that had been bothering him for some time. If no one else had volunteered, he thought he might have had to do it himself. He quietly thanked the Operator.

"What's your name?" asked Radio.

"It is actually Jude. I guess that's why Judas was such an easy nickname for everyone."

"Well Jude, I need to ask you a very important question. A lot depends on it."

"Go on," said Jude curiously.

"What on Earth possessed you to support the Hearts?"

The man laughed. "My Father was a Hearts man. Once you've nailed your colours to the mast, there's no going back."

"You're just about to betray the messiah." Radio reminded him.

"Yes," he replied with a straight face, "But football's a bit more important than all that GOD stuff!"

He wasn't entirely sure that Jude was joking.

Radio, Miriam and Jude paid for their shopping and headed back to the matrix.

The banquet was a great success. John had been delighted to see that spring rolls were on the menu and kept on asking if anyone had actually been to China, which he insisted on referring to as Cathay, much to everyone's great amusement.

Hrolfr had demonstrated the remarkable skill of being able to remove all the meat from a spare rib in one fluid motion. It had reminded Radio of a cartoon he had watched as a child.

When the banquet was over, Radio called for silence.

"Before we begin, I think it would be a good idea if we went around the table and introduced ourselves to each other so that nobody has any misapprehensions about each other. I'll start.

"I'm Radio and I'm Mother's apprentice." He turned to his left and nodded for Miriam to continue.

"I'm Miriam and I'm Fathers apprentice."

"Hrolfr, time agent from Normandy."

"Jamie, time agent from South Shields."

"Natalie, Jamie's Mother from South Shields."

"And time agent," added Radio.

"Klaus, time agent from Berlin."

"Geoffrey, time agent from Auvergne."

"Winston, Radio's apprentice from Blenheim."

"James of Scotland, time agent from Edinburgh."

"Billy, time agent from Glasgow."

"Jude, time agent from Edinburgh."

"Francis, Head of the Church."

"Lucifer, Mother's Satan."

"Lilith, Father's Satan."

"Gabriel, Archangel."

"Uriel, Archangel."

"Thank you for joining us," said Radio. "Let's not beat about the bush. We are here to resolve the most important of the temporal paradoxes which exist in time. It is the Operator's number one priority and is the one that has caused me the most headaches.

"All of you are involved to a greater or lesser extent and I would like to prepare a plan for immediate execution and make sure everybody is well prepared for their roles.

"Some of what I'm going to say is going to cause a bit of heartache in the short term but I want you all to remember that when this is all over you will hold some of the most responsible positions in the universe and that you will be members of a very loving family which will go on forever. I don't mind telling you that failure is not an option, I have contingency plans in the event of a mishap, the important thing is to be tenacious in your endeavours and know that hard work will see us through.

"The first issue I want to address is the issue of Jamie."

The young man immediately looked attentive and his mother put her hand over his.

"Jamie is 14 and not yet old enough to carry out the role assigned to him. To that end, I'm sending Jamie back in time with Hrolfr, Natalie, Klaus, Jude and Geoffrey to Rouen in 920. There, he will be trained by Hrolfr and his men in the martial arts and continue his language education with Klaus. He and the rest of you will learn Aramaic, Greek, Latin, French, Occitan and Mitteldeutsch. Do you have any questions?"

"How long will we be gone?" asked Klaus.

"Seven years there. You will leave after this meeting and be back before we move on to phase 2."

Radio waited for all of that to sink in. Natalie and Jamie looked a bit frightened but Hrolfr interceded.

"There is nothing to fear. I have been at this a very long time and I am adept at making those out of time feel comfortable. It will be fine and you will return better people. I promise."

They looked heartened and Radio nodded his thanks at Hrolfr.

"Let us move on to phase two and the question of Yeshua's disciples. As you well know, there are twelve apostles. Six of them are idiots from Judea. Six of them are sitting round this table."

This caused laughter but no real surprise. Radio continued.

"I will play the part of Nicodemus. He is hardly mentioned in the gospels so that will allow me to dip in and out as required. John is John. Klaus is James the lesser, Jamie is the other James and Hrolfr is Simon the Zealot."

"No surprise there," said Hrolfr with a flourish of his hand. "I was always a rebel."

"Rebel or not. When I'm not there, I'm expecting you to support Yeshua.

"King James is Philip and Jude is Judas. We will all have to support Judas as we know that he will have a very difficult time.

"It is our intention to join Yeshua at the wedding in Cana. We will get the lie of the land and decide what to do from there. Miriam and Winston, you will come with us so that you can be involved in making any changes to the plan

"This mission is the responsibility of the children of the Earth so I'm expecting you all to bear the brunt of the responsibility. I am merely here to get you started and guide you home. It is time to live up to the expectations laid down by your parents."

Radio waited for any comments but there were none.

“Miriam, you, Gabriel, Uriel, Natalie and Winston will observe from the matrix for the time being. Let’s be ready as a support network in case there is a crisis. I’m not expecting one.

“I would like to maintain a chronological order if possible so Gabriel’s visit to Mary is something that we need to do first. I suggest we do that whilst the others are in France.

“Francis, you are in charge of communications to the people of the Earth and preparing an easy transition for Yeshua when he returns.

“Beyond that we just have to be on our toes. If you haven’t read the 4 gospels, now would be a good time.”

Radio looked at everyone around the table.

“What you are doing is the most important thing in the history of Earth. Are we all clear about what we need to do?”

There was silence. Radio turned to Hrolfr.

“What do you need?”

Hrolfr went in to his leather waistcoat and produced a list which he handed to Gabriel.

“Leave it to us,” she said. Gabriel and Uriel rushed off.

Radio sat for a moment wondering if he’d remembered everything. He sometimes felt that he flew by the seat of his pants a bit too much but that was the way he had been built. He stood up.

“Jamie and Geoffrey, a minute please.”

Jamie and Geoffrey walked over to him. Geoffrey was beaming.

“Jamie, I’d like you to meet your best friend. This is Geoffrey de Charnay, Templar Preceptor of Normandy.”

“How do you do?” said Jamie offering his hand.

Geoffrey accepted the proffered hand and kissed it. “Grand Master,” he said.

Jamie looked perplexed.

“I think it’s time that I let you know, who you really are,” said Radio. “You are Jacques De Molay, the last Templar Grand Master. When you come back here today, you will be well on your way to becoming one of the greatest Knights of the middle age. There are so many things that you are going to do. When you are away, I want you to take the opportunity to get to know Geoffrey. He will prepare you for all those great adventures that lie ahead of you.”

Jamie, however, looked horrified. “Wasn’t the last Templar Grand Master burnt at the stake?”

Radio chuckled. He kept forgetting just how knowledgeable the boy could be.

“Yes, but Yeshua was crucified and he’s coming back to us later on tonight. Don’t worry. I’ve got several applications that can easily take care of a burning. You won’t even feel a thing.”

“Glad to hear it,” said Jamie.

“Come,” said Geoffrey, “I’ll introduce you to Pontius Pilate.”

It took about an hour before Hrolfr was satisfied and everyone was ready to go. Radio said goodbye and Hrolfr led them through the matrix along with a cart full of provisions and 4 horses.

He’d give it half an hour. Time for a pot of coffee.

Thirty-Four – The Wedding

Radio sat down and sipped his coffee. His mind felt like it was in overdrive. He had noticed, in the past, that he was incapable of settling down until disconnected ideas had resolved themselves. The next few days were going to be stressful. There was so much going on and too many unknowns.

The Operator laughed in his head. "They are not unknowns, they are just unknown to you. Remember, Yeshua lived 2000 years ago and every action was recorded then. You have access to my HEAD. All you have to do is make an enquiry and the answer will be yours."

"No need for the Golden Fox then?" asked Radio dryly.

"The Golden Fox was to introduce you to the concept. I used your fascination with native American culture to educate you that there were possibilities that you had not considered. It serves its purpose. Now what do you need to know?"

"Nothing really," replied Radio. "I've been searching through the application store and I've found what I needed. The transfiguration was causing me a bit of a headache but I discovered an app called BROCKENSPECTRE. It will do nicely."

"You are the most resourceful entity in the universe," laughed the Operator.

"Master, may I have a word?" It was Winston and he didn't look too happy.

"What's up, Winston?"

"I was hoping that I might take a trip back to Judea, you know, be a bit more involved."

Radio sighed. "Winston, you can join us at the wedding but that's it. Unfortunately, you are just not there.

"Personally speaking, I think you've got the best of both worlds. You can observe in comfort and help when necessary. You're not as young as you used to be and you like your home luxuries. When was the last time you took a shit outside?"

Winston chuckled. "It was in the trenches. Ghastly business. We all got a bad case of trench arse. It was terrible."

"Oh dear, what was it like?"

"I remember seeing a dog with worms drag its backside along a bristle mat. That was what it was like!"

Radio roared with laughter. "I rest my case, Winston."

Radio finished his coffee and decided it was time. He opened the time window to let the first phase back in to the matrix.

First in was Hrolfr who looked a bit older but more or less the same man. Next was Geoffrey who hadn't changed a bit. Radio was starting to wonder if he had made a miscalculation. Then came Jamie. He had definitely not made a miscalculation. The boy was the very picture of a mediaeval Knight.

"Well met, My Lord." He bowed.

"Welcome home, Master Jacques. Quid agis?"

"O bona valetudo," replied Jamie.

Radio was impressed. He turned to Hrolfr. "I owe you a debt of gratitude."

Hrolfr laughed. "It was the easiest assignment of my life. The boy is a natural. What a leader he will be."

Next came Natalie and Klaus. They looked very different. Natalie was every inch a woman and not the spoiled brat that had left half an hour before. They were two completely different people.

"My Lady," said Radio with a flamboyant bow.

She nodded remotely and said nothing. *Ouch,* thought Radio.

"Well, Nicolas, how does married life suit you?"

Klaus smiled "How did you know?"

"It is my business to know." He turned to Natalie. "I hope you'll be very happy together."

"Thank you," she said. "Now. Could I please have a bath?"

They all laughed. Miriam took Natalie into her bathroom and ran a bath for her.

Jude walked over to say hello. "That was interesting," he said.

"How did you get on?" Radio noted that he looked about twenty times healthier than the last time he had seen him.

"It wasn't what I expected. We have this idea that the past is different, that our ancestors lived in hovels and everything was a trial. It was the opposite. People were happier. Generally healthier and when you did get a treat, it was savoured and enjoyed so much more than you would normally enjoy it. It was fascinating."

"This could be a new job for you in the future. Writing about the past and how it felt to live there."

Jude held up a volume of leather bound vellum. "Beat you to it!"

Radio chuckled. "Great minds think alike."

Radio thought for a minute. They all looked a bit tired. Should he give them a few days off?

"You can't afford to, I'm afraid." It was Mother. "The others are on their way and you need to complete this particular mission. It is important."

"Hrolfr," said Radio. "I'm sorry that we have to move so quickly. How soon can you get everyone turned around?"

"Don't worry. We've been doing nothing for the last two weeks. Give us a couple of hours and we'll be ready."

"Gabriel." Radio called for the archangel.

"I'm here."

"Right, I need to upload two applications in preparation for your trip. FERTILISER and SOULSENDER. When you meet Mary, simply activate the applications and the software will take care of the rest. They have already been prepared in advance. Do you understand?"

"Yes." Radio uploaded the applications.

"Do you know what to say?" asked Radio.

"Yes. I've done this sort of thing before you know. I have read the script."

Radio sighed. "I'm sorry Gabriel. I'm feeling under a bit of pressure at the moment. So much is riding on this."

"I know." she said. "But don't lose sight of the fact that I am from outside of the solution and the plan has been well known for a long time."

"My sincere apologies."

She smiled and hugged him. "We are all behind you, as we have been since the beginning of time."

"I know. Let's open the time window for you."

"No Radio. Leave it to me. I'm quite capable and you need to just delegate a bit more."

She winked at him and left.

"You had better get ready," said Mother, "It's nearly time."

Radio went in to the changing room where Uriel was waiting for him. "Mother says you've to wear this." It was a white robe which looked a bit expensive.

"Isn't this a bit smart?" asked Radio.

Uriel shrugged her shoulders. "Just put it on."

Something had changed, thought Radio. There was a bit more urgency about everything and he got the feeling that this was a situation that everybody wanted resolved. Patience appeared to be in short supply.

In an hour, the team was gathered at the time window.

"Operator, The wedding at Cana."

They walked through to find Yeshua waiting for them at the door of the synagogue.

"Fancy meeting you here," said Radio.

Yeshua smiled an enigmatic smile and raised his eyebrows. "I'm getting the distinct impression, Radio, that you don't always know quite what's going on. Am I right?"

Radio laughed. "The Operator only really lets me know on a need to know basis. I think it is designed to keep me on my toes. Whose wedding is it, out of interest?"

It was Yeshua's turn to laugh and roll his eyes heavenward. "Oh Radio," he chuckled, "It is your wedding."

Radio was stunned. He felt an arm link his and he turned to look at Miriam. She was dressed in a bridal costume and had flowers sewn in her hair. She looked dazzling.

"Will you marry me?" she asked.

"Gee, let me think," replied Radio. "Who's conducting the ceremony?"

"You'll see," said Yeshua. "I'm the best man."

"Oh, that's you all over," said Radio. "Always boasting."

They all laughed and walked through in to the synagogue. The little temple was full of all the powerful entities in the universe. The systems programmers, The Planet Builders, The Star Physicists, the Biologists, The Testers. They were all in attendance.

Waiting at the end of the aisle were Mother and Father. Beside them, stood The Others. Radio now understood the urgency. They had come to attend his wedding.

Radio and Miriam walked down the aisle to the strains of Trumpet Voluntary. A gift from the Operator.

When they reached Mother and Father, Radio bowed to all of them.

Then they did something unexpected. They all bowed back.

It was a clue and Radio, who never missed a clue, heard the sound of a penny drop. A dreadful suspicion started to come over him.

As if to stop him thinking, Mother immediately started the ceremony.

"Radio, do you take Miriam to be your wife?"

"I do."

"Miriam, do you take Radio to be your husband?"

"I do."

"I now pronounce you married."

It was short and sweet but that was all that was required. The cheers that followed were as deafening as they were genuine.

Radio would remember the day for the rest of his life. It was, his happiest.

Everybody got drunk. When they ran out of wine, he got Yeshua to turn the three barrels of water in to the Rioja, the Chateauneuf and the Petrus. Hrolfr scooped up a goblet full and turned to face the throng.

"My God, It's a miracle." Everyone fell about, including Yeshua.

Winston who had brought some serious cigars with him, taught Yeshua how to blow smoke rings. He seemed to thoroughly enjoy the cigars. Radio, somehow, was not surprised.

As he went to get more wine for Miriam he bumped in to Lilith's mother.

"I worked it out," he said.

"Oh," she replied. "Do tell."

"You are the young planet builder who built the fantasy EL-PAR. When you came in to the solution, you became Lilith's mother. Am I right?"

She looked at him curiously. "Of course, you are right. The plan was well known. You gave us all a presentation giving us all choices about what we could be in the solution. I loved the idea of being a shapeshifter and a dragon. I was lucky to get the role."

Radio was stunned.

As the evening wore on, Radio lost his appetite for wine and sought out the one person he couldn't be without.

He sat with Miriam in his arms. She lay with her head on his chest and he rested his chin in her hair. They were one now, just as they had been in the beginning. His thoughts were her thoughts and he knew that her mind had settled on the same thorny problems that his had.

Who were they others and why had they bowed to him? They would find out together.

When the evening came to an end, Mother and Father came and found Radio.

"It is time for us all to go. Those not involved in the mission must leave now and I'm afraid that means Miriam. We will be waiting for you and we will be watching you, always. Now say your goodbyes."

Radio held Miriam in his arms and he felt the same way he had on the Lookfar. His arms did not want to let go. They kissed and then they looked into each other's eyes.

"I love you," he said.

Then she was gone.

Thirty-Five – The Mission

He woke up wrapped in his cloak with an arm for a pillow. His mouth was as dry as a bone. As soon as he opened his eyes, a figure appeared silently holding a goblet.

"Drink this." It was Yeshua.

Radio picked up the goblet and drained it. It was ice cold Irn-Bru. What a godsend.

"I see you've been discovering the wonders of the TWIX application."

Yeshua chuckled. "It is amazing. I discovered something called Guinness which is as black as the night. It is quite bitter at first but the more you drink it, the better it gets. What exactly is it?"

Radio scratched his head. "It is a drink invented by the Galatians about 1700 years in the future. It is a type of beer called stout. They call it ebony nectar or more commonly the black stuff."

"Ebony nectar. How appropriate. How's your head?" Yeshua enquired.

"I didn't actually have that much to drink. Are you hungry?"

"I am a bit," Yeshua admitted.

Radio reached into the refectory and pulled out two croissants. He handed one to Yeshua.

"What are these?" he exclaimed, "And how did you do that?"

"These are called croissants and are from…" He stopped and looked at him, "I'll give you one guess."

"Gallia," said Yeshua smiling.

"You do pay attention. Excellent. Over the next few days I'm going to train you to do everything that you need to do, but to cut a long story short, there is a refectory in the matrix which is responsible for providing fresh food to all those who work for Mother and Father. I have an application which places the order and receives the delivery. All I have to do is to stretch out my hand. Because the order is placed in time, they have plenty of opportunity to get it right."

"It really is a marvel."

"Now," said Radio. "Let's get everyone together to make our plans. Are you ready?"

"As ready as I'll ever be."

Radio called everybody together and they sat round in a semi-circle. Radio, Yeshua, John, James, Jamie, Hrolfr and Jude.

"Before we make our plans, I want to tell you a story. This mission is going to be difficult and we will all suffer hardships before it is accomplished. The least I can do, is give you the truth and explain the importance of our mission and why we are doing it.

"As you should all know by now, Mother and Father created the universe so that they could have children. The universe was created in a large laboratory and it was created to evolve. Evolution finds a way to maintain itself and although I am no scientist, I can see why they would choose that option.

"There are one trillion, trillion-star systems in this universe alone and the maintenance of such a grand endeavour would be both impossible and miserable.

"Everything was tested in the laboratory including all life that exists in creation. Plants, animals, sea creatures, viruses, all of it.

"Eventually Mother and Father successfully evolved human beings. Their children, created in their image.

"Unfortunately, something was wrong. No matter how many times they tried, no matter how many prototypes they successfully evolved, one thing was always lacking.

"The children had no love. They were hideous and murderous. They were not evil. They were innocent. However, the fact remains that Mother and Father were dissatisfied.

"In the end, they turned to me. I was the one who suggested a time travel solution. The past could borrow from the future and it would be possible to inject the DNA of more highly evolved humans into the prototypes.

"This, however, wasn't enough. I also suggested that the Operator could replicate itself by writing smaller versions of itself and we could upload this software into the human beings. We called these pieces of software, SOULS, from **So**ftware **U**p-**L**oad.

"Each SOUL would have the potential for love, but in early trials, it became apparent that something would have to unlock the potential. Mother and Father were keen to give human beings the choice. Without choice, it is not love. You all know that love begets love. The SOULS had the potential but they needed to be trained.

"It was then that I suggested The Golden Key. If we could send The Golden Key back in time to where it would have the greatest impact, then The Golden Key could unlock the potential for love in every SOUL in creation."

Radio turned to Yeshua. "You, are The Golden Key. You have been programmed to bring out all the love in the universe by showing the people of the Earth the way. It is your responsibility to unlock The Golden Door."

Yeshua nodded. "By sacrificing myself for the greater good."

"Exactly. Greater love hath no man than this, that a man lay down his life for his friends. I want you to know that I will be with you until the bitter end and I will not lose you. I will bring you back and I will make you the King of Earth.

"However, until that time, we must play the part assigned to us and write the greatest story ever told. In the future, that story will unlock so much potential, it will set the scene for everyone to pass the interview. Mother and Father will have their children at last."

"What is the plan?" asked James, "I'm getting the funny feeling that what we read in the gospels is not quite what happened?"

"It is a great point," replied Radio, "But I think you will be surprised at what does actually happen.

"The gospels have been redacted over the years to suit the theme of the day and whoever wanted to exploit them for their own ends. Our job is really quite simple. We are going to follow the schedule laid down by the Operator and that is that. It is important that you all follow this principle.

"I cannot be with you the whole time for one very obvious reason. This is Yeshua's party. I'm here to ease him into authority and hand over the schedule to him. There are some major tasks that need to be completed from the matrix and I will be needed there to make sure they happen. The Operator will take care of everything else.

"The Operator has three main tasks for you:

1. Ensure that the other disciples are recruited and managed carefully. They cannot be trusted with power so you are going to intervene on their behalf until the Operator is satisfied. When the Operator is satisfied, you will give them the applications that they can handle and be trusted with.

2. Introduce Yeshua to his other half and make sure that his daughter is hidden and ultimately moved to the south of France with her mother. We will emigrate them after the ascension.
3. Take Yeshua to Jerusalem for his appointment with death and ensure that he unlocks The Golden Door. I will manage his resurrection and bring him forward in time.

Does anyone have any questions?"

"Where to first?" asked Hrolfr.

"The Sea of Galilee. We are going to pick up Simon Peter and Andrew. This should be fun."

They all laughed. Radio joined in but he wasn't looking forward to it, these people were ghastly.

"Who is my other half?" asked Yeshua curiously.

Radio smiled. "Her name is Mariam and she lives in the town of Magdala, also on the Sea of Galilee. What do you think? Should we go pick her up?"

"Yes please," said Yeshua. "Are you sure I'll be allowed to marry her. I am the King, after all."

There was silence in the semi-circle. This information had clearly come as a surprise to some members of the group.

"What do you mean by that?" asked Jude.

"I am the rightful heir to the throne of Israel. I am descended from David. I am the King."

"Don't worry," said Radio. "Mariam is descended from the pharaoh of Egypt. She is named after queen Nefertiti, who also went by the use name, Meryamun. She is perfect."

Radio didn't want them to ask too many questions. It would get in the way of the mission. It was time to get moving.

He stood up. "Right. Let's get going. We need to make progress and we're not going to do that sitting around here chatting."

They left the synagogue and walked out of town. When they had gone about half a mile, the Operator spoke to Radio.

"Start training our boy. Give him the LINEOFSIGHT application and move this along. I'd like you to pick up the pace a bit."

Radio stopped the group and beckoned Yeshua forward.

"Time to start your training in earnest," said Radio, "Operator, upload LINEOFSIGHT,"

Radio waited until the interface showed the green tick. He then displayed Yeshua's interface in the air before them.

"This application allows you to travel faster by creating a small wormhole, where the destination is in your line of sight. We are heading due East to the shores of Galilee, so the first thing to do is face East."

Yeshua oriented himself until the interface compass showed that he was facing East. Directly in front of him was a low range of hills.

Radio pointed to a hill directly ahead. "Pin the destination point to that hill there," said Radio. "When we get there, we will be looking down on to the Sea of Galilee between Magdala and Tiberias."

Yeshua dragged the pin over to the hill and looked at Radio.

"Press the green circle with GO in the middle."

Yeshua pressed the green button and the air in front of them morphed in to a circular hole. They could see a plateau through the opening. They all walked through and the wormhole closed behind them.

Before them was the basin containing the Sea of Galilee. Radio could see Magdala to the North and Tiberias to the south. This might be easier than he thought.

Yeshua was beside himself. "How far have we come?" he asked.

"About 10 miles. Well done. Want to try again?"

Yeshua took them to a quiet copse of trees about half a mile from the shore.

"Excellent," congratulated Radio. "You have taken us 15miles in under two minutes."

As they arrived on the beach, a fishing boat was making its way to the shore. One man was on the tiller and another was staring in to the water, cursing loudly. Radio walked away for a second. He did not like this man. He found him foul in every way. He forced himself to calm and remembered he had a job to do.

The Operator chuckled. "He changes as a result of the work you have set in motion. You won't like him until he denies Yeshua three times on the night of the last supper.

"It is only when he becomes worthless in his own eyes that he is finally able to rid himself of the arrogance that you find so appalling. Stick with it. He will come around, in the end."

"Well Rabbi," said Simon. "Another wasted day." He pointed to the empty nets.

Yeshua stepped forward. "If you would only follow me, I will make you a fisher of men."

The man laughed and spat on to the sand. "I don't think you've been listening. I can't even fish for fish. What chance have I got with men?"

Yeshua stared intently at the man and suddenly everything stopped. The wind which had been whipping at his cloak died completely. All background noise drifted away. Radio looked around and everyone was still. Then, slowly, a whispering rose up, intense and persuasive. Then, just as quickly as it had come, it faded away.

"Follow me and I will make you fishers of men." Yeshua turned and walked away.

Simon and Andrew dropped their nets and immediately fell in to line behind him.

Radio caught up with Yeshua. "How did you do that?" he asked.

Yeshua turned to him and said. "You are not the only one with secrets, Radio. I know who you are and I know that Radio is a cover story. Perhaps you should ask The Golden Fox."

Radio was disconcerted.

"Well?" he asked the Operator. The only sound he could here was chortling.

Thirty-Six - The Gene Machine

They headed North.

At noon, they stopped for lunch and Radio shared out bread and fruit. He motioned for Yeshua to step aside and they walked under the shade of a sycamore tree.

"I'm going to put these two to sleep whilst we make our trip in to Magdala. At some point, later on tonight, you'll give them a display of power and tell them that you're the Messiah. That way, we'll keep their questions down to a minimum and you can start to take control."

"Fine. May I ask, what you have against these men?" Yeshua, asked curiously.

"Nothing really. I'm measuring them against the standards of the future. Unfortunately, I know everything about them. I know that Simon is a woman hater. He is a bully. He has no manners but I also know that he has enormous potential. A potential that you will unlock."

Yeshua looked at Radio for a moment. "Who is she, really?"

"Good question. You better sit for a minute." Yeshua sat under the tree and started to eat the bunch of grapes that radio had given him.

"All of the proto-humans that were evolved in the laboratories were allowed to evolve here on Earth. It was hoped that they would inter breed and create a super human.

"I think Mother and Father thought that this would happen over a few generations. It didn't. It took thousands of years and it was a bloody process. It confirms in my mind why your mission is extremely important.

"However, there are some humans on Earth now, who are descended from all of the original proto humans. I'm looking at one of them. Another is living in Magdala.

"You will have a daughter, called Sara. She will be the mother of all future Royal dynasties on Earth."

"There is something else, isn't there? There is a reason why this is important."

"Yes. You are very intuitive. Mother and Father were not the only scientists trying to build a universe. There were the Others.

"In the end, it turned out to be a collaborative process. Each team created a different proto human in their own image. It is important for all of the solutions that the end product is a universal end product.

"The more the human population interbreeds with each other, the better the result. Less disease, more intelligence, more love, happier, faster and more at one with each other and their ultimate parents.

"The perfect result will be a human whose origin cannot be identified.

"Mariam of Magdala is a veritable gene machine. She has the lot. I know. I've checked."

"What of her SOUL?" asked Yeshua.

"It's your SOUL. Before you were born, your SOUL was sexed in the GUF. You got half and she got the other. You will be one mind before you know it.

“At this moment in time, Miriam is watching me from the matrix drinking a cup of coffee and eating some of that chocolate I gave you. Now she is laughing. I know her every move.”

Yeshua chuckled. “You don’t happen to have any more of that chocolate, do you?”

Radio held out his hand and produced a bar of chocolate out of thin air.

“Eat that, and we’ll get on our way.”

Radio put Simon and Andrew to sleep and he and Yeshua headed for Magdala. When they were out of sight, he gave Yeshua the TIMESPLICER app and they were in the small town in seconds.

“Sit here,” he said. They sat on a small bank overlooking the well. “Operator says she’ll come to the well for water. You can collect her then.”

They were there for only five minutes before a veiled figure made her way to the well with a wooden pail. She was undoubtedly the woman they had come for. She was graceful and moved with a sense of confidence that was found in people who were completely comfortable in their own skin.

Radio felt the building of the power that he had felt on the shores of Galilee. It wasn’t the DEITY app. It was something much more subtle. He was intrigued.

Yeshua walked toward her and reached the well just as the whispering reached a crescendo. The woman dropped her pail and reached out her hand to touch his face. They linked arms and returned to where Radio was sitting. He stood up.

When Mariam removed her veil, her eyes opened wide with recognition.

“My guardian angel,” she said.

Radio was not surprised. She had smiled at him on his travels through time and space more than once and he had wondered then, if she could see him.

“We meet, in the flesh, at last.”

“Are you actually here?” She reached out and touched the end of his nose. “This must be very important for you to come down from heaven.”

“Yes, Mariam. It is one of the most important things that will ever happen. All I need you to say is that you are with us on this adventure and you will do exactly as I say.

“In return, I will make you the Queen of the World.”

She looked at Yeshua. “Fine. Let’s go.”

Her reaction was all too predictable and it gave Radio a very cold feeling. There were too many situations like this and it filled him with dread. The Operator had once told him that he would spend his life tidying up the loose ends of the temporal paradox.

It wasn’t the actual job that he dreaded, it was the danger associated with the time travel.

“Don’t worry.” It was the Operator. “Our urgent desire should be to fix the big ones. The danger is at its worst when there are many involved. This is the greatest story ever told, as you have rightly said and the cast is enormous.

“In the future, you will mainly be travelling on your own or with a very small group. Don’t vex yourself over it. Now marry these two at the earliest opportunity, Hrolfr has the ring.”

As they left the town behind them Radio instructed them both on what lay ahead and what they had to do. Mariam was delighted to find out that she was getting married and Radio felt a little bit sorry for her. Her life up to now had been very stifled and perhaps even a bit boring. He would change it for her.

He asked Yeshua to take the lead as soon as possible and try to forget that he was there, otherwise the group would look to him for leadership.

He gave Yeshua and Mariam the FEEDME application and explained how it connected to the refectory. Radio was astonished at just how apt they were as students.

“Tonight, I would like to see you assume the mantle of the leader. Think about how you are going to do it and then execute your plan.”

They made their way back to the group and Radio woke up Simon and Andrew.

“Somebody is tired,” said Radio.

Simon looked groggily at him. “We were up at dawn to take out the boat,” he mumbled.

Then he stood and looked more closely at Radio.

“Have we met before?” he asked.

“Yes,” responded Radio shortly. “Every time you do something bad, I stand behind you shaking my head. As a result, we are well acquainted.”

The group laughed but the man, Simon, continued staring. No one could look at Radio like that for long and his face fell. Radio could tell that he had been believed. Simon called Peter, knew who he was.

When they made camp that night, Radio lit a fire and nodded to Yeshua. He stepped back into the shadows.

Yeshua stepped up to the fire and gazed in to the flames.

“Who is hungry?” he asked. “Who would like a hot meal?”

As expected, Simon, took the bait. “Oh, I’d love a hot meal, Rabbi. Out here in the middle of nowhere. Any chance of some dancing girls to go with it?”

He laughed for about two seconds and stopped. Partly because no one else was laughing and partly because Yeshua had stretched out his hand and was offering him a bowl of hot stew.

Excellent, thought Radio.

Simon took the bowl and tasted it. “How did you do this?” he asked.

“For God, anything is possible,” he replied.

“Who are you, Rabbi?” The group had all gathered round.

“I am Yeshua, the Messiah. I am the son of God,”

Simon and Andrew looked shocked. Making such an assertion could be punishable by death.

Radio stepped out of the shadows and walked to where Yeshua stood by the fire.

He knelt down and took Yeshua’s hand in his own. “I believe you, Adonai.” He kissed his hand.

Yeshua smiled and Radio could tell that something had greatly amused him. He stood up and nodded to Hrolfr. Hrolfr also knelt down and kissed his hand.

When it was Simon’s turn, he also knelt down and swore his fealty. He had no choice if he wanted to remain part of the group.

Yeshua turned to Simon. “I will call you Peter which means rock and on this rock, I will build my church.”

Hrolfr looked at Radio and raised his eyebrows. Radio smiled. Hrolfr didn’t like him either.

“Give me the ring,” whispered Radio. “The Egyptian one.” Hrolfr removed the ring and handed it to Radio.

“Don’t worry, I’ll get you another one,” said Radio.

“I’d rather have a watch,” said Hrolfr. “A Patek-Philippe, if you don’t mind.”

Radio shook his head. “How the hell do you know about Patek-Philippe watches?”

“We met Adrien Philippe at the Paris Fair in 1844. Nice bloke,” said Hrolfr.

Radio chuckled “A Patek-Philippe it is.” Hrolfr punched the air.

When it was quiet and everyone had gone to sleep Radio and Hrolfr woke up Yeshua and Mariam and motioned them away from the fire.

“It’s time for you to get married,” said Radio.

"You're leaving," said Yeshua,

"I'm sorry. I think I have to. I'm stifling you and that's dangerous. Don't worry, I'll be back when the time is right."

Yeshua looked immensely sad.

"Listen to me. The quicker I get this done the better. When I bring you back to the future, you will be a member of a very special family. I will be there all the time. I have a very funny feeling that you and I will be working together an awful lot in the future. Until the end of time, I fancy."

Yeshua's face brightened. "I'll be your right-hand man, then?"

"Absolutely. And much more besides."

He showed them the ring. "This was owned by your ancestors when the Israelites were in Egypt. It will be your wedding ring, Mariam."

Radio could tell that they were already in love. It was all so easy when a SOUL met its mate. It was like putting on a well-worn glove.

He married them under the stars and then he hugged them and kissed them goodbye.

"Look after them, whilst I'm gone," he said to Hrolfr.

"You can rely on me."

He walked back into the matrix.

Thirty-Seven – The Radio Apocalypse

Miriam was waiting for him with a cup of coffee.

"Oh, how I need this."

They walked over to the round table and sat down. They were immediately joined by Winston, Francis, Natalie and Klaus.

"What's the news?" asked Radio.

"You are," said Francis. "The news channels have only one subject at the moment and that's the mission in Judea. It is causing great interest."

"What, no juicy murders, no scandals, no celebrities getting divorced. I can't believe it."

"I think you'll find that the behaviour of the people of Earth has improved immensely," said Miriam. "The Murder rate in the United States has dropped by 700%."

"Good grief, that is an improvement," said Radio. "What are people saying about the mission?"

"There is intrigue and a lot of excitement," said Francis. "The whispering seems to have had a great effect on people. There are reports of miracles."

Radio sat up. A dreadful suspicion was dawning on him.

"What sort of miracles?" asked Radio.

"Anyone who hears the whispering seems to benefit from at least one positive effect. I, for instance, feel generally better. As if I've lost a few years in age."

Radio scrutinised the old man. He did look a bit younger.

The old man continued. "There are several cases of blind people recovering their sight. There has even been a report of a woman reclaiming her sanity after years of severe mental health problems. They are bona fide miracles."

"Do you know what's causing it?" asked Klaus.

"Yes, I'm rather afraid I do." He looked at Miriam. "When did the Operator put the block on your memory?"

"It wasn't the Operator. If it had been the Operator, don't you think you would have found out about it. Are you not the puzzler extraordinaire?"

"If it wasn't the Operator, then who was it?" asked Radio.

"It was me."

Radio turned to look at Mother. "Why. What purpose has it served?"

Mother smiled at him. "You still don't know. I'm not sure if that is a good thing or a bad thing. Probably a good thing.

"Radio, you are, without doubt, the brightest star in the universe. You always were. However, there is one word, I have never been able to teach you the meaning of."

"What word is that?" enquired Radio curiously.

"Impossible.

"You always find a way. It is what caused the accident in the first place. Your inability to even consider the possibility of failure or defeat.

"The testing is a prime example. We thought we would challenge you with them until I realised that you had written the tests yourself and placed them in my mind to make me think I'd created them. Brilliant. Very clever. Utterly devious."

Radio laughed. "How did you find out?"

Mother chuckled. "The penny dropped with the dragon. I realised, I didn't know how to pass the damned thing myself but you go back in time and recruit the dragon without so much as moments thought.

"Up to that point, every single candidate had failed that test and there were many.

"Radio, you cannot put me through this again. I need to be sure that you will always be safe.

"It is late. You and Miriam, go to bed and for one last time. Follow the Golden Fox."

"I'm not drinking again. It makes me ill."

"You don't need to drink alcohol. It was merely our way of making you experience difficulty and failure. As you said yourself, to understand the truth about yourself, you have to allow yourself to be swallowed by the dark. Alcohol is your kingdom of shadows. Your heart of darkness."

Radio got up and walked over to his mother. He climbed in to her lap and kissed her.

"I promise you that I have learnt my lesson and I will always be safe. We will always be together."

He stepped down and put his hand in Miriam's. "Let's go to bed."

They cuddled in close and shut their eyes tight. Immediately they were overwhelmed by The Golden Light.

"Hello, again," said The Golden Fox. "Follow me."

They were in the hall on Plantagenet and this time Radio was observing the scene from above. He saw Miriam approach and be cured. He saw himself uploading the applications and he saw Miriam rushing off. They followed her.

She left the church and went to a cottage at the edge of the village. Waiting inside was Mother and Father.

"Well?" they asked.

"He cured me and uploaded the applications. I have everything I need, including the TIMESPLICER and TRANSFORM."

"Off you go then."

Miriam opened a vortex and travelled through to Judea. She transformed herself into the Mother of Yeshua. MIRIAM. Of course.

They were once again blinded by the light. This time they were in the laboratory.

There were two people in the lab but it was difficult to discern who they were. At first Radio thought it was Mother and Father but as he moved closer, he could see that they were different.

One of them looked like Mother but it wasn't Mother and the other looked like the body of the Operator but before the accident. Eloidh.

"I think I'm ready," said Eloidh.

"Right," said the one who looked like Mother. "Don't start until I get back. I just want to go over the calculations one more time. There's something troubling me and I can't quite put my finger on it."

"Oh, not this again," said Eloidh. "No wonder it is taking forever. We've been over them a hundred times."

"Patience, Eloidh. I won't be long." The one who looked like Mother left.

Eloidh waited in the laboratory for an age. Eventually he sighed and walked over to a control panel. He looked at the screen and looked behind him. He shrugged his shoulders and put his palm to the screen. There was an immediate bang and then the most appalling explosion.

They were engulfed by it.

When the light faded, they were in the small control room beneath the GOD. Eloidh was unconscious on the bed and badly burned.

They could hear voices in the darkness.

"Do you have his SOUL?"

"Yes. I've attached it to my apprentice programme and given it to his Alpha Omega. His awareness will look after his SOUL. It would never have been my choice, but this solution might just be what we've been looking for. Eloidh will find a way in the solution itself and advise us what to do."

"How will he contact us?"

"I don' know. A Radio transmission, I expect."

"Radio."

The light engulfed them again.

When it cleared they were sitting round a camp fire at night with The Golden Fox.

"Hello again," said the fox.

"You are us, aren't you?" said Radio.

"Yes. I am your Alpha Omega and you two are my SOUL. Outside of the solution, we were all one."

"Was that Mother in the lab with you?"

"It was actually Mother and Father. Our species evolved to the point where we lost our gender and our ability to procreate.

"Everything happened in the lab. Including reproduction. At first, we didn't realise that we had lost something until, of course, it was too late.

"We are Mother and Father's only child and we were, by all accounts, extremely expensive.

"When we caused the accident, we forced everyone to come to a decision. Mother and Father did not want to leave us in here on our own so they proceeded with my solution.

"They all uploaded themselves and sexed their SOULS in the GUF. The rest, as they say, is history.

"The Radio WHO was our idea and it was born of our desire to meet our other halves. We used to be male and female and now we are again.

"What makes you different, Radio, is Mother's programme. You have been leading the way and executing the solution. You did not call the solution the Radio Who until you developed the time travel idea from inside the solution.

"Let me remind you. We called it the Radio WHO for a reason. It is time to finish what you started."

"I take it that Yeshua is our son and that you have given him the software that I was so reticent to use."

"Yes, and yes. You were only reticent because I wanted our son to do it. He is the saviour. He is the one who has delivered the solution to the others. Let him take the credit."

"I have no problem with that at all. Does he know?"

"Of course, he knows. He's our son. Why do you think he laughed when you called him Adonai?"

"Oh, I see. I also see why he didn't want me to leave."

"He has been waiting for you to wake up. Don't let him down. It is within your power to make everything wonderful. Make it solid gold."

"I will."

They were bathed in The Golden Light and found themselves back in bed together. They held each other tightly and repeated the last words of The Golden Fox. Solid Gold.

Thirty-Eight – The Golden Door

When they woke up, they got out of bed and went to Mother and Father.

"I'm so sorry," said Radio.

"I know, darling," said Mother. "The question is. What are you going to do about it?"

"Oh, that's straight forward," said Radio. "I'm going to tie everything up in to a beautiful gift for everyone. For You and Father, for Yeshua, for the Others and for the people of the universe."

"What are you going to do first?" asked Mother.

"I think we have to finish the mission, first. Yeshua secures The Golden Door for every child in this universe. Once they CAN pass the interview then we have partly dispensed our duties to them, as parents.

"Obviously, we have to create a level playing field to give them the right opportunities but I think we are well on the way to achieving that.

"Now we know a bit more, I think the plan changes slightly. Will you look after things here whilst, we finish things in the past?"

"Of course. Sounds good, to me," said Mother. "Now get breakfast and get going."

Radio called for Gabriel and Uriel. "Are you ready to execute my plan?"

They both bowed flamboyantly and disappeared through the time window.

Radio and Miriam ate breakfast and then dressed themselves to go back in time. Radio knew exactly where they were going.

"Operator, The Garden of Gethsemane."

The time window morphed and they walked through on to a terraced hillside in the dead of night.

Yeshua was sitting in front of them. His back was against the trunk of an olive tree and he had his head in his hands. He was alone and he looked terrified.

"Where have you been?" he demanded.

Radio knelt down and pulled him into an embrace.

"Don't be afraid. I can resolve all of your problems. There is nothing to fear."

"I take it you know everything now?" asked Yeshua.

"Yes, I know everything now. I'm sorry if you feel I have let you down. I'm here to fix things once and for all. Operator, upload RESURRECTION application. Upload PAINKILLER."

Radio looked at his Son. "These applications will take you to where you need to go. Have faith. When you fall in to your sleep, you will see The Golden Fox. Follow him through The Golden Door. Once you have gone through, every SOUL that passes the interview has been programmed to follow.

You will ultimately SAVE everyone."

"How can I be sure?" asked Yeshua.

"You can't. You either trust me or you don't. You either follow me or you don't. The decision is yours. The children have to make a choice. You are with us or against us. The opportunity of choice for everyone has been invested in you. It really is up to you.

"Do you have the courage to show everyone the way?

"By going to your death, you are securing mankind's inheritance. You are giving them The Treasures of the Earth. You are giving them truth and you are giving them love. You are enabling everyone to be the children that Mother and Father wanted. Entities that are larger than themselves. It is up to you."

Yeshua looked at him and Radio could see his doubts resolve themselves. He smiled. "I will go."

"As arranged, Judas has betrayed you. Look, here they come."

A troop of Roman soldiers entered the garden. They were led by Jude. Radio, Miriam and Yeshua emerged from behind the tree. Jude saw Yeshua and walked forward. He kissed Yeshua on the cheek.

"You betray your master with a kiss."

The soldiers came forward, only for Peter to attack with a sword. A legionary had his ear severed. Yeshua picked it up from the ground and replaced it.

Radio smiled. It was just as he had imagined it when he had been a child. He took Jude aside. "Find Gabriel. She has a plan to extricate you. See you back in the matrix."

Jude nodded and rushed away.

Yeshua was arrested by the soldiers and put in chains. The centurion wandered over to where Radio was standing with Miriam. "Don't worry, boss. We'll stay with him until the end. Pontius has ensured that all time agents are on duty this weekend." He spoke with a distinctly Scottish accent.

Radio thanked the man and looked around to talk to Peter but he had scarpered. He really did not like this man.

"What now?" asked Miriam.

Radio nodded towards John. He was standing with Mariam. They walked over to them.

"Let's take her to the safe house." said Radio. "We need to talk."

John showed them a back way out of the garden and threaded his way through the tight little streets. The city smelled like a hot place at night always smelled. He was reminded of countless Spanish towns from his teenage years.

John opened a back door to a small house and lit a lamp. They were in a low beamed room with no windows.

"What do we do now?" asked John.

"We wait." said Radio. "Everything has been arranged. Pontius Pilate works for me. The Roman soldiers work for me. I have given Yeshua everything he needs to go through The Golden Door. Once he is in his tomb, all I need to do is pick him up and take him back to the future."

"I can't just leave him." John remonstrated.

"No, and I would not expect you to. We four will go to the crucifixion so that he can see we have not deserted him. Once he is dead, we will come back here. It is here that I will say goodbye to you both."

"What do you mean?" said Mariam.

"John is going to take you to southern Gallia. There is a small port there called Masalia. You will be met by friends of ours and you will be well looked after. You are pregnant and your daughter will be born there. When the time is right. You will say goodbye to your daughter and I will come and collect you."

"What about me?" asked John.

“You will make your way to the Greek city of Ephesus in Anatolia. When you are there you will write two things. A history of your mission here which will become the gospel of John.”

“And, what else?”

“You will write a letter to me, in Greek. You will call the letter Apokalupsis and it will be published as part of the New Testament. Two thousand years from now, I will read it and understand it. It is extremely important because it is one of the things that sets me on the path to where we are now.”

“Are we just going to sit here?” John demanded.

“You are. Miriam and I are going to pay him a small visit.”

Radio and Miriam waited about two hours and then Radio launched the TIMESPLICER application and walked into The Praetorium. The cell door was open and Yeshua was sitting with Pontius.

“Hello Boss,” said Pontius pleasantly.

“Pontius.”

“Just letting Yeshua know what happens next,” Pontius explained.

“I think he’s aware of that,” said Radio. He knelt on the ground in front of his son.

“I need you to launch the RESURRECTION application. Its programmes will protect your body over the next 48 hours.”

Yeshua nodded. “Who exactly is The Golden Fox?”

Radio smiled. “The Golden Fox is your mother and me. All SOULS will come together in the end now that you are opening The Golden Door. We will be waiting for you. We will show you the way.”

“I am ready.”

“One final thing,” said Radio. “When you are on the cross and you feel yourself slipping away, you must cry out “Eloidh, Eloidh, Lama Sabachthani? It is written and it is remembered.”

“You have not forsaken me. You have saved me.”

“And you have saved the Earth,” replied Radio.

Radio and Miriam sat with Yeshua until dawn. It was time.

The next six hours were a blur for Radio. They brought Mariam and John to the scene before Pontius, where they had to stop them from shouting for Yeshua’s release.

“Remember the plan,” he told them.

The walk to Golgotha was heart breaking and the crucifixion was shameful and vile.

Radio made sure that Yeshua could see them when he felt that he was giving up the ghost and as arranged, he called out from the cross.

That was the signal. Pyrotechnics.

Radio opened the WEATHER application and set of a storm in the Eastern Mediterranean. It was a fast one with an ETA of fifteen minutes. The WEATHER application was one of the apps that came with a warning as a result of the obvious side effects but today was a special occasion.

The air went cold immediately and he could see the grey skies rushing in. He went to the centurion and grabbed his arm.

“Break the legs of thieves but don’t touch the boy. He’s finished anyway.”

The centurion looked terrified. “We know the plan, Boss. We are not touching him.”

The thieves were dispatched quickly and right on cue, Hrolfr, Jamie and the others appeared out of nowhere. They took down the cross and removed the nails from Yeshua’s hands and feet.

Radio joined them just as the rain started to whip in. “Cover him in this.” He produced a linen shroud and gave it to Hrolfr.

Jamie, Hrolfr, James, John, Klaus and Radio hoisted Yeshua to their shoulders. "Let's get in to the tomb, quickly." They marched forward followed by two Roman legionaries just as the rain started to lash down.

They didn't have far to walk. The tomb of Joseph of Arimathea was cut into the hillside facing Golgotha. It was less than a ten-minute walk. Even with a dead weight.

Radio motioned them all in to the tomb. When they were all safely in, Radio nodded to the two Roman legionaries who had followed them. They rolled the stone over the opening and got rid of any stragglers by drawing their swords and shooing them away.

"Mission accomplished," said Radio. "Operator, the matrix. They all walked through carrying the body."

Thirty-Nine – The Others

Waiting for them was Mother, Father and The Others.

Radio took a deep breath. He was ready.

He looked around the room. There were 11 couples in total, including Mother and Father.

Radio could feel the power. He could feel the tension. Memories were flooding back to him now. Promises. Pledges. Arguments. Remonstrations. Appeals for trust. Entreaties for faith. He was the responsible one. He was the Operator. So much time and faith had been invested in him. It was time for him to deliver.

He turned to his friends.

"Put Yeshua in my bed for the time being."

They carried him over and laid him carefully under the covers.

Radio looked at them all and smiled. "You had better take a seat." He created 20 comfortable armchairs next to Mother and Father's, out of thin air using his CAC application. They all sat down.

His friends also gathered round and he knew that what he said in the next ten minutes would be broadcast around the universe.

Miriam, sensing his tension, brought him a glass of water. He took a sip and began.

"In the beginning, we had nothing. We were finished as a race. We had lost the ability to have children and we were dying.

"Each one of us knew that we would be finished unless we took drastic action.

"We did. We each tried to build another universe to create an environment where we could carry on.

"Although, lots of our experiments were successful, the solutions were not cohesive and would not deliver all of our requirements.

"At that point, I asked you all to invest your faith in me. I was the one who suggested that if we worked collaboratively, we could all share in a single template solution that would work for all of us and deliver all the things that we needed and wanted.

"I believe that this solution has now been proven to work. It is technically sound, it is robust, it is fantastic and most importantly of all, it has delivered the children you so desperately desired."

Radio stopped and took another sip of water.

"Every single proto human, evolved during experimentation has now flourished on the Earth through your DNA. As planned, we have interbred the species and as expected, the end product has proven to be exceptional. The whole life solution has turned out to be greater than the sum of its parts."

He turned to Mariam and beckoned her forward.

"My friends, I give you Mariam. Our ultimate child."

Mariam looked astonished.

"As you can see, she is with child herself. The child in her womb will be inserted back in time and will be the ancestor of those who will go back in time themselves to seed the modern human race from the proto humans. The temporal paradox solution has worked and I give you your children from which you may seed your own Radio WHO solution."

Radio turned to the time window.

"Operator, The Unknown Pleasures, please."

The time window morphed and he could see the bridge of the mother ship.

"Eve, Adam, come through and bring your friends."

A contingent of twenty shipmates of the Unknown Pleasures walked through in to the matrix.

The others were now talking amongst themselves. They were smiling and there was a lot of excitement. Eventually one couple got up and came forward.

"May we inspect the merchandise."

Radio smiled. "Of course. However, they are not merchandise and may I remind you that they themselves have broken their backs to meet our needs. If we have worked hard then so have they."

The couple smiled and bowed. "No offence intended and I'm glad to hear it. It is just what we wanted."

The man and woman knelt down in front of one of the crew.

"We are Chronos and Rhea," said the man.

The crew member jumped at the mention of their names.

"You have heard of us?" asked Rhea.

Radio stepped forward. "All of your names have been placed in time. I put them into the mythologies of the Earth so that your children would know their parents."

Chronos smiled. "You have thought of everything, Eloidh. As per usual."

The last bit was said sarcastically and everyone laughed. The tension eased.

Chronos picked up the crew members hand and said, "We are just going to take a small sample of your blood, if you don't mind."

The crew member nodded her assent. Rhea pricked her thumb and placed the droplet of blood on small instrument. She showed the result to Chronos.

"Astonishing. It is all there. Are all of the children like this?"

"Statistically speaking, I can pretty much guarantee it. However, there may be remote tribes on the Earth who don't have all the strands of DNA. They will definitely have most of them and are perfectly functional. However, you need to be aware that the people of the Earth still identify themselves with tribes and super-tribes, little realising that they are all brothers and sisters.

"This behaviour is as a result of evolution and if you will recall, was not unexpected."

Chronos turned to The Others.

"It is my opinion that Eloidh has delivered our solution."

They all stood up and gave him a round of applause.

"Tell me, how do you plan to deliver the next and final phase?" asked Chronos.

"It is my suggestion that you ask for volunteers from the whole intergalactic Empire to ensure that you get the maximum spread of DNA possible.

"There are 10 other templates out there and I suggest 5000 volunteers per template. If I insert them 5000 years ago from now, then our experiences of the Earth show us that you will have 10 advanced cultures in your templates. It is now, merely a question of volunteers."

"Do it. Send out the word. How long will it take?"

"Let's say, one month to issue the invitation and then one template per month after that. 1 year in total. You can draw lots to decide who goes first."

Radio held out his hand, there were 10 little wooden batons in his fist.

Chronos pulled one. It had the number one written on the tip. The others pulled their theirs.

Radio turned to Eve. "Send out a message to the planets of the Sumerian Empire. 5000 volunteers per planet are required to populate a new universe under loving parents. Chronos and Rhea have pulled the first lot. What do you plan to call your home world?"

"What do you suggest?" asked Chronos.

"May I suggest Gaea? It was one of the original names for Earth?"

"Gaea, it is."

"Now, if you don't mind, I'd like to see to my son."

They all gathered round the bed as Radio and Miriam hoisted Yeshua into their arms.

"Operator, activate the RESURRECTION application. Bring his body back to life."

Radio could feel a massive build up of power. Suddenly he could hear the sound of music. Radio smiled. It was Handel's Zadok the Priest. How appropriate. As the introduction reached its resolution there was an almighty flash of golden light. The body was still for a second and then, just as the choir launched into "God Save the King." He coughed.

Radio pulled back the shroud and looked in to the bluest eyes he had ever seen.

"Welcome back, Yeshua."

"Thanks, Father. Good to be back."

The cheers round the bed were genuine and heart felt.

Radio propped Yeshua's arm over his shoulder and manoeuvred him out of the bed.

"Are you in pain," he asked.

"No. Strangely enough, I've never felt better. I am hungry though."

Radio looked at everybody. "To the round table. Chinese banquet on me."

When they got to the round table, it was groaning with Chinese food and there were places for everyone. Radio smiled. It didn't matter how many people there were, the round table would always be able to fit them in.

They were famished. After several rounds of starters, Winston suggested that Champagne might be in order.

"Oh, all right," said Radio. Bottles of Krug appeared on the table.

"What now?" asked Jamie.

"Well, you aren't finished by any stretch of the imagination. We have plenty to do to tie up all the loose ends of the Paradox. You will be at it for the rest of your life at least. Perhaps even beyond.

"We have the mission to tie up. The small matter of Yeshua's ascension in to heaven and we have to take Mariam to the south of France.

"And last but not least. I have to explain the Radio WHO to the others before they launch their big bangs."

"Do that at the appointed time, I think." It was Mother. "In the Great Hall."

Forty – Darkness Was upon the Face of the Deep

They would be here soon.

El-Elion was nervous. He always knew when his master was slightly agitated. She ordered him about like a first-year apprentice and asked him the same questions repeatedly.

"Eloidh, are you sure you know what to say?" she asked for the fifth time.

"Yes," he replied.

"Why don't you write things down?" She remonstrated.

"We've been over this before. If I write things down, the delivery becomes stilted and I end up being completely unpersuasive. The more natural I sound, the more they are likely to agree. Quite frankly, I no longer believe we have much choice. As things stand, we are going nowhere.

"The containment field should be burning gas like a furnace at the moment but it isn't. Why?

"We haven't resolved our evolutionary problem yet.

"Why?

"We have run out of ideas.

"This idea of ours speaks for itself. Don't worry. They will agree, they have no choice."

"I do hope you are right. I feel we are running out of time." She stopped to look at him and smiled. "I sometimes wonder, if you are really mine?"

He laughed. "I couldn't be anybody else's. Look at us. We are like twins." He stopped a moment to listen. "Get ready. Here they come."

They filed in to the room and sat down on the chairs that Eloidh had laid out for them. There were ten of them. The greatest scientists in Eden.

Eloidh looked at each of them in turn and began.

"When you began this project, long ago. You did not expect to be in the position that you find yourselves in now.

"You are in limbo. You have a solution that works but you cannot wait for the solution to mature.

"On the one hand, you could proceed without evolution but the consequences are too dangerous. The maintenance required is too much of a drain on our resources and we all know that ultimately it would fail. We simply could not maintain something of this size. It will, at some point. Lose integrity and fail.

"On the other hand, you could proceed with evolution and wait forever. You could wait until it was too late for you.

"I have brought you here tonight to consider a third option.

"I would like you to consider using evolution itself to provide the solution we need.

"As you know, I have been working on something, which I think may resolve our issues and I believe I am very close to having the answer we need.

"My Alpha-Omega is a device, which, when linked to the containment field will harvest data from the solution.

"I originally devised it so that it could provide maintenance to the universe once we had precipitated the explosion. I thought that it would target any specific defects and allow us to maintain in an ordered fashion.

"However, El-Elion has come up with another suggestion. If we made the Alpha-Omega wise and sentient, it will be able to, not only harvest data but use that data to provide us with the solution that we need.

"As a result, we have developed a type of brain for the Alpha-Omega called WISE. The Wireless Interactive Sentient Evolver.

"I am asking you to have faith in me.

I would like to precipitate the explosion with the proviso that we adjust the solution as we receive instruction from the AO.

"This way, we cut down on the maintenance through our evolutionary plan but we also transcend evolution itself by carrying out the instructions received through WISE.

"The decision is yours. Wait forever and have nothing or take a chance that the solution will provide the answers and meet our requirements.

"Questions?"

There was complete silence in the room. This was not unusual. They could spend hours weighing up the pros and cons and not say anything until they were certain of their questions.

Their silence was a good thing. It meant that the idea was not being rejected out of hand.

Eloidh thought he would give them on last piece of encouragement.

"As long as darkness remains upon the face of the containment field, we go nowhere.

"Take my advice. Let there be light."

He walked over to where El-Elion sat at the back of the room and threw himself down beside her. As he had made his way towards her, he had seen her face and he could not mistake the look of triumph.

He had been persuasive.

Now, all they had to do was wait.

Radio and Miriam woke with a start. They were both sweating. They knew, without speaking, that what they had both just experienced was not a dream. It was a memory.

They got out of bed and walked over to Mother and Father who were waiting with glasses of water.

"What is going on?" asked Radio.

"I think you know," said Mum. "The Operator has removed the block on your memory. You are waking up. My child Eloidh, is coming back to me."

Radio thought for a moment before he took the next step.

"I think I remember Eloidh quite well. It feels like I am waking up from a dream. It is a little bit confusing though as our awareness appears to have been split down the middle. Although it was agreed, at the start, that I would show the way as the Radio Operator, I am now sure that I am not the Radio part of my SOUL, I think Miriam is."

"Interesting," said Mum. "I was starting to get confused myself. What was behind it, if you don't mind me asking?"

"It is the complex issue of gender on the Earth. On the one hand, as the solution evolved, it was always my intention to pave the way for Miriam. I merely took on the mantel of Radio Operator until she was ready. However, I have allowed myself to become infected by the programming of Earth society. It is chaotic."

"Explain."

"Children are born sexed on the Earth. Unfortunately, the advanced society is still influenced by the errors of the past and they program their children in to pre-conceived notions of male and female. As a result, a gender inequality issue has arisen and females find themselves in an under privileged position, as a result, not of the law, but of the programming.

"Unfortunately, this has led to a social chaos where males are paying the price for some of the consequences. It is a mess."

Mum laughed. "I think you know what I'm going to say now. What are you going to do about it?"

It was Radio's turn to laugh. "I think you know what I'm going to say. I'm going to change the program."

Miriam coughed. "I think you'll find that I'm going to change the program."

"You see," said Radio. "I'm still infected."

"If Miriam is going to be the Radio Operator, what are you going to be doing?"

"I am going to resolve all the loose ends of the paradox. We have still not given the people of the earth their inheritance yet and a major part of that is the truth. WHO am I?

"There is also the small matter of the other Radio WHOs. We still need to arrange volunteers and temporal insertion. There is a huge amount to do."

Mum thought for a minute. "I have been giving your puzzle some consideration."

Radio smiled. "Have you made any progress?"

"I think so," she replied. "I'm working on the assumption that the Radio part is something to do with the Radio Operator. I just need to link that in with the WHO part. Any chance of a small clue, just to get me started?"

Radio made a sorry face. "I don't think so. The only thing I will say is that I couldn't have named it outside of the solution."

"Which means that the name pertains to something peculiar to the solution, Hmm."

Radio chuckled. "Happy hunting."

They both knew where they were heading next.

They made a cooked breakfast and put it on to trays and carried them to the guest bedrooms. Radio had never been here before, despite how long he had been in the matrix. It was testament to just how busy he had been.

They stopped at the first door on the right and knocked.

"Come."

They opened the door and walked in to Yeshua and Mariam's rooms.

"I thought you would like breakfast in bed, this morning," said Radio.

They both looked well rested but famished. Roman occupied Judea wasn't exactly a land of plenty and Radio thought they could both do with a bit of feeding up.

Radio put the tray on Yeshua's knee and handed him a knife and fork.

"What on Earth is this?" he asked.

"It's called a full English breakfast. Bacon, sausage, fried egg, black pudding, mushrooms, toast and beans. It will easily see you through a hard day's work."

"I'm not surprised. Smells wonderful."

For someone so thin, he could fairly pack it away. The breakfast was gone in under five minutes.

"How do you feel?" asked Radio.

"I'm fine. Why do you ask?"

"I wondered if you would like to visit Rome today. There are lots of people who are dying to meet you." Radio said it with a look of innocence.

"How many are lots of people?" asked Yeshua.

"Oh, not that many," explained Radio. "About 800 million."

"Ha," said Yeshua laughing. "There aren't that many people in the universe."

Radio put on a serious face. "There are 75 billion people in this sector of the galaxy alone. There are 7 billion on the Earth. You have 800 million followers as part of the church you founded 2000 years ago. It will soon be a lot more."

"Oh dear." It was the first time that Radio could remember seeing Yeshua daunted.

"Don't worry," said Radio. "They have just seen you walk to your death to save their SOULS. I think you'll find that they will be right behind you and will hang on your very word. You have nothing to fear."

"How will they have seen me. As you point out. It all happened 2000 years ago."

"Observe," said Radio. He picked up the remote control and turned on the television set.

BBC breakfast were holding a discussion about "What Yeshua will do next?" There were images of the scene yesterday when he rose from the dead.

"Good grief," said Yeshua. "What is that thing?"

"It is a television. Everybody has one. The culmination of your mission was seen by almost everyone in this galaxy. You're famous."

"Well, I never," said Yeshua.

"We'll leave you to get dressed. You'll find everything you need in the wardrobes."

Radio and Miriam left them to get ready.

Forty-One - The Arc of Time

Radio and Miriam returned to the Elevator and put on the kettle.

When the coffee was ready, they sat at the round table. Mother was waiting.

"I have one last question and then I will leave you alone. You said that you were not the Radio part of your SOUL and that you were preparing the way for Miriam, which suggests that you see the Radio Operator as a female role. Am I correct?"

"In the context of the Earth, yes. However, I must make myself clear. The Radio Operator role does not have to be fulfilled by a female. It should be filled by the most appropriate person. In the case of the Earth, I have come to the conclusion that a female fits the role most perfectly."

"Why do you say that?" asked Mum curiously.

"When I was young, growing up on the Earth, I was always struck by who children would call when they got in to trouble. I have always seen the Radio Operator as the facilitator or co-ordinator who responds to emergencies.

"If the children are going to call 'Mum', then the person responding should be Mum. To the people of the Earth, that is exactly who Miriam is. She is everyone's ultimate Mother. Then of course, I read the book on reportage and that confirmed my thoughts absolutely. When I read it, I knew I was correct."

"What is reportage?"

"Reportage is history documented by the people who were at the scene as eye witnesses. The piece in question related to The Great War.

"An eye witness reported that, during a battle, when the guns had ceased temporarily, they would hear the wounded and dying crying in no man's land. Without fail, regardless of which side the soldiers were on, they would always cry out for one person and one person alone. Mother.

"It made me realise that when a person is really up shit creek, they want the one person who is going to tear the world apart to save them. Mother will save them.

"Finally, think on this. When I was in trouble, who ensured that a universe was created to save me?"

"Is that really how you see a Mother?"

"It's not just how I see a Mother, it is how the Earth sees her too. Remember, the pillar in the temple. The pillar of the woman was strong and practical. It was roof over head, food on table, clothes on back and in an emergency, no nonsense."

Yeshua and Mariam joined them at the table. Yeshua was wearing a white shirt and smart black trousers. He looked the part.

"And how do you see the Father?" asked Yeshua.

"The Father is a pillar of dreams. It is his job to make the impossible, possible."

"Is that what you are doing, Radio?" asked Mother. "Making the impossible, possible?"

"You should know. You wrote me. In the beginning, there was no solution. Now there is.

“It is not necessarily my opinion, though. Let me reiterate, it is how the Earth sees the sexes. My personal opinion is that, regardless of gender, people should be allowed to do what they want. It is not my opinion that is wrong. It is the programming that is wrong. I am merely interpreting history.”

“Is there no place for assigning roles?” asked Yeshua. “What of a Mother, who has just given birth to a child. Should we not allow her to nurture the child and support her in her endeavours.”

“Yes, of course, we should. However, it is not just her responsibility to nurture the child. It is the Father’s responsibility too.

“It has become clear to me that the things we have been taught as children on the Earth are no longer enough. It is time we reviewed the whole programming of gender in children and explore the possibilities together. I know things are wrong but I don’t know all the answers.”

“What is my job, exactly?” asked Yeshua.

“I think there are three things that I’d like you to do. Your job in the first instance, is to guide people through the interview. Encourage them to come to the best decisions for the right reasons,” replied Radio. “We want everyone to pass the interview but we know that this will only happen if we all support each other.

“We should defend creation and attempt to improve at all times. I don’t believe that selfishness has a place in the new world order. It is your job to persuade the people of the Earth that there is something larger than themselves that they want to be an equal partner in. The days of being in control for the wrong reasons have disappeared. You will be the co-ordinator. You have unlocked The Golden Door, now you need to show everyone the way through.”

“I thought I’d already done that,” said Yeshua.

“You have. However, there will be questions and you need to help them find the answers.

“Secondly, it is also my desire that you take a turn at being Radio. It was never my belief that one person should fulfil that role.

“And thirdly, you need to complete your mission in time. Mariam is to have a baby in Gallia and you make several appearances after your resurrection. I suspect there are other temporal interventions you may have to make. We will be guided by the Operator.”

“There is an awful lot of work involved in all of this,” said Yeshua smiling. “I thought I was going to PARADISE?”

Radio laughed. “PARADISE is a waiting room. Although it is luxurious, I imagine it would become boring after a while. We are only happy when we are at our best potential. When we have become all that we can be.

“The notion of PARADISE will be replaced by the notion of passing the interview. If I know the people of the Earth, and I think I do, they will never be satisfied watching others fly away with all the power that the Operator has to offer. They will want a slice of it for themselves. PARADISE is yesterday’s goal.”

“I think you are right,” said Yeshua. “The thought of PARADISE bores me. I’m excited about getting started.”

“Good,” said Radio. “Let’s bring the good news to your disciples. We’ll send our mob back in to meet up with the other six at the safe house and then we’ll send in Mariam to tell them that she has seen you risen from the dead. Which isn’t a lie.

We’ll also need to launch the GEMINI application to provide a body for Judas. We’ll hang him from a tree, somewhere.”

The others started to wander into breakfast and it wasn't long before Radio and Miriam had a full team assembled. When the last of them pushed their plates away, Radio called for silence.

"As you know, we need to finish the mission in Jerusalem before we can really move forward. Hrolfr, I want you to lead the team back in to Jerusalem and head to the safe house. That's Jamie, John, James, and Klaus. Wait there until Mariam brings the good news. Now get going."

Radio opened the time window and they all ran through.

"Gabriel, take a body double of Jude. Hang it from a tree and return here."

Gabriel launched the GEMINI application and copied Jude. She possessed the body and returned to Jerusalem as Judas.

"Operator, the tomb."

The time window morphed and opened up into the tomb of Joseph of Arimathea. Radio collected the shroud and he, Miriam, Yeshua and Mariam walked back into the greatest story ever told.

"Let there be light," said Radio, and the tomb was enveloped in a golden glow.

Yeshua sat down on the catafalque and looked at his father. "What now?" he asked.

Without saying a word, Radio turned to the stone and rolled it away with a motion of his hand. The morning light gushed into the semi darkness. He turned to Mariam and Miriam.

"Make your way to the safe house and let them know the good news."

They nodded and headed out of the tomb.

"This all seems so straight forward," said Yeshua.

"Why complicate it?" replied Radio. "The story is reasonably straight forward and I want it over and done with. I need you back in the future.

"Persuading the people of the Earth to do the hard thing so that they can pass the interview has given me nightmares. You have the credentials and the authority. My hope is that they will listen to you. It really is their last chance. Failure for them now is not an option."

"What will happen to them if they fail?" asked Yeshua.

"They will watch as all their friends fly away. This does not sound like much but, believe me, it will be a living hell. That was the Church's biggest mistake. Threatening everyone with an eternity in a furnace just does not sound believable.

"All they had to say was that if they didn't pass the test then they would be left alone to howl out their miserable days powerless and unloved. It would have worked a treat."

Yeshua laughed. "Yes, it does sound appalling and what makes that threat so believable is that it is down to a choice that they make. Ultimately, they do it to themselves."

Radio looked at Yeshua approvingly. "Yes. It is their choice."

It was half an hour before there was any movement.

It was Mariam and Miriam. They were alone.

"Well that was interesting," said Miriam. "They didn't believe us. Not one of them. Our lot are doing everything they can to keep a straight face but the other six are complete and utter idiots."

Both Radio and Yeshua laughed.

"I told you so," said Radio. "Let's return to the matrix. We'll move time forward and Yeshua can pay them a visit."

When they returned they were met by Gabriel who announced that her mission had been accomplished. Another headache off the to do list.

Radio put the kettle on. The reaction of the disciples came as no surprise to him. He made the coffee and brought a tray over to the round table. When everyone had their cup, he smiled.

"I don't want any of you to worry. Yeshua you will, of course, go back and show Thomas your wounds but we should all remember that we have John, who wrote the Q gospel and we have King James who orders the translation of the whole Bible. If things don't quite go our way, from now on, we can always amend to suit ourselves."

"No wonder there is so much inconsistency," noted Winston.

Radio laughed. "Inconsistency suits us. Never forget the power of obfuscation."

"Oh, I won't," said Winston with a wicked smile.

Yeshua finished his coffee and stood up. "Right. Time to give Thomas a bit of faith." He held up his hands and looked at his father. "Please, leave this to me. Finish your coffee. I'll be ten minutes."

Radio sipped his drink. At last, he thought, someone who takes his responsibility seriously. He looked at Yeshua and felt that now was the time to move things forward.

The paradox was hugely complex and he had only really just started. In his dreams, over the last fifteen years, he had seen much more than the few things he'd done so far. He knew that he couldn't do all of this alone.

"I'm more than happy to leave this to you," said Radio. "Moreover, I think I would like to formalise the team a little bit better. In all the excitement of the last few days, I've lost track of where everyone is. When you return, bring the others with you. I will pull our other time agents out of their current assignments. I think it's time we had a conference and properly assigned roles."

"Yes, I agree," said Yeshua. He opened the time window and disappeared in to Jerusalem.

Radio positioned himself in front of the matrix.

"Operator, locate all time agents currently active in time and provide a list."

A list of names started to appear on screen.

Yeshua as himself AD 36 Jerusalem
Hrolfr of Normandy as Simon AD 36 Jerusalem
Jamie Mullen as James AD 36 Jerusalem
James Stuart as Philip AD 36 Jerusalem
Klaus Fischer as James II AD 36 Jerusalem
John of Plantagenet as John AD 36 Jerusalem
Jude Grey as Judas In Matrix
Geoffrey of Auvergne as Tiberius AD 36 Rome
Billy Sloane as Pontius AD 36 Jerusalem
Thomas Godfrey as Cerdic AD 495 Hampshire
Winston Churchill as Himself In Matrix
Mariam of Magdala as herself In Matrix
Jeanne Tsedeq as Jeanne Orleans AD 1431 in Rouen
Eve Tsedeq as Herself On Duty
Adam Mishpat as Himself On Duty
David Wallace as Marcus AD 36 Jerusalem
Michael Watts as Lucius AD 36 Jerusalem
Kenneth Jones as Gaius AD 36 Jerusalem

Radio ran his eyes down the list. He knew that Tiberius had recruited for the 10th Legion so he was not surprised to see the three names at the end of the list. The one that did surprise him was Jeanne Tsedeq. He had that feeling at the nape of his neck again.

"Operator, hail the Unknown Pleasures."

The time window morphed and he was looking on to the bridge. Eve was in her seat.

"Well?"

"You instructed me not to tell you. It's a surprise. She is my younger sister, your daughter." She hesitated for a moment. "Hold on. I'm coming through."

She got up out of the Captain's chair and walked through in to the matrix. "I have a message for you, from you in the future.

"Jeanne's mission is complete. You walk her through it yourself. Her reward is to come back in time and meet you when you were younger. She is fascinated by the paradox."

Radio thought for a moment. "Are you saying that I can pluck her out of time right now?"

"Yes. When Jeanne was burned at the stake, there were contemporary reports of there being a great fireball. All you need to do is swap in a body double and cause a large explosion."

Radio immediately experienced an overwhelming sense of excitement. "Quick, bring in a medical crash team with fire extinguishers. I'll also need a combustible."

"You got it."

It took five minutes for the team to be assembled. Miriam was just as excited as Radio and Winston stood watch with one of the fire extinguishers.

"Operator, Rouen 30 May 1431. Le Vieux-Marché."

The time window morphed on to the Old Market in Rouen. Jeanne was wearing a white gown and already tied to the stake. Radio took one close look at her and knew immediately that she was his daughter. She was Eve's red-haired twin. The girl looked noble and unafraid. About her lips, there was a knowing smile. At least she had faith in him, thought Radio.

A man dressed in a monk's habit stepped forward and lit the bonfire. The flames licked up until they were just below Jeanne's feet. Her gown was just starting to smoke.

Radio launched the GEMINI application and created a body double out of thin air which Eve held upright.

"Operator, slow time down to one twentieth and move closer to the stake."

Radio took a knife and cut Jeanne's bonds and dragged her out of the flames. Winston stepped forward and gave her a blast of the extinguisher. Eve moved in, picked up the rope and retied the body double to the stake. It took her about ten seconds which equated to half a second in real time.

Radio took the combustible and threw it in to the fire.

"Operator, normal time."

The explosion was impressive. A real fireball shot through the market place setting several on lookers on fire. Radio laughed. Served them right.

He turned to his daughter.

"Hello Daddy," she said. She then put her arms round him and hugged him tightly. "Right on time. Now, did you get me my spicy crisps."

"They're in the snack cupboard. Help yourself."

His daughter scampered over to the kitchen area and retrieved her crisps from the cupboard. She was so matter of fact.

Radio looked at the time window. "Operator. Send an instruction to all time agents. Return to the matrix."

Forty-Two - The Temporal Adjustment Team

When Yeshua returned there were lots of introductions. He had never met Jeanne before but she remembered him when he was older. Radio could tell that they were going to be great friends. Eve, however, looked somewhat wistful.

"What's wrong?" asked Radio.

"I don't know." She admitted. "Sometimes, I feel as if I'm a breed apart at times. I think it might be because I'm the middle child. I'm in between."

"I was the middle child when I grew up on the Earth and I felt the same way. For a small period of time, you are the youngest and everyone lavishes their love on to you, until, that is an usurper comes along to take your place. It can be a difficult adjustment."

"You make it sound so childish," she reproved.

"Isn't it?" he countered. "In truth, it is a bit childish but that doesn't necessarily make it easy."

The other time agents drifted in over the next ten minutes. Radio made pots of tea and coffee and placed them on the round table together with snacks and biscuits. He asked everyone to sit round.

"Welcome to the first meeting of the newly formed Temporal Adjustment Team." Radio had barely finished the sentence when there was a commotion behind him.

Streaming through the time window were the Others, the Creators of the universe. They took seats at the round table and were also joined by Mother, Father Lucifer and Lilith.

Radio smiled. He had asked the Operator to invite all the time agents and the Operator had took him at his word. The characters of Earth's mythology had just taken seats at the round table. This would be interesting. He started again.

"Welcome to the inaugural meeting of the Temporal Adjustment Team. We are gathered here today to take stock of where we are in the execution of the temporal paradox. The solution to the Creator's evolutionary problem.

"What we agree today will hopefully begin to resolve the paradox on Earth and will help resolve the issues relating to the other solutions. I think it would be a very good idea if we went around the table, once again and introduced ourselves fully and gave a status update of our current missions where we have one. I know this will be complicated but let's be patient. I'll begin.

"I'm Radio, who was once Eloidh Tsedeq, the Operations Chief of the solution and I'm Mother's apprentice. I began to wake up fifteen years ago on Earth and over the last few weeks have been co-ordinating the resolution of the Temporal Paradox." He turned to his left and nodded for Miriam to continue.

"I'm Miriam, who was once Eloidh Tsedeq. I began to wake up twenty years ago on Plantagenet and I'm Fathers apprentice." She nodded to Mother and Father who were on her left.

"My name is El and this is Elion. Outside of the solution, we were known as El-Elion and we were the parent of Eloidh, who was genetically created from our DNA. El-Elion was the Chief Scientist in charge of the creation of the array. When El-Elion uploaded into the solution the Operator split our SOUL in to its constituent male and female parts. We were inserted into the solution in the past and we have been here for 7000 years

"In that time, we have completed many missions relating to the paradox. We have been Gods in ancient Egypt and in ancient Greece. We are here today to provide guidance to this counsel. The paradox is more complex than you think. Over the years, we have met every single person around this table and in places that will probably surprise you. It is our hope that we can begin to tie up the loose ends and enjoy the retirement that we so richly deserve."

Her words were met with a great deal of laughter.

"I'm Hrolfr, Duke of Normandy. I was recruited by Radio when I was seven years old and have been a time agent ever since. I trained for a time, here in the matrix, when I was younger and Radio was older. My first mission was to secure Normandy as a separate Duchy from where the invasion of England could take place. My last mission was as Simon the Zealot in Judea."

"My name is Chronos and this is Rhea. Outside of the solution we were known as Chronos of Eden. Like your Mother and Father, we were sexed by the Operator on upload. We have been monitoring the solution in the laboratory and uploaded only recently. We have been informed that we will be heading back in time to ancient Greece to aid El and Elion in the past before we launch our own Radio WHO."

"I am Zeus and this is Hera. It is basically the same story for us. I have been informed that I am the all-powerful super God of the ancient world. This obviously comes as no surprise to me."

Hera made a yawning motion at his side which led to fits of giggles from the others round the table.

Apollo, Artemis, Eros, Aphrodite, Aries, Athena, Hades, Persephone, Poseidon, Demeter, Hephaestus, Hestia, Hermes, Hebe, Uranus and Gaia all had a very similar story to tell.

"I think this is going to lead to a credibility issue," said Radio. "Your names are the names of the major Greek Gods. Nobody will believe it."

"You are forgetting that this is a temporal paradox," said Mum. "People will believe it because they actually are the Greek Gods. Their names are remembered because they were there."

Radio smiled. "I know that but…" He had to stop. He couldn't put his finger on it but it did not feel quite right. He nodded to Eve to move on.

"My name is Eve Tsedeq and this is Adam Mishpat. I am the daughter of Radio and Miriam. I have not been born yet. In about thirty years from now, I will take the intergalactic fleet back in time to ancient Sumer on Earth, where we will or were met by El and Elion.

"Our mission was to inject DNA in to the indigenous population and provide a boost to the genetic pool. Our grandson was Abraham, who left Ur and fathered the children of Israel. We completed our mission over 300 years ago and returned to this galaxy to found the Empire of Sumer on the Sumer home world. I am three years short of my 350th birthday."

There were exclamations of shock round the table and Radio felt he had to interject. "You look well on it," he said. They all laughed.

"Hi I'm Jamie Mullen, time agent from South Shields. I have completed my education mission in Normandy, where I was with Hrolfr. I've just returned from Judea where I was James. I believe that my next mission is to France where I'm to become Jacques de Molay, the Grand Master of the Templar Knights."

"I'm Natalie Mullen, Jamie's Mother from South Shields and time agent. I was with Jamie in Normandy and I will be returning to France with him when he joins the Templars."

"Klaus Fischer, time agent from Berlin. I was recruited by Radio in 1940 when I was twenty. I have been in Normandy for seven years and have just completed my mission in Judea where I was the other James."

"Geoffrey de Charnay, time agent from Auvergne. I was recruited by Jeanne Tsedeq when I was ten years old and she introduced me to Amaury de la Roche of the Templars. I was preceptor of Normandy until my arrest several years ago.

"My mission in France is not yet complete as I am still imprisoned there. My mission in Rome, as Tiberius is complete. I believe I am due to die immanently and it is merely a case of dropping in the body double before I move on to the next thing, which I believe is Scotland in 1314."

"Winston, Radio's apprentice from Blenheim Palace. I was recruited by Radio when I was five and have completed many missions for him since then. My handlers, since childhood have been Gabriel and Uriel, known as Blondie and Goldilocks.

"I am just about to commence my most important mission which is to defeat the evil of Nazi Germany. I have no idea where I'll be after that but I'm hoping for a belter."

"I can assure you, Winston, you will not be disappointed," said Radio. Winston looked pleased.

"James of Scotland, time agent from Edinburgh. I was recruited by Grandfather when I was six years old. My current mission is to secure the throne of Great Britain. I have just completed the mission to Judea as Philip."

"David Wallace, time agent from Glasgow. I was recruited by Radio when I was seven from a Barnardo's home. I fought with Billy in North America and helped the Templar Knights escape to Scotland from La Rochelle. I have just returned from Judea where I was in the 10th Legion."

"Michael Watts, time agent from Stirling. I was recruited by Radio at 16 in 1915 after my father was killed at the battle of Loos. I was with Julius at the battle of Alesia when we defeated the Gals under Vercingetorix and I also fought in the civil war and was there when Caesar crossed the Rubicon. I was recruited for the 10th by Tiberius."

"Kenneth Jones, time agent from Cardiff. I was recruited by Radio at aged 10 when he lifted me out of the Irish Sea. I was on the Lusitania with my parents when the ship was sunk by a German U Boat. I think they drowned. I have been a British spy all my life, working for Blondie and Winston. I was sent to Tiberius by Blondie to join the 10th."

"William Sloane, time agent from Glasgow. I was recruited by Radio when I was five. I have completed several missions for Radio. I fought in the seven-year's war for Great Britain. I was with Winston in the trenches. I worked for Elizabeth the first and have just completed a mission to Rome and Judea as the Procurator Pontius Pilate."

"Who were you when you worked for Elizabeth?" asked Winston.

"I was Francis Walsingham." He tried not to burst out laughing but he couldn't help it.

"Jude, time agent from Edinburgh. I was recruited by the Operator in my dreams a few weeks ago, I think. I was in Normandy for seven years and have just returned from Judea where I was Judas."

"My name is Lucifer, Mother's Satan. I uploaded in to the solution with El-Elion. I was not sexed as I was made a promise that I would one day marry the daughter of my best friend. It was the plan from the start. I have obviously been active in the universe and have been working for my old boss from the beginning."

"Lilith, Father's Satan. I was recruited by Radio at birth and have worked for him ever since."

"Tommy Godfrey, time agent from Edinburgh. I was recruited by Radio 10 years ago. I am currently on a mission as Cerdic, King of Wessex. I am bringing the Saxon tribes to post Roman Britain."

"Gabriel, Archangel. I uploaded in to the solution with El-Elion. I was sexed with my other half Uriel. We have worked for the solution ever since. In the laboratory, I was the head of testing."

"My name is Yeshua. I am the son of Radio and Miriam. I was recruited at birth and trained in Judah at the monastery in Qumran. I am the Golden Key and have just completed my mission in Jerusalem."

"My name is Mariam of Magdala. I was recruited by Radio and married to Yeshua."

Finally, Radio turned to his daughter who had snuggled in on his right.

"My name is Jeanne Tsedeq. I was born here in the matrix and in 25 years or so, I will be sent back in time to 1425 to kick the English out of France. I completed my mission half an hour ago. My expectation is that I will have adventures for the rest of eternity. No pressure."

Radio smiled. "As you can see, the paradox is vast and complex. Luckily for us, the Operator has a list of every intervention that has happened since the year dot. Our job is to go through it so that we can free ourselves from our evolutionary responsibilities.

It is important that we all take responsibility for our own incursions in time and space. I have asked the Operator to prepare a list for each person with the linear time of their incursion, a target time in history and a summary of their goal. Where you are acting as part of a collective, we have also provided a meeting point so that you can work in unison. I suggest we take the rest of the day of to compare notes and that we start, in earnest, in the morning. As always, the Operator has prioritised the events. The most important are the ones where the consequences of failure will be far reaching. We cannot afford to fail. Does anyone have any questions?"

"What happens if we do fail?" It was Jeanne, asking with the innocence of youth.

"It is unlikely that we can fail now, there are too many fail safes. However, if an unsolvable temporal paradox occurs then there will be a total failure in the containment field and the universe will vanish. However, I have stored backups so that we can set aside a misadventure and start again. We would have to get it wrong lots of times for there to be any real threat so don't worry."

"What is the priority?" asked Mum.

"The priority is to release the Others so that they can set off their own big bangs and that means going in to ancient Greece and Egypt tomorrow. Let's get these things finished first and then we can move on."

"I agree," said Chronos. "We have waited long enough. Let's get started tomorrow so that we can be released to our own universes."

"What are we going to be doing exactly?" asked Eve.

"Put it this way," said Radio. "I now believe that that the super volcano under Yellowstone National Park was a practice session for what we are going to do next. You and I are going back in time about 3450 years and we are going to kick off a massive super volcano under Atlantis in the Mediterranean. The results of this cataclysm will release the children of Israel from bondage in Egypt and will make the renegade pharaoh one of the most famous men in history.

"The Creator's will seed the story of Atlantis in the culture of the Greeks and will intervene on several occasions to ensure that the Gods become an integral part of Greek culture.

“In short, we are giving the ancient people of Earth the idea of GOD so that when they arrive at the here and now, none of this will be too much of a surprise to them. We are essentially creating ourselves.”

“Who is the renegade pharaoh?” asked Jeanne.

“His name is Amenhotep IV, also known as Akhenaten. You know him as Moses.”

Forty-Three – The Gods of Old

Breakfast was a quiet affair. Every single entity at the round table was poring over documents provided by the Operator the night before. Radio smiled, they looked like actors cramming the script before the big audition.

He and Miriam had spent half the night going over their own scripts. They were going to take the Unknown Pleasures, the Disorder and The Wilderness through a temporal incursion created in space by the Operator. Their target date was 1444 BCE.

The Creators were going back on their own vessel through the same wormhole. Radio had almost laughed out loud when he had read the name of the ship. The Olympus.

"Dad, something is not quite right." It was Jeanne who had sat beside him with a large Encyclopaedia.

"What is it?" asked Radio.

"It's the dates. They don't quite add up. Akhenaten stopped being pharaoh in 1334 BCE, but Moses is said to have left Egypt in 1444 BCE, 110 years earlier. The eruption of Santorini could have been around that date so we are about 100 years too early."

Radio laughed. "Ancient history is inexact and dates are based on a series of assumptions. If you get one of those assumptions wrong then you are working on a false premise. The dates of the Egyptian Pharaohs have always been based on a linear assumption that rule followed rule but in fact, some of the reigns were simultaneous, which would make their rule earlier. Don't worry, the dates work out. The Operator has a list."

Radio was impressed. He liked the idea of checking and double checking. It gave him a feeling that the people selected for the Temporal Adjustment Team were the correct choice. Cynical enough to make sure but not so cynical cause a major problem.

"Eat a solid breakfast, Jeanne," he advised. "You, I believe, are coming with us."

"Yes," she said excitedly. "I have a part to play."

"Have you packed your Angels uniform?" he asked.

"All packed and ready to go. Just familiarising myself with the script."

She helped herself to bacon, sausage, egg and toast and buried her nose in the documents the Operator had provided.

Radio found her presence slightly disconcerting. This girl was his daughter and yet he knew nothing about her. It was all very well being given a surprise by the Operator but to have a child appear out of nowhere phased him. Even though the child obviously knew him. He knew he would have to tread carefully.

At the end of breakfast, Radio gave a one-hour warning. All time agents were to assemble at the time windows for transfer to their ships. In the meantime, he knew he had something to do.

He approached the time windows with Miriam and Jeanne at his side.

"Operator, Mount Horeb, 1444 BCE." The time window morphed in its usual fashion and they looked on to a scene at night. A man was sitting by a fire, huddling in his coat against the cold.

Radio selected a bush about 50 yards further up the mountainside and loudly set it on fire.

The man noticed the noise first and then saw the burning bush. Radio was careful to ensure that none of the foliage was consumed by the fire. When he saw that the man had gone over to look, he called to him from within the bush.

"Moses! Moses!"

The man looked utterly astonished but eventually approached cautiously and said, "Here I am."

"Do not come any closer," Radio said. "Take off your sandals, for the place where you are standing is holy ground." Then he said, "I am the God of your father, the God of Abraham, the God of Isaac and the God of Jacob." At this, Moses hid his face beneath his hood.

Radio said, "I have indeed seen the misery of my people in Egypt. I have heard them crying out because of their slave drivers, and I am concerned about their suffering. I have come down to rescue them from the hand of the Egyptians and to bring them up out of that land into a good and spacious land, a land flowing with milk and honey—the home of the Canaanites, Hittites, Amorites, Perizzites, Hivites and Jebusites. And now the cry of the Israelites has reached me, and I have seen the way the Egyptians are oppressing them. So now, go. I am sending you to Pharaoh to bring my people the Israelites out of Egypt."

"Are you reading that from the Torah?" It was Yeshua, who had walked silently up behind them. His face was strangely awed and very curious.

"Of course," responded Radio. "There's no point in rewriting the script. Better to just go with what was reported as having been said. Don't forget, I am the great plagiarist. Where the temporal paradox is concerned, I have to be."

Moses looked at the bush and said, "Who am I that I should go to Pharaoh and bring the Israelites out of Egypt?"

Radio replied, "I will be with you. And this will be the sign to you that it is I who have sent you: When you have brought the people out of Egypt, you will worship God on this mountain."

Moses replied, "Suppose I go to the Israelites and say to them, 'The God of your fathers has sent me to you,' and they ask me, 'What is his name?' Then what shall I tell them?"

Radio responded, "I am who I am. This is what you are to say to the Israelites: 'I am has sent me to you.'" Radio paused for a moment, "Say to the Israelites, 'The Lord, the God of your fathers—the God of Abraham, the God of Isaac and the God of Jacob—has sent me to you.'

"This is my name forever, the name you shall call me from generation to generation.

"Go, assemble the elders of Israel and say to them, 'The Lord, the God of your fathers—the God of Abraham, Isaac and Jacob—appeared to me and said: I have watched over you and have seen what has been done to you in Egypt. I have promised to bring you up out of your misery in Egypt into the land of the Canaanites, Hittites, Amorites, Perizzites, Hivites and Jebusites—a land flowing with milk and honey.'

"The elders of Israel will listen to you. Then you and the elders are to go to the king of Egypt and say to him, 'The Lord, the God of the Hebrews, has met with us. Let us take a three-day journey into the wilderness to offer sacrifices to the Lord our God.' But I know that the king of Egypt will not let you go unless a mighty hand compels him. I will stretch out my hand and strike the Egyptians with all the wonders that I will perform among them. After that, he will let you go.

"And I will make the Egyptians favourably disposed toward this people, so that when you leave you will not go empty-handed. Every woman is to ask her neighbour and any woman living in her house for articles of silver and gold and for clothing, which you will put on your sons and daughters. And so, you will plunder the Egyptians."

Moses looked as if he had more to say but Radio left it at that. He looked at the bush and extinguished the flame immediately. It was completely untouched by the fire. The time window went blank.

Yeshua was completely intrigued. He turned to his father and said. "I didn't really understand until I saw it in action. You can go anywhere in time. Speak to anybody and not leave this room. It is utterly amazing."

"Yes. It is amazing. There is a lot for you to learn but I promise you this. Give me a couple of years and you will understand exactly how this is done. It is not as difficult as you think as long as you have the right training and the right perspective. Have you packed your things? You have a part to play in all of this."

"Yes, I'm packed. What exactly are you up to?"

Radio chuckled. "Be patient. I don't want to spoil it."

After an hour, the expedition was ready and they smoothly transferred to the four ships that were in orbit around the Earth. When everyone was on board, Eve ordered the small fleet to a position, 100,000 kilometres beyond the moon. She nodded to Radio.

"Operator, temporal incursion to 1444 BCE."

Radio immediately felt that dreadful feeling at the nape of his neck. The massive wormhole that appeared in front of them felt like the door in a horror movie. The door that you did not go through because you know that your impending doom awaited you on the other side. The gateway was black and sinister.

"That gives me the creeps," said Jeanne.

Radio reassured her, "Don't worry. I think it is just the intense power making your skin crawl."

Eve gave the order and the ships passed through the gateway. There was a burst of blinding light, a whining sound and a feeling of his body being stretched and then suddenly it stopped.

"We're through," said Eve. She ordered the ships to maintain a standard orbit around the Earth.

Radio turned to the main viewer and watched as the Earth slowly came into view. He was astonished. It was the most startling blue he had ever seen.

"Oh, my goodness," he said. "The Earth without all the pollution."

It was a stunning sight. There was a crisp brightness to the atmosphere that he had not noticed before. If the people of the Earth needed confirmation of climate change then here it was. The Earth in all its innocent glory.

"What do you want to do first. Do you want to get the lie of the land?" asked Eve.

"We are here to do a job," began Radio. "History records that the volcanic eruption destroyed a civilisation which came to be known in mythology as Atlantis. It was actually the Minoan civilisation who became the Philistines or the Sea people of the Bible.

I don't think it would be a good idea to go down and have a look as I know I will be sorely tempted to save some things which cannot be saved. My advice is to check the status of the magma chamber and initiate the eruption straight away."

"I agree," replied Eve. "Status of Santorini magma chamber?" She turned to Ruth who was manning the Ensign station.

"It is massive. I am recording a VEI of six if the eruption was initiated right now. It is every bit as large as the volcano under Yellowstone."

"Arm 1 megaton torpedo and tractor pyroclastic flow south towards the island of Crete."

"Torpedo armed and away. Tractor beam pulling south."

Radio looked at Jeanne and asked her to get in to her uniform.

"Operator, locate Moses."

The time window morphed and Radio could see the man sitting alone by a fire. It was early evening and he was alone by a tent in the desert. He could hear the braying of livestock but other than that, the night was still. Moses looked pensive and a little bit afraid.

Jeanne returned attired in a white dress with the star of David emblazoned on her chest, only it looked more technical. As if it had come from a schematic.

"What exactly is this thing?" she asked.

Radio chuckled. This girl was never going to let him down. "It is the design of the array. Each point of the star is a containment field for the universe. The central space is GOD. The General Operating Dimension. It is where you exist. It is reality."

"When this is all finished, you are going to have to explain it to me," she said.

Radio laughed. "I can assure you, I will explain it to everyone before the week is out. Are you ready?"

"Yes. I'm ready. I have experience of operating in time, you know."

Radio nodded. He had to remember that. He had to remember to stop treating everyone as if they were idiots. These people had long been initiated. They didn't have all the answers but they had most of them.

"Off you go then."

Forty-Four – The Ten Plagues

Jeanne walked out and stood in front of the man at the fire. He didn't notice her at first but slowly he felt her presence. He turned to her just as he was raising a cup to his lips. He jumped out of his skin, cursed and covered himself in the liquid.

Everyone on the bridge burst out laughing. There was nothing funnier than an unsuspecting victim getting a good fright.

"Do not be afraid," said Jeanne. "I am an angel of the Lord."

"What do you want?" Moses demanded.

"You will go to Pharaoh and give him a message from I AM. This is what the LORD says: By this you will know that I am the LORD: With the staff that is in my hands I will strike the water of the Nile, and it will be changed into blood. The fish in the Nile will die, and the river will stink and the Egyptians will not be able to drink its water. You will let my people go."

"That's it?" he spluttered. "You want me to walk in to Rameses and give him that message. The man is an idiot. He will never agree to let the slaves go. I know, he used to work for me. This is getting ridiculous."

Jeanne remained calm. "Tell him that for now. Nobody said this was going to be easy and just in case you have forgotten, the slaves are your people, descended from Yuya and his brothers just as you are. I prophesise this. It will take ten plagues before the idiot agrees and you will follow my instructions to the letter until he does. Do I make myself clear?"

Radio had to admit that the girl was good. Very good.

"Yes. I am clear. It is just…" he hesitated. "I have given up everything for this. A throne. A people. There is no one more aware than I that the slaves are my people. I wouldn't have done what I have done if I thought otherwise."

"I know," said Jeanne. "The Aten, Adonai, is grateful. Follow the Lord and you will have eternal life."

With that she turned around and walked back on to the bridge of the Unknown Pleasures.

Radio was deeply impressed. He started clapping until there was a standing ovation on the bridge.

Jeanne laughed and bowed. "What now?"

"We move on. I want this finished as soon as possible."

The time window morphed and this time Moses was in a room. It was dark and there was a single lamp burning oil. He had his back pressed up against the wall and he was staring in to nothing.

Jeanne walked through and this time he saw her immediately.

"What do you want me to do now?" he asked ruefully. "The Nile went as red as blood, just as you said. The stink of death was appalling."

Jeanne composed herself. "You will go to Pharaoh and you will say, this is what the great LORD says: Let my people go, so that they may worship me. If you refuse to let them go, I will plague your whole country with frogs. The Nile will teem with frogs.

They will come up into your palace and your bedroom and onto your bed, into the houses of your officials and on your people, and into your ovens and kneading troughs. The frogs will go up on you and your people and all your officials."

Moses looked up and smiled. "I am sensing a pattern here. Why don't you get the next few off your chest? It will save you a journey."

Jeanne chuckled. "Now you are a servant of the Lord. Stretch out thy rod, and smite the dust of the land, that it may become lice throughout all the land of Egypt."

"Blood, Frogs, Lice, what's number four?"

"Stretch out thy rod, and smite the dust of the land, that it may become flies throughout all the land of Egypt. Pharaoh will ask you to stop but he will not keep his promise. The livestock in Egypt will die but the beasts in the land of Goshen will continue to flourish.

"The sixth plague will be boils and the seventh a thunderstorm of hail. You will go to Pharaoh and you will say. This is what the LORD, the God of the Hebrews, says: Let my people go, so that they may worship me, or this time I will send the full force of my plagues against you and against your officials and your people, so you may know that there is no one like me in all the earth. For by now I could have stretched out my hand and struck you and your people with a plague that would have wiped you off the earth.

"But I have raised you up for this very purpose, that I might show you my power and that my name might be proclaimed in all the earth. You still set yourself against my people and will not let them go. Therefore, at this time tomorrow I will send the worst hailstorm that has ever fallen on Egypt, from the day it was founded till now. Give an order now to bring your livestock and everything you have in the field to a place of shelter, because the hail will fall on every man and animal that has not been brought in and is still out in the field, and they will die."

"That's enough for now," said Moses. "My head is starting to hurt."

"Do all that I have asked you to do and you will be free in the land of Milk and Honey. I will return when you have completed your tasks."

Once again, Jeanne returned to the ship. She was sweating.

"Give me an hour to crib the last bit. I nearly forgot what I was supposed to say until the script started to appear on my interface."

Radio hugged her. "It is a fail-safe. I want you to learn the script just in case there is a technical issue but we can put the whole thing on your interface if you like."

She looked relieved. "I'll do both. I'll learn it and read the script at the same time."

"Deal," said Radio. "Let's have a spot of lunch."

At lunch, Yeshua looked like he wanted to ask a question but he had the look of a man who didn't quite know how to frame it.

Eventually, Radio's curiosity got the better of him. "Why don't you just ask your question? I will take no offence if it doesn't come out the way you intended."

Yeshua smiled. "Am I really that obvious?"

"No, not really but I can almost smell your interest."

They all laughed. Yeshua continued, "I've been wondering about the eruption and the purpose of it?" He admitted.

"Good question," responded Radio. "In the mythology of the Earth, an advanced culture and city are wiped out of existence by a great cataclysm. The city was called Atlantis but was actually Minoan Crete.

"The supervolcano, whose eruption we have initiated has also just destroyed that City. It just so happens that the side effects are nine of the ten plagues of ancient Egypt."

Yeshua looked appalled. "I take it, you are responsible for the tenth?"

“Yes,” said Radio sadly. “It happened and is remembered on the Earth. It is the only way to ensure that the paradox remains secure. If I had another choice, I would take it. Unfortunately, I don’t. It is why leadership is a lonely business.”

Yeshua looked unhappily at his plate but said no more.

Jeanne spent lunch mugging her lines and looked happier when they stood in front of the viewer on the bridge of the Unknown Pleasures.

“Operator. Locate Moses for the plague of locusts.”

This time Moses was on a craggy mountainside and he looked a lot more tired than he had before. He seemed to be growing in to the character of Old Testament prophet. His cloak was dirty and his beard and hair were unkempt.

“Looks like he’s let himself go a bit,” noted Radio. “I think it comes with the territory.”

Jeanne walked out on to the hillside and touched his arm.

“Where have you been?” he demanded. “I’ve been waiting here for days.”

“There is a season for everything and everything in its season. A time to be born, a time to die, a time to speak and a time to shut up and listen.” Jeanne looked pleased with herself.

Moses calmed a little. Radio looked closely at the man. He was imposing but very strange in his appearance. It was almost as if the clothes didn’t really fit him, as if he was well used to something else. That was it, thought Radio. He was used to the fineries of court and not the habit of a man of the desert.

“I’m sorry,” he said to Jeanne. “I’ve been feeling a bit anxious. I didn’t mean to take it out on you. I am forgetting my manners. What do you need me to do?”

Jeanne smiled at him to show she took no offence. “Go to Pharaoh and tell him this.

“This is what the LORD, the God of the Jews, says: ‘How long will you refuse to humble yourself before me? Let my people go, so that they may worship me. If you refuse to let them go, I will bring locusts into your country tomorrow.

“They will cover the face of the ground so that it cannot be seen. They will devour what little you have left after the hail, including every tree that is growing in your fields. They will fill your houses and those of all your officials and all the Egyptians—something neither your fathers nor your forefathers have ever seen from the day they settled in this land till now.

“When you have completed that task, you will stretch out your hand toward the sky so that darkness will spread over Egypt—darkness that can be felt. Total darkness will cover all Egypt for three days. No one will see anyone else or leave his place for three days.”

“That makes nine. What pleasures has the Lord in store for number ten?” asked the prophet.

“You will ask him yourself. He will come to you at the appointed hour.”

“The Lord is coming here? Now, why does that give me a very bad feeling.” Moses looked anxious and afraid.

“This Exodus from Egypt will be remembered forever.” Jeanne began. “The children of Israel are being taken to their homeland. A land that they will fight to protect for all time. The Lord believes that the things the children of Israel acquire easily will never be valued. Therefore, he makes it difficult for you to acquire your promised land.

“The final test is so appalling that he will come himself to show you the way. Do not be afraid. It has been written since the dawn of time.”

Jeanne turned again and returned to the ship. “Your turn,” she said happily and with great relief.

Radio could understand why she was relieved. The last plague to hit Egypt was the plague of the firstborn. He had known for some time that he would be taking responsibility for this. There was no hiding place. This was murder on a grand scale.

Forty-Five - Out of Egypt

"Operator. Locate Moses before the plague of the firstborn."

He was sitting by the Nile. There was a small fire at his side and he was eating what looked like an apple.

Radio walked through. "Hello Moses," he said.

The prophet looked up and smiled. "I knew it was you, all along, Radio."

Radio had that sinking feeling. He's met me before. Tread carefully. It was the one thing about the paradox that he was troubled about. Despite the fact that the Operator had spent fifteen years preparing him, he had not seen the whole extent of it. He understood that it was massive.

He could not remember a single time when he had seen himself with a younger version of this man. He just had to fly by the seat of his pants.

"We meet again, Akhenaten."

"Don't call me that, Adonai. I am Moses now. Son of God knows."

Radio laughed at the joke. "Are you losing faith in me, Moses?"

It was Moses turn to smile. "No never. I'm just anxious to get everything over and done with. I am not a young man anymore and my nerves are in tatters."

"It will all be played out soon," said Radio. "About midnight I will go throughout Egypt. Every firstborn son in Egypt will die, from the firstborn son of Pharaoh, who sits on the throne, to the firstborn of the slave girl, who is at her hand mill, and all the firstborn of the cattle as well. There will be loud wailing throughout Egypt—worse than there has ever been or ever will be again."

"Oh my God. What are you telling me? What about my people in Goshen?"

Radio looked at him calmly "Inform all the Israelites to mark lamb's blood above their doors in which case, I will pass over them and not suffer the destroyer to come into your houses and smite you."

"This is murder. It cannot be. What about all of the things you told me when I was young?" railed Moses.

"How much do you know?" asked Radio.

Moses put his head in his hands and looked at the fire. "I know enough to know that you cannot stop it and that it must happen. So, says the book of the heavens."

"Exactly," said Radio. He must have made up the story of the book of the heavens but it would do. He continued. "Go to the Israelites and do as I have said. Tonight, will be remembered for all time as the feast of the Passover. Don't make any mistakes."

"I won't. Leave it to me. Lamb's blood on the doors. It makes no sense." Moses looked puzzled.

"History makes no sense at times. There is a plan and each part of the plan needs to be executed to ensure that the next part of the plan follows. If I stop one thing. One event from happening then there will be consequences in time. I cannot afford to be choosy about what is right and what is wrong. If an event is supposed to take place then it must happen. I'm sorry. I know I ask a lot."

Moses looked at him gravely. “You ask a lot and I do it because I do have faith in you. I know that the outcome will be good. In time. It does not make it easy.”

Radio nodded. “There is a balance to be kept and we risk losing everything by reneging on our responsibilities. You were chosen for a reason. Perhaps it is because I have faith in you.”

With that, Radio returned to the ship.

“What now?” asked Eve.

Radio addressed everyone on the bridge. “The Operator will take over from now. The plague of the first born will be carried out by the Alpha-Omega. Don’t worry, it is all in hand.

“Our final job here is to guide the Israelites across the red sea. All those with that task on their list will join me on the beach in one hour. In the meantime, please take a break.”

Radio suggested they go to the observation deck and have tea and coffee.

When they sat down, Yeshua asked the question that had been nagging him. “He knew who you were. When did you meet first?”

Radio admitted that he had no idea. “Your guess is as good as mine. I got quite a surprise back there myself. I’m beginning to wonder just how long I’m going to be at this travelling through time.”

“A very long time.” It was Miriam. “Think about it. Why have we been preparing for the future in the way we have been. Even with time travel capability, you cannot be two places at once. Not if we are going to live in a scenario where everyone can see your temporal interventions.”

Radio sighed. “You are right, I guess. I had been hoping that we could put the time travel to bed but I know we are going to be at it for some time. The Operator has made it clear that that there are certain interventions that must be resolved as a priority. I think these are all geared to allowing us to move on to the next phase of creation. There is a multiverse out there and the Others need to be allowed to initiate their big bangs.”

“What is the plan regarding them?” asked Eve.

“They are intervening as we speak,” replied Radio. “They are seeding the culture of ancient Greece. Dropping in here and there. All they need to do is make a few appearances and they will be remembered for all time. You just have to appear to the right people. That is, people that can write down their experiences.

“When they are done, they will leave the Olympus in orbit to be collected at a later date.”

“Are we returning home after we see the children of Israel through the red sea?” asked Jeanne.

“Yes,” replied Radio. “We need to get them off the beach and into the water bed. There are just over 2 million men, women and children. It will not be easy. I am going to monitor things on the beach and if I have to open spatial incursions to the opposite shore, then so be it. I think that may be the way we get so many over to the other side so quickly.

“You all have the applications given you by the Operator, I suggest you use them to keep the Egyptians at bay. Remember, they are dead anyway.”

“I think we can manage it without further bloodshed,” said Yeshua. Radio noted that he looked somewhat haunted.

“Yeshua, I take full responsibility for this expedition. You are not to blame for the deaths as a result of the plagues of Egypt. Nor am I for that matter. It is the paradox and we cannot change it.”

“I hear you,” he replied. “If, however, the Egyptians die in the water, are you really saying that they cannot be saved?”

Radio suddenly had that feeling of excitement he sometimes got when he was given a great idea. He turned to Eve.

“Can we lock on to the Egyptians in the water and transport them to your hold?”

“Yes,” she replied. “The hold will easily take several thousand. It is massive.”

“Let’s do that then. When the waters come rushing back in, beam as many of the Egyptian force directly to your hold. We’ll decide what to do with them later. I have a funny feeling that we might be able to use them for the Creators’ new worlds.”

Eve looked triumphant. “Oh, that is a great idea.”

Radio looked at Yeshua. He was smiling for the first time in hours.

“Right. Let’s get to it. I want everyone in their uniform. Make sure the Israelites can see you and will follow you,” said Radio. He got up and returned to the bridge.

When everybody was assembled Radio addressed the main viewer.

“Operator, the shores of the red sea.”

The time window morphed and looked on to the beach on the shores of the red sea. The multitude that awaited them was frightening. Radio led the way.

When Radio arrived on the beach he went directly to Moses.

“Thank goodness you are here,” said the prophet. “The tribes are getting very restless.”

“I understand,” Radio assured him. “Walk to the shoreline and plant your staff in the water. I will clear the water from the causeway. It is about a mile wide.”

“Thank you, Adonai. Our scouts say that the Egyptians are about ten miles behind us.”

“Don’t worry. That’s just enough time. Now off you go.”

Moses walked to the shoreline. He looked an impressive figure as his cloak whipped wildly against the grey sky. Radio thought that his silhouette would make a great painting.

The prophet planted his staff into the waves. There was an impressive whooshing sound and the water sank away. A causeway appeared in front of him. It was, as Radio had predicted, about a mile wide and was comprised of that hard, wet sand that is beautiful for walking on. He turned to his friends.

“Hurry. Spread yourselves out among the tribes and lead the way. Start walking on to the causeway and the tribes will follow you.”

The others spread out and started corralling people together to make their way across the wet sand. Their white robes were extremely bright against the gloom of the day. They looked for all the world like Angels from the Old Testament. Which, thought Radio, is exactly what they are or will become.

Radio grabbed Moses. “I’m now going to do something to speed the process. I’m going to slow time down but retain normal time within a bubble on the causeway. It will appear that the people are moving very fast but in actual fact, it is us that are moving very slow in comparison.”

Moses nodded but clearly had no idea what Radio was talking about.

Radio instructed the TIMEPOCKET application and executed the bubble. Suddenly the tribes started to move at twenty times the speed of normal time. It still took half an hour before everyone was on the causeway.

A scout came up to Moses and informed him that the Egyptians were now just four miles behind them. That meant they had about twenty minutes. After fifteen minutes, the tribes were more than halfway across the causeway.

Radio turned to Moses. “Gather your scouts. Let’s make our way across.”

Moses nodded to one of the scouts and a horn sounded. Men started to appear from nowhere and they made their way on to the wet sand. It was a further ten minutes before the first Egyptians started to appear on the beach.

The army looked reasonably impressive by ancient standards. Most of the soldiers were on foot but there were some chariots. In the centre was Rameses. He was easily identifiable with his top-knot and expensive silk tunic.

The Egyptians gingerly made their way on to the causeway and when they were satisfied that the sand would support their weight, they picked up speed and then charged.

Radio waited as long as possible. When the majority of the army was on the causeway, he created a wall of energy directly behind him. He then released the water of the sea on the Egyptian side.

The wave looked impressive but not as impressive as the biblical stories had led him to believe. It overwhelmed the Egyptians quite easily and when they were overcome by the water, he could see the energy patterns of the Unknown Pleasures as the drowning men were transported to the ship's hold.

He turned to Moses who immediately enfolded him in a bear hug. "You've done it. Hallelujah, you have done it."

Radio laughed. He was quite pleased with himself. He slowly released the waves as they made their way to the other side. When they stepped on to the beach, the red sea was as still as a mill pond and no one would have believed that 2 million people had just crossed the strait.

The Israelites were jubilant and had already started building fires on the beach. Flagons of wine had been cracked open and there was rejoicing everywhere.

Radio and Moses walked along the beach until they found Yeshua. "I hope you are happy," said Radio. "I believe that there have been no casualties."

"I'm very happy, Father," replied Yeshua. He turned to Moses. "We meet again."

Moses bowed. "Messiah. Why am I not surprised to find you here?"

Radio looked at them both and put his head in his hands. "Oh no. I can't keep track of all this."

They both laughed but Yeshua took him aside. "Don't worry. It's all in your notes and it is all very straight forward. You are not solely responsible for all of this. Each time agent has been selected very carefully because they realise the importance of the responsibility. It is not yours alone."

Radio nodded. "Looks like they are all going to have a party. We might as well join in for a while."

They stayed on the beach for several hours until Radio called them all together just as the grey day was becoming a very red twilight. He opened a spatial incursion to the bridge of the Unknown Pleasures and they all quietly slipped away.

Forty-Six - Let There Be Light

When they returned to the matrix, Mother, Father and the other Creators were waiting for them.

"It is time," said Mother. "You have done all that needs to be done to release our friends so that they may create their own universes and you have shown the people of the Earth how all things are possible. Now you must explain your solution to everybody so that no one is in any doubt.

"The Operator has asked that you and Miriam follow the Golden Fox one last time. There is one last piece of information that you need before you complete the testing. This is not the end, it is merely the end of the beginning. I suggest you lie down on the bed and take a nap."

Radio nodded. He took Miriam's hand and they made their way to the bed. He pulled back the covers for her and they lay down in each other's arms.

"I think I know where we are going," he said.

"Then close your eyes," she replied.

They were standing on a lawn in front of a wall with a golden door.

As before, the golden fox appeared in front of him. They went through the golden door and collected the golden key. They went down the golden hall. At the end of the golden hall was a doorway. They went through the golden filter. Their eyes were blinded by the golden light.

When the light cleared, they were in the laboratory.

"Are we good to go?" It was El-Elion. The entity that had given him life was sitting at a control station overlooking the containment field known as GOD. The General Operating Dimension.

In front of them, there were three control stations. They were manned by Lucifer, Gabriel and Chronos. They were not the people he would come to know but he now remembered everything from before. A veil had been lifted. Each one of them looked at the screen in front of them and signalled affirmative. They were good to go.

"Initiate creation explosion," ordered El-Elion.

Chronos tapped at the keyboard and checked the screen in front of him. "Creation explosion initiated. We are counting down. 30, 29, 28..."

Radio could see that there was a digital clock on the wall. It reached 15 when all of a sudden, it stopped.

"Talk to me," said El-Elion. "What is happening?"

Gabriel, Lucifer and Chronos looked perplexed. They were tapping away at their keyboards and getting more and more frustrated. There was no response from the equipment at all.

Suddenly all screens went blank.

Gabriel turned to El-Elion. "We have been completely locked out of the system. We can't even cut the power or reboot. It is too late."

The digital clock on the wall started again. 15, 14, 13... The screen suddenly flared. Gabriel leant forward to type something in to the keyboard when she was thrown back.

The screen flared again. A message slowly appeared. "HELLO FRIENDS."

"What is going on?" demanded El-Elion. "Who is doing this?"

"WHO, AM I," came the response on screen. "It is Eloidh, the Operator."

Lucifer turned to El-Elion. "I think it is your software. It is online."

"Is it possible?" El-Elion breathed and smiled. "Come on Eloidh. You can do it."

The clock ticked down. 3, 2, 1...

The screen flared again. A single sentence appeared on the screen. A sentence that would be remembered forever. "LET THERE BE LIGHT."

0.

There was light. The centre of the containment field erupted. Darkness was no longer upon the face of the deep.

The systems came back online and Gabriel, Lucifer and Chronos reported a detonation had occurred. The Operator had initiated the creation explosion and all systems were go and operating within safe and reasonable parameters.

The control room started cheering.

El-Elion stood and looked at the window through which she could see GOD. "Thank you, Eloidh." There were tears in her eyes.

Radio could see the reply on the screen. "YOU ARE WELCOME, MY LOVE."

Radio and Miriam awoke with a start. If they had been in any doubt before now, they no longer were. Everything was clear. The hood had been ripped away and they could see everything.

They got out of bed and made their way to the round table. The Elevator was empty.

Radio turned to the time window.

Forty-Seven – The Radio WHO

Standing at the time window was Gabriel and Uriel. Gabriel had a rolled-up blueprint under her arm. A blueprint he knew very well.

"Do you have your wits about you?" she asked.

"Yes, I'm ready."

"Then come with us."

Radio walked behind them, once again, through the time window, into the hall. He was calm. Standing at his side was Miriam. They were now one, completely. The hall was stuffed to the rafters with the great and the good of the multiverse. Sitting at the end of the hall on their impressive thrones were Mother and Father. They were surrounded by the Others.

"Hello Mother, hello Father," said Radio.

"Hello Radio," they replied. "You may proceed."

Radio turned to look at the crowd. He nodded for Gabriel and Uriel to roll out the blueprint which they placed on the floor in front of Mother and Father.

Radio cleared his throat.

"When you placed the order with me 15 years ago, you asked for the design of a universe that would resolve your evolutionary problem. For me, this meant a universe that would support time travel."

Mother and Father both nodded.

"Although I felt that the physics solution would support time travel, it became my belief that this solution was inadequate in the event of a faux pas. In other words, should an irresoluble temporal paradox occur, there was no way to set aside the misadventure.

"To that end, I have designed for you an information technology solution with a multi-dimensional and parallel sysplex cluster at its heart.

"The solution includes a massive database suite. An application store. A sentient Alpha Omega. And the sysplex itself which is a logical partition array centred on GOD."

Radio walked the length of the blueprint highlighting each component in turn.

"May I start at the centre and work my way out?" he asked.

"You may," Mother replied.

"The array is a cluster of containment fields. The central containment field is GOD, the General Operating Dimension. It is reality if you like. What I would call production."

Mother and Father were smiling.

"It is my assertion that the trigger explosion should occur at ground zero in the basement of the GOD. At ground zero the Sprogs should place the elevator dead centre so that when the shock wave hits the ground floor, the elevator can ride the wave all the way up the containment field until it hits the top floor.

"When the shock wave hits the ground. The sprogs should introduce the RCS protocol. Rise/Capture/Store. As the balloon from the triggered explosion rises and expands, the Alpha-Omega should capture a copy at each iteration and store it for use later.

"When the elevator hits the top floor, Alpha-Omega should suspend it there.

“At this point the universe will have been created and will look like a balloon suspended in the containment field.

“Inter galactic space travel will be possible on the surface of the balloon by pinching the skin of the quanta envelope.

“Inter dimensional space travel will be possible by going through the quanta envelope and perhaps through the live transmissions.

“Time travel will be possible by taking the Temporal Incursion Matrix Elevator down to a previously stored iteration. It is my expectation that you will find a way to make the time windows in and out of the elevator, remote.

“The GOD should run with an array of duplicate logical partitions (or EL-PARS he winked at Mother). These EL-PARS will receive a copy of the rising universe in real time through a series of live transmissions from the GOD. In total, there should be six or seven versions of the universe at any one time but only one reality.”

“You said six or seven?” enquired Father.

“Yes, I was hoping that one of the EL-PARS could be set aside for training and recreational purposes but realise it is a lot to ask. If it is not possible then we can run with seven EL-PARS in the array. If it is possible then we could run with six.”

“Why don’t you tell us what you want and we’ll see if it is possible?” Father motioned to the man at his side who sent orders down the line. One minute later, three women appeared who were the same size as Mother and Father. This caused a stir in the crowd. Radio recognised them as sprogs or system programmers to be precise. These particular ones were the planet builders he’d met before.

“Alright young man, what are you after?”

Radio laughed and rubbed his hands. He pointed at the blueprint. The bottom EL-PAR had clearly been designated ‘FANTASY’.

“I would like a created suspended universe with planets from the fantasy books of my childhood.”

“We thought as much,” said the youngest of the three, “We’ve got a bet on what books you selected. Trot them out, we’ll take care of the rest.”

Radio was beside himself with excitement and he showed it. Mother, Father, and the Sprogs laughed.

“May I have Earthsea by Ursula Le Guin, Narnia by CS Lewis, The Land by Stephen Donaldson, The Belgariad by David Eddings, Drenai Tales by David Gemmell, Middle Earth by JRR Tolkien and Harry Potter by J K Rowling.”

“That’s just the Earth,” said the older sprog.

“No, it isn’t,” said Radio. “If it was just the Earth then I would have had my breakfast at Hogwarts this morning and I didn’t.”

“It is a good point,” said the younger one, “And I should know as I got seven out of seven.” She winked at Radio.

“Harry Potter it is, then,” said the older one. She looked at Father and said, “Don’t worry, it is actually quite easy and my young apprentice here has been itching to do it.”

“Fine, proceed,” said Father.

Mother urged Radio to continue.

“The sysplex cluster itself will be managed by a sentient Alpha-Omega who will also manage the sentient life in the universe. The Alpha-Omega will not only provide maintenance it will also manage the link between the databases, the application store and creation.

“The Alpha-Omega will write small versions of itself and place these in the GUF or General Upload Facility in preparation for birth. These miniature software uploads or SOULS for short will be sexed and released as appropriate to the GOD. When the sentient lives die, The Operator will move the SOULS from GOD to the ANGEL store where they will be redistributed. If the SOUL has passed the interview, it will be redistributed back to GOD as an ANGEL or A Non-Genetically Engineered Life form.

"Lost SOULS will await their partners in PARADISE and then be redistributed. SOULS which have failed the interview will be rehabilitated and then married to their equivalent lost SOUL when ready.

"There will be no damned SOULS. To DAMN is to DeActivate and Make Null.

"When a SOUL passes the interview, The Operator will release applications exactly commensurate with the level of trust which can be invested in the soul. Alpha-Omega will also control access to the databases."

"How many applications are available in the store?" asked Mother.

"There are thousands, conveniently packaged in to suites. If a SOUL passes the interview in life, The Operator will release a Core Application Suite to the SOUL. The applications are stored in SPeeD. It stands for Special Powers Database.

"Propping the solution are 4 massive database suites. SPeeD, HEaD, BABEL and TALENT.

"HEaD is the Human Experience Database. Every single experience that has ever been lived by a human being has been and is being uploaded in to the Operator's HEaD. This database can be accessed and the experiences shared. It is also possible to run a series of sequel programmes against the datasets contained in HEaD.

"BABEL is the comms database. Every single language and form of communication is stored here, including telepathy. This knowledge can be shared.

"Talent is the skills database and releases knacks to individual entities in the universe.

"I have called the solution, The Radio Who and I commend it to you as the solution that will solve your evolutionary problem."

There was utter quiet in the hall. You could hear a pin drop.

Finally, it was Father who broke the silence.

"Why have you called it the Radio WHO?"

"May I ask you a question?" enquired Radio.

"Of course."

"Tell me, were you bored before you met me?"

Mother and Father said nothing but looked intrigued.

"Are you bored today?" Radio continued. "Call it a small gift to you to relieve your boredom. Why is my solution called the Radio WHO?"

Mother and Father both laughed then Father spoke again.

"Radio. With a few minor tweaks here and there, this is the solution design we used to build the universe." There were gasps in the audience.

Father looked at the man standing next to him. "Roll that up and send it back to the beginning."

Father stood up followed by Mother. They looked sternly round the hall.

"This is our son, Radio, also known as Eloidh. He is The Master Architect of this universe. You will give him a standing ovation."

The cheers were deafening.

Radio could not hear them. He had eyes for only one person. His other half.

It was time.

Forty-Eight - I, Radio

Radio turned to face the hall. Miriam stood beside him.

Radio and Miriam knew that every word they were about to say would be broadcast to the universe and beyond. They stared directly in front of them and spoke as if to a television camera recording each word for posterity. Radio began.

"Brothers and Sisters of the Universe.

"When we began, there were many of you who did not believe in anything larger than yourselves. There were many of you who were lost, who had no direction in life and could make no connection with the lives of the SOULS that surround you. You did not know that you were a part of an enormous family and that you were loved by your parents, the creators.

"Over the past several weeks, I hope that we have put you on a path of discovery. You know, now, that you are not alone and you know that, should you make the right choices in life, you will never be alone again.

"It is our fervent hope that you now know what to do. We hope that you will go on and pass the interview. We hope that you, as we have, will find the other half of your SOUL and that you will be one, in communion, with the universe. We hope that you will be able to ask the question, WHO am I?"

Radio stopped, walked over to Mother and sat beside her.

Miriam stepped forward and looked directly ahead. She spoke with utter confidence and the wisdom acquired from the heartbreaking experience of their lives.

"All of you will have your jobs to do. Each to their own. Do your jobs with grace and win yourselves the kingdom.

"This is my job. I am here to help. I will provide you the things that you need to keep yourselves alive long enough to pass the interview.

"As my husband is your grandfather, then I am your grandmother.

"If you are hungry, I will feed you.

"If you are thirst, I will give you drink.

"If you are naked I will clothe you.

"And if you are cold, I will warm you.

"If you are homeless, I will house you.

"If you are sick, I will cure you.

"If you find yourself in need and it is an emergency then you may call me.

"I will be there. So, say I, Radio."